PARALYSED

First Published in 2023 by Echo Books

Echo Books is an imprint of Superscript Publishing Pty Ltd
ABN 76 644 812 395

Registered Office: PO Box 669, Woodend, Victoria, 3442

www.echobooks.com.au

National Library of Australia Cataloguing-in-Publication entry.

Creator: Tracey Roberts, author.

Title: Paralysed

ISBN: 978-1-922603-75-3 (paperback)

A catalogue record for this
book is available from the
National Library of Australia

Book and cover design by Andrew Davies.

Tracey Roberts

PARALYSED

A tale of forbidden love and one woman's courage through adversity

For Peter

Young, old, or anywhere in between, women need to know it's okay to stand up for themselves and say no to abuse.

ACKNOWLEDGEMENTS

Books don't magically happen overnight. They take the encouragement of friends, the support of loved ones and the knowledge of those you seek most.

Thank you, dear friends – those named, referenced and unnamed, I count on you in the days ahead.

Thank you to Pamela Barnard, Derek Taylor and Damon Chamberlain for your incredible support and faith in this project. Always willing to listen and to read yet another draft. I am forever grateful for your enthusiasm and know how.

Heartfelt gratitude to Roger L. Price for your wordsmithery and regard for details. Your extensive knowledge astounds me.

For your kindness, generosity and friendship, my special thanks go out to Richard Burgmann, Grant Pollitt, Lou Larrosa, Sonya Drysdale, LeeAnn Lynch, Barbara Mackin and Nikki Lacey. I deeply value your encouragement.

To Perry Cross AM and Professor James St John who help so many; you have my profound admiration. Thank you for your dedication to the field of Neurobiology and Stem Cell Research.

As always, grateful thanks to Tony Landolfi whose unfailing belief in me and this book kept me going.

To Kenny Derley what can I say, thank you for having my best interest at heart and always looking out for me.

Special thanks to Rosario Ivaldi who has been a paragon of patience and support.

Thanks to my family who continues to be supportive and enthusiastic even after so many years-thanks again, David, Mel, Alex and Ava.

Tom Flood, this book would not be possible without your writing and editing skills. Thank you for your literary counsel. You saved me.

I am grateful to Sharon Blain for directing my manuscript to my publisher, Marcus Fielding, who combined great editorial wisdom and pure publishing know-how to a degree I would not have believed possible.

This is what dreams are made of.

She scans the master suite, tiny tealights softly flickering throughout but is taken by surprise when his soulful eyes grow hungry, primal even, causing her to catch her breath. She dares not say a word, as if to speak will break the magic unfolding between them.

Taking her by surprise, he pins her up against the wall, then slowly lifts her closed hands above her head and peruses her body seductively.

Confronted by his desire, her heart races in anticipation, sending shivers throughout. Her lips part under his eager gaze, her eyes shimmering with desire.

He traces the pad of his thumb seductively across her bottom lip. Leaning into her body, he hears the release of her breath as he slowly kisses along the line of her neck, almost licking, leaving a trail of moisture towards her mouth. She arches into him, and he ravenously kisses her mouth for the longest time before lifting her silky dress up and over her head. 'I've wanted to see you naked since we met.'

The tension blossoms between them. The rise of her chest causes her breasts to jut forward in reveal, nipples erect.

He looks at her naked breasts with such want, she feels dampness between her legs. His fervent grip suddenly whisks her away from the wall and across the room. Lying her down on the bed and kneeling over her, he slowly releases her long mane from the restrictions of the band. Watching her auburn locks tumble gracefully onto the sheets, he bends down, kissing the line of her shoulder tenderly, then pulls back and gazes down at her with consummate love.

She catches a sigh and bites down on her lip, feeling she might die with need, grateful the noise of the distant waves against the rocks is louder than the pounding of her heart.

Bending low, he devours her mouth ever more passionately.

Melded to him, she sensuously whimpers: a moan of lust from deep within.

He runs his hand down over her body, loving the softness of her skin, the heat radiating from her flesh. Moving the flat of his hand slowly along the edge of her silk panties, he teases ever so gently, arousing her need and taking pleasure in seductively slipping the silk down her legs, never taking his eyes off her form.

She can't believe how sexy he is when, without warning, this incredible man stops, teasing her with need. Suddenly, he stands at the end of the bed, and she watches him remove his belt, the whipping sound, as he rapidly slides it through the keepers of his jeans, sending tingles across her skin. 'Ah …' She catches her breath and waits, luxuriating in the way he removes his top ever so slowly, taunting her, shaking his muscular shoulders forward and out, shirt falling to the floor.

He stares naked from the end of the bed. His tan only enhances his remarkable physique, his reassuring thighs heralding they'll support the love she craves. At first, he doesn't move, and for a moment she thinks she sees a tear in his eye.

She beckons him to her. Her eyes shimmer in the candlelight.

He moves onto the bed beside her and levers up on one elbow, gazing at the object of his desire in the soft light.

Brushing a hand across her body, she licks her lips and moans, feeling his penis resting against her, his hands exploring her freely.

He wants nothing other than to touch and caress the softness of her skin, warm hands moulding the shape of each breast: one and then the other. His fingertips trace back up to the line of her neck.

Leaning in, their lips touch in a long-extended kiss. It's the strongest sexual attraction she's ever felt.

His penis presses against her hip. Moving slowly down her body, tracing with the tip of his tongue, needing to taste her sweetness, he presses his mouth between her thighs, smooth and silky. His lips gently search the moist folds that begin to swell under his touch. Twisting beneath him, her fingers harsh on his shoulders, holding the force coursing throughout her body, his lips devouring her delicious scent, he hears her gasp.

The sensation between her thighs grows stronger, more intoxicating. Longing. Wanting ... Needing.

He breathes her in, caressing gently, tasting, pushing her aroused body into a state of bliss, her hips moving with need.

She catches her breath, too rapt to notice him stealing a glimpse of her writhing in pleasure at the anticipation of their love.

He kisses one last time before moving back up her body. His full weight positioned evenly, he presses gently inside, slowly and carefully, for the first time. She is deliciously warm, embracing his sensuality. Aroused, he moves his body carefully, going deeper. The more he gives, the more she wants. Sounds of pleasure fill the room, their bodies in perfect harmony.

She's never experienced such tenderness mixed with such raw passion. A moan escapes her lips, like music, and his chest bears down upon hers as they move together, slowly and rhythmically. Running her hands along the smoothness of his muscular back, she cries out for his love, pulling him into her, his tenderness beautifully proportioned to her needs, his groans of desire gliding over her body.

Bodies bathed in candlelight, he withdraws, turns her away from him and brings her to her knees, catching a glimpse of the moisture of their loving. His breathless tongue tenderly follows the outline of her neck and down the length of her back. And there it is, the signature of her pain and suffering, the scar that holds the full story of the horrific injuries sustained at the hand of a monster. He surprises her by tenderly kissing the welt-like scar in its entirety. His light, delicate touch floats easily over the soft curves of her body, tingling her skin as he moves slowly up the line of her form.

She writhes sensuously beneath him, hungry for his touch.

He grips her hair, gentle but firm, his fingers tighten, and she arches her body in surrender as he re-enters her body, placing his wet mouth to her lips.

She sighs, her tongue swirling to meet his, softly, gently arousing.

Moans of pleasure fill the space. His demand causes an onslaught of intensity so overwhelming he's suddenly overcome with exhilaration and buries himself deeper and deeper.

Stiffening in ecstasy, she feels an explosion of love between them, her face tight with pleasure, both lost in a blinding orgasm. She falls limp beneath him, their trembling bodies collapsing slowly onto the bed in bonded passion.

In that moment, she knows this is the man she's been waiting for her entire life.

CHAPTER ONE

Stepping out from the elevator into the corridor of Whittakers Publishing House, designer handbag dangling from her shoulder, Vanessa remarkably believes herself to be one of the luckiest women in the world. The elegant 40-year-old looks gorgeous. However, even after challenging herself by writing and successfully publishing a best seller, the whip-smart author believes she still needs to do more for the cause.

A man rapidly brushes past her causing Vanessa to suddenly lose her balance. 'Oh, I'm so sorry.' Arms outstretched, the debonair stranger attempts to steady her. 'Are you okay?' He looks up, realising she's the most stylish creature he's ever seen.

Clutching at her handbag, Vanessa is struck by the stranger's subtle, elegant scent. Fragrance is very important, men and women alike. Sure, she's aware perfume is vastly over-scented alcohol, but this refined beauty has always had a keen nose for fragrance. As early as five, she had discovered her grandmother's exotic French soap wrapped in white tissue paper in the underwear drawer.

Her theory is that perfume provides the ability to attract a whole new level of attention, an intangible quality, a *je ne sais quoi*. Inexplicably, her senses in the clandestine world of scent have been truly heightened of late.

The stranger is still holding her hand when Vanessa turns, faces him, their eyes lock, and they're immediately struck by a chord resonating between them.

'Creed! You're wearing Creed! One of the best perfumes in the world,' she says, surprised by her sudden outburst of aromatic wisdom.

Releasing his grip, Vanessa is awestruck as he goes about straightening his blue silk tie, askew across the shoulder of his navy suit.

His eyes never leave her.

'I'm sorry,' she says.

Sensing her discomfort at having made such a personal observation, he gives her a reassuring grin. 'It's me that should apologise.' He looks into her magnetic eyes, a striking shade of green.

Handsome, charming, and sensitive; there's an aura of kindness about his masculine, chiselled features. Smooth, olive complexion, and sporting a recent tan, it's as if he's just flown in from some exotic destination. Perhaps he has, and he has quite an air of confidence.

Coup de foudre: love at first sight. Those magical French words suddenly make sense to her. She studies his sparkling, brown eyes and is reminded how much she misses the romantic attention of the opposite sex. Starved for affection, she realises a dormant fire has been ignited deep within.

Groomed to perfection, he cuts a dashing figure dressed in a dark blue suit, like a man who isn't afraid of anything, except perhaps dirt.

Aware of something more, his presence is making Vanessa self-conscious. She feels a sudden flush of heat cross her face. Everything else in the corridor fades into insignificance.

A passing man gives William a knowing smile.

Composing herself, Vanessa flicks her long, auburn hair back over her honey-toned shoulders, glances at her watch and realises she is running late for her meeting.

'William Fuller Whittaker, pleasure to meet you. I'm sorry about this. Are you alright?' he asks a second time, finding any excuse to gently touch her hand again.

'It's nothing. I was daydreaming.' She tries to sound in control, mindful of the nervousness in her voice on feeling his hand linger. 'I can't be late for my meeting.'

'Uh-huh. Vanessa T. Albert, is it not?' William says in acknowledgement, removing his hand.

Aware she hasn't introduced herself; she frowns. 'I'm sorry. You're making me nervous.'

'Ahh, my grandfather is waiting for you.' He points to the unmarked door at the end of the corridor.

'Yes, that would be me.' Embarrassed, she offers her hand in greeting. *Christ! You're more handsome than the tabloids portray.*

'My grandfather speaks very highly of you.' He appears reluctant to let go of her hand.

The stunning author is grateful when an energetic woman appears and interrupts the conversation, handing him a cream folder. 'Here's the paperwork for Sandersons. You'll be needing this.' She raises a discreet eyebrow.

'Thank you.' He barely acknowledges her before looking back to Vanessa.

'He's told me the detail in which you write, and your natural narrative flair, is remarkable.'

Embarrassed by his candour, she clears her throat.

'The very touching autobiography, *A Woman of Courage* – is it not?' He seems somewhat disappointed he hasn't read it.

'Yes.'

'Gramps is very touched by your body of work.'

Did he have to use that turn of phrase? There's no mistaking the Whittaker charm; it's certainly a family trait. 'Please call me Vanessa.'

'Vanessa. Well, it's been a pleasure to meet you. I'm sorry I won't be joining you today, but I've been called away on an urgent business matter.' He sounds disappointed. 'I'm sure we'll be seeing more of one another in the not-too-distant future.'

'Indeed,' she says, unsure of what he means. Feeling her heart warm, she half-turns in the direction of Mr Whittaker's office, then back again. 'Okay, I better head on in.'

'Enjoy your meeting,' he says, proceeding down the hallway.

Outside the office door, Vanessa's heart is still a-flutter as she glances over her shoulder and catches a glimpse of William, at the other end of the corridor, staring back. In a split second, he's gone. Checking her blouse, the leggy beauty gathers her composure and knocks on the impressive door. *No name – heck! The sheer solidity suggests power.*

She hears Mr Whittaker's voice, distant on the other side. 'Come in.'

She pushes the mahogany door open with unexpected effort.

'Ah, there you are, my dear,' Thornton says, his deep voice directing her focus towards him.

Warmly received, Vanessa's entire demeanour relaxes as she enters the high-ceilinged, corniced room overlooking the city below.

Thornton, seated in his wheelchair over by the window, seems dwarfed by the heritage building opposite.

Thornton's office always makes me feel safe. She skims the spectacularly rich collection of objects, hundreds of books forming the space of a life well lived. The Jacobean style never fails to remind Vanessa of the similar personal library in the latest film adaptation of *The Great Gatsby*. Unlike F. Scott Fitzgerald's character, she assumes there's old money respectability here.

Thornton, of English descent, is a well-known collector of Australian art, antiquarian books, and most notably the founder of Whittakers Publishing. The initial success and magnitude of his publishing house is due in part to his obvious determination to not let his disability define him. Since its beginnings, the company has survived many incarnations, including the early 80s when his son, Montgomery Whittaker, was introduced to the business. His extraordinary knowledge of international business broadened the scope of an already respected establishment. Almost two decades later, and fresh out of university, grandson William joined forces, injecting new enthusiasm.

Once a tall, imposing figure prior to his horrific attack, Thornton's sporting interests had been varied. He had been a notable polo player in his day, and it's said, the biggest drawcard to every match. A true lover of gentlemanly sports, he'd taken up golf as a youngster and had become a number-one-ranked golfer.

Now in his late eighties, Thornton could best be described as a Christopher Plummer-style of man, that charismatic, smooth-talking, award-winning Canadian actor. Like Plummer, Thornton has a fascination for stories that are insightful, often about human nature and human predicaments. There is also a sweet, tender side to him, a smooth softness with strong overtones. He's fascinating, articulate and eloquent, with a depth of care that comes from all manner of experiences, including having suffered a life-altering injury.

This magnanimous character has sensitively melded together a business space full of soul. These hallowed walls, complete with bespoke floor-to-ceiling bookshelves, exude a great deal of charm having been carefully planned right down to his old, scarred writer's desk and plume. His extensive library contains a diversity of tomes on history, sociology, and philosophy, as well as a most impressive collection of antiquarian books, including magnificent old vellum dating back to the early 1500s, but he also remains a great admirer of many literary contemporaries. His collection is replete and greatly admired.

A nineteenth century Tom Roberts oil portrait of a mysterious woman hangs above the imported eighteenth-century oak-panelled walls. Australian-born artist Bertram Mackennal's bronze sculpture sits to the side of the clock on the mantel. No more noteworthy than all the other riches in this office, a John Glover oil on canvas of rubbery gum trees is placed on an easel set to one side, as if to imply its transitory existence. There's no mistaking this library is his life, and these works of art are like old friends to Thornton.

'Mr Whittaker, lovely to see you again, sir. Sorry I'm a little late,' she says, hoping for forgiveness.

Vanessa observes Thornton eyeing the exceptional black slate antique clock sitting pride of place on the carved mantel. She locks on the French *frères* movement which reads three minutes past the hour and blushes.

'No problem, dear. Do sit down,' he says in a manner that suggests not to make it a habit.

She gives him an apologetic smile and notices a large pile of uniform pages on his desk. She's seen various stacks there on previous visits and wondered if these have been read or left unopened. Some are tied with traditional tough, pink ribbon used by lawyers and the others secured with black, foldback clips positioned perfectly to the left of the pages in the hope of being chosen by their mere exactness.

A bright pink, foldback clip she's not seen before jumps out at her, the very same shade a favourite of her deceased sister, Monica, whose presence she can feel so acutely.

Thornton Whittaker leans back in his chair to flip through her latest manuscript.

CHAPTER TWO

The weekend has come and gone in a flurry. Vanessa makes her way through the busy foyer, past the towering floral arrangement, towards the art deco elevators. The coolness of the old building is welcome relief from the summer winds.

Dinner with Michael had been as strained as usual. A massage to help ease the pain in her neck. Pilates, followed by coffee with a woman from a recent writers' group, then in a blink of an eye, she is delighted to be back at Whittakers Publishing House.

Romancing the Writing had been a decision made on impulse one evening over a large glass of chardonnay. Vanessa had started to feel some of her literature was a tad risqué and it might be a good idea to dial her style back a notch. Going over her notes on the weekend, perhaps she needs to dial it back quite a bit. She certainly doesn't want to be perceived as an erotic writer, so the idea of learning when to leave a romantic scene at a closed door, giving it a less-is-more kind of feel, seems the way to go, hence taking another course.

Having a keen eye for people watching, Vanessa looks around the busy foyer, eyes scanning everywhere because simple things appear unexpectedly. It's chaotic at this time of day, a sea of angst with people in choreography with one another bustling in all directions, and business attire at its best for a Monday morning.

She feels the moment and stares off to the side at a middle-aged chap with wavy, grey hair sitting in the foyer café, which triggers an obscure thought. *I wonder why some people manage to lead relatively ordinary lives – normal even. Nothing much ever seems to happen to or around them. Not that I know the man, but dressed in a drab, cheap, grey suit, almost the same colour as his hair, staring blankly off into space, he merely blends in and seems non-controversial. Quiet. Perhaps a little on the dull side even.*

Suddenly a short, pretty woman, wearing bold red lipstick and a bright yellow dress, approaches the man and his face lights up like a Christmas tree, becoming instantly animated as he stands to greet her with a cheeky kiss.

So much for my perceptions.

Vanessa's thoughts skip back to the weekend, having experienced another one of Michael's spectacular walkouts. She's fed up with the repetition of it all. It's not as if she consciously hunts down drama, it just seems to find her wherever she goes. Her mother, Diana, always says to rise above any storm with dignity, but when it comes to Michael, well, he makes it damn near impossible. In some ways, you could go so far as to say that's why the author seems to have a mania for self-improvement. She never wants to be regarded for her beauty alone.

All of a sudden, she stops dead in her tracks when a young man in a very smart suit trips and goes flying across the foyer. Papers strewn everywhere, his colleagues try desperately, to no avail, to save him from plummeting face first onto the marble floor.

'I'm fine, I'm fine,' he says, desperately scurrying to get up.

Vanessa watches as he rounds off with a jump to attention. Red-faced, he quickly sets about collecting the litany of documents in the hope of saving them from being trampled by the traffic of stilettos and business shoes tracking through the lobby.

Pleased he's okay, she sets about her business, waiting by the elevator, fidgeting with her gold bracelet when unexpectedly she gets a whiff before spotting him. The loud ding of the elevator startles her as she realises the Australian-born powerhouse himself is standing immediately to her left.

'That was some tumble,' William says thoughtfully.

'Indeed. Poor man. I hope he's not hurt.'

'Just his pride.'

'That can be mighty painful, you know.'

Bearing witness to her humour, he gives a closed-mouth chuckle. 'We have to stop meeting like this,' William says.

Do we? She gives him a gentle smile.

'How was your weekend?'

They step into the crowded elevator.

'Ah, not without interest.' She watches him reach across to push the top button.

'Sounds intriguing?'

'No. Not really. It was lovely, thank you. And you?'

'Terrific. I had a function interstate so I ducked away for a couple of nights.'

Wonder who the lucky woman is?

'It was nice to have some time to myself,' he adds, as if reading her mind.

Feeling his eyes on her, she tries to remain professional. After several stops, the elevator arrives at the designated floor.

Captivated by her grace, William takes pleasure in allowing Vanessa to go first. 'I'm coming to today's meeting. I hope you don't mind?'

'No, of course not,' she says as they walk nervously together.

At the end of the corridor, William knocks once, then turns the stylish brass handle. Pushing with brute force, he steps to one side and holds the hefty door wide open for Vanessa to pass.

Vanessa offers an appreciative glance.

'Gramps, look who I found downstairs.'

Thornton looks over his black-rimmed glasses. 'Lovely to see you both.'

'Hello, Mr Whittaker,' Vanessa says.

'Come in and shut the door, William. There's an awful draught that comes through there.'

Vanessa shoots an empathetic grin. Given her uncle's suffering from the demon grip of paralysis, she knows only too well it's hard to regulate your body's temperature when living with a spinal cord injury.

'Did you have a nice weekend, Vanessa?'

'Yes, I did. Thank you, sir.'

'Good.' He turns to William. 'And how's my favourite grandson? Did you have a nice time away?'

'Need I remind you I am your only grandson, and yes, I did. It was pretty relaxing really. Aside from having a few too many drinks at the fundraiser, it was good to get away and tuck another book under my belt.'

'Oh, what book was that?' Vanessa asks, interested.

'A best seller.'

'Oh?'

'Yours actually.'

'Oh dear, not exactly soothing reading material.'

'I must confess I haven't quite finished it yet, I'm afraid, but I will. I did give it a bloody good nudge and in return, it's given me a fair idea of what Gramps has been talking about.'

'I'll take that as a compliment,' she says confidently.

William offers an admiring smile.

'Vanessa, please take a seat,' Thornton says, the timbre of his mature voice provocative. 'Would you care for something to drink: tea, coffee?'

'Thank you, no. I'll help myself to some water if I may?' She points at the silver water pitcher, steps across to the mahogany sideboard and fills a crystal tumbler. 'Would either of you gentlemen like one?' She looks back over her shoulder.

William appears deep in thought and simply shakes his head.

'No, thank you, dear. I'm fine,' Thornton says, now positioned behind his desk.

Vanessa feels a certain closeness to Mr Whittaker senior, a deep connection that she can't quite explain, like he's in accord, appreciating the good, ignoring all her shortcomings. Taking her work seriously means a great deal to the author, but he doesn't fool Vanessa. This stoic, gentle man has a sentimental streak that runs deep within. She senses he belongs to the ages. She takes a seat and crosses her legs, only to realise Thornton is pointing at something which appears to be a very old, long-barrelled pistol on a metal tripod.

He spins it around and asks, 'Do you know what this is?'

'A gun?' She studies the older man's intensity as he strokes the barrel with an unsteady hand. Acutely aware he's an avid collector of all things rare, Vanessa savours his knowledge and senses it pleases him to have an enthusiastic audience.

William smiles. 'Good start.'

She takes a sip of water.

'Well, it's not just any old gun. This, my dear, this is the Puckle gun, a recent acquisition of mine.'

'Puckle gun?' Vanessa quizzes. 'I've never heard of such a thing, but then again, I don't know much about guns, full stop.'

'I'm not surprised: very few have. It was invented in England way back in 1718 by an influential gentleman, lawyer, and I might add, a writer, Mr James Puckle. Bizarrely, it takes square bullets. Isn't that extraordinary?'

'Really, how odd,' she tests, imagining the coldness of the revolver in her hand, the weightiness of it.

'Do you know why it uses square bullets, my dear?'

'No, but you have my full attention.'

'Well, I'll tell you. It's a most curious thing. Two versions of this gun were made: one used conventional round bullets and was used to shoot Christian enemies; the other fired square bullets, like this one, and was used against the Muslim Turks to cause considerably more damage.'

Her brow furrows.

'How primitive,' William says.

'If you don't mind me saying, sir, that is somewhat macabre.'

Thornton hands his grandson a copy of the original patent. 'Yes, of course, by today's standards it is. But, like many things, some changes are for the better and some, well, let's just say are still in the Dark Ages.'

'Well, hopefully the tide is about to turn, sir,' Vanessa says, under no illusion of the latter.

'Says here "A portable gun or machine called a defence, that discharges soe often and soe many bullets, and can be soe quickly loaden as renders it next to impossible to carry any ship by boarding ..."'

'The devastation of history is the absolute loss to the face of humanity,' Vanessa says.

'Indeed,' Thornton says.

William looks up from the paper. '... quickly loaden, and *so* is spelt s-o-e.'

'Well, it was written in 1718. Language is always evolving. Anyway, enough of that. Let's get down to business, shall we?' Thornton closes the glass cabinet and locks the gun away on its tripod.

'Please,' William adds, respectfully showing a sense of relief.

Following a somewhat casual discussion and satisfied with the detail changes Vanessa's made thus far, Thornton offers a few more suggestions and it's time to wrap up.

Extremely pleased by the Whittakers' enthusiasm, Vanessa stands and bids Thornton a fond goodbye, turning to William to do the same.

'I'll see you out,' he says, holding the door open.

'Thank you.'

Vanessa looks Thornton's way. 'Goodbye, sir. It's always a pleasure. I'll make the relative amendments and see you again tomorrow at noon.'

Regular face-to-face meetings is the old school way of doing things. Vanessa is aware this is how Thornton likes to roll, so she never pushes for online communication. Besides she likes being able to dress up and spend time in the presence of such a dignified man. Thornton nods and Vanessa makes her exit.

'I won't be a moment, Gramps.' William steps out after Vanessa through the open door, letting it return to a soft close. 'Well, you should be pleased.'

'I am, and he seems to think the manuscript's worthy enough.'

'Of course.'

'Thank you.'

Halfway down the corridor, he stops and asks, 'Vanessa, I was wondering if you'd like to have a bite to eat this evening?' William senses her reserve. 'To discuss business, of course.'

'Oh ... I have other arrangements.' She feels his disappointment. 'But I can easily change my plans.'

'Please don't throw your plans out for me.'

'Business always comes first,' she says.

'I hope not.' He gives a cheeky grin.

She's taken aback.

'I do, however, find good decisions are often made over a bottle of fine wine, are they not?'

'Yes ... I believe they are,' she adds, somewhat confused.

William takes the lead by pressing the down elevator button. 'Done! It's a date. I'll pick you up at seven sharp. I know where to find you; it's on file.'

Vanessa is grateful the elevator is quick to arrive.

'Until tonight then,' he says.

She turns and calmly nods.

"It's a date." Odd terminology for a business dinner. She looks out through the closing doors, taking his breath away.

CHAPTER THREE

Having only ever written non-fiction, Vanessa sits alone, happily taking notes over a quiet café lunch in the city and pondering how to write fiction that people can't put down. Fiction that's responsible for bedside lamps being kept on long into the wee small hours. Looking up from her notes, she observes a tall gentleman arriving, who joins two striking women at the next table. With hands almost feminine in swiftness and structured elegance, he hikes the crease in each trouser leg and takes his seat on the booth side of the table.

Vanessa believes by observing people, you get little gems of truth. She pictures in her head her characters, even x-ray parts, down to their voices: the softness, sincerity, honesty.

She's spotted staring. Embarrassed, Vanessa remembers her food and picks up her fork, but can't help stealing another glance for the sake of it.

The Whittaker's evidently believe I have what it takes. She contemplates her notes positioned to the side of her salad bowl. *The great man himself said it loud and clear. I write a sentence and then turn it around and turn it around again until I'm dizzy with confusion. I can't be that bad, given William is taking me out this evening for a so-called business dinner.*

Her mind drifts to what she might wear. *Beige trouser suit or black, fitted number perhaps.*

Having savoured her chicken salad, she crumples her napkin, places it on the empty plate, and pulls a fashion magazine from her bag, opening it for inspiration, or better still, to stop herself from staring. After a few minutes of page turning, she's conscious her neighbours are eyeing her quizzically.

Service is slow, so she doesn't bother having coffee. Instead, she places the mag back in her bag, grabs her things, and pays the bill at the counter.

'Have a nice day,' she says to the interested group as she walks past with a ready smile.

Outside, the heat of the day is almost nauseating, so she chooses to take the opportunity to make a quick stop at the city library. The cool air flow is welcome relief, and the place is reasonably quiet, considering the throng of people milling about.

'It's so unbearable out there,' she hears an older woman say to her partner, gripping his upper arm. She notices a black and white poster displaying Charles Laughton in the old classic tale, *The Hunchback of Notre Dame*, currently showing in the auditorium. A smile crosses her face as a rush of beautiful memories fill her head – of staying up late with her mother and sister to watch it.

Vanessa pushes through the crowd, then at the top of the staircase, squeezes past a group of schoolkids engrossed in what their teacher is describing to them. *Christ! They must be cooking in those felt caps and heavy blazers*. She feels the heat coming off their bodies as she brushes past, the smell of the teenagers repugnant as she makes her way downstairs to the administration desk.

She hands a modest woman a small list of titles she'd decided on earlier. As the librarian peruses the list, Vanessa can't help noticing the woman's unusually high, round forehead that reminds her of Shakespeare.

'I think you'll find we have all of these on the shelves,' the librarian says, looking up at Vanessa with a blank stare.

'Oh, good.' Vanessa is somewhat surprised because two of the books have only recently been released. The other, Nabokov's *Lolita*, is a sure in. She's not read it in over a decade, but remembers it being one of the most captivating books ever and she could never understand why it is so misunderstood. *Christ, people, it's not erotica; it's a special class of satire.*

'If you go over there to that computer,' the woman says, pointing at the near distance, 'you'll find everything you need.'

'Thank you kindly.'

Vanessa makes her way across to the computer, sets her bag down at her feet and begins scrolling through the relative titles. Bingo! Everything is currently available, so with a fine-tip pencil, she jots down in her notepad where to find them.

With her books tucked under her arm, she decides to hang out for a bit and take in a photographic exhibition. On second thoughts, she looks at her watch and realises Victor Hugo's gothic tale about the misshapen bellringer is about to start. The poster shows it runs for two hours, which means she'll have enough time to make it home and get ready for dinner. *What the heck! Let's do it.*

Throughout the film, she often tears up, not just at Quasimodo's tragic love for Esmeralda, but the memories the movie holds of watching re-runs with her mother and sister as they sat in the dark on the couch, eating ice-cream together. After the film, a melancholic Vanessa drifts out onto the street, pleased she took the time to stay back, and jumps in a stray cab. She races through the lobby of her apartment block, calling jubilantly to Richard, 'Hi there,' as she scoots past, before he gets a chance to look up from the front desk.

He's a darling. Even though he's responsible for all the resident's needs in her block, Vanessa is forever grateful for his charm and concern towards her.

'Good evening, Ms Albert,' Richard says earnestly, stepping out from behind the desk and striding forward in an attempt at holding the elevator doors open. 'Been to the library again, I see.'

She smiles. It's no secret Vanessa loves to read and always has something tucked under her arm.

'How was your day?'

'Fabulous!'

'Good for you,' he says.

Once the doors close, Vanessa gives an excited twirl.

Having had a most fruitful meeting that morning, and a nostalgic afternoon, Vanessa is simply glowing. Now she can focus on the evening ahead. *Sure, it's supposedly a business dinner thingy, but the mere thought of dining with William Whittaker makes me feel almost skittish. What could be more ideal? Michael's having dinner with his mother and never bothers to call when he's with Mummy dearest for fear of reprisal from the wicked witch. Having never been extended an invitation to join the mother and son team, I've grown accustomed to his lack of commitment. Long gone are the days when I wished he'd get some starch in his spine. With his cul-de-sac take on life, some might say he's a man of many secrets. However, his familiar paranoia is very much working in my favour now, especially tonight.*

Michael's mother, Constance Keats-Dickens, is old school and her late husband, George Dickens, hadn't done her any favours by loving her despite the extra pounds. Unlike her name would suggest, constant and steadfast, she's really a capricious woman by nature.

A right royal pain! I've never felt comfortable around that woman ...

Constance is the direct descendant of her namesake, the notorious Constance Keats from England, responsible for the chilling murder of her baby half-brother back in 1860. Constance Keats the First killed the little boy of four with her father's razor, almost decapitating him, when she was only sixteen. She later moved to Australia after serving many years in the English prison system.

Maybe it's the only child thing, but I hate the way Michael revels in his mother's line of infamy, even though he displays an unhealthy fear of her. Listening to him relay the historical story is like being privy to an unspeakable secret world for which he holds some twisted form of regard. Given any serious thought, it creeps me out that I am dating the great, great grandson of an infamous killer, particularly knowing Constance dislikes me so intensely. God only knows how unbearable the old girl would be if she ever found out her son asked to marry me early in the relationship. Who knows what she's capable of if the apple of her eye were to marry a divorcee? Hell! According to Michael's twisted logic, being related to some gruesome throat-cutter is far more acceptable.

Inside, Vanessa falls flat against the closed door, letting out a long sigh.

I've got to make the break. I'm sick to death of his bombastic character. Christ, no one likes him. Even Lizzie repeatedly tells me to get away from him. Lizzie's smart and only wants the best for me. She pinned him long ago; this relationship is non-existent.

Shaking off her insidious reverie, she peels herself away from the door and makes a beeline for the bedroom. Switching on the bedside light, she tosses her things on a chair and undresses quickly. Naked, she heads for the bathroom. The ensuite door swings open at her finger-touch and the overhead light automatically illuminates the space, revealing no outward signs of shared occupancy.

It's odd Michael's never even left so much as a bloody toothbrush here, let alone PJs or a t-shirt: something, anything!

She douses a cotton wipe and carefully removes her make-up before stepping into the shower. The warm water washes over her, bringing a sense of calm to a remarkable day. Glancing at her reflection in the mirror opposite, Vanessa feels confident. After all, she walks most mornings, lifts weights every other day, and if time permits, weekend Pilates with Lizzie. That is, of course, when her friend can make it. *She always seems so busy lately.*

The hot water suddenly surges, and she quickly turns the faucet off, stepping out onto the large, soft, white bathmat. *I need to get this hot water system fixed.* 'Richard!' she says aloud.

Happy with her summer glow, Vanessa grabs a towel and dries off. She pours her favourite body lotion over her pert breasts and runs a gentle hand down the curve of her frame. 'Ah, that feels better.'

Tossing on a robe, she thinks about today's meeting, pleased she's making headway with this current manuscript. Her thoughts immediately jump to William. *Mm. I'm really looking forward to this evening.*

Wiping away the steam from the make-up mirror, Vanessa stares at her skin and applies moisturiser before skilfully applying a thin, even layer of foundation. *Ah, the power of make-up is undeniable, but it's all about showing the woman and not the products.* Bronzer. Blush. Highlighter down the bridge of her nose, across the tops of her high cheekbones and the inner corners of her eyelids. Radiant, she adds the final touches. Minimal eyeshadow. With the sweep of a steady hand, she carefully draws a fine line across each eyelid. Adding black mascara, her green eyes seem to pop. She then preps her pouty lips. *Red? Yes, I think matt red is the go tonight.* To even out the colour, she rubs her lips together and leans into the mirror for closer scrutiny, blotting with a tissue before using an index finger to clean a smudge of colour from her teeth. She hangs the towelling robe behind the door, stands naked in front of the mirror and takes considerably more time with her hair, tying it up soft and high.

Satisfied, she marches into the bedroom and takes a quick glance at the small clock revealed by the ambient bedside light. *Ten minutes to the hour. William is due any minute. I'll wear the little black dress. No need to press it. Indestructible and perfect for occasions like this when time is of the essence.*

A swift spray of perfume and the buzzer startles Vanessa as she's slipping her feet into her new, black silk slides. One last squizzy in the full-length mirror. Pleased, she straightens her dress and heads to answer the intercom.

'Come on up,' she tells him before dashing to her jewellery box for a chunky gold choker and placing it quickly around her neck, where it sits high, illuminating her face.

Vanessa is already at the open door as William steps out of the lift. His mouth opens, and he's openly spellbound by her appearance. 'You look a million.' A gaze full of promise this is more than just a business dinner.

Dormant emotions stir as she touches her heart with an open palm. 'Oh, thank you. Come in.' Stepping through the doorway, Vanessa places a gentle hand on his upper arm, more as an acknowledgement this is a date, than a welcoming gesture. Inhaling his scent, it's different this time. *Very earthy, but I do like it.*

She's only ever seen him in a suit and admires his casual sense: jeans, white shirt, navy blazer. *Mm, loving the matching suede loafers, no socks. I know who looks a million. Must have cost a pretty penny too.*

William looks around the room as she closes the door. 'Nice place.'

Her apartment exudes an air of timeless elegance. Following her sensitive redesign and signature style, she's carefully created a tasteful home filled with various treasures. Amassing a collection of books, rare archives and vintage photographs amid family paraphernalia, Vanessa hopes it gives off a sense of luxury. A large, crystal leaf-drop chandelier creates a welcoming warmth, transforming the rudimentary into a tranquil refuge. *Mini-mansion, Lizzie likes to call it. Behind her tough exterior, Lizzie really is a romantic at heart.*

On the fireplace, Vanessa keeps a bell jar containing pearly seashells collected from her many travels. Nearby, in proud proclamation, a bronze figurine gracefully pirouettes next to a large, framed photograph of her deceased sister, Monica.

William stops and stares at the picture of the pretty, young girl. He looks to Vanessa, then back at the old photograph. It's evident he recognises the likeness but chooses to say nothing.

Vanessa is grateful, but she takes a moment, remembering what a loving, happy, and gifted child Monica was on the threshold of the rest of her life. *Wow, that's thirty years ago.*

With only ten months separating the girls, Monica would have been forty-one this year, had she lived. Monica was only ten when she was involved in a terrible motorbike accident in Bali. It was Good Friday, but on this occasion, instead of all of them going to the beach together by car, Vanessa refused to go, wanting to stay back at the resort swimming pool in the care of trusted staff while their mother, Diana, took Monica on the back of her motorbike down to the beach for the usual early morning surf. The girls were regulars to Bali and lived for the sunshine, but although Diana and Monica loved the surf, Vanessa opted for the calmer waters of the pool.

Tragically a small pickup truck sideswiped their bike, clipping the surfboard attached to the side, causing Monica to fall off and be hit by an oncoming car. Her sudden accidental death was a shock to all who knew her, her loss acutely felt by locals who aptly referred to her as Goldilocks because of the honey streaks through her light brown hair.

Diana was unscathed physically but was left reeling from grief and her bohemian heart never recovered. Blaming herself for her daughter's senseless death, Diana became an over-protective mother to Vanessa.

Vanessa also blames herself and lives with the useless idea of what if I'd gone that day. Monica would still be alive today. Futile in its legitimacy, she has never been able to utter her sister's name since.

Vanessa remembers, with horror, the scene when she and villa manager, Maddie, arrived at the Indonesian hospital to find Diana running up and down the corridor screaming 'Monica's dead', pain Vanessa couldn't spare her from. Diana did not want to be touched. She needed to release her grief.

Tormented Vanessa has always tried to draw down on the good stuff to help keep Monica's memory alive, her hair smelling of peaches and her eyes sparkling in the light on a summer's day. Her distinctive laugh always lifted the spirits of those around her. A kind girl, a loving sister, Vanessa's best friend. Missing that special bond, she has secretly searched for that closeness in every female friend since.

'Are you okay?' William asks, surprised by her distracted mood.

'Yes, yes, I'm fine. Martini?'

'Lovely, thank you.'

'Vodka or gin?'

'Vodka, thanks.'

She steps behind the bar.

'This apartment is exactly how I envisaged it. A perfect reflection of who you are. It tells me a lot about you,' he says genuinely.

This is how he envisaged my apartment? 'Thank you. I wanted to create a space for my art and my world.'

'I can see you are a woman of many talents, but I already knew that.'

She smiles. 'Please take a seat.'

William sits on the plush, navy lounge. 'Have you been here long?' He runs the flat of his hand in line with the velvet.

'I've been here for a few years, but I could only recently afford to refurbish the place. I extended the kitchen for practical reasons which unfortunately diminished the size of the terrace. But I feel it looks better for it, or at least I like to think so.'

'Is this navy or black?'

Vanessa recognises William's look of admiration and welcomes his attention to detail. It's always nice to feel your efforts are appreciated. *Michael never notices anything.* 'Navy, but you'd be forgiven for thinking it's black.'

'An effortless mix of antiques and modern sensibilities – eclectic synchronicity.'

'You're starting to sound like a decorator.'

'Well, I have been known to dabble.'

'Oh, really.'

He holds his thumb and index finger a couple of centimetres apart. 'I had a decorator do my place but did have a small amount of input.'

'And where is home?'

'Whale Beach.'

'Nice part of the world.'

'I think so.'

'Still a bit of a drive to the city though.'

'Oh, I don't need to be at the office most days, but when I do, I enjoy the drive.'

'Nice.'

'So, tell me about your vision for this place.'

'Well, this place was never going to be about minimalism, more an unbridled diversity. I needed it to feel warm and inviting, especially when my living space is also my workspace, so certain design priorities demanded to be met.'

'Ah, and I love this painting. What a statement piece.' William points to a large still life over the dining table.

'It's very old.'

She would love to share with him the provenance of her acquisition but he's too quick. 'Really. They say the richness of the world is tied up in art, the poetry of everyday life.'

I'm sensing nervousness here. No, not William Whittaker, surely.

'Research shows that great art and design can induce the same brain activity as being in love,' he says.

If my place is going to induce love, bring it on, baby. His back turned, Vanessa chuckles to herself at how cheeky she feels. Trying to remain sensible, she clears her throat. 'I find that decorating is very much like writing. You find yourself in front of a blank page having a story to tell, something coherent and natural.'

'True.'

There's an awkward silence where Vanessa feels a necessary input. 'I know some people think of luxuries and fine art as status symbols. But we are only the custodians of the treasures our ancestors leave behind. Luxuries can often be the little things we can't buy: hand-written cards from a lost loved one or a tiny pencil drawing like that sketch of a Splendid Fairy Wren my aunt gave me as a child.'

William tracks Vanessa's finger pointing at a small, unframed drawing resting up against the wall, taking pride of place on a side table.

'Things that are unexpected and come from the heart,' she says, swirling a drop of vermouth in each glass and tipping the residue out into the bar sink, then adding the chilled vodka. *Gosh, now I'm rambling.*

'Ah, a sentimentalist,' he says with a disarming look.

He may be nervous, but he certainly sits comfortably in my eyes. She studies his deliciously handsome profile. 'Here we go,' she says, handing him a martini. Her hand touches his fleetingly, sending a chill through her body. She sits alongside him.

'Cheers,' he says, clinking glasses.

Exquisite hands. She gazes at him gripping the stem. *Long, masculine fingers.* 'Cheers,' she says, sensing the sexual tension resonating between them.

'Mm, that's good.' He takes another sip before setting it down on the coffee table. 'So are you hungry?'

Hungry for you. 'Yes, I am. It's been a big day.'

'Good. I like a girl who loves to eat.'

Well, I'm that girl.

After a great deal of frivolous flirting, they decide to head off to the restaurant. Vanessa feels a bit lightheaded and fleetingly wonders if she's made a blunder accepting William's dinner invitation. *The last thing I would ever want is to be deemed disrespectful to Thornton Whittaker.*

He holds the front door open while she grabs her purse and keys off the console.

Stepping out, the lift doors open.

'This lift really spooks me, the way the doors open without me pushing the call button.'

'The eyes have you,' he says spookily, pointing his index and middle fingers towards her eyes.

Yep, he's nervous.

Richard looks up from his desk and steps across to open the entrance door for them as they walk through the foyer laughing.

Vanessa delights in introducing the men to one another. 'Richard, I'd like you to meet William Whittaker.'

'Pleasure, sir,' Richard says in a professional tone.

Vanessa realises William's car is parked right out front.

'The restaurant is nearby, but I thought we'd drive. You never know with this weather of late.' William looks up at the patchy cloud formation.

'Splendid idea.' Opening the door, the smell of new car hits her immediately.

William slides in behind the wheel and notices Vanessa running her hand along the leather panelling of the door frame.

My car might be special, but this is pure luxury. 'Nice car,' she says.

'Yes, it's brand spanking new.'

'Smells like it,' she says, still touching the leather.

'It's a good smell, isn't it? Do you drive?'

'Yes, of course.' She's not certain what he's implying. 'I drive an old car.'

'Why an old car?'

'Because I avoid new cars, the way I avoid drinking Sambuca. No offense.'

'No offense taken.' He's unsure of the analogy. 'Seatbelt.'

That reminds me I must get that faulty buckle fixed sooner rather than later. She straps herself in.

'So, what sort?'

'Sorry?'

'Your car.'

'Oh, an old '68 silver convertible Mercedes, a gift to myself when my book was published.'

'That's not an old car. That's a classic.'

'Well, a classic then.'

He thought for a moment. 'You don't mean the Pagoda?'

'Yes. How did you know?' Her eyes glitter with amusement.

'That's a real classic.'

'The colour is called astral silver.'

'So what colour interior?'

'Red.'

'Now you're talkin'. That's a statement piece.' He raises his eyebrows, suitably impressed.

They make easy conversation and before they realise it, they've already arrived. William finds a park directly in front of the old, glass-fronted restaurant nestled amid picturesque gardens. 'It's more good luck than good management.' He looks at her with a cheeky grin.

They step down the ambient-lit pathway and through the wisteria-covered loggia to the busy restaurant. Vanessa is so physically striking that William notices the sight of her causes a brief silence in the room as diners pause and take in her presence.

Seated by the window with the promise a waiter will be with them shortly, William squeezes Vanessa's hand reassuringly under the table and she's instantly taken aback.

Business dinner, my foot. Staring into his warm gaze though, she can't help considering he's a most seductive character. As the waiter approaches and sets down the wine list and two menus, Vanessa discreetly withdraws her hand.

'Do you have San Pellegrino?' William asks.

The waiter shakes his head.

'Okay. We'll have a large bottle of Perrier?'

The pencil doesn't move.

'A bottle of sparkling water?' William enquires.

'Ferrarelle,' the waiter replies.

'Ferrarelle! There you go,' William says. 'I've been absent for too long.'

The waiter goes to step away, but William stops him. 'Wait, wait, wait; I'm not done yet.'

'Pardon me, sir.'

William looks at Vanessa. 'Do you like white or red wine?'

'White.'

'Good. So do I.'

He turns to the waiter. 'And a bottle of Penfolds Yattarna Chardonnay.'

'If I may say so, sir, a most excellent choice.'

William turns his attention to Vanessa. 'So, I thought today's meeting went very well. Gramps is pleased and we all seem to be on the same page.'

'I like your grandfather's advice. I think he really gets where I was coming from with this manuscript.'

'Yes, we both do.'

'He's so supportive.'

'Look, there's a raft of great books out there, but clearly your work resonates with him. I've known him to chastise writers for drowning their readers in trivia, but your book is different. You don't swamp the reader at all, and let's face it, when a piece of writing rocks the world, it's a glorious thing.'

She feels his sincerity sweep across her. 'I am truly humbled.'

'Vanessa, it's certainly time to bring to light the plight of so many living with domestic violence. As the narrator and the victim, you have a genuine voice and you're able to reach the reader. The sales tell the story; it's flying off the shelves. Look at Gramps suffering from the demon grip of paralysis. He welcomes good literature that empowers others living with disability.'

'Yes, it must have been so hard for your grandfather. He's amazing. Thankfully I didn't suffer any spinal cord damage and whilst my back was broken, I'm blessed the surgeons were able to put me back together.'

'It boggles the mind to think your ex could have killed you.' He wants to kiss her pain away forever.

'Yes or put me in a wheelchair.'

'Christ!' He's outwardly rattled by the thought.

'That's precisely why I reference my uncle in the book, who sadly did suffer from paralysis. He had permanent loss of voluntary muscle movement in certain regions of the body,' she says seriously. 'In the book, it's a means of highlighting the differences.'

'And that's why the book resonates with Thornton: the detail with which you write and the understanding of the architecture of your work.'

She finds it interesting how he fluctuates between calling his grandfather Gramps and Thornton.

'You must remember, Vanessa, he's well into his late eighties now, but when he first had his accident, forty odd years ago, there was very little literature out there about paralysis. It was almost shameful and kept behind closed doors. Most people, at best, were institutionalised, and that's if they were lucky enough to survive.'

The waiter returns, pours the wine, then asks if he can take their orders.

'Yes, please,' William says. 'Vanessa, are you okay if I order for us?'

'Yes, I'd like that.'

'Anything you don't like?'

'Nothing.'

'Good.' He turns his attention to the waiter.

He hasn't even opened a menu and his eyes glimmer in the low light as he reels off their order.

Vanessa had Googled Thornton Whittaker the day before they first met:

It's no secret Thornton Whittaker, a very private man, has lived as a T6 paraplegic since breaking his back in a car accident many years earlier. Rumours circulating in Sydney's society circles say it was during a heated argument with his then wife, Ava. Believed to be a bit of a 'tear away', she flew his much-loved navy Aston Martin DB5 convertible airborne off a cliff. It's assumed his wife had been having an affair with Thornton's best friend and then business partner, Martin Banks. It's alleged when Thornton confronted her, she became so outraged she accelerated the car, losing control, resulting in her own death. Mr Whittaker, however, suffered horrific injuries, leaving him a paraplegic with complete paralysis of his lower body and legs, and needing to be in a wheelchair for the rest of his life.

At the inquiry, there was speculation Thornton may have been driving, but that was later quashed. He was already a notable businessman, employing hundreds of people worldwide. With insufficient evidence, it's thought he was worth more to the community as a free man. The grief-stricken Thornton and Mr Banks parted ways and never did business together again. Without Thornton's genius, Banks soon went into slow decline, and ultimately receivership, while Thornton's crisis led him to find a direction for his shattered life.

Vanessa notices William's smile is wide and almost bashful, with dimples halfway up his cheeks.

'You know what? Make that a large serve.'

She has no idea what's just transpired.

'So where were we?' he asks.

'I'm not quite sure.'

William looks around the busy room. 'I thought being close to your apartment would be a good idea, and of course the food is pretty good here, I must say.'

Vanessa catches herself glancing at an elderly couple on a nearby table who are endearingly whispering to one another and holding hands, seemingly oblivious to anyone else.

William nods their way, 'tell me something. Wouldn't you give anything to be like them? To still be in love at their age?'

At any age. 'Absolutely.'

The elderly lady catches a glimpse of Vanessa glancing across at them and gives an elegant nod.

'Guess what I did this afternoon?'

'What?'

'Whilst I was in the city, I went to the State Library to borrow some books and ended up seeing *The Hunchback of Notre Dame*.'

'What? In the library itself?'

'Yes, the original 1939 classic.'

'Gosh, Vanessa, I haven't seen that for decades.'

'I know, right.' She laughs and touches his arm in a gentle gesture.

The waiter returns. He places a large dish in the centre of the table.

'Splendid!' Williams says. 'I hope you like mussels?' The delicious lemon and parsley aroma fills the space.

'Lucky for you I do,' she says cheekily.

It occurs to him her response, though deliberate, has double meaning.

'I knew that,' he says, laughing.

'Sir, would you like me to serve you.'

'No, I'll take it from here, thank you.'

The waiter retreats.

'Do you always do the ordering for your dinner guests?' Vanessa asks.

'Only the ones I like.'

'Ooh!' she says, feeling spoilt.

'In all honesty, I would never be so impertinent, but these are good, and I had a gut feeling you'd like them. And if I got it wrong, it could be easily fixed.' He forces his attention back to the mussels. 'Would you like me to serve you?'

'Thank you, but I'm fine.'

They each reach across, taking a crumbed mussel in its shell, and scoop out the flesh.

'Good, huh?' William says.

'Oh yes. With a hint of chilli. Delicious.'

'This time of the year, they're always lovely and fat.'

'Why are some mussels white and some orange?' He pinches his face. 'Isn't it something to do with the sex? Males are white, I think.'

'It's actually one of nature's little tricks,' she says.

He waits and watches as she takes another. 'And?'

'Well, interestingly, there hasn't been any exact research done to date. But they have found both male and female to be orange.'

'Aren't you a wealth of information.'

'More like useless trivia.'

He laughs.

Having spent almost three hours together; they barely touched on business. Vanessa enjoyed the time immensely, finding him easy going and such a delightful man in every sense of the word. The restaurant had been abuzz when they first arrived, but glancing around the room, there are only three others that civilise the dining room now.

'William, that fish was amazing.'

'Good.' He takes her hand and gently squeezes momentarily before signalling the waiter for the bill.

While William is busy paying, Vanessa takes the opportunity to check her mobile. Four missed calls: three from Michael and the other from Lizzie. She reassures herself everything is okay. *Elizabeth probably wants to debrief from her day, but she'll be fine until the morning. I have no idea why Michael can't stick to his routine. What could possibly be so important? Surely nothing's wrong with the dark doyenne?*

'Everything okay?' William asks.

'Yes. William. Thank you for a beautiful dinner, but we really must be going. As you know, I have a deadline again tomorrow and I don't want to disappoint your grandfather.'

'Never.'

She still has minor edit changes to make, but it's nothing of any real consequence and shouldn't take up too much time, but she'd rather be on the safe side and get home in case Michael's lurking about. Ignoring his calls could end disastrously.

In the privacy of the car, William says, 'I've really enjoyed this evening. I'd like to do it again.'

'Yes, it was lovely.' Vanessa, somewhat distracted, turns and spots her neighbour's old dog, Rex, nonchalantly sitting kerbside, two blocks from home. *I must ring Bob and let him know where Rex is.*

Silence prevails as William parks the car but doesn't switch off the engine. He draws a long breath, turning her way. 'I think I need to be a little clearer. I'm wondering if I could take the liberty of asking you out on a real date?'

Is he kidding me? Gazing into his eyes, he possesses something quite different to the other men she's dated, and she's feeling quite drawn to his light. 'Yes. I'd like that,' she says with a genuine warmth in her eyes.

Pleased, William places his hand on her knee. 'Good. Can I call you and we'll make plans?'

'Yes, of course.'

'I'll call you in the morning when I have a clearer idea of my schedule,' William says.

'Until tomorrow then.'

Vanessa moves from the car so easily; he's taken by her elegance. She looks back at William in brief flirtation. Taking a last glance, he proceeds to pull away from the kerb.

For a split second, she thinks she hears her name being called from the opposite direction, but chooses to ignore it, putting it down to a simple case of paranoia.

CHAPTER FOUR

The unexpected buzz of the intercom startles Vanessa. Stopping her in her tracks, she takes a deep breath to compose herself before answering. *Maybe it's William returning for a nightcap.*

Picking up the receiver enthusiastically, she's halted by a cold shiver that unexpectedly runs the length of her spine and she refrains from using his name. 'Hello?'

Michael's voice is like a sonic boom. 'Vanessa, it's me. Let me up, please. I've been calling you all night!'

Pleased she's never given him keys, she reluctantly hits the small silver button on the wall. There is a tragic side to this tortured relationship. Even after three tedious years of dating, they still only ever see one another on weekends, and she certainly doesn't have any real desire to push for a shift.

Preferring Michael doesn't know she's been out, she's out of her shoes, off with her dress, and grabbing her bathrobe from the back of the bathroom door by the time she hears the lift arrive.

Michael suddenly bursts through the open door in a flurry, pointing a quivering finger mid-air. She finds his gruff, barbaric manner scary and tries not to wince as she ties her sash.

'Who was that guy in the black Mercedes?'

Her relief at having returned home undiscovered is short lived. *Ah, not your usual self-gratifying tone used to impress clients in the courtroom.* Her mind is racing, but having witnessed this type of behaviour before, she recognises Michael is eager to quash his own fears. Trying to remain outwardly calm, she considers confessing. On second thoughts ...

'I had dinner with the Whittaker family tonight. They took me out to celebrate book sales and I didn't call you because Wednesdays you're always at your mother's.'

He lets out a sigh and seems relieved.

'They're already going into second print. Isn't that marvellous?' she says enthusiastically.

As if to halt the roar within, Michael tries to take a deep breath. Instead it catches and sounds more like a grunting noise. Appearing to accept her explanation, in exasperation he waves an agitated arm and asks for a whisky. 'Give me one of those Ardy-fardy ones.' He waves his fingers dismissively towards the bar.

'Ardbeg,' she says, indignant over his dismissal of her recent purchase for him. Vanessa walks across the carpeted floor on shaky legs towards the bar. She leans in against the edge of the countertop as a means of stilling herself, watching him pace the floor as she opens the bottle. The lid is stuck, requiring more effort than usual.

'When you didn't answer your mobile, I was worried.' He un-intentionally raises his voice again.

You? Worried? That would be a first. More like you thought I was up to something.

His back turned, looking out through the open terrace doors, his suspicious nature breaches again like a whale. 'Vanessa, you never go out and leave the doors open?' He turns sharply.

'I didn't. I just opened them.' She steadies her hand pouring a double. Swallowing hard, she decides to go on the defence. 'Anyway, you were busy, so what's the big deal. It didn't impede on your evening with Mummy.'

'Don't start that again,' he snaps.

She spots the empty martini glasses and quickly hides them below, before making her way to the fridge for some ice cubes. She hates his lack of respect towards the magical dram, but she's given up trying to educate the man long ago. 'Start what?' she calls from the kitchen with an air of confidence she's felt of late. *Bloody fridge won't close.* She tries again. *No.* She runs her fingers through her hair in frustration before trying a third time. *No.* She walks away until the beeping sound calls her back in frustration. 'Damn it!'

Michael brushes past her in haste to see what's wrong and lets out a spicy dinner belch as she shoves the whisky glass into his hand.

'The bloody door's jammed,' she says in exasperation.

'Let me look.' His tone is less threatening. He takes a swig of whisky. 'Oh, that's good.'

Shame you fuck it up by having ice with it. It's like feeding strawberries to pigs. She hopes he'll drink up and go. Leaving him to it, she heads to the bathroom in preparation for bed.

Michael attempts to fix the fridge, realising a loose magnet has fallen into the rubber seal, preventing it from closing properly. He slams the door with such force, the magnet falls back down into the seal again. 'Shit!' Irritated, he picks up the bothersome piece, tosses it in the bin, heads into the bedroom and taps on the bathroom door.

'What? Are you shaving your legs or something?' He listens to the tap running.

'No.'

'So are we screwing tonight or what?'

She's so repulsed she doesn't even dignify the condescending ignoramus with a response. When she eventually turns the running water off, Vanessa hears an odd noise on the other side of the door and steps closer to listen, only to realise it's Michael snoring. *Christ, he's staying!*

She waits a minute before opening the door carefully. Tiptoeing across the carpet, she retreats to the edge of the bed. Wary not to wake the sleeping giant, she disrobes down to her chemise and climbs in alongside him. *It's time to make a change. I must find the courage to get out of this dysfunctional relationship.*

Vanessa wakes at first light. Her terrace doors are still open and a cool breeze, almost cold, is blowing through the apartment. *Thank God he's gone.*

Comfortably tucked up in bed, alone with a sense of excitement, thoughts of William and their little flirtations in the car arouse a secret longing. Vanessa decides to play out her desires. No guilt. William at the fore.

Her body in sensory overload, a stirring of physical emotions, once quiescent, are ignited. Running her hand down over her ivory chemise, she slides it easily beneath the sheets, allowing it to ride up and over her silk panties. She touches the warm mound beneath.

Slipping her panties off, her breasts rise in jubilation at the mere thought of William touching her naked flesh. Biting down on her bottom lip, she suppresses a moan as her fingers, smooth and soft, begin moving, searching through the silken folds of flesh. She is a woman lost in her own fantasy, her own touch. A woman who likes to be teased, aroused by a slow hand. She touches herself, her eyes closed, burning with need. She sees his face, sublime, his body strong. Primed, she imagines his lips moving down over her body, his tongue circling where the moisture pools, his touch prevailing to the slick sounds beneath. He kisses it, licks around it, teasing tenderly.

As lustful images play out, she lets her legs fall further apart, feeling her juices spill from her body, teasing her nipples with the other hand. Bracing in quivering expectation, lust heightened, bursting with desire, she lets forth a low, drawn-out sigh.

Lost in the moment, stilled in thought, there's a hush as Vanessa catches her breath. Needing to gather her composure, she drags the doona across herself, enjoying the sensation as she waits a moment for her body to settle.

'Time to get moving.' She sits up, sliding her legs from under the covers. A little tired perhaps, but nothing can quell her excitement for the day ahead as she heads into the bathroom. When she opens the door, she sees Michael has habitually left a foul mess, a reminder she can't stand him a minute longer. Tracing her steps back through the loungeroom and out into the kitchen, a distinct taste of toothpaste is still on her tongue. Standing at the sink in a peaceful daze, she rinses her favourite porcelain mug her grandmother gave her. The Chelsea Garden mayflower scene never disappoints. Deep in thought, enjoying the warmth of the water as it washes over her hands, she looks through the closed window to the bright, beautiful day, causing her to smile.

Unfortunately, her whimsical thoughts soon drift back to Michael, who thankfully left early, leaving her alone in peace. *Huh, he says he hits the gym before heading into Chambers. Like the notorious criminals he represents, I'm not convinced. The stout, little, arrogant bastard is probably lying and doesn't work out at all. Certainly not as often as he professes.*

In the past it had occurred to her she ought to make a better job of finding out, but she'd never bothered. This morning she's far too content to even bother calling him. *William, on the other hand, looks so goddamn buffed he must work out all the time.*

A bee appears on the outside of the window and distracts her with its buzzing, like a rubber band pinging up against the glass. It's as if it's trying to get in and she wonders if the tall sunflower, perched on the inside ledge, is the attraction. 'Like bees to a honey pot.' She dries her hands. *Mm, like me to William. I'm hearing you.*

Vanessa turns and leans up against the sink with her mug and sips at the water, eyeing her open laptop on the coffee table in the loungeroom, reminding her of the work she has left to do.

I wonder if William will be there today. Before jumping online, Vanessa heads to the front door to grab the morning papers and is delighted to see a large bunch of beautiful, soft pink roses. *Oh! Francis Meiland's.* She'd recently sent her best friend, Lizzie, a bunch, only in peach, for her birthday. Closing the door behind her, Vanessa checks for a card in amongst the folds of white tissue and is surprised there's none. *They couldn't possibly be from Michael. William? I hope Michael didn't see them.*

She calls downstairs to check with Richard.

'Always happy to oblige, Miss Albert. The tall gentleman that was here last night dropped them off to reception around six and asked if I would place them at your door.'

Relieved to hear it would have been well after Michael left. she could almost see Richard smiling down the other end of the line. 'Oh, before I forget; the water is surging again in the shower.'.

'I'll call the plumber for you today.'.

'Good. I'll be out until at least lunchtime, so if you could get someone to come ...'

'Consider it done, Ms Albert.'

Distracted by the kettle's shriek, she thanks Richard, hangs up politely and races to turn the gas off. Reaching up inside the kitchen cupboard, she grabs a crystal vase that once belonged to her grandmother, fills the beautiful bowl with water and arranges the flowers. Carrying them steadily into her bedroom, she sets the vase down on the bedside table. Delighted, she steps back, admiring their glorious paleness against the backdrop of the soft grey wall. *Ever since I can remember, flowers never fail to bring a smile to my heart. Now where was I? Ah yes, tea.*

Pleased the bee seems to have given up, Vanessa opens the window to the delightful sounds of the children on the ground floor playing and giggling. She stops to listen to their joyous squeals and quickened feet scurrying around the courtyard as their father hollers, 'Look out, I'm coming to get you.'

Vanessa has always wanted children, but she knows it's probably out of the question in view of her age, not to mention a responsible partner to co-parent with.

The laughter eventually dies down. She grabs her tea and heads out onto the open-air terrace to her favourite spot. The day is glorious, not a cloud in sight. It's just starting to get hot, but it's not humid. Eyes closed; she turns her face upwards to gather a hint of warmth as she nestles into a recliner.

I love this feeling; it's like being on holidays, somewhere exotic, where the sea lies deep and clear, inviting you to plunge. Gosh, I need a holiday. Michael never wants to go anywhere. If I dare to suggest I go alone, all hell will break loose. It's not worth it. It's been two years since we've set foot on foreign soil. My, time flies.

A tiny urban bird, a superb fairy wren, sweeps down into the garden. Vanessa observes his iridescent blue and black plumage as he flits in and out of the low bush line, keen to find his breakfast. Two little brown wrens, obviously female, are quick to join him and it makes her laugh. *Bloody males, they always want more than one girl.*

A lone fly zigzags overhead, oblivious to the dangers below. Her attention is diverted to her forgotten herb garden, causing her to frown. The neglected sprouts beg to be watered. Remnants of rosemary, continental parsley, cilantro, chives, and mint all struggling for her attention. *Even my red-thumbed grandmother couldn't kill off the bevy of mint growing wild in an old cast iron bathtub in her backyard. The old leaky tap took care of that. Maybe I should plant some chillies? Forget it. I'd kill them too. Having successfully killed off the unkillable, perhaps I should admit I'm not cut out for gardening.* She pulls at the only visibly green thing: a weed. 'This, my friend, needs work.' *Which reminds me, I have work to do.*

Vanessa rallies and heads inside to check the time on the kitchen wall clock. *It's still way too early to buzz Lizzie. She'll be livid if I call her before eight. Ah, Lizzie has the life. I would love the luxury of having lunch with friends every day. Not really. Who am I kidding?*

Pleased she's not part of the sisterhood, Vanessa chooses to have very few girlfriends, convinced the most difficult part of a woman's life is, quite frankly, other women. Following her time in rehab after the attack, the decision was made to be more discerning, carefully choosing the women with whom she spends time. In her treasured group is Georgia Scott, a retired schoolteacher. The forty-one-year-old was born in the state of her namesake in the USA but raised in Australia from the age of thirteen. Following her father's death, her mother made the heartbreaking decision to return to Sydney, her place of birth. This meant having family support for Georgia throughout her awkward teens. Georgia is a blonde beauty and Vanessa smiles, thinking of her eyes. Blue-silver, not dull, they are shimmering orbs of light. Delightfully, her American accent has never waned, and along with her delicious southern twang and fun personality, she keeps everyone in stitches.

Sadly, ten years ago Georgia suffered a stroke, resulting in an ever so slight facial paralysis, believed to be caused by taking the pill, the very same oral contraceptive credited with accelerating women's liberation.

Georgia recently parted from the love of her life, husband of twenty-one years, Paul Scott, who ran off with a much younger woman. Unfortunately, Georgia feels old and somewhat vulnerable, especially since Paul never wanted children, only adding to the depth of her despair. However, she always puts on a brave face and is fun to boot.

Then there is the more recent addition to the group, the ever-flamboyant Francesca Scicolone. Vanessa met the leggy forty-year-old over cocktails at an art exhibition three years ago. Francesca is a hugely successful luxury lifestyle consultant who specialises in developing private art collections for wealthy investors. She's never married, having curiously been guided from an early age by her Italian mother to work hard and earn enough money in her chosen career to oversee her own destiny. 'Because if your husband is cruel, you can leave him immediately,' her mother told her, and like a dutiful Italian daughter, Francesca heeded her mother's words.

And of course, the infamous, blonde Elizabeth La Monte, known as Lizzie. Also a divorcee, but unlike Georgia, Lizzie has been gifted squillions from her divorce settlement, and through clever investments will never have to work again. Distinctly different to the other women, this flirtatious character wouldn't be caught dead without a full face of make-up. Lizzie is often featured in the Australian tabloids and most describe her as the single most hated woman in Sydney for her nefarious practices with married men.

Vanessa is a good friend and chooses to see past the hedonistic gossip, looking to the greater good by whipping up her own personal dialogue about her best friend. *Lizzie's always dolled up to the nines for any occasion. I wonder what "dolled up to the nines" means?*

Curious about the phrase, she Google searches on her mobile. *Ah, here it is. "To the nines is an old English idiom meaning to perfection or to the highest degree. The phrase comes from the nine yards of material a tailor needed to make a good suit."* She reads another story referring to the 99th Lanarkshire Regiment of Foot, a British army regiment established in 1824, known for the immaculate condition of their uniforms. *In other words, nobody is sure.*

Before work threatens to steal her away, Vanessa decides to take a quick shower. Out of habit, she observes her body in the vanity mirror and wonders if William will ever see her naked. The intense longing, since they met, is a first. *Locking eyes with him, the desire was so raw. I can't deny what I'm feeling.*

Drying off, she hears the phone in the other room, drops the towel and rushes to pick it up.

'Hello, Vanessa speaking.'

'Hi, Vanessa, William here.'

The second she hears his voice, an image pops to mind of his handsome face and a pleasurable warmth drifts throughout her naked body. 'Hi,' she says joyfully.

William is brief, sharing his thoughts on how lovely the previous evening was.

'It was divine,' she says.

'So ...'

Vanessa politely interrupts, thanking him for the beautiful roses. 'I've placed them on my bedside table, and they look simply stunning.' She's saddened she'll have to dispose of them before Michael returns for the weekend ritual.

'My pleasure! An exquisite woman should always be gifted beautiful flowers.'

She feels her cheeks blush.

'I've spoken to Gramps and he tells me today's meeting shouldn't go for more than an hour. So I was wondering if you'd like to meet me for lunch when you're done?'

Vanessa is surprised and curious as to how much he's shared about their private connection, William is quick to allay her fears with the assurance that Thornton is more than fine; he's pleased.

'So I take it you're not coming to the meeting?' She's beginning to feel quite vulnerable, standing there naked.

'Unfortunately, no. But if you're free afterwards, I'd love for us to grab a bite to eat.'

'Sounds lovely. Yes, of course. Where and when?'

They agree to meet at the plush Hyatt conveniently situated not far from the publishing house. Vanessa hangs up and squeals with delight before checking the time. Realising it's a quarter of an hour before she can call Lizzie, she throws on a silk robe, pours another cup of tea and pops on some soothing music.

CHAPTER FIVE

Vanessa grabs her laptop on the way to her office and plugs it in. Waiting for the machine to start up, she sets her tea down and picks up a small brass plaque her mother gifted her recently with the words etched into the alloy:

We Rest In Trust.

Directly underneath are the initials W.R.I.T. for *write,* a reminder of her mother's everlasting support for her work.

Sitting in her eighteenth-century armchair, Vanessa starts making necessary changes to her manuscript by culling and layering, layering, and culling. Suddenly dizzy with inspiration, she sets out pounding the keys enthusiastically. Not realising the passing of time, she looks down at her watch set to the side of the computer. The elegant, silver-toned dial shimmers back as she fixes her gaze on the Roman numeral markers. It's already gone half eight, so she decides to stay a little longer and use the extra time to propel her creative roll.

I'll call Lizzie this evening. That way I'll have more time to chat and a great deal more to tell in the wake of today's lunch.

Lizzie is constantly urging Vanessa to get out of her dysfunctional relationship. She assumes her best friend will be delighted by the news.

Pleased with her work and resolute she's done all she can today, she proceeds to email a copy to the publishing house and prints off a hard copy to take with her. Fanning through the pages with her thumb, she hopes Thornton will be happy with the amendments. Vanessa places a large, black foldback clip to the top left-hand corner and sets the manuscript out on the console nearest the front door in readiness.

'Time to get a move on.' She races to the bathroom to fix her makeup. Fishing about in her closet, Vanessa looks for something that will impress. 'Cream pants suit: check. Everyone loves this.' She hopes William will like it, and if the truth be known, Thornton too. She's not silly, having noticed the old man's flattering eye from time to time. *Being in a wheelchair doesn't mean he's stopped being a red-blooded male and it never hurts to impress the boss, no matter what his age.* Holding the suit up to the light for further scrutiny, she glances at the watch on her wrist. 'Good. Just enough time to dress.'

Ready, she orders an Uber. She's almost out the door when the landline rings. It's Lizzie.

'Hello, darling.'

'Oh, hi.'

'Where were you last night?' Lizzie asks suggestively.

Oblivious to her friend's tone, Vanessa says, 'Hold on a second, honey?'

'Sure.'

Setting down the phone, Vanessa wanders across the room, grabs her mobile and turns the music off. 'Hi, hi, back again. Lizzie, I'm sorry, honey, but I have a car waiting downstairs. Can I call you this evening? I have so much to tell you.' she says, adding pitch to her excited voice. 'Damn! I forgot to call Bob.'

'Who's Bob?'

'Oh, my neighbour, his dog. Oh, never mind. I'll call you tonight.'

'Anything for a friend,' Lizzie says with cynical dismissal.

Vanessa fumbles to hang up the receiver, glad of her savvy friend's understanding nature, but she'll have to wait to tell her the good news. Grabbing her handbag, she scoops up the manuscript and hurries out the door. The air hits her rosy cheeks with a blast of heat. Vanessa no sooner hops in the car, the driver about to pull away from the kerb, when she spots Bob striding down the footpath with Rex on his worn-out leash.

'Stop the car,' she says to the weather-beaten driver.

He hits the brakes hard as she hastily puts down the window.

'Hi, Bob,' she says cheerfully, then looks down at the dog despairingly and deepens her voice. 'Rex, you naughty boy.' She eyes the dog like they share a state secret. 'He was out gallivanting around again last night, Bob.'

'I know. I found him asleep on the front steps around eleven, probably escaping the heat.' He wipes his sweaty brow with a crumpled handkerchief. 'So bloody hot.'

'I'm so sorry I forgot to call you. Anyway, he's safe now.'

'He's a bloody cat, I'm telling you, Vanessa, not a dog. I'm certain of it. He has nine lives, this one.' He looks down at Rex with a wry grin.

As Vanessa follows Bob's gaze, they both spot a five-cent piece facing heads up. Bob bends wearily to pick it up and hands it to Vanessa. 'It's good luck.'

'I need a bit of good luck,' she says, taking the coin in gratitude.

Rex beams up at Vanessa, wagging his tail vehemently, then back at his owner like they're talking about him.

Vanessa laughs and indicates to the driver he can proceed.

Satisfied with how her meeting had gone with Thornton, Vanessa strolls through the gorgeously appointed hotel lobby, very much looking forward to catching up with William. She stops at the entrance point of the restaurant. *Where is he?* She pans the architecture of the room and is immediately distracted by the enormous arrangements of magnificent flowers throughout. Their stunning swathes of colour fill the vast space beautifully, some all the way up to the ceiling. *Spectacular! If only flowers could talk. They get front row seats at our most significant moments: thank yous, apologies, arrivals, farewells, funerals, birthdays, proposals, and weddings. Petal power speaks volumes when love is in bloom.* This sparks a thought about this morning's delivery.

Smiling, she looks around. The maître d' is nowhere to be seen so she ventures a little further, her dazzling rope of pearls gracefully draped down her decolletage, transforming her outfit to classical simplicity.

Passing a table of gentlemen, she's unexpectedly overwhelmed by the smell of hops dancing in the air as the men down their boutique beers like it's a competition. *The scent of flowers is preferable.*

Several tables, peppered about, are filled with confident, well groomed, physically fit older women sipping vodka martinis in between salon appointments and nibbling on poor excuses for lunch, tittering to one another through a wave of diamond fingers. *Asparagus and lettuce on enormous plates seems to be the order of the day. I wonder if Lizzie is in amongst this lot.*

The most delicious man in the room stands with a broadening smile and nods with a slightly raised hand. 'Vanessa.' He motions her to join him. 'Over here.'

She waves in acknowledgment just as another woman strides past, flipping her bleached blond hair across her bare shoulders, almost knocking Vanessa over as she demands to the nearest waiter to be seated. If looks could kill, Vanessa would be trampled over without even a thought. She squeezes her eyes shut. William is dressed impeccably in a navy suit. He stays standing as Vanessa crosses the room. Feeling his eyes follow her every move, she admires his calm, considered manner.

'Lovely to see you,' he says, leaning in and kissing her cheek before she gracefully slides along the grey velvet booth. He follows and they sit close. 'Coming across the room, you look like a slender punctuation mark against a blank page.'

She laughs at his imagination.

'You are quite the head turner,' he whispers in her ear.

Who isn't? 'Thank you,' she says, her eyes dwelling on an unopened bottle of champagne chilling in an elaborate ice bucket.

He notices. 'You did mention you like champagne, so I thought I'd get a head start and ask the waiter to put a bottle on ice. But if you prefer something else, I can change it?'

'Champagne is fine. Thank you.' *Did I say fine?*

'Good.' He gently touches her hand resting on the table.

Uncomfortable with public affection, she thinks about moving her hand, but William's seductive gaze is so engaging, it weakens her reserve. There is something very sensual and enticing about him. She can clearly sense he likes her, although she doesn't feel in his league.

He signals the sommelier, indicating he may proceed.

'Roses, champagne. William, I could get very comfortable with this if you're not careful,' she teases.

'That's the plan,' he says seriously. 'Do you know it's the first time I've ever actually had a meltdown choosing flowers: Meiland roses or calla lilies?'

Perusing the room, she just catches the hem of his comment, but it is beautiful. She rests her hand on his. 'They're stunning. Thank you.'

As the sommelier pours, a formally attired waiter stands to his left and waits.

Mesmerised by Vanessa, William leans in and whispers, 'You bother me.' His eyes search hers.

She feels his concentration, however they have an audience. Clearing his throat, the waiter excuses himself to recite the specials of the day. Vanessa doesn't hear a thing, watching William listening fixedly to a litany of choices.

'We're not in any great rush, Jonathan, so could you give us a few minutes, please.'

Vanessa is loyal to a handful of selected favourites herself, locally and across town, restaurants that are worth traveling an acceptable distance for, but certainly not to this standard.

'Cheers.' William holds his glass in salute.

'Cheers.'

He draws a contented breath and announces, 'Well, you certainly pleased the old boy today with those manuscript changes. He said you can feel the vitriol of the man leaping from the pages.'

'Tell me more?' she asks excitedly, under her breath, like someone much younger than her years.

'He loves it.'

'I worry, because he's told me I'm notorious for turning sentences around and I fear it distracts from the story.'

'That's what editing's for.'

'I know, but still, you'd think I would have figured it out by now.'

'Listen, you're a storyteller, Vanessa, and if this is anything like your last, you're a powerhouse to look out for.'

'Really?' Her eyes widen, liking the way he makes her feel. It's a nice change.

'Let's toast to that.' He holds up his glass.

Moving past matters of work, they talk about their expectations, having witnessed the changes since moving into their forties: work, friends, and touching on the future. When referencing her book, she notices his mood changes.

'I couldn't help wondering how you found the strength to openly write about what happened.'

'Well, they say all serious daring starts from within.'

'Eudora Welty.'

'I love her work: her words, photography, and the like.' Choosing her words carefully, she looks at William. 'The transitory more and more becomes one with the beautiful.'

'Remarkable artistic vision.' He shakes his head. 'Most of the time we look for neat answers.'

'Neat? What's neat about life?'

'True.'

'William, when you occupy a space that demands a voice, then you have a call to arms.'

'And that's what Thornton looks for. He has to find something exceptional in the work before he even considers publishing it, something that triggers his enthusiasm.'

'Well, I try to keep it real.'

'It shows and that's why your reviews are so extraordinary.'

She blushes.

'When the reader is able to concentrate on the inner life of a deep book by a serious author, it can be life-changing and far more powerful than any self-help book.'

Wow! She's flattered by his support.

'Did you decide to write while you were still in rehab, or afterwards?'

'I started taking notes in rehab because of the pending hearing.'

'I see. Most people would probably have ended up getting a ghost writer.'

'So I've come to realise. For me, that wasn't an option.'

William decides to lighten the mood. 'Here we are, the author and the publisher having lunch together, and for the record, I've never dated an author before.'

I think he's racing ahead of himself here. Vanessa feels far too drawn in to pull back now. 'Is that what this is? Because I've never dated a publisher before.'

The waiter returns and they decide to start with the Pacific rock oysters, then settle on the fresh fish of the day. Snapper. 'Right away, Mr Whittaker. Can I get you a garden salad perhaps?'

'Yes, please, Jonathan. Oh, and some of that lovely, crusty bread.'

The waiter gives a knowing nod and returns almost immediately, placing a roll on each of their side plates.

'Life's one long complicated journey, huh?' William says.

'Well, I had plenty of time in rehab to think about what had happened and came to the realisation of my certain mortality.'

'Mm. Well, if anything is going to make you reassess your life, that will. So are you all okay now?'

'I'm good, unless something else knocks me down along the way.'

'None of us know what's around the corner. It's how you handle it when you get there that counts.'

'That and outlook. My husband tried to end my life that day. But, in fact, that's when my life really began.'

'Yes, but I like that you haven't made this just about yourself.'

'I'd like to think so.'

He looks at her seriously. 'Courage is to recognise your own weaknesses and to do something about it, to live for something bigger than yourself.'

She thinks about what he's said and the detail with which he reasons.

'That's what I got from your book: your exceptional courage. Hence the title.'

'Thank you, but I have your grandfather to thank for that.' Though the title of the book says so, she's never really considered herself to be courageous. Coming from William Whittaker, she takes it as a compliment. 'Look, no one chooses to go to the darkest depths, and it's not what I signed up for, of course, but I think I found my own narrative out of survival.'

'I imagine it was an extremely cathartic process for you.'

'Yes, it was. So, by the time I got to rehab, I decided to write down everything I could remember while it was still fresh in my mind. It was the first time I'd caught a glimpse of something I might do with my life and that's how I became a writer.'

'Your vocation.'

'Yes.'

'Well, there's nothing greater than knowing what you want to do.'

She appreciates he's a good listener, observing her as she speaks, as if to encourage her to continue revealing more about herself, her writing, her family, and life in general.

'We're very grateful to have you.' He attempts to break the crusty bread roll. The bread virtually explodes, propelling crumbs everywhere. 'Arghh! I always do that.' He brushes crumbs from his trouser leg.

'Perhaps you should try a different kind.'

'But I like this one.'

'What's neat about life, huh?'

He bursts out laughing. 'You're funny. I like that about you.'

The waiter notices the spill, like he expected it. Giving William a nod, he approaches, crumb scraper in hand, and proceeds to remove the offending tidbits.

'A man of habits,' she says, still laughing.

'Mm, I have to agree there.' He picks up a large crumb from the tablecloth, setting it on the edge of his plate. 'Let's get back to you.'

'Well, I decided if you set about diarising your thoughts and feelings and were diligent about keeping a record of your life, suddenly you have a body of work, a book even.'

'Well, it's not that simple and not everyone has earth-shattering lives,' he says, lowering his eyes a little.

'My uncle Harry used to say little actions big things create. As you know, my uncle was paralysed, much like your grandfather.'

'What happened to him?'

'Diving accident.'

'That's certainly a life changer.'

'I had little or no idea about paralysis until his accident. Unfortunately we, the family, had to learn the hard way.'

He frowns.

'We live through emotional leftovers, battle through ignorance, and resurrect ourselves from pain.'

'You should write that down.'

She smiles. 'Well, I guess that's a conversation for another time.'

'So at what point did you realise you were a confident writer?'

'Tomorrow.'

He laughs.

'There's no magical moment. I think in your youth you have hubris, and sometimes false drive, but determination and experience or wisdom displaces a lot of that.'

'So had you written other things before *A Woman of Courage*?'

'I've always crafted short stories and had bits and pieces of editorial work published in the past, but nothing of any great significance.'

'Now there's a talent, making short stories leap off the page, creating compelling narrative with so few words.'

'True. Naively I used to have this idea a writer had to have lots of money, a beautiful room, and magnificent, unobstructed views of the ocean or the vineyards in Tuscany to write anything of worth.'

He laughs. 'Many great writers were stuck in some damp, dingy hide-away somewhere.'

'Oh, I hope not.' She cringes.

The slight movement in her brow tells him she has a kind heart. 'Vanessa, you're such a natural, I think you had a book in you no matter where you were.'

'Well, I have you gentlemen to thank for that.'

'We're so pleased the book has been well received and you're keen to keep writing.'

'I have to. William, you'd be amazed. I'm flooded with emails daily from people all over the world, sharing their stories of abuse. Quite horrific really.'

'I'm not surprised. '

'Are you really?' she asks, surprised.

'Of course. People are living in a pressure cooker these days.'

'Oh, I hate the thought, but I guess it's everyone, men and women.'

'Of course. But now, more than ever, women are able to speak up and there's great power in women's voices rising in tandem. People are being forced to listen. That's what storytelling is. And I noticed you have an enormous following on social media as well.'

'Yes. Look, I'm not the voice of a generation and I never will be. But I do think it's important to unmask the powerful forces of angry men and the vulnerability of those subjected to their emotional attentions.'

'I think you are underestimating yourself.'

'I'm just lucky to be embroidering my little square of the quilt. By that I mean casting hopeful visions for people reclaiming their lives.'

'I feel writers are always in some sort of subconscious psychosocial construct of how the world is put together and how the lives before you brought you to the here and now.'

'William Whittaker!'

Vanessa looks up to see the voice belongs to a heavily made-up woman with red hair, green eyes, and tanned skin that is hard and lined, like weathered leather. In contrast, she's wearing a very expensive, soft silk dress, but far too much gold jewellery. She strikes Vanessa as a woman who is in desperate need of attention.

She plonks her designer handbag down on the table as a bold statement. 'Well, hello there,' she purrs, her hand going to her weighty necklace that hangs low to her cleavage.

William doesn't get a chance to speak.

'You're William Whittaker! Do you come here often?'

'Um, yes.' He looks up at the imposing character before him.

'So do I, but I've never seen you here before.'

'Oh, I'm sorry; I didn't get your name.'

'Beverly. Beverly Watts.'

'Well, Beverly Watts, if you don't mind, I'm in the middle of –'

'Oh, I don't mind,' she says, bending at one hip.

'Okay. All right.' William is somewhat perturbed by her lack of understanding.

'Cheeky,' the woman says, self-assured.

Vanessa observes William staring at the woman in disbelief and clearing his throat.

'Oh, how silly of me,' the woman says, looking at Vanessa unapologetically. She proceeds to forage noisily through her bag, pulls out a business card and winks. 'Call me.'

'Thank you. Goodbye!'

The heavy-thighed woman walks off, click-clacking across the marble floor like her stilettos are in desperate need of heeling.

Vanessa observes her giving a wide wave across the room, then proceeding to sit at a table with the bare-shouldered, bleach-blond woman who almost bowled Vanessa over earlier. William simply slides the card across the table in complete disregard.

'Do you get that often?' Vanessa asks, tongue-in-cheek.

'All the time. One day I even had a woman following me into the bathroom.'

'No.'

'Some people have no shame.'

'Well, she certainly doesn't.'

'Astounding.' He shakes his head in embarrassment.

'It would appear you are a person that everyone has an opinion on.'

'Yes. Nobody is neutral, I can assure you. When someone asks me a question, I have this instant fear that they are looking for something to give the tabloids.'

'So tell me a bit about yourself, William.' She smirks.

'Oh.'

'No, really. I know you adore your grandfather, so that's a good start. Tell me more about your relationship with him.'

William is always open to the opportunity to sing his grandfather's praises. 'Well, he's emotional. Life touches him, moves him, and upsets him. He's a deeply serious individual. Oh, and don't be fooled. Beneath that calm exterior, he can be quite stern when he wants to be. But he's always there for us, no matter what, so what's not to love?' He opens the palms of his hands.

'I hope this doesn't sound strange, but he's become quite dear to me,' Vanessa says.

'Trust me, you bring out the best in him too.'

She smiles warmly. 'Family is everything.'

'Indeed. What I admire most about Gramps is his accomplishments, having ignited a dream that, to this day, has been relentlessly pursued by each generation of our family. He founded this business on a shoestring and successfully created an empire under difficult circumstances.'

Vanessa listens intently, shocked to hear he founded the business on a shoestring. *I always thought Thornton came from old money.*

'Nearly 60 years ago, he established a small publishing house on George Street, Sydney. Did you know he is the grandson of an English suffragette, my great-great-grandmother, Cristobel Whittaker?'

'No,' she says, astonished.

'Gramps was brought up to believe men and women alike have the right to vote and the right to freedom of speech.'

'Of course!'

'His core beliefs were forged by his grandmother from an upper middle-class background who was frustrated by women's antiquated social and economic circumstances.'

Ah, so I was right. He was exposed to money.

'I'm sure you know women were once deemed to have no place in a world made for men. The suffragettes' battles for change within society were demonstrated by women activists, comrades soldiering on in all manner of ways, chaining themselves to railings and setting fire to mailboxes. It's said one woman, the infamous Emily Wilding Davison, died at the Epsom Derby when she was run down by the King's horse. Many of the women were detained in Holloway Prison, London, and force-fed after going on hunger strikes. Can you imagine the abuse they endured?'

'Shocking!'

'You have to remind yourself it wasn't that long ago. And it's what those women managed to do, and the sacrifices they made fighting against the antiquated beliefs of old, that took decades off the suffering of women and the generations to come worldwide.'

'Absolutely. I think here in Australia, if I'm not mistaken, it was 1902 when parliament passed the bill enabling women to vote.'

'Something like that, yes. But from a very young age, Gramps saw his mother work tirelessly at the grassroots level for the rights of women – a belief she too inherited.

Apparently as a lass, she passed out pamphlets, her mother Cristobel had written and distributing them throughout London, including to local newspapers and editors. Cristobel was also a woman with a good mind and an advanced degree. She was a wonderful speaker, and I'm told, a very attractive woman. But coming from money didn't matter; she felt she needed to do more with her life.'

'A rebel with a cause,' Vanessa adds.

'Yes. In turn, this gave Gramps an enormous admiration for strong women like yourself and the need for them to express themselves with the written word. There's rich literature about women fighting for their rights, written by women, for whom it represents emancipation.'

'I've read bits and pieces, but I must admit, not in any detail. Do you think your grandfather would chat to me about what it was like back then?'

'Of course. He's so proud of his heritage. You can see why you've struck a chord with him: women fighting for their rights.'

'And rightly so.' Vanessa looks at him admiringly. 'The respect you have for him is so inspiring, William.'

He grows pensive. 'Vanessa, I remember, as a little boy, I would watch him, with such admiration, shave every single morning. He'd carefully sharpen his cutthroat razor on a long, leather strop and meticulously shave without ever cutting himself, applying hot towels to finish and some fresh-smelling, oily lotion. Having observed his level of precision, I couldn't wait to grow up and try it myself.'

She grasps the enormous respect sparkling like diamonds in his captivating, brown eyes. Such love and admiration moves her and she reaches across, rubbing his upper arm endearingly.

'The business of life is the acquisition of memories,' he says.

'I like that.'

'Gramps says it all the time.'

'At fear of sounding silly, I'd like to take a USB and plug it into his brain to download what he's seen.'

William breaks into a belly laugh. 'We all would. And I might add, he never forgets anything.'

'I noticed that, William. I don't mind telling you I am often rendered mute in his company.'

'Oh, I get that. I think he has that effect on a lot of people.'

The waiter appears and centres the oysters on the table as the sommelier simultaneously tops up their glasses.

Vanessa grins at the spectacular display on show.

'Oh, you'll love these.' William reaches across to grab one of the oysters. He looks at the waiter. 'Jonathan, they look exceptional today.'

'Thank you, sir. Will there be anything else?'

'No, this is perfect. Can you not rush our main meals, Jonathan, thank you?'

'Of course, Mr Whittaker.'

'Try these, Vanessa. They are so fresh. They shuck them immediately before serving.'

'They're so plump.' She places an oyster on her plate, scooping it up with her oyster fork and letting the delicate morsel slide across her tongue before swallowing. The sweetness is a delight to the senses.

'Mm. They're like taking a dive into the ocean,' he says, looking at her.

'William, I don't want this to come out the wrong way, but you're nothing like the press portray you.'

'Thank Christ for that.' He reaches across for another oyster. 'I remember, years ago, my poor mother saw the first negative news article about me and was devastated. When people were cruel, I'd tell her, "Mum, tomorrow that newspaper will be wrapping for fish and chips".'

'Or the potty for the puppy.'

He laughs.

'Sounds like it might have been pretty tough on your mum.'

'It was. According to the press, I'm a philandering playboy motivated only by my libido, living a cavalier lifestyle. Apparently I'm out at lunch every day and living off my grandfather's wealth.'

'A real womaniser?'

'No. A notorious womaniser for my Lothario-like antics. Oh, please let's not go there. While I can expound the many glories and scandals in my family history, I am conscious of doing the right thing by them and I live with a clear conscience. I have my truth.'

'Granted.'

'Vanessa, I don't know what your experience is with family businesses but let me tell you this. They can be notoriously treacherous waters to chart.'

She gives an intrigued nod.

'Sure, we have our own internal politics but we each have a role to play. Above all else, we have respect for one another.'

She watches as he moves an empty shell to the side of his plate and looks at her seriously. 'Do you know Gramps has a team that reads every single manuscript that comes through our doors?'

'Really?'

'Yes. After the crew have made their comments, Gramps then oversees the manuscripts himself. No unnecessary slush piles at Whittakers, I'm proud to say. He's a font of information and his knowledge of books, old and current, is remarkable.'

Another shell is set down on the plate.

'Yes, I noticed some on his desk yesterday.'

'That was last night's read for him.'

'Really.'

'On the other hand, my father is a different kettle of fish.'

'Oh. How so?'

'He's a little on the quiet side, but don't let that fool you. He's a deep thinker and one shrewd businessman.'

Definitely no underlings in this family. 'He sounds interesting.'

'He's the number-cruncher and takes care of the promotional side of things, both here and overseas, believing in ongoing expansion. It's paramount, he says, and I might add, I don't think he's ever read a single manuscript.'

Vanessa is interested to meet his father, Montgomery, whom the press often has a field day with as well. According to William, his father is pleased her book sales demonstrate the interest in her work. *Obviously, it ticks a major box for Montgomery if you are making money for the company. Clearly the Whittaker men are distinctively different but equally dazzling. Each one appears cut from the same cloth, having a marvellous approach to the way they do business.*

Unlike the usual trash written about the family in the paparazzi magazines, Vanessa read to the contrary in one of the financial mags, an excellent article on the moral code of the men behind the empire:

> Whittakers high net-worth is well founded, whether it be first generation or third. These outstanding men hold their own singularly and collectively, possessing a business and investment savvy based on longstanding values. It is the age-old, dependable process of a lifetime of knowledge handed down through the generations. Their prosperity has clearly amassed comfortably from generation to generation. For that reason, the best investments over time have been those that provide a sense of security, longevity, and asset appreciation.
>
> Whittakers are most notably revered for caring passionately about the product, the written word, and the person behind it, often going out on a limb by supporting unknown writers. Other publishing houses simply toss potentially praiseworthy manuscripts away after only having read the first line, showing no compassion for the devastated soul behind the work.
>
> Evidently some publishers don't even bother to respond or return the work these individuals have spent years developing and fine tuning, thereby leaving the writer in a state of perplexed limbo.
>
> Whittaker Publishing is a well-oiled machine that obviously cares about creative individuals, and the risks often pay off, delivering readers some of the best bodies of work on offer.

William clearly has good business acumen, but Vanessa can't help feeling uneasy about what the press have said about him making bad personal choices. *He said it himself, the women he's dated were all striking to look at, but there was always something missing on a deeper level. Why is that?*

William continues. 'Part of the reason for the stability of Whittaker Publishing is the family ethics, imbued into every facet of our business and personal life.'

Well, that tosses the Chinese's theory out the window! Wealth lasts but three generations. The first earns it, the second builds it, and the third spends it. The Whittakers, it would seem, continue to disprove this dictum.

'As for me, everyone was expecting me to break the rules. But I have a vast array of interests. I tend to gravitate to certain projects I think reflect some of the attitudes of my grandfather. Publishing is where I fit. It's my world.'

'Have you always felt this way?'

'No. Not really. Most twenty-somethings don't.'

She laughs, taking another sip of her drink, delighting in the texture of the bubbles. 'Twenty-somethings?'

'Yes. At the insistence of my mother, I travelled far and wide.'

'Really? I thought you joined forces straight out of university.'

'I did. But took a gap year and it's the best thing I could have done.'

'Wow!'

'Well, not that I tried to shirk the weight of inherited responsibilities. It was a great decision driven by my mother's wisdom. I was totally independent as a kid. We travelled a lot, so I wasn't ambivalent about her encouragement to spread my wings. But at some point, I had to decide what would be my legacy.'

'Interesting. Tell me about your mother.'

'That's a whole other matter for another time,' he says. 'Eventually I returned home and knuckled down. At the fear of sounding conceited, I took my family's business in the direction it needed to go, into the 21st century, championing consumer confidence with regard to holding a book. The visibility of owning something someone has spent years creating, instead of simply downloading, I feel is invaluable.'

'Absolutely, and for the record, I don't think you're the least bit conceited.'

'You are sweet. There's nothing quite like holding a book in one's hands and smelling it, say turning the pages of Keats and breathing in the decades.'

Did he have to say that name. I don't need Michael in my head today.

'If I hadn't stepped up, I'm certain my father would have sold off to the highest bidder and retired to the beaches of Bali. I simply couldn't see my grandfather retire and lose his soul to boredom.'

'I'm with you. He's too great a man.'

'His passion for life and his enormous drive come from having something to go to every day. Publishing is in his blood; it's what he knows and loves.'

Vanessa taps her temple and gives a questioning look. 'How does that saying go?'

He shrugs his shoulders.

'Ah, yes:

Give a man someone to love,

And if you can't,

Give him hope,

And if you can't,

Give him something to do!'

William smiles. 'You are gorgeous.'

Their fish and salad arrive with an unordered side of crispy, herbed chips, causing William's eyes to light up.

'Excellent! A bonus!'

The confused waiter glances at a nearby table. *Oops!*

'Don't take them away!' William raises his eyes playfully. 'You can't put them down and then take them away. All right, take them to the rightful owners and we'll take another one.'

The chips stay.

William smiles. 'In gratitude, I'll eat them.'

His easy charm makes Vanessa chuckle. 'No willpower, huh?'

'None whatsoever!'

She laughs. 'William, I'm very pleased I went with Whittakers because I don't mind telling you I've heard some horrible stories of people being taken for a ride. As you would know better than most, there's an awful lot of stress that goes hand-in-hand with writing tell-all biographies. So for someone to simply toss years of your work into a bin must be heart-wrenching.'

'Sure, it is. There's a lot to consider with publishing. I was reading a recent report from the UK about widespread bad practice among hybrid publishers that manipulate and charge authors to publish their work.'

'Oh, do you mean vanity publishing?'

'No. I'm talking about aggressive, strategic tactics where the writer ends up out of pocket.'

'Oh dear. That's awful.' She's intrigued about the industry and remembers a heated discussion regarding plagiarism at one of her writers' groups recently. 'I heard plagiarism goes on as well.'

'Oh, don't get me started,' he says, annoyed. 'I had an issue with a fairly well-known author recently.'

'Oh, do tell. Who is it? Anyone I know?'

'Yes, that bloody Fiona Ca–' He stops short. 'I shouldn't really say.'

'Quite frankly, I'd rather not know. They're the scourge of literature as far as I'm concerned.'

'Sadly, it goes on all the time.'

'Wasn't it Nora Ephron who wrote, 'Everything is copy.'

'You needn't worry about that at Whittakers; we've got your back.'

'Sounds like a promotional slogan.'

He laughs.

'I think it must have been the Strawberry Sponge Fingers that did it,' she says with a chuckle.

'Forgive me while I scull my champagne,' he says, surprised.

'Oh, so they're a regular indulgence.'

'Ah yes. The dreaded Ladyfingers. They're amazing! Gramps' secretary, Donna, makes them for him on occasion. You're bloody lucky he was willing to share. You are a star.'

'We bonded over cups of tea and cake that afternoon.'

'Good on you.'

'After the first bite, believe me, I willingly indulged. In fact, Thornton inspires me to do a lot of things I ordinarily wouldn't. And not just eating cake.'

'Like dining with his grandson?' He grins cheekily.

Vanessa laughs. 'Ah, no, this is all your own doing.'

'Right now, I'm feeling quite chuffed with myself.'

'Your grandfather is very encouraging, but there are moments when I still find him a little daunting, like a bold uncle figure at family gatherings.'

'Vanessa, he'd hate to think he intimidates you.'

In the distance there's an almighty crash. They look around to see a tray of glasses on the dining room floor. Several men cheer, then one man starts tapping the side of his glass with a knife, drawing further attention.

'Don't you hate that?' Vanessa says.

'Yes, it's total unnecessary and only adds insult to injury.'

Vanessa likes William's consideration.

'Who was that man I saw running towards you last night? He was calling out your name, but you didn't see him.'

Vanessa is suddenly caught off guard. 'Pardon?' Her voice trails off and she seems quite vague.

'When I dropped you home?'

She stares blankly at a lot of farewell double-air cheek kisses taking place over at the lady's luncheon table – *looks a bit like Beverly Hills Housewives* – and finally says, 'Oh, him. It was probably my girlfriend's partner. He was out looking for her. Thought she may have been with me.' *Dear God, what possessed me to say that.*

Her thoughts on speed dial, she traces back to William checking out all the photographs in her apartment. *Christ, it's not likely anyone would keep a framed photograph of their best friend's boyfriend. I need to explain myself. We still have a business arrangement.*

Picking up on her clumsiness, William intuitively changes the subject. 'So what have you got planned for the weekend?'

'Ah, not sure yet.'

Her mind is ticking over, and though she's only taking in half of what he's saying, she is grateful he keeps talking.

'Again, this is short notice.'

'You're good at that.'

He laughs. 'I'm wondering if you'd like to head up to Whale Beach for a couple of days. The weather has been beautiful lately and my place overlooks the beach, so it's ideal. I can pick you up Friday evening and you stay for the weekend.'

Christ! What about Michael?

Sensing her reluctance, he decides to explain further. 'Since my mother passed away, Dad usually comes down on weekends. I'm company for him, I guess. But as it happens, this weekend he has other plans, so we'll have the place all to ourselves.'

'Oh, where does your father live?'

'In the city. He has an apartment at Circular Quay.'

'Nice.'

'He likes it, but personally I much prefer being near the water. So will you come?'

'William, that sounds great, but —'

Believing her prompt response is an acceptance, he says, 'Done. I'll pick you up at seven. That way we'll miss the peak hour traffic and have dinner along the way.'

Even knowing he's played court to some of Sydney's most glamorous women, she's feeling strangely connected to him and simply can't bring herself to refuse. 'Okay then, why not.' *Lizzie is never going to believe this.*

After a long, animated lunch, William drops Vanessa home. Before hopping out of the car, he reaches across, taking the opportunity to kiss her on the cheek. 'I'm really looking forward to spending time with you.' He looks deep into her eyes.

The feeling is mutual. 'Me too,' she says in the sincerest tone. She gives him a warm smile, opens the door, and says goodbye with a gentle wave.

Upstairs, Vanessa heads straight to the main bedroom, kicks off her shoes and puts her bag down on the bed. Suddenly she thinks of Michael and frowns. *I have no idea what to tell him.* 'Michael, I'm going away.' *Let alone with whom.* 'With Sydney's most eligible bachelor. Christ, If I had a cat, I'd kick it!' She screams.

Glancing across at the roses on the bedside table, her face turns from frustrated to delight, and she remembers telling Lizzie she'd call her back. *On second thoughts.* Instinct taps her on the shoulder. She decides to keep details to a minimum and say nothing about William. *I can't afford any slip-ups.*

The landline jolts her out of the self-chatter. It's Michael wanting to know how the meeting went.

'Great,' she spews forth unrehearsed. 'In fact, I've been invited to go and stay at their Whale Beach property this weekend. They're having some international writers get together and have offered for me to join in and chat about my book and the circumstances that led me to write a tell-all.'

Silence.

'Michael, are you still there?'

'I'll give you tell-all. I knew when you wrote that bloody, goddamn book things would go from bad to worse, Van.'

She loathes being called Van. It's something her fly-by-night stepfather used to say whenever he wanted to take her down a peg or two.

'And what is that supposed to mean, Mick?' *I wish you'd take your foot off my fun.* 'You know, Michael, whenever something special comes my way, I can always count on you to smash it mid-flight. Thank you very much.'

'Pleasure! Have a nice life!'

Holding the phone away from her ear, Vanessa hears a distant click. *I hadn't planned on arguing, but this might well turn out to be fortuitous. Now I can go away without having to explain myself, and this way I'm not obliged to call him.* She heads directly for the liquor cabinet. *I think a bloody good gin and tonic and a long soak in the tub is in order.*

Reclining in the bath, feet up against the opposite edge, she goes over the day's events and how relaxed she feels in William's company. *But going away is a whole new ball game.* She looks down at her knobbly knees. On one is a tiny scar, reminding her of Bruno and trying to drag herself through the garden bed on that fateful day. *Yep, life's too short.* She resigns herself to going away and having some fun for a change.

Feeling relaxed and somewhat tingly from the water, Vanessa steps out, dries off, and retreats to the bedroom. She tries to read for a bit. Her eyes skim the words on the unbleached pages:

> "Beyond the ugliness in this world, is the incredible
> beauty of love and friendship — that is where I live."

She yawns. *No offence, Nan Witcomb. You write beautiful poetry, but* Thoughts of Nanushka *never fails to put me to sleep. Perhaps that's why it's taken up permanent residency.*

Vanessa places the book on the bedside table, switches off the light and falls sound asleep.

CHAPTER SEVEN

At last it's Friday morning and Vanessa is overcome with childish glee, so the first thing she plans to do is zilch. Wanting to look her best for this evening's dinner, she thinks it wouldn't hurt to indulge by giving herself an extra languid twenty minutes. After all, there's nothing too pressing, other than her manicure and pedicure appointment scheduled mid-afternoon, so she reaches across, hitting the snooze button on her phone. *I love that naughty button, it's like a drug.*

Just as she snuggles into the softness of her favourite pillow, a narrow beam of warm light bursts through the curtains in line with her eyes, causing her to open them suddenly to dust motes dancing in the sunlight.

Her thoughts skip to the need to pack. *I won't need much. What am I thinking? I've never packed light in my life.*

She sits bedside, looking down at her beige toenail polish, and crinkles her nose. *I need to change to a soft pink.*

She stretches before pulling her overnight bag down from the wardrobe and plonking it on her unmade bed. Sleepy-eyed, she proceeds to fumble through her clothes and is soon colour coding a theme and laying her things out on the white doona. The blues and blacks pop, but she decides to inject some more colour here and there. Before folding them into her bag, she laughs at herself for packing almost the same for a weekend as she does for two weeks abroad.

Feeling her tummy rumble, she checks the time on the bedside clock. *Lovely. I have plenty of time.*

The quiet leads Vanessa to put on some soothing music. Checking out the contents of her fridge, she wiggles her bottom and harmonises to the melody. Looking at two ripe tomatoes, she decides on making a *pico de gallo*. Laying everything out on a wooden chopping board, Vanessa dices the tomatoes, takes a small, white onion, and dices it finely, adding it to the bowl. A green jalapeño, finely minced, is added along with a dash of fresh lime juice, salt and pepper. It's then set to the side. Bringing a pot of water to the boil, she gently lowers in two eggs and toasts an English muffin. When it's nice and crisp, she layers the muffin with sour cream, avocado, the *pico de gallo* mixture, shredded Gouda, and the softly poached eggs, then finishes with a dash of her favourite hot sauce.

Peeking at the sunny terrace, she decides to take brekky out. Grabbing a place mat, napkin, some cutlery, and her plate, she heads to the outdoor table.

'I do love it out here,' she says, taking the first bite. 'Gosh, this is good. Glad I thought of it.' *If my neighbours heard me chatting to myself, they'd have me locked up.* She looks at her plants in desperate need of water. Between mouthfuls, Vanessa jumps up, places the copper watering can under the dripping tap, and sits back down to finish breakfast.

'I'm so excited about getting out of town.' *Especially with William.* 'Gosh, it's a long time since I've gone anywhere.'

Listening to the rhythmic sequence of the soothing music through the outdoor speaker, Vanessa sets her cutlery down and settles back in the cast-iron chair. Closing her eyes, the steady cadence of the drums is almost hypnotic, until she hears her cutlery tinkle and opens her eyes to see a little sparrow on her plate, picking at the leftovers.

'Shoo! Don't eat that,' she cries, waving a gentle hand at the intruder. 'The jalapeño will kill you.'

She watches as the bird flies off to the watering can and drinks from the dripping spout. Vanessa sits long enough for him to quench his thirst before watering her herbs and plants.

'Okay, enough. Time to get some work done.'

'You pick colour,' requests the familiar nail artist, Cindy, as she preps the warm water into the foot basin, adding blue bath salts.

'Pale pink, please,' Vanessa asks, feeling relaxed.

'You pick, you pick,' the Vietnamese woman says more urgently, waving the back of her hand at the array of colours displayed on the wall.

Vanessa spots the perfect shade and hands it to Cindy before sitting down and popping her feet into the warm water.

'How's your boyfriend?' Cindy asks in a high-pitched tone.

Vanessa has a sudden wave of empathy for Michael; it soon passes.

When she doesn't answer, Cindy grows quiet. Aware her client needs space; she douses a cotton pad with polish remover to make the chipped colour disappear.

Vanessa is mindful she and Michael have reached a critical point in their relationship. It has become far too combative and there is simply no justification as to why they're still together. Meeting William has stirred dormant emotions and she isn't prepared to walk away from the prospect of a happy future together.

Another manicurist arrives to begin her manicure. 'You look very beautiful today,' says the young woman cheerily.

You say that to everyone. 'You speak with fork tongue.' Vanessa chuckles, waving a jesting finger.

The two Vietnamese women laugh along with Vanessa, then exchange words in their native tongue.

Vanessa's thoughts move back to William. *He's such a darling man: considerate, handsome. I cannot believe I'm going away with this man, and for two whole nights!*

She looks to the front of the salon as half a dozen women simultaneously try to squeeze through the doorway. Judging from the level of bantering taking place, it's a bridal party. The last woman to appear is wearing a *Bride to Be* tiara.

I'm out of here.

Several young Vietnamese women appear through a colourful beaded curtain from the back of the salon, casually work their way, in pairs, to the front of the shop and set about seating the women at the various nail stations. As the women's voices escalate, Vanessa is glad she's done.

Vanessa spots Richard bent down behind the front desk as she enters her building.

'Hi, Richard. How's your day?'

'Good. And you?' He looks up.

'Great. Richard, I'll be away until Sunday evening, so don't worry when you don't see me about.'

'Thank you for letting me know.'

'I know I don't need to say this, but I would appreciate your utmost discretion.'

'Of course, Ms Albert.' He makes a zipper movement with thumb and forefinger across his mouth.

'Oh, and by the way, thank you for getting the plumber in. The shower's working perfectly now.'

'My pleasure, Ms Albert.'

Vanessa gives him a warm smile and enters the lift.

Inside her apartment, she calmly sets about getting ready to go away. After a quick shower, she adds minimal make-up and decides to choose something *très chic* from her underwear drawer. *Oh, I am naughty.* Her fingers lace easily through the silk; the softness of the fabric a pleasure to the senses. *Red? No, too bold. White? No, too innocent. Black? Mm, perfecto! What am I thinking?* She shrugs her shoulders. Pairing black pants with a matching silk blouse, she teams it with a pair of gold stilettos.

True to form, Vanessa is not surprised in the least when William buzzes the intercom a few minutes early. Not one for faffing about, she checks herself in the mirror and gives a nod of approval, then races to answer the intercom.

'Come on up.'

Within minutes, William is at the door, left ajar with a very large book. He hesitantly pushes it open and peeks around the corner. 'Hey,' he says, catching his breath as she looks up, glancing in his direction.

'Hey. Come on in.' She gives him a flattering smile while trying to close the clasp on her gold bracelet.

William steps inside, picks up the weighty tome, presents it flat between his open palms and says, 'Only you would dare to use this as a door stop.'

'Oh, you noticed,' she says cheekily.

He places the heirloom, her old family bible, on the console with care, then takes advantage of the warm hug on offer. Inhaling a whisper on the side of her neck, he says, 'You are beautiful!'

She looks up into his eyes. 'Beautiful things should remain at the fore and in our hearts forever.'

In that moment she knows she has him, but is taken by surprise when he tilts her head and steals a kiss on the lips for the very first time.

'Sorry. I had to do that,' he says, gazing at her.

Leaving her spellbound, a second or two is lost, until she draws back an unforgotten breath.

'You look stunning, by the way,' he says.

'So do you.' She pulls back slightly, admiring what he's wearing. Navy polished cotton jeans, crisp white shirt, navy linen blazer and brown suede loafers.

'Are you ready?'

'Sure am,' she says, like she's been woken from a deep sleep.

He scoops up her leather overnight bag situated nearest the front door. 'Is this it?'

'Yep.'

'Got your keys?'

'Yes.' She jangles them enthusiastically.

In the confines of the lift, William raises Vanessa's hand to his lips, kissing the back of it tenderly while breathing her in. 'You smell good.'

I really like everything about this man. Faultless. A spontaneous chill runs up her back. She doesn't ever remember feeling so intensely aroused in any man's company before.

As the lift doors open, William squeezes her hand tightly, reluctantly letting go.

Vanessa clears her throat, acknowledging Richard standing over by the concierge desk.

'Sir, can I get that for you?' Richard asks, stepping forward to help.

'No, thank you. We're good,' William says, walking towards the glass doors.

Richard nods, steps through the entrance to open the car door for Vanessa while William flicks the boot open.

She leans back in her seat and draws down on a sigh. *My God, I'm going to hell.* Trusting Richard implicitly, she gazes at him through the window and gives him a grin.

He grins back at her before saying goodbye to William.

He's never said in so many words, but I know he never warmed to Michael.

'Let's get this weekend started,' William says, pulling away from the kerb.

'Let's,' she says, pleased to be getting on their way.

A few minutes out, William turns the volume down on the steering wheel control. 'Busy day?' He's aware he needs to keep his eye on the road and not the curve of her breasts.

'As a matter of fact, no. Quite cruisy really.'

'Sounds cool. So what sort of music do you like? I got Phillip to organise a new playlist for me.'

'Phillip?'

'I'm sorry. You've not met at the office?'

'No.' *I do seem to remember hearing his name tossed about from time to time.*

Surprised, he pulls a curious frown.

'He works for the family. Has done for years. Come to think of it, I don't think he's ever worked for anyone else. And he has impeccable taste, including music, new and old.'

A falsetto voice floats easily from the speaker.

'Curtis Mayfield,' she says. 'I really like his music.'

'You have good taste.'

'Did you know Curtis Mayfield was paralysed?'

'No. Really?'

'Terrible,' she says.

'How?'

'From the neck down, after stage lighting equipment fell on him at a concert. Tragic. In the US, I think it was.'

'That's awful.'

'Yes, it is.'

'And he was still able to sing after that?' William asks. 'How?'

'He actually recorded an album lying down.'

'You're kidding me,' William looks her way, astonished.

'Incredibly, gravity pulled on his chest and lungs, enabling him to still sing.'

'That's rare, right?'

'Yes, absolutely. It's remarkable.'

The traffic is unusually smooth for a Friday evening and Vanessa is far away, relaxed in thought, when it occurs to her she's seen an article in a magazine about the Whittakers' home, *Oceana*. Conscious of William's hand gently stroking her lower thigh, she attempts to remember the publication. *Damn! I wish I'd remembered. I would have re-read it.* She does remember the house being touted as magnificent.

William is chatting away beside her.

'Sorry, I was listening to the music,' she lied.

'Are you looking forward to dinner?'

'Yes, I am.'

'Well, I'm famished. I booked this great restaurant overlooking the water near my place.'

'How lovely.'

'The lobster there is the best. They fly it in from Western Australia.'

'I love lobster.'

'Good. There's a start.' William turns off the main drag and the roads become more intimate, more localised, friendlier even. Taking the bends comfortably, William suddenly brakes at the top of the hill.

A boy about ten is trying to coerce his sleepy dog off the middle of the road. He waves a cheerful thanks, like he's done it a thousand times.

Vanessa smiles.

William waves and accelerates, taking one last turn up a steep hill before pulling into a small driveway. The sign over the door reads *The Waterview*.

Vanessa hasn't been to the northern beaches in such a long time and is instantly delighted to see it's the acclaimed restaurant she recently read about.

'Here we are,' William says, parking out front.

A casually dressed couple exit the car next to them, behaving somewhat rowdily, having obviously kick-started their evening with a few drinks already.

'For God's sake, people, put on a jacket and leave your tracksuits at home,' William says quietly, checking the couple out. 'This is not Macca's.'

'I thought it was just me, but I guess most restaurants these days invite a level of casualness,' Vanessa says.

'Yes, and for that I'm grateful. But if you're not going to put on your best for *The Waterview*, then when?' He slides from the vehicle and makes his way around to open her door.

Vanessa jumps out and peruses her surroundings. *It feels familiar.* It strikes her she's been here before as a small child, with her sister, mother, and a tall gentleman she can't quite put a face to. *No matter, I'm here with the man of my dreams now.*

Entering the restaurant, hand in hand, they're immediately greeted by a self-assured maître d', a tall, skinny man with a ready smile of large, crooked teeth.

'Good evening, Mr Whittaker. Good evening, madam.'

'Good evening,' William says.

Observing William's confident manner towards the maître d', she nods politely.

'Right this way. please,' the man says, extending his arm in an outward direction and almost knocking a patron in the face.

'Oh, sir, my apologies.' He whips around, watching as the stooped man regains his composure.

'Quite alright,' the man says, nervously fidgeting with his oversized jacket.

In view of the maître d's formality, Vanessa holds back a giggle at the absurdity and the couple follow him through the busy restaurant.

A low buzz of mingled voices is unexpectedly broken by loud, alarming laughter coming from a bosomy woman in a polka-dot dress over by the corner. Delicious aromas waft from the direction of the kitchen. Comfortably seated, Vanessa watches the flair with which the maître d' places a large, white linen napkin on each of their laps.

'Your waiter will be with you shortly.' With a bow, he excuses himself.

'For a moment there, I thought we were in a scene out of *Fawlty Towers*,' William says good humouredly.

'I wondered if perhaps I was supposed to be laughing, seeing the maître d's deadpan reaction.'

'It was funny.'

The waiter soon appears in a white dinner jacket and says his name is Lenny with a Y, pointing to his name tag in proud confirmation.

The only Lenny with a Y I've ever heard of is Kravitz and they sure as hell don't look like they're related. Perhaps his mother's a fan, much like mine? The absurdity of this place. Vanessa watches the short man hand William the wine list.

William waves him no and asks for a bottle of their finest Sancerre. 'Oh, and a large bottle of sparkling mineral water, please.'

As the waiter retreats, William is quick to ask if she is okay to go straight to wine.

'Yes, perfect.' *I shan't be drinking much this evening. I'd like to keep my composure.* Again, she loves that he likes to take the lead. *Strange. Until meeting William, if any man ordered for me, I'd find it downright presumptuous.*

Vanessa scans the intimate room, admiring the large window framing the vast expanse of water below. In stark contrast to the hum inside, the view is a lonely one. The sea is pitch black, except for two ocean liners in the distance, their guiding lights creating silver shadows reflecting across the water.

'Isn't this beautiful,' she says, luxuriously draped across the white chair. *It's a pretty defining factor in a man when he has the consideration to plan such an evening.*

He takes her hand lovingly in his. 'You know you're beautiful?' He gazes across at her.

When the waiter returns, William samples the wine and nods approvingly.

Conscious of the romance between the two, the waiter speaks a hairline above a whisper. 'Wine, madam?'

William squeezes her hand before raising his glass to make a toast. 'Here's to a wonderful weekend.'

In the company of such a charming man, she questions why she's stayed in such a dysfunctional relationship for so long. After her brutal marriage to Bruno, it could be said she worked her way back to some form of normality until she met Michael, another self-absorbed male, and everything seemed to go into a slow decline. *It's time I recognise my success and all that comes with it: financial and professional security. And keeping company with a more dignified man has got to be worth taking a chance on ...*

'Vanessa, you look preoccupied.'

'No, no, I'm fine. Let's order.' She glances across at the meals being served at the next table. *Whole snapper: nice.* When their meals arrive, Vanessa gazes down at her plate and is delighted with their choice. 'My God, William, this looks amazing.' She glances at him, then back at the lobster. She's tickled. Feeling his eyes upon her as she scoops the white, meaty flesh from the shell, dripping in garlicky, herbed butter, she takes a first mouthful.

'Good?' he asks.

'Delicious!'

But her crazy thoughts suddenly dart to an essay piece, *Consider the Lobster,* as Wallace's thought-provoking words arise:

"Is it alright to boil a sentient creature alive just for our gustatory pleasure?"

Setting her fork down on the edge of the plate, she tries to brush aside the disturbing consideration and swallows hard, looking across at William who is about to take his first mouthful.

'It's amazing!' She picks up her fork, moving past the absurdity. 'I have no doubt you appreciate certain foods more when you don't have them very often,' she says, clearly a means of justification.

'I couldn't agree more.'

'What's that quote by Hippocrates on excess?'

"Everything in excess is opposed to nature," they say simultaneously.

William picks at the salad, then stabs at a slice of tomato with his fork.

'Take this tomato, for instance ...'

Trying to be discreet with a mouthful, she nods.

'In Italy, one of the things I look forward to eating the most is their rich, red tomatoes, particularly in the south, Sicily.'

She swallows.

'Oh, I know. That's why they make the best sugo.'

'It's got to be the collaboration of the rich mineral soil and tantalising weather conditions that make it a perfect place to produce tomatoes.'

'The mouth-watering local produce makes Sicily a gastronomic paradise' she says exaggeratedly while pinching her thumb and forefinger together and tipping her head sideways.

He laughs. 'That, and love.'

She smiles.

'Seriously though, when you're in a foreign land trying new things, eating food you've never tasted before, it's all part of the travel experience,' he says.

'Like early mornings in Rome. At dawn, while the city still slumbers, I like to climb to the top of Pincian Hill via the Spanish Steps or Piazza del Popolo.'

'I know it well,' he says with an acknowledging grin.

'I love standing on the terrace with the ancient domes and crowded rooftops below, sharing the city with a lone streetsweeper tidying the Tridente, young romantic couples still out from the night before. From that vantage point, at that hour, it's possible to inhale the true splendour of Rome.'

'There are many cities where centuries collide, but few like Rome,' William adds. 'Like the obelisk that dominates the Piazza del Popolo. Did you know it dates to the 14th century?'

'13th,' she says.

'Well, there you go. I didn't know that.' He's most impressed by her architectural wisdom.

'Don't get me started. The Vatican and St Peter's Basilica, the greatest temple of Christendom, are amazing. Beauty built by hands over centuries steeped in history reminds me how insignificant I am.'

William takes her hand. 'There is absolutely nothing insignificant about you.'

Blushing, her eyes give off a seductive light.

'For instance, do you like this wine?' He holds up his glass.

'Yes, I do.'

'Same principle. You can taste the richness of the soil in Italian wines, quite distinct from, say, this delicious wine from the Loire Valley, or an Australian wine, or even a New Zealand drop.' For a moment, it almost seems like he wants her to fulfil his checklist of common interests. 'A superb French wine married with Australian West Coast lobster. What could be more perfect?' He tilts his glass to the light.

Married. Christ! I'm bloody well infatuated. The wine no doubt helps, and as the evening progresses, Vanessa grows more and more comfortable talking about books and movies, the pleasure and pain of travelling, then religion.

'So are you religious at all?' he asks.

'I have a very strong interconnectedness to certain things, but not a formal religious belief. No, but I do believe in finding meaning to the universe and I think people do that spontaneously.'

'True.'

'And you?' she asks.

'No. I think we're pretty much on the same page when it comes to beliefs.'

Thank God for that, having gone to hell and back with the hypocrisy of Bruno's extreme beliefs.

The waiter appears. 'More wine, sir?' discreetly holding up the empty bottle.

William looks to Vanessa. 'Shall we wait? The house is only a few minutes down the road. We can continue this chat there and have a nightcap. Dessert even.'

'Sounds like a plan.' She sets her almost empty glass down on the table.

The waiter notices William glance at his watch while furling his napkin and he attends to clearing their plates pronto.

'Could I have the bill, please?' William asks.

'Certainly, sir. Coffee, dessert?'

'No. Thank you. Just the bill when you're ready.'

'Of course, sir.'

Vanessa chuckles, watching Lenny with a 'Y' almost click his heels together like a soldier.

As they cruise through the exclusive streets following the curves of the coastline, Vanessa observes several cliffside residences with spectacular water views that sculpt the landscape, giving Whale Beach it's characteristic, stately prosperity. *There's an obscene amount of wealth here.*

William suddenly slows down and pulls into a steep driveway. 'Here we go.'

Vanessa tries not to let her mouth drop. *Impressive.*

William pushes a button inside the car and the imposing gates, bearing the familiar family crest of the letter W, open slowly before gracefully coming to a stop.

When it comes to putting a personal stamp on anything, this family are the ultimate perfectionists. 'Oh, William, this is incredible.' She looks up at the commanding outline, a bold home surrendering to its glorious surrounds.

William pushes another button before hopping out, and steps to the rear of the car, grabbing Vanessa's bag from the boot as she slides out excitedly.

'I told Phillip we wouldn't be needing him this evening. In fact, if you like, I can ask him not to bother coming over until after we leave Sunday evening. That way we'll have the place to ourselves. Or would you prefer he comes in and takes care of our daily needs?'

'I thought you said we'd be here by ourselves.' Vanessa follows him up the stairs.

'Well then, I have my answer. I don't mind having you all to myself.'

Good.

They're met with pin-drop silence. The room is softly lit. Vanessa waits for her eyes to adjust as William pushes in the code on the alarm system and turns on another small lamp. She scans the hush of the enormous space, her eyes immediately drawn to the kitchen that runs the length of the room to a showstopping focal point, a bespoke collection of wines displayed in a special wine walk-in, glass climate room. *This is one serious aficionado.* She's startled when more lights suddenly come on.

'You okay?'

'Yes. I just got a fright, that's all.'

'Nervous, huh? Don't be. This is a very calm house.'

It's not the house I'm nervous about.

Outside, the lights on the terrace illuminate a designer ice bucket on a tall, silver stand by an enormous glass window. A bottle of champagne is chilling, with a small cheese platter, dates, and an assortment of delicacies set to the side on a table.

Feeling a slight sense of unrest in Vanessa, William gives her a reassuring squeeze. 'Stay here. Don't move.' He walks across the room to where he strikes a long taper to the candles of a large candelabra.

Vanessa is spellbound. *What an amazing ambience. This special kind of alchemy doesn't happen effortlessly. It requires close observation and attention to detail, something the Whittakers have in spades.*

There are many outstanding homes on the northern beaches, but this lavish idealism is another level again, very Mediterranean in its simplicity of line and texture, an absolute tribute to its location, due in part to the geography with its outrageously impressive views.

I knew places existed like this, but it's a totally different world.

When William opens the glass sliding doors, sheer white linen curtains flow softly in the breeze, giving it a romantic, relaxed feel while simple base lighting around the spectacular infinity pool sets the mood ...

Vanessa notices a huge double sunbed. *How lovely it will be to relax there by the pool tomorrow.*

'Come outside and take a look,' he says proudly.

'Gosh, William, this is remarkable.' She's still taking in her surrounds. Everywhere she looks screams style.

'*Mi casa es su casa.*' Placing his arms around her waist, he holds her close and is delighted when she doesn't resist. With a gentle hand, William tilts her head up to meet his gaze and grows pensive. 'Vanessa, I've wanted to hold you all night.'

Feeling safe, she looks into his wanting eyes and whispers, 'I know, it feels right.'

'It's crazy, but I've been walking on air since we met.'

'William,' she says, lost for words, relaxing into his arms. His warmth is nurturing, but she is delicate as he tenderly kisses her for the longest time.

Sensing her fragility, William pulls back and settles himself. 'Forgive me.'

Feeling his sudden reserve, Vanessa is grateful. Somewhat embarrassed, she turns around and he hugs her from behind in an intimate embrace.

Looking over her shoulder, she gazing back towards the house, he feels her flinch suddenly.

'My God!'

'What?' He releases her.

She turns and her excitement rises. 'Lempicka!' Catching her breath, she looks from the painting to him in astonishment. 'You have a Tamara de Lempicka.'

On the inside wall is one of the world's most renowned art deco paintings.

'Yes, I do. You know the artist?' With a big smile, William watches as she observes the clear luminous colours of an elegant face staring out from the canvas.

'Do I know the artist? My God, William ...' She's lost for words.

'Do you know much about her?'

'Do I know much about the Baroness with a Brush?' she says, validating her sentiment and growing quiet in thought.

William is impressed by her passion for such things. Better still, he's pleased she appreciates the woman on the wall, but realising her brain is ticking over, the gap in conversation is still a little frustrating.

'First things first, let me get you a drink,' he says, stepping inside to open the champagne.

Hearing a tweaking noise, Vanessa reluctantly tears her eyes away from the painting to see William uncoiling the hinge and trying to ease the cork out of the bottle of Krug. It doesn't budge as smoothly as expected. He tries again, then rushes to fill their glasses before the golden liquid fizzes all over the marble floor.

'Here you go. I nearly lost the lot.' He hands her a glass.

'Good save.'

'Here's to beautiful moments not yet shared.' He raises his glass.

Vanessa cheekily raises her glass in the direction of the painting. 'And to the Baroness.'

Looking across at Vanessa's exquisite profile, he smiles warmly, and for all the reasons she's yet to find out.

'Cheers,' he adds, clinking softly.

Having only ever seen images of her favourite 1920s artist online, or in art books and journals, Vanessa is overjoyed to be in the presence of a genuine Lempicka. 'How did you come to own such an exquisite picture?'

'I bought it.'

'Yes, but how?'

'From a friend, of a friend, of a friend.'

'Nice friends,' she says, dazzled by his world.

'I promise to tell you all about it tomorrow. Now let me give you a guided tour of the house. Bring your champagne with you, sweetheart. I'll grab your bag.'

Vanessa likes the sound of sweetheart; she's not heard it in a long time. Truth be told, right now she'd rather hear the Lempicka story, but doesn't dare express herself.

As they pass the painting, Vanessa takes the opportunity to stop for a moment, nearest the picture, raises her glass in honour and says, 'I'll be back, my new friend.'

William smiles at Vanessa's open delight. At the top of the stairs, he pushes open a large door to a dimly lit bedroom, a space that's warm, lit only by a bedside lamp, and sets Vanessa's bag down on the king-size bed.

'This is your room; I hope you'll be comfortable here.'

Comfortable? Is he kidding me? This is remarkable. 'Yes, of course. Thank you.' She places her glass down next to his as he lights a natural burner that throws off a seductive dance of shadows across the darkened walls.

'The bathroom's in here.' When he switches on the light in the adjoining ensuite, she is again impressed by the spectacular design, enhanced by a lush garden and a small private infinity pool, the dark background of the ocean in line with the view.

'Just beautiful, William.'

'It's different, isn't it?' he says, turning the lights off again as they re-enter the bedroom.

She spots an enormous vase of red roses dominating the sideboard, a small card attached bearing her name, and blushes. 'Oh, William, you shouldn't have.'

'I wanted to ...'

She isn't sure what he is about to say next, but bends to smell the roses before opening the card, which reads:

> *Vanessa,*
> *To the first of many magical weekends together, William x*

Taking her in his arms, he holds her firmly to his body so she feels his passionate heat. The hunger in his eyes makes her heart skip a beat. Pressing his lips to hers, savouring her mouth with such tenderness, she feels herself coming alive. The sudden physical connection is all consuming and she doesn't want him to stop as his kiss grows more intense by the second.

William releases his grip slightly and the timbre in his voice changes, telling her he's never felt this way towards any woman before.

Vanessa is speechless, knowing no words are needed.

'Darling, I've turned off all the phones and you have my undivided attention for the next two days. Let's not waste a moment,' he says sincerely, aware of his serious attraction, but willing to take it slowly, mindful of her fragility. 'I feel we're building special memories here and I want nothing to hold us back.' His eyes are hauntingly warm and loving, but he refrains from an avalanche of words before his emotions take over completely.

Sensing his self-control, she too is grateful as much as wanting. 'Let's take our time, William,' she says, kissing his cheek softly. *No need to rush.*

'Would you like to go back downstairs for a nightcap? Dessert perhaps?'

'You're very sweet, but if you don't mind, I think I might finish my champagne and retire for the evening, if that's okay?'

'Run a bath if you like and relax.'

'Thank you. I appreciate that.'

'Well, I'll say goodnight. I'm sure you'll find everything you need. Oh, and the main light switch is over by the bed.'

'Okay, got it.'

He kisses her again. The tenderness of his mouth stirring their emotions, she presses back softly. Feeling her vulnerability, he slowly withdraws and picks up his glass to leave. 'I hope you have a good night,' he whispers, retreating to the doorway. 'I'm next door if you need me. I thought we'd take it easy tomorrow, so come downstairs when you're ready.'

'Lovely.'

'Sweet dreams.' Chivalrous to the core, he stays true to his word and calls it a night, closing the door behind him.

Vanessa leans against the closed door, smiling at his obvious restraint, but acutely aware she is in over her head now. She places her hands over her mouth to stop herself from squealing. The subtle scent is William's aftershave. *Delicious! There are so many things that impress me about this man. But knowing how special this is, we need to take this slowly ...*

CHAPTER EIGHT

Cloistered from the everyday tensions and concerns of the big city, Vanessa slides easily between the sheets, then stretches like a cat, exhaling slowly. *Life can bring the most pleasant surprises if you allow it.*

Having slept like an indulgent princess, wrapped in the purity of Egyptian cotton, the feel of her silk nightie, soft against her skin, makes her tingle with pleasure. She's grateful to be relaxing in such a wonderfully embracing bed, luxuriating alone under the covers as the aroma of freshly ground coffee and bacon hang in the air.

She thinks about last night and how, after soaking in a hot bath, she crawled into bed with the sound of the ocean an exquisite lullaby that slowly put her to sleep. She smiles at having William in her room before he graciously retired to his own. *This man is starting to get under my skin.*

On every level, he appeals to her, but given her current circumstances, and out of self-preservation, she's decided to impose a slower courtship on William than he's probably accustomed to with previous women. *But I must admit, something gels between us.*

With the smell of breakfast calling her, she looks out at the sunshine glistening across the ocean, feels almost giddy about the day ahead, and pushes the covers from the bed.

Dressed simply in a short, white sun frock and wearing very little make-up, she places her hair up in an uncomplicated ponytail and slips on a pair of white sandals. She follows the delicious aromas down to the next level into the enormous open-plan room that leads onto the sweeping terrace.

As the dazzling view comes rushing into sight, Vanessa notes that it is quite a different viewpoint during the day. Stepping outside, she can't help noticing things are strangely silent, and she's surprised to see there's no sign of William. On the terrace, the table is set for breakfast under a bright orange, fringed umbrella, typical of the ones in Bali. *Perhaps he's down at the beach?* Venturing further, she looks about. *Ah, there he is.*

William is looking relaxed, huddled over in a sunny corner enjoying the newspaper, which he folds quickly when he realises Vanessa is there. He's casually dressed in white linen shorts and a pale blue t-shirt complimenting his already golden tan. His dark brown hair is wet and swept back.

He's obviously been for a dip and up for some time. I hope I haven't kept him waiting for long.

'Hi there,' he calls, watching her approach.

She takes him by surprise when she gracefully leans down to his eye level and stills herself. Without words, she waits, staring intimately into the depths of his delicious eyes before gently kissing him.

He welcomes the softness of her mouth and the gentle touch of her hands on his warm, muscular shoulders as he becomes lost in the smoothness of her moist lips.

When they surface, their eyes meet again.

'Mm. Good morning to you too,' he says, coming up for air.

'Have I kept you waiting?'

'You're worth the wait.' He focuses on her emerald eyes.

'Patience; I like that.'

'Herculean!'

'Mm, better still.'

'How did you sleep?'

'Like a baby,' she says.

He reclines in his chair and clasps his hands behind his head, still looking up at her. 'Good. At least one of us did,' he says with a wink.

He's so sexy! She watches the flex of his arms, then looks out at the view, growing pensive, 'Sounds silly, but I feel very safe here.' She shrugs her shoulders. 'I guess it's just being away from the city.'

'The beach will do that to you.'

'I'm sure.'

'No outside voices here,' he says and scoots across on the sunbed, patting the chair, indicating to sit. 'Vanessa, you deserve some peace of mind.'

'Thank you. I think so too.'

He stretches. 'Fearing the walls weren't strong enough to keep me away,

I decided to get up early, head down for a swim and a run along the beach.'

Vanessa smiles at the idea of him entering her room. 'That sounds refreshing,' she says, a twinkle in her eye and a sense of teasing in her heart.

'Mm.' He curbs his fanciful thoughts. 'Then I hit the gym for a workout.'

'What? This morning?'

'Yes.'

'Well, you have been out and about.'

'It's just downstairs.'

'What? Here, in the house?'

'Yes.' He's surprised that she's surprised.

'Any wonder you look so fit.' She tries not to ogle his remarkable triceps and changes tack. 'What a glorious day.'

'You should have seen it earlier. When I went down, the sun was just beginning to show itself: a bright orange dome on the horizon. When the sky brightened, it was quiet and the beach was mine for a moment. It was pure magic.'

She admires his magnificent jawline. 'Did you take any photographs?'

'No. I couldn't; I left my mobile here on the kitchen bench.'

'That's a shame.'

'Unfortunately, most weekends it can be like a zoo, but this morning it was fantastic.'

'That's pretty much all Sydney beaches though.'

'These days it is.'

'The sky looks like it's been washed.' She looks up. *It's as if the light itself has the power to strip away dust and grime.* 'It feels like someone has hit the refresh button on the world.'

The slap of his open palms on his knees startles Vanessa out of her dreamlike state. 'Now, what can I get you? Would you like a coffee, fresh juice – orange or watermelon – or would you prefer English breakfast tea?'

Vanessa raises her nose to the air. 'Smells good.'

'I'm having coffee, but you have whatever you like.'

'Watermelon juice? Gosh, I haven't had that since I was a kid.'

He winks.

Ah, he must have read it in my book. 'So many choices, but I'll start with a watermelon juice, and then a white tea with breakfast.'

'Okay then.' He leaps from the sunchair.

Vanessa looks up at him. 'I love the smell of coffee, but I much prefer tea first thing in the morning.'

'I'm a coffee man myself.'

'Yes, it was that and the smell of bacon that stirred my taste buds.'

'It worked!'

'You haven't had breakfast without me, have you?'

He doesn't answer but waves her in as she follows him across the terrace towards the kitchen.

She points to The Baroness on the wall and says, 'We must talk about this a bit later.'

'We must! Now, I've partially cooked some bacon.'

'Oh?'

'For two reasons. You are going to meet my geek side.' He gets the juice from the fridge.

Does he have one?

'My mother taught me to pre-cook the bacon and drain off all the nasty fat onto a paper towel before cooking the eggs.'

'That's always a good idea.'

'She used to say, "Eggs wait for no-one, William, so keep the bacon waiting".'

Vanessa chuckles. 'I like that.'

'Second, and more importantly, I knew if I didn't tempt you with the smell of breakfast, you would never get out from that big bed.'

'Your mum sounds like she was a special woman.'

'She was.'

Vanessa is eager to hear about her, but something in the way he's responded suggests she shouldn't probe.

'Anyway, enough about that. You'll learn all about my mother in due course, but now is not the time.' He slides the juice towards her.

The loss clearly affected him in a big way. 'You're very respectful, William. I like that about you.' She perches comfortably on a stool at the kitchen bench and takes a sip. 'Mm, that is beautiful.' A flood of memories flow, of her mother making it for her and Monica when they were young.

He looks at her as if seeing her for the first time, before picking up a vase of fresh herbs and smelling them. 'Goodness knows how many times I've made the mistake of picking the coriander over the continental parsley.' He plucks a sprig of green.

'I hear you. I keep them in the fridge in water, a plastic bag over the top. That way they last longer.'

'Good idea.' He clicks his fingers and points mid-air.

Contentment washes over Vanessa as she watches him prep the herb. He's gone to so much trouble, she doesn't have the heart to tell him she's craving toast. *Mm, with lots of hard, unsalted butter and a decent lashing of good old-fashioned Vegemite.* Turning towards the terrace, she observes the reflective light dancing off the marble floor. 'William, I love the bones of this home, the original detail, the layout, and the way it opens up as you walk onto the terrace. I have a sneaking suspicion you had a lot to do with styling this place.'

'I'm interested to know why you would think that?' He rests a wooden spatula face down on a plate and looks quite pleased with himself.

'Because it has your signature all over it.' She believes the enviable location makes it as much a place for soirées as it does for romantic interludes.

'I had a very talented decorator by the name of Robert Bradfield from New York come in, so I can't take all the credit.'

'Where have I heard that name before?'

'Sometimes there's articles written about him in design mags.'

Ah yes, in the article I read about Oceana.

'One might say it was a meeting of the minds and a huge dose of respect for one another. Robert usually prefers to be briefed and then have free rein to go it alone from there. But I convinced him I needed to be a part of it for personal reasons, so we agreed to give it a shot. He initially wanted to strip the space back to a bare white shell and layer it quietly from there. I pointed out some of the building's original features, noting the ceilings and beams, so we saved those and magically, it worked.'

'Personal reasons?'

'Yes, because this was originally Gramps' weekender. Then it became my parents' place, so it's where I have the fondest memories, and there are certain things in this home that needed to stay.'

Must be something to do with his mother.

'But my father insisted on adding one touch.' He points an oily spatula in the direction of the orange umbrella. 'That bloody thing is a Balinese influence from his love of all things Indonesian.'

'Yes, I know them well. My mother has one.'

'Really? So he's not the only person on the planet with garish taste. Poached or fried?'

'Poached, if it's not too much trouble.'

She swings back in the direction of the umbrella, appreciating it against the clear blue sky.

'I would have preferred something, say, a little more neutral.' He closes his eyes in frustration.

'Oh, stop. Let your father have his thing if it makes him happy.'

He laughs.

'Can I help?' Vanessa asks.

'No. I've got everything under control.' He sets the breakfast plates down on the bench top.

'As you can see, I set up outside, but it's getting quite warm now that sun is really beating down, so are you happy to eat here?'

'Here's fine,' she says, finishing her juice.

After breakfast, William makes another pot of tea and they retreat to the sunbed with their porcelain mugs. Observing the surfers below waiting for the next set of waves, they sit content, chatting to one another.

'Vanessa, I'm feeling quite chuffed I was able to steal you away for a couple of days.'

'I'm always gathering information, so this is great, William. Let's just call it a research break.' She taps her temple with her index finger. 'That way I won't get an attack of the guilts.'

He looks at her admiringly. 'You never stop, do you?'

'Never. I'm inspired by everything around me. Everyone has a story.'

'Speaking of stories, I actually finished your book last night,' he says seriously.

'What did you think?'

'I have no idea how you managed to write the thing. It must have been like reliving the nightmare all over again.'

'I had to.'

'So let me get this straight. Your back was broken and yet you have no obvious signs of paralysis?'.

'Yes. I'm very lucky considering the height from which I was pushed.'

'Remarkable! So clearly a broken back doesn't necessarily mean you end up in a wheelchair.'

'No. That's when there is spinal cord damage, say, in the case of my uncle or your grandfather.'

'I see. I really should know this, given Gramps' injuries.'

'William, you'd be amazed how many people don't. That's another reason why I wrote the book.'

'Aha.'

'For instance, think of an electrical cord. If you cut the cord to your vacuum cleaner, it won't work, right? The spinal cord works like that, allowing signals from the brain to the various parts of the body.'

'Yes, I read that bit last night. You outlined that very well, by the way.'

'You have to understand everyone's spinal injury is unique, and their body's response depends on the site of the injury, age, and fitness prior to their accident, especially to what degree the damage is in the spinal cord. In my uncle's case, he was what you call a T6 paraplegic which affected many of the muscles in his legs and lower torso.'

He listens, taking it all in.

'Whereas in my case, it's a spinal fracture at L1, but there was no spinal cord damage. Surgeons fused my spine and I am pretty much fine.'

'Even so.' He shakes his head in contemplation.

'It could have been worse. At least I wasn't left drinking through a straw for the rest of my life,' she says seriously.

He openly cringes.

'I'm not to be pitied.'

'I admire your strength.'

'I'm pretty pleased with what I've managed to achieve.'

He smiles in genuine admiration. 'It's refreshing to hear you say you're pleased with yourself.'

'William, life goes on. After spinal injury, it's all about adapting your lifestyle, and more about what you can do, not about what you can't.'

'Just can't seem to grasp the difference between a C injury as opposed to a T or L.'

'What's your grandfather's?'

'I think he's a C7. Would that be right?'

'Could be.'

'I think that's right, but I have no idea what that really means.'

'Put simply, the spine is divided into five areas. Your cervical which runs from the stem of your brain down your neck. Thoracic which is your upper and middle back. Lumbar which starts below the shoulder blades. Sacral is lower back to tailbone, and of course, your Coccygeal which is your Coccyx, the bottom of your spine. Each area consists of numbered vertebrae, so if your grandfather is a C7, it means it's his 7th vertebrae that's damaged in the cervical area. And he'd be an *incomplete* because he can still move his arms, so signals are getting through from his brain.'

'I see.'

'By the way, does he ever come here?'

'Never.'

'Why?'

'Long story, *and* definitely one for another time, but basically, after my grandmother died, he couldn't bring himself to come back here. Too many memories, I guess.'

Vanessa looks openly moved.

'Excuse me for a minute while I get some cold water. Would you like some?' William asks.

'Sure.'

When he returns, he sets down a glass jug and two tumblers. As he pours, she watches the slices of lime and lemon bob around in the jug.

'Thanks,' she says.

'Please go on. I'd like to hear more.'

'You sure I'm not boring you?'

'No, I'm genuinely interested,' he says sincerely.

'Well, do you remember Australian athlete, John Maclean? He was hit by an eight-ton truck when he was out training on his bicycle and suffered incomplete spinal cord injuries?'

'Yes. Yes, I do. I'm sorry, you said incomplete spinal injury. What does that actually mean?'

'It means the spinal cord isn't completely severed.'

'I see.'

'He's a T12 paraplegic who went on to become the first person in a wheelchair to complete the Ironman World Championship, and even swam the English Channel. He's a miracle because now, through sheer determination, he's walking again.'

'So let me get this right. He has an injury in the Thoracic area of his back in the 12th vertebra.'

'Yes exactly. There are many inspirational stories of how they still manage to live life with some degree of normality while hoping that a cure will soon be found. Enormous progress is being made in this field and a 'cure' would appear to be closer than ever before.'

'Really?'

'Yes, there's research here on home soil actually. It's still in its infancy, but scientists have discovered that special cells from the olfactory sense of smell nerve can dramatically increase growth and function in the spinal cord. The olfactory nerve is located within the nasal passage so it means they can easily use the patient's own cells by taking a simple biopsy from inside the nose.'

His eyes widen.

'These olfactory ensheathing cells, or OECs, as they call them, together with a three-dimensional nerve bridge made from these same cells, are transplanted into the spinal cord at the site of the injury. Excuse my use of words, but they almost work like a Pacman of sorts, eating away at damaged tissue, cleaning up the site, and rejuvenating the damaged area, so messages can hopefully get from the brain to other body parts. I know, as we speak, in Queensland they're in the midst of organising human clinical trials.'

'So why those cells?'

'Because the olfactory nerve cells are the only cells of the nervous system that rejuvenate every day as part of their normal function, and it is the OECs that help the olfactory nerve cells find their correct targets.'[1]

'Fascinating!'

'And not before time.'

'So there's light for the very first time in history, huh? That's huge!' he says, astounded.

'Well, if the human trials are successful, it is. I'll email you some data, if you like, which explains it all in greater detail.'

The ring of laughter and banter in the distance distracts.

'Something's going on down there,' William says, moving across to the balustrade to see what's happening. 'Come take a look.'

From where she stands in the blaze of the sun, the beach runs away like an old, dusty country road: metres and metres of amber sand speckled with people. Lost in the blue haze, she follows her line of view back to the sounds of joy directly below at the shoreline.

It turns into a hive of activity as an excited crowd gather on the beach looking out to sea. William immediately spots the blue table of water is broken by the presence of a humpback whale. Pointing in its direction, he guides Vanessa's eye just as the whale launches its 30-tonne bulk out of the water again, both pectoral fins spread wide. Then two, no, three humpbacks breaching.

'I see them,' she squeals.

Two of them splash like crazy to draw attention, showing off their tails in a breathtaking display, determined to put on a show as they call, click and squeak. Overhead, cawing seagulls swoop with delight as another coastal bird hovers mid-air and sounds reprimand. Other than one odious heckler on the beach, the atmosphere is contagious.

William raises his voice so he can be heard. 'Outstanding, isn't it?

---

1 Personal communication from Professor James St John, Griffith University, Queensland.

'Glorious. I've never seen a whale before, let alone three.'

'You're kidding me?' He watches her clap with joy as she looks skyward and appears to delight as three upward-spirited seagulls circle overhead in high, graceful arcs over the water, then dive as if to dare the whales to reach for them with their enormous grey fins.

'This is why I love living here.' William looks down at the throng of revellers below.

Holding her palms up in the air, a radiant smile spreads across her face. 'Woohoo! Whales, budgie smugglers, and the big surf: Australia's traps and treasures.'

He loves her spirited ways he finds so refreshing.

Vanessa hears a woohoo echoed back from the beach and leans over the railing, as if moving in closer will allow her to identify the culprit below.

William takes the liberty of moving in behind her, and with an element of surprise, pulls her to him in a gentle hug.

The sound of the cheeky whale breaching again doesn't distract.

'Let's not rush down there. We can take our time, laze about, and enjoy what's left of the morning together.'

She looks over her shoulder at him. 'Whittaker, are you having a dig at me for sleeping in?' Vanessa had caught him watching her sometimes in thoughtful study, and wonders what goes on inside his head.

'Never.' He has a chuckle as she looks back down at the beach.

'I'm more than happy to enjoy the breathtaking show nature has in store,' she calls out, nodding towards a woman attempting a star-jump. Vanessa notices the woman's partner is trying to capture the perfect pose with the whales showing off in the distance, and she laughs at the woman.

'If we head down a bit later, the crowd should have dispersed.'

'Sure,' she says as he turns her to face him.

'Tonight, I have a surprise for you.'

'Mm. Sounds intriguing. Where are we going?'

'Well, then it wouldn't be a surprise, would it?' He kisses her brow.

'How will I know what to wear?'

'Casual.'

Avoiding William seeing her expression, she turns back towards the water, thinking about Michael and what he's doing. *I'm surprised I haven't heard from him since the tiff. Not that I expect to. He seemed so quick to have a dummy spit and hang up the other day. Perhaps he has plans of his own. No way, he's such a loner: no friends. It's such a dysfunctional relationship, but it's never easy to cut ties with someone who's been a significant part of your life. Maybe I need to do more than simply leave it up to the universe? Oh heck, it's normal, I'm sure, to contemplate a fresh start when you have an infinite ocean in front of you aglow with the burning sunlight. It's enough to stir any heart, but I shouldn't get ahead of myself here.*

Feeling the tension in her body, William turns her to face him again, his passionate embrace comforting. She responds to his warmth as he brushes a stray lock of hair from across her cheek.

'Kiss me,' he says, not wanting to wait for a response.

His mouth finds hers and for the first time, she lets his tongue explore hers: long, luscious strokes with the sounds of moisture making them hungry with need.

'I need you so badly,' he says.

Her chest beats thunderously. Suddenly she feels more than her own heart and isn't sure whether she should pull away, somewhat relieved when the decision is made for her. He calms the pace by kissing more gently, tenderly, his self-discipline evident as he eventually pulls back.

'On second thoughts, let's go for a swim.'

'Good idea.'

'Vanessa, why don't you go and throw on your swimmers? I'll meet you back here in ten.'

'Okay.' She heads up to her room to change, where she takes a moment to stand in front of the bedroom mirror, regarding her body in her new one-piece bathing suit, feeling her new training regime is finally paying off. William's attentiveness is certainly helping to give her a new level of confidence. *If he keeps this up, I might consider buying a bikini.*

Vanessa throws on a sheer blue sun frock, slips on a pair of white scuffs, grabs two beach towels stacked neatly on the bathroom shelf and heads downstairs.

William is waiting on the terrace, looking breathtakingly masculine in only his navy, boy-cut bathers, his six-pack highlighted by his tan.

'Ready?'

'Sure am. I've brought you a towel.'

'Thank you.' He takes both and secures them under his arm, leading the way through the private gate, gripping Vanessa's hand, steadying her behind him down the immediate cliff face.

'Are you okay?'.

'Tickety-boo.'

'You come out with some funny things at times,' he says.

Vanessa grips his hand tightly, enjoying the coolness of the breeze on her face as they make the steep descent. At the bottom of the stairs, a group of teenage boys are jumping about, pushing one another in jest and flicking towels at their sandy calves.

'Scuse me, boys, comin' through,' William says.

'Hey, man,' one boy says, nodding at William.

Vanessa stops on the last step, smiling at the boys as they promptly step to the side. She laughs at one of the boys, whose colourful boardshorts are dripping wet, covered in sand, and look like they're about to fall off.

'Hey, watch this,' one boy says coolly, but threatening.

'Dude!' the first boy says, trying to hold on to his pants.

Judging from his mate's cheeky grin, there's no doubt he will assist as soon as Vanessa steps past.

'How's your father doing, Pete?' William asks one of the strapping lads.

'Good, Mr Whittaker. Real good,' the boy replies happily. The boy is earnest and good-looking and could be forgiven for seeming older than his teenage cohorts.

'Say hi to him for me,' William says.

'Sure thing, Mr Whittaker.'

I like William's chain of command. She takes one last step onto the golden, grainy sand.

As they get closer to the water, it gets surprisingly warmer. Really warm. It's as though the lack of pollution allows the sun to beam down more strongly. The sand radiates heat through Vanessa's shoes. William looks for a spot to set the towels down like he's done this a thousand times before.

He has. 'It's so hot, Mr Whittaker,' Vanessa says in jest, squeezing his hand.

'That's a good thing, right?'

'Of course it is. It's respect.'

'His dad's a good bloke too.'

'No doubt. The boy has manners,' she says sincerely.

'His dad's actually my dentist.'

'Really?'

'And his grandfather was local gentry, hugely powerful in his day.'

'Also a dentist?'

'No, no, his grandfather came from big money and was responsible for inventing something to do with heart surgery. I think it is ... Gramps would know; they were friends.'

'Oh.'

Were. She didn't want to dig any deeper.

Vanessa shimmies out of her sundress, rests it on her towel before kicking off her scuffs, and hurries to the water's edge, glad of the cool, foamy liquid bubbling up between her pedicured toes.

The whales have long gone, and thankfully the crowd has already thinned, just an odd couple here and there sunning themselves.

Sharing all this with a man like William feels almost dreamlike. She watches him run past and plunge.

He's quick to surface, spinning around as Vanessa eases herself into the water. They swim out past the break together. He opens his arms as she nears and they float in the water, bobbing up and down with the current.

A lone swimmer paddles past with a warming smile. She's elderly, clearly a local, and evidently fit enough to swim alone out here in deep water.

Vanessa smiles back.

'You know, William, I rarely go in the surf, but I do like this.'

'Salt water is good for you. It awakens the soul.'

She breaks free and floats alongside him, looking out to the horizon as the breeze carries his scent towards her.

As their bodies brush against one another, their thoughts ringing with intimacy, he presses his lips to hers: soft, silent kisses, perfect in their quietness.

'Don't waste this time, Vanessa,' he says, his breath so near.

'I won't,' she mouths, hushed by the roar of the distant surf.

Conscious the sun is shifting, William suggests a short walk along the beach, mostly as a means of distraction.

'Let's go then.' She takes off. At the shoreline, she picks up her pace to avoid a set of waves. Not looking back, she makes her way to their things.

'Wait up.' He's quick to catch up and hands her a towel.

'William, this is what I call living.' She's drying her hair off. She pulls a band from around her wrist and casually ties hers up in a knot.

'I'm so glad you came. It's much nicer sharing it with someone than being alone.'

'I can't imagine you ever being alone,' she says, surprised.

'Trust me. That's one of the best things about living away from the city.'

'I guess so.'

'Occasionally I have people over on weekends; it's a great party house. But lately Dad's always down here.'

'It sure looks like the perfect party house.' She rolls her eyes with a telling smile.

William flicks his towel at her legs like the teenage boys. 'You're pretty cheeky, you know that?'

'No, not me.'

He laughs, suggesting they leave their things on the sand until they return. Strolling along the water's edge in companionable silence, Vanessa radiates calm as William takes her hand and lifts it to his mouth, affectionately kissing the back of it. She feels her heart flutter. Further on, she spots a lone shell at her feet and stops to pick it up. Twirling it around in her fingers, her thoughts dart to Monica. She looks out to sea in contemplation.

William feels a shift in her mood and takes the liberty of moving in behind her, wrapping his arms around her waist. She leans back against his body, and overcome with contentment, they look along the beach, strangely empty now.

Reaching for the shell, he allows his fingers to slowly intertwine with hers as he hugs her to him securely. The warmth of his breath is like a whisper tickling the nape of her neck.

Feeling his muscular body against hers, she's dizzy with desire and bites down on her bottom lip.

Gazing out at the salty, mist-filled air on the horizon, he squeezes her to him and their breath-held silence is broken when he murmurs in her ear, 'I want to hold you for the longest time.'

She listens.

'You already mean a great deal to me.'

A feeling passes through her, one she can't quite identify. Not happiness exactly, more like the absence of worrying about finding happiness. She wants to say something profound. Instead, she remains silent, embracing the moment and enjoying the texture of the wet sand beneath her feet and his strong arms supporting her at the water's edge.

If I dare look up at him, I'll caress him, kiss him again and tell him I want him.

William takes the shell in his hand and unexpectedly tosses it out to sea.

'Hey!' she protests, turning to face him.

His eyes lock on hers lovingly.

Feeling a well of emotion so strong, she dares not speak.

When he pulls back, she notices a change in him, his desire evident as he presses her body to his, growing more intense as everything else around them seems to go quiet, disappear almost. Her parted lips give him the advantage, letting his tongue slip in deep, moving lazily around hers. His kisses scream intimacy.

'William,' her voice a breathless whisper, uncertain, 'I need time ...'

He squeezes gently. 'I hear you.' He releases his hold and brings her hand to his mouth for a kiss.

They continue along the beach, absorbing their surrounds in a tranquil way, and savouring the warmth of the late afternoon sun on their skin while enjoying the stretched-out silence.

'Rusty, Honey,' calls a woman from behind as two wet, long-haired retrievers bound past the couple, ignoring their owner's cries.

Skittishly, Vanessa leaps into William's embrace as the dogs excitedly chase one another, kicking up sand as they go.

'They shouldn't be off the leash.' He takes the opportunity to hold her tight. Concerned the dogs might knock her over, William suggests they head back. 'It can sometimes get cold when the sun gets a bit lower.'

They walk back. Gathering up their things, they stop and look up at the base of the stairs rising towards the house.

Vanessa can't get over the enormity of them. 'Gosh, did I actually walk down that!'

'Sure did, all 175 of them.' He pouts. 'Unless you want me to carry you, you're walking back up.'

She takes the first step and stops in playful protest, knowing if she really wanted him to, he would. There's a faint, pleasurable offshore breeze at their backs as they begin the ascent and with every step, she takes gratification in their bodies brushing up against one another. Halfway up, she stops, looks across at him and smiles, catching her breath.

'Come on. You're tougher than that,' he says, urging her on.

By the time they are inside the gate, William closes the gap. Drawing her close, he kisses her the way he's wanted to. His tongue swirls, soft, gentle, then he sucks at her lip, feeling her nipples harden against his chest.

God, he's hot! Using every ounce of willpower, she pulls away slowly and kisses his shoulder before heading up to her room to take a shower.

'Take your time,' he says, head swimming with a tidal storm of emotion.

From the stairs, she looks back and for a moment, she almost feels timid.

'This surprise of yours is intriguing me.' She places an index finger to her bottom lip.

'Well, you'll find out soon enough.'

I love surprises. The warmth of the water cascading over her body is generous relief from the freshness of the ocean. Washing her hair is such a leisurely thing to do. She takes her time. It's one of her most complimented assets and she likes using it to her full advantage. *I wonder why William is keeping tonight's plans so close to his chest.*

Rinsing off with a blast of cold water, Vanessa steps into a light blue silk kaftan that floats easily around her. It's designer, no less, but you'd never know. She prefers a less is more approach. Opting for a pared-back, elegant take on beauty, her make-up is fresh and her hair swept back gracefully in a loose bun. She steps into a pair of stylish silver slides and hopes she has the dress code accurate. Spraying her points with perfume, she suddenly has the excitement of a woman twenty years' younger.

From the landing, she hears muffled voices and stops to listen, recognising there are women chatting away, appearing to be taking direction from William as to where he would prefer to dine, inside or out.

'Probably outside; it's such a beautiful evening. But I'll double check with Vanessa that it's not too cold for her.'

Mm, considerate too.

Hearing Vanessa, he looks up and catches his breath. 'Here ... she ... is,' he says, feeling overwhelmed. It's obvious to everyone in the room, he is spellbound by her beauty. He takes her hand and whispers, 'Stunning!'

'Thank you.' She notices there are three women in total, all dressed in white aprons. The one at the other end of the room is holding a taper to the candelabra, while the others are in the kitchen preparing what appears to be a feast.

I wonder who'll be joining us. She's relieved to be dressed appropriately. 'Ladies,' Vanessa says in acknowledgement.

The women reply in sync, all smiles. 'Hello.'

'As you can see, they're busy at the moment, so I'll introduce you a bit later,' William says. 'Champagne, darling?' A small table with two old fashioned champagne glasses is at the ready.

Mother has the exact same glasses. She delights in the bubbles as they work their magic up the hollow stems. 'Goodness, William, this all looks so impressive.'

'I thought we'd dine outside. Are you okay with that?' he asks, certain he's got it right.

'Yes, of course.' she says in a whisper.

'Good.'

'Who else is joining us for dinner?'

'Dinner for two, madam.' He hands her a glass, wrapping his free arm around her waist and guiding her outside.

'Oh.'

'You're just in time. I don't want you to miss this.' He points in the direction of the magnificent sunset. 'Here's to you, Vanessa, and the enormous success that comes with being a great writer.'

'Thank you.'

'Fortunately for us, there's a full moon tonight.'

They look towards the horizon and raise their glasses.

'Spectacular!'

'Talk about timing.' He holds her to him in a warm embrace as the sun slips swiftly away.

'The bright day is done, and we are for the dark,' she says as one of the women approaches with a tray of delicious-looking *hors d'oeuvres*. Vanessa selects a small portion. 'These look amazing. Thank you.'

'You're very welcome,' the young woman replies, handing her a small linen napkin.

William picks up a delectable morsel. 'Here, try this one first.' He proceeds to hand-feed Vanessa the baby black beauties of beluga caviar that have been carefully spooned onto small buckwheat blinis.

The tiny pearls explode on Vanessa's tongue. 'Oh, a mouthful of bliss.' She closes her eyes for a second before taking a sip of champagne. 'My God, William, where did you come from?'

He silences her with a gentle kiss.

She's hushed momentarily before stealing a glance back across the terrace, noticing the women in the kitchen discreetly smiling out at them. 'Who are those women, William?'

He discreetly points in the direction of each woman as they go about their business. 'Well, that one right there is Jo and the lady next to her is Tess. The other is the lovely Sunny. I'll introduce you a bit later.'

Clearly there's a protocol to this sort of thing. 'Will they be here all evening?'

'They're caterers my family have had the pleasure of using for decades.'

'Oh.'

'That sounded terrible. I should say we have enjoyed their culinary delights over many years.'

'Decades? But they're far too young, they must be only in their late twenties, early thirties?'

'Well, yes, they are, but it was Jo's mother who, for many years, was my parents' personal chef. Sadly, she passed away a couple of years ago, and now Jo has thankfully followed in her mother's footsteps and started a catering company with the other two lovely ladies. As luck would have it, whenever we want something special, and God willing, Jo is available, she prepares these gastronomic feasts for us.'

'How divine. I want your life, William.'

'That can be arranged!'

'That's thought provoking.'

'It should be.' He gives her a considered expression that says her life is about to change for the better. 'Your taste buds are in for the time of their life. You are going to have to loosen your belt.'

'You, kind sir, sound almost too pleased about that.'

He tosses his head back, laughing, then hands her an orange carry bag emblazoned with the word Hermes. 'A small gift to thank you.'

She hesitates before taking the bag. 'Whatever for?'

'I hope you like it..'

'I'm sure I will.' She gazes down at the bag.

'Go on then. Open it.'

She is almost too scared to, but she sets her glass down and pulls a thin, square box, also orange and marked Hermes, from the bag. She carefully opens it, folding back the delicate tissue paper embellished with the notable H. Inside she finds a blue silk scarf large enough to use as a wrap.

'Oh, William, it's absolutely beautiful!' The cross-dyed finish is in the strongest blues she's ever seen. One blue is like looking at the sky on a summer's day, the other like the deep ocean before her.

William places it around her shoulders, now tanned from the day's sun. 'I'm so glad you like it.' He kisses her shoulder.

'How could I not. And look, it matches my dress,' she says, enjoying its softness against her skin.

'I knew that.' He hands her back her drink. 'Cheers.'

She can't ever remember feeling so incredibly spoilt.

CHAPTER NINE

Candlelight shimmers over a plate of yabbies with shaved fennel, broad beans, asparagus spears, and a delicious citrus dressing. This is followed by a main course of poached lobster and baked snapper *en papillote*.

'It's so beautiful out here, especially in the evening,' Vanessa says softly. She is startled by a woman's voice.

'Excuse me, sir. Will that be all?'

'No, it won't. Sunny, this is Vanessa. Vanessa, this is Sunny.'

The pair exchange pleasantries.

'Sunny, would you please ask Jo to come out here for a moment?'

'Yes, of course, Mr Whittaker.'

Jo approaches, minus the chef's apron.

William stands to introduce the women. 'I'd like you to meet Vanessa. Vanessa, this is the very talented Jo Mackenzie.'

She is a tall, handsome woman with long, brown hair pulled back in a neat ponytail. She has firm, tanned skin and looks like she'd be comfortable on a surfboard.

Jo extends her hand with a warming smile.

Vanessa responds in kind. *Mm, no wedding band, but loving the silver arm band.*

'Vanessa, I do hope dinner was to your liking?'

'It was absolutely superb. Thank you, Jo. That yabby salad was sensational, as was the fish: so tasty. An unqualified joy from beginning to end.'

'Well, I hope you have room for dessert. Given you like chocolate, I made a chocolate and date torte which I recommend you have with a dollop of fresh cream to offset the sweetness.'

Vanessa gives William a quizzical glance. *Nice one.* 'Thank you. I do admit to having a passion for anything chocolate.'

'Good.' Jo smiles, 'I will give you some time to let your mains settle. Mr Whittaker, when you're ready, we'll set it aside and you can help yourselves.'

'Thank you, and we'll chat during the week re next month's cocktail party.'

'Of course. Good evening to you both,' Jo says and retreats.

'She's a dream. I'm so glad you met as you'll be seeing a lot more of her in the future,' William says, sitting back down.

'William, they all seem so lovely, especially Jo.' Vanessa looks back through the kitchen at the women quietly chatting as they go about finishing up.

'The girls were concerned you wouldn't want seafood two nights in a row.'

'Oh, you didn't tell them?' She looks concerned.

'No, but when I mentioned we were at The Waterview last night, it was a given.'

'I feel so bad. They've gone to so much trouble.'

After plating up dessert, the women discreetly leave.

'William, you have such a gifted life.'

'I do. However, it's not without its shortcomings.'

She grows serious. 'How so?'

'I'm pretty much noticed wherever I go and not for all the right reasons. Sure, there are lots of amazing women out there, but it's very hard to truly get to know someone, given my circumstances.'

'Poor baby,' she says sarcastically.

'That came out the wrong way, didn't it?'

'Ah, yes.'

'I better quit while I'm ahead.'

Raising her eyebrows, she gives a little laugh.

'Can I redeem myself by getting you dessert?'

'That won't cut it,' she says playfully.

'Why not?'

'You didn't make it. Jo did.'

'I did cook you breakfast though.'

'True.'

'So would you like some dessert?'

'Yes, absolutely!'

Unable to take her eyes off him, she glances across, and a tingling sensation courses throughout her body. She leans back and sighs with delight. *Yes, there is a God.*

William returns with only one plate of dessert, but two heart-shaped spoons, and they decide to move across the terrace, curl up on an enormous outdoor lounge and share the chocolate torte together.

She likes the way he kisses her on the bridge of her nose before taking the liberty of spoon-feeding her.

'Mm.' He watches her take the first mouthful, and closing her eyes, savour the smoothness of the chocolate as it melts in her mouth. 'This is a poem in my mouth.' She opens her eyes to see William admiring her. Her gaze fixes on his mouth as he takes the next spoonful and she waits to gauge his reaction. The pleasure that crosses his face says it all. Instantly she feels the need to be closer to him.

To her surprise, William sets the plate down on the small table between them. 'Is that it?' Vanessa asks, her eyebrows knitting. In cheeky response, she flirtatiously runs an index finger through a glob of cream and seductively licks it.

'You are so goddam sexy.' Hitting the volume button on his mobile, the music softens, and he summons her to dance. Her dazzling smile captivates him.

She slides into his open arms as a sudden breeze kicks up, causing a strand of her hair to rise like the flame of a candle.

With his hand gently stroking the small of her back, they begin to move rhythmically.

Vanessa looks up at the evening sky and William meets her gaze. *Talk about pinch-me moments.*

'*La tristesse durera toujours.*'

Vanessa pulls a slow, questioning look.

'The sadness will last forever.'

'Oh.' Her face falls.

'You've not heard that before?'

'No. Never.'

He seems surprised. 'It was Van Gogh's last words before he died in Auvers-sur-Oise, France.'

'Tragic!' She feels him pull her in closer. 'William, I feel so lucky to have met you.'

'This is not luck, Vanessa. It's a meant-to-be moment in our lives.'

She's taken aback by his seriousness.

'I feel it in here.' He places her cupped hand to his heart as he presses his lips to hers.

They stay there for the longest time, in connected silence, moving to the music. Sensing his longing, she grows quiet.

Under the moonlit sky, the lure in her eyes tells him she feels as strongly about him as he does her. 'This might sound ridiculous, Vanessa, but I was drawn to you long before we even met. The minute my grandfather mentioned your name, for some reason I had an overwhelming sense that we'd have a deeper connection than just business. Then when I saw you for the first time, I was overcome. Aside from being the most glorious creature I've ever seen, something was telling me I'd be a fool if I ever let you out of my sight.'

'That's quite extraordinary.'

'Trust me. The best is yet to come.' William kisses the top of her head, resting in a moment of affection, then looks down, admiring the softness of her lips. Feeling her reserve, he whispers, 'Vanessa, I have no intention of hurting you.'

She relaxes into his arms. 'William, there's something —'

He kisses her quiet, obliterating her concerns. 'Vanessa, I know it's difficult for you to trust. After all, we haven't known each other for very long, but I need to feel you, love you. I want us to go with our hearts. I'm sure you sense this is very special.'

But once we cross the line, there'll be no turning back. 'I'm just cautious.'

'I promise I will take care of you.'

Other than Michael, she hasn't sought the comfort of another man since her marriage and feels it only fair to tell him about her current circumstances. Placing a gentle hand to his cheek, she gazes into his eyes to see a deep longing there. 'I ...' She sees it because she feels it too.

Words are no longer necessary, and he silences her by exploring her mouth lovingly with his tongue.

Out of starvation for genuine emotion, she gives in and responds in kind.

Wanting to feel her hands on his bare flesh, William takes her by the hand, kisses the tip of her nose, leads her inside and up to his bedroom, closing the door behind them.

This is what dreams are made of. She scans the master suite, tiny tealights softly flickering throughout but is taken by surprise when his soulful eyes grow hungry, primal even, causing her to catch her breath. She dares not say a word, as if to speak will break the magic unfolding between them.

Taking her by surprise, he pins her up against the wall, then slowly lifts her closed hands above her head and peruses her body seductively.

Confronted by his desire, her heart races in anticipation, sending shivers throughout. Her lips part under his eager gaze, her eyes shimmering with desire.

He traces the pad of his thumb seductively across her bottom lip. Leaning into her body, he hears the release of her breath as he slowly kisses along the line of her neck, almost licking, leaving a trail of moisture towards her mouth. She arches into him, and he ravenously kisses her mouth for the longest time before lifting her silky dress up and over her head. 'I've wanted to see you naked since we met.'

The tension blossoms between them. The rise of her chest causes her breasts to jut forward in reveal, nipples erect.

Vanessa will never forget the way he looks at her naked breasts with such want she feels dampness between her legs.

His fervent grip suddenly whisks her away from the wall and across the room. Lying her down on the bed and kneeling over her, he slowly releases her long mane from the restrictions of the band. Watching her auburn locks tumble gracefully onto the sheets, he bends down, kissing the line of her shoulder tenderly, then pulls back and gazes down at her with consummate love. 'You are so beautiful.'

She catches a sigh and bites down on her lip, feeling she might die with need, grateful the noise of the distant waves against the rocks is louder than the pounding of her heart.

'You're safe,' he says softly. Bending low, he devours her mouth ever more passionately.

Melded to him, she sensuously whimpers: a moan of lust from deep within.

He runs his hand down over her body, loving the softness of her skin, the heat radiating from her flesh. Moving the flat of his hand slowly along the edge of her silk panties, he teases ever so gently, arousing her need and taking pleasure in seductively slipping the silk down her legs, never taking his eyes off her form.

She can't believe how sexy he is when, without warning, he stops, teasing her with need. All of a sudden, he stands at the end of the bed and she watches him remove his belt, the whipping sound, as he rapidly slides it through the keepers of his jeans, sending tingles across her skin. 'Ah ...' She catches her breath and waits, luxuriating in the way he removes his top ever so slowly, taunting her, shaking his muscular shoulders forward and out, shirt falling to the floor.

Appreciating his defined chest, Vanessa lets out a sigh.

He stares naked from the end of the bed. 'You're perfect,' he says. His tan only enhances his remarkable physique, his reassuring thighs heralding they'll support the love she craves. At first, he doesn't move, and for a moment she thinks she sees a tear in his eye.

She beckons him to her.

'Vanessa, give me this moment, my love. I want to look at you.' He rubs his chest while stilling himself for a second. 'Tell me you want me.'

She nods. Her eyes shimmer in the candlelight.

He moves onto the bed beside her and levers up on one elbow, gazing at her in the soft light.

Brushing a hand across her body, she licks her lips and moans, feeling his penis resting against her, his hands exploring her freely.

He wants nothing other than to touch and caress the softness of her skin, warm hands moulding the shape of each breast: one and then the other. 'I love your breasts' he says, watching her nipples grow taut. 'So sexy.' His fingertips trace back up to the line of her neck.

Leaning in, their lips touch in a long-extended kiss. It's the strongest sexual attraction she's ever felt. *He's like a Celtic warrior.*

His penis presses against her hip. Moving slowly down her body, tracing with the tip of his tongue, needing to taste her sweetness, he presses his mouth between her thighs, smooth and silky. His lips gently search the moist folds that begin to swell under his touch. Twisting beneath him, her fingers harsh on his shoulders, holding the force coursing throughout her body, his lips devouring her delicious scent, he hears her gasp.

The sensation between her thighs grows stronger, more intoxicating. Longing. Wanting ... Needing.

He breathes her in, caressing gently, tasting, pushing her aroused body into a state of bliss, her hips moving with need.

She catches her breath, too rapt to notice him stealing a glimpse of her writhing in pleasure at the anticipation of their love.

He kisses one last time before moving back up her body. His full weight positioned evenly, he presses gently inside, slowly and carefully, for the first time. She is deliciously warm, embracing his sensuality. Aroused, he moves his body carefully, going deeper. The more he gives, the more she wants. Sounds of pleasure fill the room, their bodies in perfect harmony.

She's never experienced such tenderness mixed with such raw passion. A moan escapes her lips, like music, and his chest bears down upon hers as they move together, slowly, and rhythmically. Running her hands along the smoothness of his muscular back, she cries out for his love, pulling him into her, his tenderness beautifully proportioned to her needs, his groans of desire gliding over her body.

Bodies bathed in candlelight, he withdraws, turns her away from him and brings her to her knees, catching a glimpse of the moisture of their loving.

So damn sexy.

William's breathless tongue tenderly follows the outline of her neck and down the length of her back. And there it is, the signature of her pain and suffering, the scar that holds the full story of the horrific injuries sustained at the hand of a monster. He surprises her by tenderly kissing the welt-like scar in its entirety.

There's something about this man that makes her feel at peace with her injuries and her heart is elevated.

William knows her broken past will not affect their future together and he wants to love her forever and celebrate what he finds most beautiful, her diversity, resilience, and strength embracing every part of who she is as a woman.

His light, delicate touch floats easily over the soft curves of her body, tingling her skin as he moves slowly up the line of her form. She writhes sensuously beneath him, hungry for his touch.

William grips her hair, gentle but firm, his fingers tighten, and she arches her body in surrender as he re-enters her body, placing his wet mouth to her lips and whispering, 'Taste our love.'

She sighs, her tongue swirling to meet his: softly, gently, arousing.

'Taste it!' he commands. Moans of pleasure fill the space. His demand causes an onslaught of intensity so overwhelming, he's suddenly overcome with exhilaration and buries himself deeper and deeper. 'Take me,' he says, harsh against her body, pushing deeper.

Stiffening in ecstasy, she feels an explosion of love between them. 'Oh!' she cries out, her face tight with pleasure, both lost in a blinding orgasm. She falls limp beneath him, their trembling bodies collapsing slowly onto the bed in bonded passion.

'I love you, Vanessa.'

In that moment, she knows this is the man she's been waiting for her entire life.

The sun streaming in through the corner of the heavy grey drapes causes Vanessa to stir, realising William is curled up next to her with his body moulded to hers. Contentment at the fore, knowing the day is theirs to share, her thoughts kick in. *This feels so right.*

William feels her move. 'Good morning, darling.'

'Good morning,' she murmurs.

'You know what? I've never said that before.'

'Will,' she says, crinkling her nose in recognition.

'Will?'

Will has a special ring to it. She laughs, tucking her head in under the covers in a spirited gesture.

'Coming from you, I think I quite like it.' He pulls back the sheet and joyfully smothers her naked body in kisses.

'You think?'

'Maybe it's your seductive tone.' He kisses her décolletage. 'It gets me every time. I adore you.' He strokes her hair away from her cheek.

Right now, feeling the way I do is worth risking a broken heart.

'What would you like to do today?'

'Oh, I don't mind. What's on offer?'

'Well, we can stay in bed for the rest of the day.' He winks.

'Or drive down to Palmy and have lunch or – simply hang out at the pool and take the day as it comes. The choice is yours, sweetheart.'

Vanessa puts her middle finger to her lips.

'So long as we are together, I don't mind,' he says.

'What could be better right now than being curled up in bed together, sweetheart,' she says. 'Well, you are my sweetheart, aren't you?'

'Am I?'

'I hope so.'

He straightens the sheet across her chest. 'Vanessa let's be serious for a moment. It's important to me you're armed with the facts. I've never brought any other woman here before. This is going to sound tasteless, but I'm going to say it anyway. Usually, I get very bored very quickly, so the women I meet don't make it anywhere near this place.'

'What, never?'

'Never! This,' he says, roaming the flat of his hand over the bed, 'is very different. I feel an enormous connection to you. Contrary to public speculation, I do recognise a good woman when I see one, and Vanessa, you're most definitely the real deal.'

She is moved by his candour.

Smoothing the flat of his hand slowly across her chest, solemnity comes over him. 'Vanessa, when I'm with you, I literally feel the intensity of your beautiful heart – right in here. This here, this is what I adore most. This is where I want to be.'

'This feels so right I'm actually scared.'

'I know. But you dazzle me.' He lifts his head, drawing breath in thought, then looks back into her eyes.

Vanessa considers his words. 'My life isn't quite so clear cut, and what concerns me is this is all happening so fast.'

'I'm a patient man, remember.'

'So you've told me.' *I hope so.* Her voice softens to a whisper. 'I love being around you, William.'

'Don't overthink it. Let's just run with that.'

'You make it sound so easy.'

'It is. If you just let it be.' He kisses the corners of her mouth.

She relaxes. Vanessa is all too aware William is different to most men and, given his upbringing, assumes he doesn't know a thing about insecurity, but for her, her reality is very real.

'I would have thought you'd prefer to be with some twenty-five-year-old,' she says, breaking the spell resonating between them.

'Vanessa, give me some credit.'

'Come on, William, it's true. Most men prefer younger women.'

'I'm not most men and I prefer someone a bit more cerebral.'

Feeling the line of conversation is growing far too serious, she pulls the sheet up and over them in jest and says, 'Really?'

'Yes, really. Your age is one of my most favourite things about you,' he says, flicking the sheet off. 'I read where women are at their sexiest in their 40s and I tend to agree. You've proved it, Vanessa. You're clever, confident, witty, strong, feminine, and inspiring, with a kindness of heart I've not seen in most.'

'Thank you,' she says, feeling flattered.

'And need I say, confidence in a woman is key for a man, and you are all that and more.'

So much for my self-confidence. Her mother's words resound; "remember confidence is sexy, Vanessa."

William kisses her forehead, climbs out of bed and retreats to the bathroom.

Through the open door, she hears running water and, curious, waits until he returns.

'Let's take a bath,' he says, moving around the bed naked and taking her by the hand.

What a body. 'What a bath,' she says. The infinity hot tub looks more like a small swimming pool. She steps down slowly into the water, feeling the warmth close around her body. *Oh, this feels so good.*

With his body pressed against her nakedness, he nuzzles at her ear, then moves back to her mouth, slowly flicking her tongue with his. Stilled by his feelings, he searches her eyes, embracing her lovingness, kissing tenderly.

She turns her back to him. Buoyant in his arms, she feels relaxed as he cradles her body, the heat of his face resting against her cheek. She loves the feel of his body, his scent, and his attentiveness in and out of the bedroom.

'You're such a beautiful woman.' He lifts her hand and allows droplets of water to run through their intertwined fingers over her breasts.

Secure in his arms, she finds it intoxicating knowing his loving heart is open to infinite possibilities.

'I love your body; it's so sexy,' he says looking down the line of her form through the shallow water.

'Pardon?' She pulls a wry look.

'You know exactly what I said. You just want to hear it again.'

'Maybe.' She rests her cheek back against his.

He laughs.

'So should I let you have some space, and leave you be for a bit while I go and shower in my room?' she teases.

'Are you kidding me?' He kisses the top of her head. 'I'm not letting you out of my sight.'

CHAPTER TEN

It's a magnificent day and the arc of the fuchsia bougainvillea on the terrace provides a dramatic splash of colour against the ocean and the bright blue sky. Nothing can dispel the peace and tranquility Vanessa is feeling right now as she pokes her fork at the remnants of chorizo sausage, parsley, and egg in a large, cast-iron frypan at the centre of the table.

'William, this is delicious. Would you call this an omelette or a frittata?'

'It's more like an Italian frittata, but without the potato.'

This man is something else. Is there nothing he can't do?

'Do you always cook?' She sets down her fork and takes a sip of her Bloody Mary.

'When I'm not eating out, I do. No one else to do it.'

She pouts. 'Poor baby.'

'Cook much?' William asks.

'A little. I must have you over for dinner soon.'

'Plenty of time for that.'

'For me, it's about the easiest way to the most pleasure. If you have a capsicum that's full of flavour, fresh and crunchy, then eat it raw in a salad. Don't roast it. Eating seasonal fruit and veg has always been my thing.'

'Mm, maybe, but I do like roast capsicum.'

She reaches across the table, and with her index finger, rubs a tiny, white, sticky spot from his chin. 'What's this?' The smell of peppermint is released. 'Toothpaste?'

'Ah, so it is.'

'I don't think it goes with the chorizo.'

'Good in Bloody Marys though.' He holds up his glass.

From the sun-drenched terrace, Vanessa surveys the pristine waters below, enjoying the bright sunlight on her body and having breakfast with a gorgeous man. She loves the heat burning through the umbrella.

'All this must make you feel like you want to live forever?' She points out to sea.

'Like it's possible, at least.'

'And the hair of the dog always helps.' She tilts her glass, feeling it's almost scandalous to be drinking so early in the day.

'Well, the weather has certainly turned it on this weekend.'

'Australia is a blessed place. I know our country has a ruggedness, and in some places, a brutal landscape, but you'd never know it, sitting here looking at all this beauty,' she says.

He watches as Vanessa grows quiet. 'Are you okay?'

'William, are you in any way concerned about the scar on my back?' Maybe it is the enormous level of trust she's feeling, or maybe it's the hit of alcohol that's giving Vanessa Dutch courage to put it out there. She toys with the celery stick in her drink.

'Well, I figured you'd talk about it when you were ready.'

'Considering my ex-husband is in prison, how do you feel about being associated with me?'

'To be perfectly honest, Vanessa, he's where he belongs, and this will never be a problem for us unless you make it so.'

'But what about the press?'

'Leave that to me.'

'Right.' She feels somewhat relieved.

'It matters more to me that you're okay, psychologically and physically.'

'Well, I won't break, if that's what you're thinking.'

'I would never want to hurt you, sweetheart.'

'I know that, but you needn't worry. I'm fairly robust. Sure, I get upper body pain from time to time, but that's why I make sure I train daily. It keeps the demons at bay.'

'I think your scar, it's a testament to your strength.'

She lifts her sunnies and parks them on top of her head. 'William Whittaker, how do you do that?'

'Do what?'

'Say everything I want to hear.'

'Darling, I have every intention of always giving you the emotional support you need,' he says, implying some form of future permanency. 'I think you're the strongest woman I've ever met. It amazes me how you've come through something so utterly horrendous, and still look to the future the way you do.'

'Thank you.' She looks deep into his eyes.

'How you ever learnt to trust again is beyond me.'

'I can assure you it wasn't without its challenges, but I recognised long ago you can't stay angry forever, or fear will literally paralyse you.'

He takes her by surprise when he suddenly stands, and then she realises it's to re-adjust the umbrella, to shield the noon sun from her eyes. *Michael wouldn't even think to do that.*

'Darling, I have no intention of breaking your trust,' he says, sitting back down.

'William, I believe that. Truly I do.'

Reading all the gory details in her book, of how she had been thrown off the balcony of her marital home by her then husband, Bruno Salvi, had sent shivers up William's spine.

Landing nine metres below, feet first in the garden bed, had resulted in her suffering a spinal fracture. The shock had travelled instantly through her legs and spine, shattering her lumbar 1 vertebra, or L1 as it is referred to, causing a burst fracture.

With no distinct pain at the time, Vanessa hadn't grasped the severity of her injuries but was, in fact, fighting for her life. Her body had gone into defensive mode, shielding her from the onset of pain.

Realising she couldn't move her legs and fearing they had been broken, she tried desperately to get to safety by dragging herself across the lawn. She couldn't move her lower body at all, and her legs and lower torso were lifeless.

As Bruno's cold, hate-filled eyes had peered down at her from the balcony, a convulsive movement had alerted him to the fact she was very much alive, and he needed to finish her off.

Suddenly she heard a piercing scream, only to realise it was her own. *Scream! Yes, scream!* Her voice was all she had. Feeling her life blood was ebbing away, her cries for help had reached a fearsome crescendo.

Bruno had appeared next to her just as she'd felt herself weakening and her cries starting to fade away. Standing over her, he had repeatedly kicked her limp body with brute force. When the kicking hadn't completely silenced her, he'd dropped to his knees, seizing her by the throat in a manic attempt to crush the life out of her.

Fortunately, a nearby neighbour had heard her screams of desperation and had rushed to her aid. When Bruno had become aware of the man's footsteps on the gravel drive, he'd released his grip and fled, turning the air blue with his language. If the quick-thinking neighbour hadn't come to her aid as rapidly as he did, who knows how things would have played out?

Later, the neighbour had told police he likened the gurgling sounds to that of a wounded animal.

After a mammoth five-hour operation involving spinal fusion and placement of metal rods and screws, Vanessa had been finally able to leave ICU and move into the rehabilitation ward. This is where the real work had begun, but through sheer determination and hard work, Vanessa had been finally able to walk again, unaided.

Emotional relief had come the week of Christmas when she read in the newspapers:

> On December 21, after a gripping three-month trial, Supreme Court Judge Rebecca Pritchard found property developer Bruno Salvi, 42, guilty of the attempted murder of his wife, Vanessa.

Only then, as a victim of domestic violence, had she openly admitted her marriage to Bruno had always been fettered, humiliating, and full of terror.

William reaches for Vanessa's hand. 'Look, darling, if you don't want to discuss this, I totally understand.'

'No, I'm fine. In all honesty, I think it helps to talk about it.' She takes another sip.

He can't help noticing she still carries the sadness that sits in the eyes of a woman who once loved this man.

'To live a life which is a perpetual falsehood is to suffer unknown tortures. Being Mrs Vanessa Salvi was like being Alice in chains, looking out through prison bars to a distant life I'd once known. I'll admit it was hell at times, however I took my role as his wife seriously, and told no one. I was simply powerless under his constant control and somehow, I managed to accept his abuse. I am, by temperament, not a victim, however fear anchored me to him, and I felt I had no other choice. And like so many, the marked walls of our home absorbed the pain, tears, and fears of a dysfunctional marriage.'

'Was it always like that?'

'William, it was never one big outburst. It was a series of intermittent spurts of abuse and dismissive behaviour, and up until that day when all hell broke loose, I thought I could deal with it privately.'

Squeezing her hand gently, William listens, horrified by her story, as Vanessa continues to purge her feelings.

'Bruno is certainly an intelligent man, not educated, but he definitely stands out because of his ability and level of power in business to get things done. That's what I fell in love with. However, he was very controlling, and before long, I was made to feel like a nuisance, so I guess dependency ensued. And that type of co-dependent male needs to always satisfy his narcissism. It's highly destructive.'

William winces at the thought, shaking his head in disbelief. 'Why didn't you leave?'

She is quiet for a moment, then looks at him. 'You know, Bruno was always so confrontational I didn't feel I could.'

'That's how narcissists roll.'

'Yes, absolutely. It's their *modus operandi*. They're predators.'

He compresses his lips and nods pensively. 'Scary stuff. What goes on in their heads?'

'Oh, trust me, you'll never understand a narcissist.'

'The man is clearly a psychopath.'

'Arrogant, conceited, self-centred, and haughty.'

'Didn't you see any red flags before you married him?'

'No. And that's what they're good at, manipulating people.'

'I'm astonished it didn't send you off the deep end.'

'It nearly did.'

'You're a very strong woman, Vanessa. Do you get that from your mother?'

'I guess I inherited from somewhere.' She sits in thought. 'Whilst I was in rehab, my mother handed me a handwritten note and said, "I want you to keep this." It read: One day you will tell your story of how you overcame what you went through, and it will be someone else's survival guide.'

His eyes widen. 'Wow! That's powerful!'

'Spooky, huh?'

'This calls for another drink.' He reaches for the bottle of vodka, adding more to the jug. 'Would you like a top up?'

'Yes, why not.' She watches him add a splash to her glass. 'William, in all honesty, I have mixed feelings about Bruno. One, a certain anger because I haven't seen any regret or sorrow on his behalf, and two, from a human point of view, sadness and compassion for his miserable life.'

'Really,' he says in astonishment.

'I don't think I'll ever understand why he did it.'

William is lost for words as much as Vanessa is reflective.

'All I remember is a montage of angry incidents. We'd been tussling over my mobile phone because a friend had sent a photograph of Bruno and another woman in an intimate embrace at some restaurant somewhere. I refused to delete the image and threatened to show his mother, Anna, if he didn't end the affair. Well, you can imagine Bruno was seething, and whilst we were tugging at the phone, he suddenly snapped, and with overwhelming rage, spun me around and seized me from behind by the throat. All I remember is being launched off the balcony.'

'Christ!'

'It happened that fast.'

'That day I didn't just land in the garden. That day is a metaphor for what my life and marriage had become – rock bottom. Later I found out Bruno had been having the affair for the entire time we were married!'

'How long did he get?'

'Twelve years, with a non-parole of six. He's coming up for parole soon,' she says somewhat nervously.

William cringes, his mind in overdrive suddenly.

After the incident, Vanessa was initially stalled in a kind of limbo and had no idea what to do with her life. Then, one day when her mother handed her the note, she decided instead of concealing her shocking tragedy, why not write about it, in the hope of helping others.

She had done the same thing as a youngster. Scribbling thousands of words in spidery handwriting, covering every inch of her exercise books as a means of grieving the loss of her sister. A sister she still can't bear to utter her name.

However, what she wrote back then had been for her alone. Now she writes for millions. Initially, when the book was released, she had no idea it would be an instant success. Within a short period of time, women around the nation put it on the best seller list and now everyone is crying out for her to write another.

The tabloids read:

> Here is a woman who had been tortured throughout her marriage, flying solo on the wings of a very dark secret. Having come close to death at the hands of her violent husband, Vanessa T. Albert has fought her way back, physically, and emotionally.
>
> However, due to bruising she was temporarily confined to a wheelchair, and thus privy to the realisation she escaped paralysis. Through sheer determination she has learnt to walk again.

'William, these last few years are not what I would exactly call happy, but in some strange way, they have been my happiest yet. Now I'm all about living my dash.'

'What does that mean?'

'You know, the dash they inscribe on your head stone. Born 1973, dash, and then the year you pass away.'

'Live your dash,' he says with a grin. 'Hey, maybe you should think about writing a book of quotes for your stronghold of followers.' He reaches for her hands and kisses the back of both.

'Not a bad idea. I'll give it serious consideration.'

'I'd like to revisit this a bit later, but for now, I think we need to get out of here and go for a walk,' he says, standing.

'Give me a minute. I'll go and freshen up.'

'Oh, while we're out, remind me to grab some fresh bread in case we get a bit peckish later.'

'William Whittaker, all I've done is eat since we met.' She pats her washboard tummy as she heads inside, a spring in her step.

The minute they're back and through the gate, William shucks his thongs off and wanders into the kitchen.

'That was a great walk,' Vanessa says, stepping out of her runners.

William sets the bread down, adds more ice to the Bloody Mary mix, grabs the jug and the daily papers, and follows Vanessa onto the terrace.

'Why don't you read the news on your tablet?'

'Remember, it's all about supporting the printed word.'

'Some might argue trees vs paper, books vs e-books.'

'True, but I like holding a paper.'

'You're so old-fashioned sometimes.'

'Don't you talk.'

'True.'

'That's a good thing, right.'

'In a lot of ways, yes. It's certainly a quality to be admired.'

Standing by the railing, breathing in the salty air, Vanessa contemplates how much she's enjoying being away with William, and is certainly not looking forward to facing Michael, nor the interrogation that will ensue when she returns. *With a bit of luck, he's probably spent the weekend at Mummy's place and not even noticed my absence. I can only hope.*

Suddenly a deep voice disturbs the calm of the afternoon. 'Hello, hello, anyone home?'

Vanessa looks at William, somewhat concerned. 'Who's that?'

He smiles, then calls out, 'Phillip, come on in, buddy. We're outside. Come and meet the lovely Vanessa.'

A tall, blond, handsome man, casually dressed in board shorts and a t-shirt, wanders barefoot through the house. William leaps to his feet and waves him in with one arm, placing the other around Vanessa's waist and gently moving her towards him.

'How do you do, the lovely Vanessa.' Phillip raises a sun-bleached eyebrow with a very friendly grin.

'Please call me Vanessa,' she says hesitantly.

'Okay, Vanessa it is.'

'William has told me so much about you, Phillip.' She's a little shocked by his sudden appearance.

'Has he now? Mate, sorry to barge on in, but I tried calling and your phone's off. I was starting to get a little concerned. It's not like you.'

Phillip looks at Vanessa, then back at William.

'Anyway, now that I know you're okay, I'll get going. I'm sorry for the —'

William doesn't give him a chance to finish, 'No, buddy, I'm glad you did. I'm having problems getting the spa to work in my room. It keeps spluttering like somethings caught. Can you take a quick look?'

'Sure, it's the least I can do.'

'Come have a drink with us first. I've just made a fresh jug of Bloody Marys.'

'No thanks, mate. Too early in the day for me. I'm heading out for a surf soon.'

Sensing Vanessa's reserve, Phillip takes his cue to check out the spa and heads straight upstairs, striding two steps at a time.

'Does he have keys?' Vanessa asks, slightly vexed.

'Yes.'

'William, I thought you were going to tell him not to bother calling in over the weekend. Lucky we're both dressed and not fooling around out here on the terrace.'

'Now, there's a thought,' he says with a boyish grin and heads after Phillip.

Halfway up the stairs, he looks back. 'Trust me. It's all good. I'll be back.'

Vanessa grimaces and grabs her glass, taking a sip. *Boy, that's got some kick!* She decides to take advantage of the view, sets down her glass, and with a glossy magazine, retreats to one of the sunbeds under the umbrella by the pool. Enjoying the freshness of the sea breeze rising to meet her bare feet, Vanessa languishes on the chair, admiring her soft pink toenail polish. The vodka has begun to take effect and she feels slightly embarrassed, inwardly cringing at how silly she's been. *Clearly my feelings of insecurity are still just below the surface.*

With the warmth of the sun caressing her feet, a delightful sensation of calm pervades, and she struggles to focus on the words on the page. Allowing the feeling to take hold, she soon drifts off.

When she wakes, William is nowhere to be seen, so a sleepy Vanessa decides to look for him. *I have no idea how long I've been out to it.* Hearing the muted sounds of soft music, she heads upstairs. The heady scent of aromatherapy oil hits her first. Pushing the half-open door, she's shocked to see William on a massage table over by the infinity pool. Embarrassed, she stops in the doorway.

He has a white towel draped across his lower body and Phillip is standing shirtless beside the table, oiling William's body.

Phillip looks up. 'Here she is.' He continues to massage his buddy's back.

She's at odds with a man rubbing William's body but can't help thinking the sunshine only applauds his nakedness. The men are in no way being secretive, but something feels off.

William lifts his head. 'Darling, would you care to join me? I'm sure Phillip would be happy to indulge you with his expertise. He has the hands of a God.'

He looks like a God. She's glued to the spot and feeling somewhat vulnerable. 'No, thank you,' she says her air of impregnable self-confidence gone.

She quietly slips away, but not before the men notice her troubled eyes.

Vanessa decides to take a swim and makes a quick dash to her room to change. Swimmers on, she grabs a sports cap, threads her hair through the hole in the back, and fits the cap on her head, tucking up the loose strands of hair on either side, trying to calm her racing mind. *I consider myself a smart woman with highly developed powers of discernment, but am I missing something here? Is there something going on between these men?*

She reaches into her bag, pulls out a pair of designer shades, and tosses them on her face. Grabbing a towel on the way out, she heads downstairs, only to find William is already on the terrace waiting for her.

Phillip has the smarts to make a quick exit. 'See you guys. I'm off for a surf,' he says, leaving the lovebirds alone.

William's forehead is beaded with perspiration. He picks up a towel from the nearest chair, uses it to mop his face, and follows Vanessa out through the side gate. When he attempts to take her hand to steady her descent, she prefers to hold her own, precariously making her way towards the beach below.

The closer they get, the louder the surf becomes. It's so loud that if you want to speak, you have to raise your voice to be heard, so he doesn't bother. At the bottom, she quickens her step and walks ahead. William calls for her to wait, but she doesn't hear him as she drops her towel, hat, and shades on the sand.

Over the rumbling of the waves, she is relieved when she meets the freshness of the sea, the soft, hissing ripples washing at her feet. Stilling herself at the water's edge, she observes three children in sunsuits playing in the fizz. The atmosphere is filled with a hazy, wet mist and a timeless purity hangs in the air.

William suddenly races past and plunges into the water. The saltiness stings his eyes as he meets the surface. Barely able to see, he spins around quickly, his eyes clear, and he looks back at Vanessa, melancholy at the water's edge.

William makes his way towards the shoreline, takes her in his arms and pulls her close, seizing the opportunity to hug her for the longest moment. Under the weight of his arms, he's pleased to feel her relax. 'Vanessa, I don't know what you thought you saw back there, but it's not what you think.'

She looks closely. Assured he's sincere, she tempers her reserve.

'When can I see you again?' he asks.

Soon, I hope. She dares not say.

'Would you like to have dinner tomorrow evening?'

Vanessa takes comfort in knowing he still has to drive her home. The idea of catching up again tomorrow pleases her. 'I'd love to,' she says, giving him an embarrassed grin.

Secure in his grip, he pulls her closer, kissing her lips tenderly as the water laps around their legs. A rogue wave suddenly knocks their legs out from under them. It's fast, jolting her out of her dreamlike state. They give in and roll around freely in its dynamic power. For a time, they're happy under the glare of the afternoon sun, laughing and frolicking about in the water as it washes off the coarse red sand.

'Let's go for walk,' he says.

'Okay.'

Vanessa, in close step behind, watches William walk up the beach, water dripping from his taut body. *I can't believe I've met such a beautiful man. That was plain silly of me to be suspicious.*

As they're towelling off, a breeze whips up from nowhere, allowing the heat of the day to cool. They decide to take their towels with them in case they want another swim further along the beach.

'William, I've thoroughly enjoyed being here. Thank you.' She watches two small boys, squealing with excitement, run ahead of their mother. Their father calls them back from the water's edge.

'I'm so pleased you were able to get away, but I don't mind telling you, you had me worried back there with that scolding glare of yours.'

'I'm sorry. Strangers make me nervous.' Believing she still has trust issues she makes a mental note to do something about it.

'Of course. I should have taken that into consideration.'

'I was thrilled to bits when you asked me to come away,' she says, needing to deflect.

Their chat is suddenly interrupted by a conspicuous, screeching sound. 'Yoo-hoo! William!'

The shouting, from a long way ahead, reminds him of his childhood when he went off on his own at the beach and his mother called him back.

'William! William, over here!'

William spots them immediately. It isn't his mother.

Vanessa squints into the afternoon rays and notices a messy couple, silhouetted by the sun, striding towards them.

William recognises his next-door neighbours, and for a split-second, he tries to ignore them. 'My bloody neighbours,' he says under his breath.

The woman is insistent. 'Yoo-hoo!' she calls again, waving a big, fleshy arm in an attempt to catch William's attention.

He's reluctant to stop. 'Oh, hi, Marj, Mauri,' William mutters, acknowledging them with a nod as they near.

With the woman is a pale, short man with a vast stomach that marches on ahead of him. Vanessa can't help noticing he has slightly splayed feet, Scotch-drenched eyes, and tufted, grey eyebrows. He wears a scruffy, grey shirt with white buttons that look like they might pop open at any minute.

Marj is schlumpy and chubby, with glowing cheeks, her neck haloed by a cheap, chunky strand of purple beads that match her sandals. Her big right toe hangs over in stark contrast to the rest of her scaly digits. She has had too much sun in her time, resulting in her resembling a jowly, mahogany-hued mastiff.

'Well, fancy,' Marj says, eyebrows arching towards her dishevelled, bleached hair.

'Vanessa, these are my neigh —'

'Fancy seeing you here, William; the famous bachelor with a beautiful woman,' pants Marj, ogling Vanessa.

Her fat husband stands silent, peering over his grimy, bifocal sunglasses, closely eyeing Vanessa.

William turns to Vanessa in obvious frustration and lifts his tone. 'Vanessa, as I was about to say —'

'Shoosh! I'm Marj and this is Mauri,' the woman says, waving a dismissive hand at William.

Vanessa felt it right for William to raise his voice slightly when he was so rudely silenced. 'How do you do.' She's acutely aware of William's reluctance to stay and chat.

'So, William, do tell. We've not seen you lately unless it's with a crowd of partygoers or that fellow of yours. What's his name? Phillip, isn't it? Nice chap, but it is so much nicer to see you keeping company with the opposite sex. Makes a pleasant change. How do you know Vanessa and where and when did you meet?' Marj shows no shame.

After what's just happened up at the house, William needs to draw down on his inner strength. Instead, he grows indignant. 'To set the record straight, *that chap* happens to work for my family, and yes, his name is Phillip.'

Not wanting to take his eyes off Vanessa, portly Mauri is gasping for air like a pug dog, waving a sandy, indignant hand at William. 'How do you know William? You know a beautiful woman like you needs to be careful around this Casanova.'

Mauri's comment felt like chalk on a blackboard. *You may pant like a pug, but you look like a bloody albino dugong that's been beached.*

'Thanks for that, Mauri,' William says annoyed, joshing back.

Mauri suddenly snorts, making Vanessa jump. 'Can I give you some advice?'

William holds up an objective hand. 'Ah – no!'

Mauri frowns. 'Oh, lost your sense of humour, hey, William?'

'Okay then, we'll be off. Need to get a walk in before we head back to town tonight. Cheerio,' William says. He smirks and walks away, almost pulling Vanessa along with him. A few seconds out – 'Bloody sandflies,' William says under his breath.

'What?'

'That's what they are. Annoying insects that distract from a beautiful beach day.'

'Sorry?' Vanessa's taken aback.

'I feel like a bloody tourist attraction.'

'Are they always so rude?' she asks, discreetly looking back at the sweaty pair waddling along the beach.

'Don't ask. Let's just say I don't like them one bit.'

'Well, they seem to delight in pushing your buttons.'

'They're complicated.'

'It's complicated?'

'No. They're complicated!'

'Oh.'

'Look, we're flattering them by even talking about them.' He peers back over his shoulder as they walk on. 'Christ! Watching them navigate the stairs, juxtaposed against the stunning beachside setting, is borderline insanity.'

She laughs. 'You should be a writer.'

'I'll leave that up to you.'

Judging from his tone, there's something else, something I can't quite put my finger on. Maybe they're just nosy Parkers? As for the Phillip comment, I think it best I leave that one well enough alone.

There's a long moment of quiet as they walk on, until Vanessa suddenly breaks the lull. 'As I was saying, I've really enjoyed the last couple of days, William.'

'Me too! In fact, I don't think I have ever felt more at ease.'

'Other than earlier,' she says jokingly. *Why did I say that?*

'Yes, well.' He shoots half a smile.

'I guess all good things must come to an end,' she says.

William stops at the shoreline and pulls her in close. 'Sweetheart, this is only the beginning.'

She feels her heart starting to melt. They linger in place, her lips suggestive and wanting. And with the enveloping sea mist giving off a pleasant, mystic feeling, he presses his lips to hers and she has a sense of being lost for all eternity.

Pulling back slightly, he looks at her with a telling smile. 'Let's go back,' he says, taking her hand and leading her back along the beach.

Reaching the stairs, the intensity of need is distracted by a group of young children whose mother is vigorously brushing sand off them. The woman ignores the couple as they keenly weave their way around the family and begin hastily trekking up the steep incline.

William unlatches the gate as Vanessa looks back across the water.

I don't want to go home.

Tossing their towels over the railing, he wastes no time in taking her in his arms under the outdoor shower, he kisses her earlobe, nibbling on it.

His lips trace sensuously down her throat as he loosens the neck strap of her swimsuit, letting the Lycra triangles fall forward. Taking delight in cupping her breasts gently in the palm of his hands and feeling the sensation of her nipples hardening under his touch, he fondles lovingly.

She feels a great tenderness well in him, a tenderness for the spirit of the woman standing in front him. In silence, they stand together in the light, looking at one another tenderly.

His face fractured by the water, the steam soon fills the space around them as he bends and seductively suckles on one of her rosebuds, teasing sensually as her moans of pleasure excite. Everything male in him expands – excitement, need. He steps out of his trunks and turns the shower off, grasps her hand and leads her upstairs to his bedroom.

Stirred by his muscular body, Vanessa watches as he reclines on the bed naked. His insatiable appetite exciting her, she quivers with need as he extends his hand, beckoning her to him.

No words are exchanged. He watches her seductively peel her swimsuit off, climbing onto the bed and slowly straddling his centre. Her hands settle on his muscular chest, loving the way he stares up at her. Her moisture is his guide. He eases her body down and is swift to penetrate.

Gazing up, her breath comes fast, warming his skin. Her eyes are half-open, feeling the warmth of the room from the late afternoon light. Moving leisurely at first, throwing back her head, she lets out a long-pleasured sigh. She looks back suddenly to see his desire-filled eyes taking in her form.

Feeling the last shard of sunlight catching the side of their bodies, casting captivating shadows, her rhythm builds causing wet hair to slap against her back. The swishing sound exciting them, she moves back and forth. With the knowledge she is lit perfectly, she cups her own breasts seductively. Her body, irresistible, is in every sense hungry for nurturing.

He feels her arousal.

Vanessa reaches behind and gently fingers along the crease of William's thigh, teasing, sending shudders of intense pleasure throughout his body.

He arches his back, penetrating deeper and deeper. 'Darling, you feel amazing. Slow down; it's too good,' he cries as groans of passion whisper across her body, exciting her more and more. Breathing harder and consumed by pleasure, William's body tightens as he grips her hips. Anchoring her to him, they begin to rock keenly and heat rushes throughout her body. William feels her shaking.

Looking up at her quivering lips, her eyes nearly closed as she pushes down, working together in intensity, the passion builds. Breathing so hard its palpable, they can't hold back any longer. The pleasure is so intense, she begins to tremble as their orgasms rage throughout them simultaneously.

When she opens her eyes, he looks up at her and says in a hushed, exhausted tone, 'You are —'

She places a gentle finger to his lips.

He needn't say a thing.

Nothing is of any consequence.

They are in love.

Waking just enough and trying to get her bearings, Vanessa squints, expecting to hear the ocean. *It's not there.*

If realising she's home isn't disappointing enough, feeling the empty bed beside her and discovering she's alone brought about an unusual feeling of melancholy.

Lying for a minute, staring at the white ceiling, she considers how much things have changed these last few days and is almost coy about wishing William was there. *It's unusual; normally I like having my bed to myself.* Surprised by how quickly she's grown fond of him, Vanessa smiles at the flickering bits of life that have taught her to grab this moment with both hands and go for it.

Thoughts of their time away together bring a much broader grin to her face. With joy in her heart, the commotion of life seems to have trickled away with the sun, surf, his tender touch, the food and wine, everything. Feeling refreshed from two days away, she excitedly kicks her feet rhythmically under the covers, letting out a delighted squeal. She felt young and carefree again.

Aside from the Phillip situation, the weekend was positively glorious. We are so close! Vanessa sits up, positions her cushions accordingly and looks around her room. *I can't wait to see him again.*

The joyous sounds of children downstairs float through the open window, alerting her to the fact she should be getting on with her day. Bouncing out of bed, she takes delight in grabbing a slice of bread and popping it in the toaster. Grabbing a slab of her favourite French butter, a jar of Vegemite, she laughs at how much she needs a yeasty fix right now.

'No bloody potato-less frittatas and Bloody Marys in this kitchen.' She closes the fridge door with a laugh. *I adore that man, but he's got to get a grip on the good old basic Aussie brekky.*

The smell of toast wafts throughout the kitchen, filling it with a sense of blissful homeliness. The sound of toast popping up is music to her ears, and she sets about prepping breakfast. 'Come to mamma!'

As she's about to take a bite, her thoughts are abruptly interrupted by the disturbance of the intercom. Vanessa puts down the toast and marches through the living room to see who it is. 'Yes, hello.'

'Morning!' Michael sings sarcastically down the receiver, adding pitch to his already excitable voice.

Annoyed by his sudden arrival, her chest automatically tightens. 'I'll let you up.'

In that moment, something changes.

Unbeknown to the cocky little barrister, Vanessa is about to buzz him into a world that no longer exists. She opens the front door and waits uneasily for the lift to arrive. *I need to clean house. In fact, I need to disinfect!*

Michael bursts out from the elevator like a barking dog is at his heels and strides past Vanessa, straight into the kitchen to pour himself a cup of tea.

No kiss hello, bite your bum, nothing. She's become accustomed to bad behaviour of late and is acutely aware of the lack of respect. *There is no escaping the fact everything has changed!*

Michael's brashness throws Vanessa. Concerned about her recent change of circumstances, she starts to over-think things and wonders if she's able to appease him as to what she's been doing all weekend.

I'm certain of one thing. I've found my Prince Charming and nothing's going to stop me, not even this smug little narcissistic barrister. Observing his agitated state, she rapidly has second thoughts. *It might be smarter to let the dust settle. Perhaps now is not the time and I should discuss my next move with Lizzie first.*

Standing transfixed in the doorway of the kitchen, Michael begins to laugh hollowly.

Unable to look him in the eyes, she focuses on the point of his left ear.

'So, Van, how was your weekend? Did you captivate all the other writers with your stories of survival?'

Vanessa cringes, trying to ignore his attempt at stripping her of any self-confidence.

He picks up her toast and takes a great bite.

I know exactly what you're trying to do, you sneaky, self-righteous prick.

Huge globs of melted butter and Vegemite stick to the corners of his mouth.

She winces. 'You're acting very weirdly, Michael.'

Ignoring her, he grunts and takes another bite, then gulps his milky tea down.

Enough is enough! The present is as good as any. 'Michael, we need to talk, and we need to talk now.'

He holds up a hand, palm facing her, and closes his eyes.

Vanessa finds it so frustrating when he does this. It's impossible to have a conversation with someone whose eyes are shut. It's as though anything she has to say is of no consequence.

'Now there's an understatement,' he says, ignoring her seriousness. Propelling himself past her, he gives off the aroma of another woman.

She deliberately bites her tongue.

'Not now, Van, I'm in a rush and I have more important things to do. I'm needed in Chambers. Just popped by to pick up my new reading glasses.'

'What are you talking about?'

Muttering to himself, he stomps through the living room, frantically lifting cushions off the sofa, then shifts everything on the coffee table in a frenzied search. Without any concern for her handwritten notes or regard for her work, she is astounded when he tosses reams of words skyward. 'You know the new grey rimmed ones; they're round. I left them here the other night.'

You never take my work seriously. A much-loved, antique version of *Notes on Novelists* by Henry James topples to the floor and the hard cover splays open. She flinches when he kicks it to the side. *This is a never-ending battle.* Eyeing a hard copy of Usher's *Letters of Note*, sitting to the side, a black, felt drink coaster sitting on top like a full stop, she hopes the borrowed book won't fall victim to his vitriol. 'Michael, stop!'

Fastidious to a fault, everything at her fingertips, Vanessa would know if his glasses were there. They would have leapt right out at her. After three drawn-out years, Michael doesn't have much more than a couple of heavy-duty law books cluttering up her bookcase. 'Michael, our lives have changed, but you're so self-absorbed, you haven't even noticed,' she almost pleads.

He stops, turns, marches straight up to her and says dogmatically, 'You've changed, not me. I'm still the same man I ever was, Michael Keats-Dickens.'

There's nothing she loathes more than when he states his name like some bloody descendant of nobility.

Abruptly his face changes in recognition, and without making eye contact, he turns and marches out through the front door, banging it shut as he leaves.

She is bewildered, like a tornado has ripped through her apartment. *Why the pathetic, whirlwind exit? Probably another of his excuses to call in and check up on me. He's been acting so strange lately.* Vanessa squeezes her eyes shut till they hurt. *By dragging this out, there's no winners or losers, just hangovers.*

Distracted, she slams the door of the dishwasher in marked relief, then eyes the half-eaten toast sitting precariously half on, half off the bench top. In disgust, she picks it up with thumb and forefinger and tosses it into the open kitchen tidy.

I'm not going to let Michael spoil my day. Not today. I have too much to look forward to, which happens to include dinner with William.

First things first, I'll see if Lizzie's free and pop over for lunch before my hair appointment. I'm so looking forward to sharing my newfound happiness, especially the details of my time away. She'll be able to give me some sound advice on how to handle the situation.

She puts the kettle back on the gas cooktop and sets about making a fresh fruit salad. Cutting through the silence, the kettle quickly shrieks to the boil. *Instant teabag for speed, no sugar, milk. Full cream? Check.* Placing everything neatly on a tray, she elects to sit out in the morning sun and read the book reviews in the daily newspapers. *Why not? I'm a sucker for punishment. Sure, the book has been out for, what? Six weeks now, but with the literary awards pending, the journos love rehashing this stuff. People can't get enough of personal tragedies. Good in one way, because that's the precise purpose of the book, to make others more sentient.*

Comfortably seated, she sits upright, back straight, closes her eyes, and takes a moment to take some deep breaths in the hope of stilling her chaotic mindset. Centred, she opens her eyes and looks down at the splash of colour in the bowl, admiring the strawberries, blueberries, watermelon, and papaya, all cut into small pieces and drizzled with fresh passionfruit. *It's like looking at jewellery.* She daren't touch and decides to ping a photo off to Lizzie with a message:

> Girl, this is breakfast, so you better get something naughty for lunch because I'm coming over. If you're free, of course.

After the first mouthful, she sits back and opens the paper to the Review section.

True to form it reads:

> Vanessa T. Albert's book, *A Woman of Courage*, has winner written all over it. An autobiographical account of how the author survived her brutal husband's real-life attempt at murdering her. The author works through multiple layers in confronting dialogue and does not disappoint. The reader is able to get up close and personal through flashbacks and feel what it's like to suffer at the hands of someone she trusted. There is a real physical presence to this as Albert reveals her story, layer by layer. She charts her horrific circumstances as to how, with a broken back, she struggles to get help, fearing her spouse would come to finish her off. This goes beyond one woman's survival story and her fight

to walk again. It is the rarest of insights as her level of courage is revealed through this intimate read.

Another:

A stunning heart-wrenching debut about a shocking tragedy and one heroic woman's desperate fight to survive and be heard. If this book isn't a winner, I'll eat the first page myself!

And another:

How this work made it past Whittakers' slush pile, I'll never know. Her work deals with the scar of personal history. Boring.

Oh, icky! How narcissistic! She holds the paper away from her as if it were contagious. *Fancy finding gratification by calling someone's personal tragedy boring and not considering the skill of the writer. Takes all sorts.*

She hears the landline from a distance and races to answer it. To Vanessa's delight, it's Lizzie saying she'll be home around noon.

'Got your message. Any preferences?' Lizzie asks, panting as she speaks.

'No, honey, see you at noon. No, wait. None of that delicious bean salad for me. I'm wearing the wow dress tonight and can't afford to have a bloated tummy.'

'Oh.'

'See ya soon, honey.'

Vanessa arrives right on noon as Lizzie is stepping out of an Uber, her arms loaded with goodies. Greeting each other with exaggerated air kisses, she helps Lizzie inside to her ground floor apartment, placing the groceries on the kitchen bench. Eyeing the Gourmet Life bags, she goes in for a hug, careful not to let Lizzie's clown make-up mark her outfit, before moving to the opposite side of the marble counter and sitting on a swivel.

'Hm, I'm starving. So what's my best friend been up to?' Vanessa watches Lizzie remove her lightweight jacket and hang it on the back of the opposite stool.

The smell of new carpet and fresh paint lingers in the air of the stylish apartment, almost overriding the delicious aromas wafting out from the brown paper bags.

'Oh, nice roses. I didn't see them there,' Vanessa says with a smile.

Lizzie deliberately ignores the comment. 'Well —'

'Oh, bloody Michael called in unannounced this morning. Sorry, honey, I cut you off but —'

'Really. What did he say?'

Vanessa is unable to contain her excitement. 'Oh Lizzie, I had the best weekend.'

'Really, do tell,' she says, intrigued.

'I'm sorry, honey. You go first. I'm prattling on. Forget about bloody Michael. How was your weekend? What did you get up to?' Vanessa tries to contain her excitement.

There's a long moment of silence. The quiet envelops them.

'Nothing much,' she says in a disconnected huff, pulling the takeaway containers from the bags. 'I went over to Mum and Dad's, and as usual, Mum nagged me incessantly. I came home mentally exhausted and curled up watching Alfred Hitchcock movies all night. And, I might add, couldn't help wondering what and whom my rogue girlfriend was up to on the northern beaches.'

What is this obsession with Hitchcock movies? 'Is there something wrong, Lizzie? You don't seem yourself.'

'I'm fine, honey.' She tries a distorted grin, not making eye contact.

Vanessa has so much to share with her friend, she doesn't labour the point. *Wait till I tell her about William.* 'Lizzie, I'm sorry but I have to use your bathroom. I drank so much water this morning.'

Lizzie grabs two plates and starts serving up lunch. 'Use the ensuite; the paint in the main bathroom is still drying.'

'Oh, how are the renos going, by the way?'

'Good.'

Vanessa heads towards the bedroom and ducks into the ensuite. Closing the door, she notices the toilet seat is up. *Ah-ha, new man. I knew it! Go Lizzie! So much for alone movie night. Oh well, everyone's entitled to their secrets.*

Retracing her steps back through the bedroom, Vanessa sings out, 'Lizzie, you are going to love what I'm about to ...'

The words are barely out of her mouth when she feels like she's been punched in the stomach. Everything moves in slow motion as her eyes dwell on Michael's new glasses, in full view, perched on the bedside table at the far side of the bedroom. She stops in her tracks, bewildered for a second, her thoughts resounding. Her legs feel like they're about to buckle. Suddenly she feels like she's going to be sick.

Holy Shit! I need to get out of here. She tries to take a deep breath in the hope of easing her churning gut. Instead, it rushes from her in a deep sigh.

Vanessa recovers her balance and marches out to the lounge room, shooting Elizabeth a knowing, angry, needle-sharp stare.

As Elizabeth meets her gaze, denial isn't an option.

Vanessa has an overwhelming desire to rush over and poke her in the eye. Instead she eyes the roses, and with a trembling hand, picks up her handbag and races out the front door, leaving it wide open.

Seeing the look on Vanessa's face is enough to make Elizabeth almost pass out. She collapses on a nearby stool and her eyes well with tears that burn like acid rain. She knows their friendship is over forever.

The fresh air hits Vanessa's face like a bucket of cold water. *Betrayal!* Her knees are trembling with barely the strength to move. She decides to seek sanctuary in a nearby park to calm her nerves. Steadying herself kerbside, she looks up and notices the sky is a remarkable blue.

Vanessa learned not to cry a long time ago. She learned how little tears help and she learned how miserable they make her feel, and that no one else really gives a damn anyway. Taking a deep breath, she straightens up, and semi-dazed, steps off the kerb towards the park across the road.

The grass beneath her trembling feet, in contrast, is a brilliant green, shimmering reflective light from the sunshine, and the air is filled with birdcalls that echo in the distance of her confused mind. Everything seems magnified and she begins to shake uncontrollably before taking refuge on a park bench. *Hitchcock; glasses; Christ!*

Turning her face towards the sun, she tunes in to a nearby sprinkler spouting jets of water under a tree and begins to tear up, questioning why she has been so blind.

Piecing together what's happened, and her bitter regret at having made yet another emotional error, Vanessa resists the impulse to shout out as two curly-haired teenagers, dashing past on their skateboards, add a deafening roar to her inner screams. Silenced by the rumble of the wheels on the pavement, she couldn't be heard anyway.

Her internal chatter takes over as she casts her eyes downwards. *I had no inkling. Elizabeth has been having a sordid affair with him right under my very nose and I didn't even see it. My best friend: a double whammy. Why? How long has it been going on? How could I have been so stupid?* A million questions that ultimately need no answers. She wonders if this has been wilful blindness on her behalf.

Staring off into the distance, she catches a glimpse of the university through the trees, but her mind is too busy churning in circles to be bothered taking in the beauty of its old-world charm. Sitting in a confused state for what seemed like mere minutes, she looks down at her watch and realises it has been more than an hour. *You know what? If it could fall apart this easily with Michael so that I needed to seek the comfort of another, then the screws were already loose.*

She considers her options, but ultimately her choices are to give Michael the benefit of the doubt or leave the damaged goods behind and start anew. *The choice is less difficult now. The goal posts have been well and truly moved.* Faced with moving on with the next phase of her life, what falls to her now is not the burden of the affair, but the perfect opportunity to offload Michael. *My God! My life has shape and it suits me perfectly.*

Vanessa takes a deep breath and runs her index finger under each eye to wipe away the evidence of mascara. *This might well be my next chapter.*

With instant clarity, she springs from the bench, walks to the kerb, and pings an Uber.

CHAPTER TWELVE

While Vanessa readies herself for dinner, she takes a moment to reflect on what's happened today. *My pride is hurt, that's a given, but there's an enormous amount of relief Michael is finally out of the picture. Certainly, stooping so low as to have an affair with my best friend wasn't on my radar. Michael and Elizabeth have clearly made conscious choices, having created an untenable situation with no regard for me. Sadly, she's not to be a friend after all.*

Vanessa grabs her bag and keys. *With me out of the picture, I wonder if the affair will continue. Especially now they're free to do whatever they please. Anyway, that's their business. I know in my heart it's time to look forward, not back. Elizabeth can have him all to herself, including an unhealthy side order of his mother!*

Stepping out into the foyer, Vanessa's somewhat disappointed Richard isn't anywhere to be seen. She enjoys his sunny disposition and their little chats from time to time.

Sliding into William's car, her friend Francesca's words were never more apt: 'Lovers are like buses, honey. If you wait a short while, the next one will come along.'

Vanessa looks across at William and has the strongest feeling her future is brighter than ever. As a personal seal, she reaches across, surprising him with a gentle, seductive kiss.

'Mm.' He sighs, pulling back slightly, keeping eye contact.

She gives him a look he's not seen with her before, a look of a woman that's content in herself.

'You look fabulous.'

'Thank you.'

Pushing back her hair, he notices she's wearing a detailed gold bracelet. 'That's beautiful.'

'Yes, it is. A precious gift from my wonderful uncle just before he died.'

'It's lovely. So unusual.' He touches the gleaming band. 'So you like jewellery?'

She gives him a quizzical frown. 'William, name me one woman who doesn't.'

He tosses his head back laughing as he pulls away from the kerb. 'True, very true.'

Vanessa nestles comfortably in the leather seat, feeling right at home listening to Julio Iglesias' version of *Begin the Beguine*. 'You have no idea how much I love this song.'

'It's one of my favourites. I love the older stuff.'

'So do I.' *Nothing could be more perfect.*

Sitting in comfortable silence, driving through the streets of the eastern suburbs towards the restaurant, the trees have the advantage over the footpaths, creating a romantic take on the area.

William turns the music down. 'How was your day?'

'Interesting.'

'I hope that's a good thing.'

Looking across at him, she finds his masculinity infinitely appealing. *But there's a playfulness too: such spirit, such dignity.*

With not a single red light, they are quick to arrive at the restaurant and surprised to get a park right out front.

William jumps out and scoots around the car to open the door for her.

Vanessa looks up and gives him a warm smile.

William is taken aback when the headwaiter and the maître d' immediately fuss over Vanessa like a long-lost friend.

'*Ciao*, Vanessa. *Come stai?*'

'*Ciao*, Antonio, I'm well. And you?'

The maître d', true to form, shrugs his shoulders, and with a wave of the hand says, 'Ay, I can't complain.'

At this point, Vanessa introduces William. Two young waiters, out of earshot, whisper to one another and give an acknowledging grin.

'I've known Bella since she was a baby,' Antonio says to William.

'A baby?' William asks.

They all laugh. Vanessa is chuffed Antonio openly shares such obvious affection towards her.

'Vanessa, please, right this way,' Antonio says.

They are seated in one of the cosy private alcoves in the wine cellar. It's a small but special area lined with an extensive collection of vintage wines all the way up to the low ceiling, providing a unique setting for a romantic dinner.

The headwaiter confirms Vanessa will have the usual, then turns to William for his drink of choice.

'Scotch, straight, no ice,' William says.

'Any particular Scotch, sir?'

'Yes, do you have Johnnie Walker Blue?'

'Yes, sir.'

As the waiter steps away from the table, Vanessa looks at William. 'Warms the cockles of your heart.'

'Scotch?'

'Yes.'

'And you call me an old soul.'

'Well, you are.'

'I think we both are.' William places an outstretched hand on the table and Vanessa, feeling a little warm and fuzzy, rests hers in his. 'You're a regular here. Aren't you full of surprises?'

'Why?'

'Don't know. I would never have picked it.'

When Antonio reappears, Vanessa discreetly pulls her hand back from William's so he can place their drinks on the table.

'Vodka martini with a twist for you, Vanessa, and a straight Scotch for you, sir.'

Antonio, a passionate Italian, straightens his back and proceeds to recite the evening's specials like a Shakespearian verse, then steps away in a decorous manner to give them a moment to decide.

Vanessa never tires of dining out, whereas Michael never cared much, preferring to stay in, so with him out of the scene, she's free to go wherever she pleases.

'Mm. They make the ultimate martini here.'

He notices her bracelet again. 'You were telling me the other day that your uncle Harry was a paraplegic.'

'Yes, a T6 complete.'

'Explain that to me again.'

'Well, the spinal cord was completely severed so he needed to be in a wheelchair.'

'How did it actually happen?'

'It was a diving accident. He dived into a riverbed, and it's believed he attempted a backflip and hit his back on a submerged rock.'

'Oh dear.'

'Fortunately for him, my mother was there and was able to drag him out, otherwise he would have drowned.'

'Tough on your mother though.'

'Yes, she's had to deal with some pretty terrible things during her time. He passed away a couple of years ago.'

'Oh.'

'Yes, he had all sorts of complications, and his failing body eventually gave out. He became an alcoholic, developed cirrhosis, and eventually liver failure.'

'That's terrible!'

'Anyway, let's talk about something else, shall we?' she says, wanting to get off the topic.

In acknowledgement, he looks around the room, 'I'm pleased Donna booked this place.'

Vanessa's chuffed Whittakers' secretary made the reservation and didn't even realise it's one of her favourite restaurants. 'William, how come your grandfather refers to Donna as his secretary and not his PA?'

'Habit, I guess. Donna has worked for Gramps for decades and he's always called her his secretary, so it's stuck.'

'Old school, huh?'

'Oh yes, very much so.'

'She's lovely,' Vanessa says.

'She's bloody good, too. Looks after all of us. Gosh, we'd all fall to pieces if she ever left. You know this place is an old favourite of mine, but for some reason I never remember it. But not Donna.' William touches his temple with his index finger. 'She's got it all stored in here. We're very lucky to have her.'

'Indeed.' Vanessa looks up at the wines displayed on wooden racks. 'Look at all these amazing red wines.'

'A bit of money there.'

'I love old-fashioned Italian restaurants with their dignified waiters. There's a fine line between being in someone's face and delivering great service. I think the lighting is very important too. it's so intimate here.'

'This place has a great ambience,' he says.

'Why is it that the cheaper the restaurant, the brighter the lights?'

'Apparently bright lights make you eat more. That's probably why food courts have such stark lighting.'

'Is that right?'

'Sounds pretty right to me.'

'This type of old school charm is often hard to find in Sydney. Lot more places like this in Melbourne,' she says.

'We should scoot down there for a weekend. Maybe in winter.'

'Why not? I adore people watching, and Melbourne's the best. I like sitting in a quaint, suburban café watching the old men sitting in the sun, canes by their sides, caps pushed back to reveal faces sculpted by hard work.'

'That sounds more like Italy.'

'You know, I was only sixteen when I first came to this restaurant.'

'So, you *were* a baby.'

'Not quite. My slightly older boyfriend and I had very little money, but still, out came the old silver cloche. It was the skill and theatricality with which the waiter revealed the spaghetti that made it so memorable. Years of training, applied to a few strands of pasta, turned an ordinary action into a ritual. Like they do in Europe.'

'Yes,' he says, clearly enjoying listening to her tell the story. 'There's no doubt this restaurant is a love letter to the decades in which this kind of dining is king, and an extremely poetic one at that.'

She likes the way his mind ticks. They chat fiercely about all things European, especially Italy.

'Whenever I'm here, I have a burning desire to revisit. I'm certain the Italian consulate should give the owner a cheque for tourism.'

He laughs. 'Well, I guess restaurants transport you. It's a way of getting away if you're unable to travel. Speaking of which, Vanessa, I was wondering if you would consider taking off for a week's break to Bali?'

Her mouth opens.

'Granted it's not Italy, but it's a start. Italy can come later.' He sips his Scotch.

The idea of withdrawing from life and relaxing for a week is something Vanessa often fantasises about, but the thought of leaving her computer behind could almost make her freeze. Writer's block is a very real fear for her.

'And before you say a word, you're welcome to take your laptop and keep working while we're away. I certainly wouldn't want to take you away from our next bestseller. My grandfather would have my head on a block.'

Vanessa is delighted. It's the same excitement she had as a child, heading across to Bali with her mother and sister. 'I'll give the idea some serious consideration.'

Antonio appears and Vanessa suggests they share an entrée: her usual, angel hair pasta with fresh crabmeat.

William agrees. 'I wouldn't want to miss out on the theatrics of the silver dome. Vanessa, why don't you do all the ordering this evening for a change?'

Her eyes sparkle, and with a cheeky grin, she looks up at Antonio. 'You know what that means.'

'The usual?'

'Yes, please, *due*.'

'May I suggest a bottle of the —'

Vanessa gives Antonio no time to finish. Instead, she gives him a knowing nod.

'Of course, madam.' The waiter retreats.

'What was that? Morse code?' William asks.

She shrugs her delicate shoulders with a sassy sideways glance. 'It's a surprise. Seeing we're having the pasta to start, I ordered something slightly lighter for our mains.'

'I'm intrigued.'

'Don't be. Trust me; it's simple but tasty.'

'And the wine?'

'Again, you'll have to trust me.'

'I'm certain you'll make the right choice with whatever you decide.'

She wonders if his choice of words may have another meaning.

'What was so interesting about your day?' William asks.

Before she has a chance to respond, a young waiter appears and presents the wine. His Italian accent is strong, straining his hoarse throat. 'The 2014 Pieropan la Rocca Soave.' They are shocked when his voice breaks like an adolescent boy.

Vanessa raises her eyes, but the waiter waits for a response from William. 'That will be fine,' Vanessa says.

The waiter proceeds to remove the cork from the tall, thin bottle. 'Care to try the wine?' he asks William.

'No, the lady will, seeing she chose the wine.'

The waiter looks slightly embarrassed, turns Vanessa's way, and pours enough to taste.

William watches as she observes the colour, swirls the glass by the stem, then confidently savours the aroma before putting it to her lips. She sets the glass down on the white linen tablecloth, allowing the wine to roll across her taste buds. 'Yes, that's fine, thank you,' she says.

'It's a good drop, this one,' William says in acknowledgement.

The waiter pours the wine and places the bottle in a silver ice bucket on a service table nearby. Two apron-clad waiters appear, also quite young, apprehensively manoeuvring the mobile trolley. On it is a large silver dome. Antonio watches from a professional distance as one man lifts the cloche, then pours the creamy crabmeat sauce over the pasta.

Vanessa hears the ring of the silver pasta server drop on the plate and the hiss of Antonio's indrawn breath. She keeps her eyes glued to William, too polite to risk a glance in the waiter's direction. Frustrated, Antonio takes over and skilfully finishes plating up the dishes.

'Antonio, it smells delicious,' Vanessa says.

'I have to agree it looks and smells amazing,' William adds.

'*Buon appetito.*' Antonio steps back as the embarrassed waiters bow slightly before wheeling the trolley away.

William notices Vanessa giving them a warm smile and he touches her hand softly. 'You are sweet.'

'Poor things. They're clearly new here.'

'Well, it's very difficult to get good staff these days.' William withdraws his hand and looks down at his dish in appreciation. '*Buon appetito.*'

'*Grazie. Spero che ti piaccia,*' Vanessa says, confidently.

'Ah, so you do speak Italian?'

'After years of being married to a Sicilian, that's the extent of it, I'm afraid.' She sniggers and lingers over her food, waiting for William to taste, observing waterfalls of saffron sauce dripping from his pasta.

His eyes light up. 'Oh! What ...' With a mouth full, he proceeds to mumble to his meal in rapture.

'It's important not to offend the pasta. You don't want to hurt its feelings.' She laughs at his delight.

'This is good. Real good.'

'Watch that sauce doesn't swing off the linguine onto your white shirt.'

He swallows hard, widening his eyes at the thought.

Vanessa tastes tentatively, afraid of burning her mouth, but it is so delicious she twirls her fork efficiently.

'This is their signature dish,' she says.

'I can well understand why. It's sensational.'

'There are many dishes that pass from restaurant to restaurant, from country to country, but I've never had this anywhere else.' Vanessa excitedly takes another mouthful.

'I've now added this dish to my mental Rolodex,' he says.

'Has it ever occurred to you,' she asks him, 'that we are shaped more by our pleasures in life, than our happiness?'

'Aren't they the same thing?'

'I don't believe so. When I look back over my life, my fondest memories are the little pleasures, like this.'

Watching him indulge in the enjoyment of the dish, perhaps marking the moment, makes her smile.

He sets his fork down and leans in as if he's about to say something profound.

She waits.

'Vanessa, tell me, do you like where you live?'

Her demeanour instantly changes. 'Yes, why?'

'Just asking.'

She quietly ponders his line of questioning and resumes eating.

'Oh, don't get we wrong. It's a beautiful suburb, one of the best. I was merely wondering if you like living so close to the city.'

'That's what I love most.'

'Really. How so?'

Antonio reappears, clearing his throat to speak. 'Is everything to your satisfaction?'

'Yes, delicious,' William says, sitting back in his chair with a satisfied grin.

'*Perfetto,*' Vanessa adds.

Antonio removes the empty plates.

William reaches across the table, taking her hand again. 'I love the beaches, the smell of the surf, sea, open spaces ...' He trails off in thought.

'So do you surf?' she asks, having noticed a surfboard at his place.

'No, not my thing. I guess I like having my feet on the ground.'

'Each offer different things. Personally, I'd like to have the benefit of both, city living and the beach.'

He smiles. 'That can be arranged.'

Antonio reappears at that precise moment with their mains.

'Oh good. Yes, this is something light,' William says, looking down at his fish.

'I thought it would hit the spot nicely,' she says, savouring the delicious creamy spinach being served.

'Yes, but where are my fries?' he teases.

'Stop! You are so naughty.'

Antonio gives a quizzical look.

'Don't worry, Antonio, it's an in-house joke,' she says.

Suddenly they're aware the restaurant has become very busy and the couple seated beside them are incredibly irritating, totally disrupting the mood. She on her mobile phone and he a very noisy eater, a real chomper, who sounds like he's on wash cycle with his sloshing and slurping.

William asks for the bill.

On the way home, William can't stop laughing at Vanessa's candid description of the other diners.

'OMG, with the cacophony of sounds coming from the other table, and let's not leave out the visual effects. Watching that man chew his meat felt like I was at a Wet n' Wild theme park.'

'That's hilarious!'

Her excitement escalates. 'What are the seven deadly sins again? Gluttony, greed, ah, lust. Oh, I know; envy, that's four. What are the others?

'What?'

'Come on, William, you must remember them.'

'Why would I?'

'Because you're very clever. Come on, what are they?'

'Okay, okay, here goes. Greed, wrath, lust,' he says, taking the perfect opportunity to wink her way.

'Come on, be serious for a minute,' she urges, nudging his upper arm.

'Okay, okay.' He rests the base of his hand on the steering wheel and uses his fingers to count. 'Sloth, pride, gluttony.'

Vanessa counts them off. 'Six.'

'That describes those people perfectly,' he says.

'One more!'

'Okay, okay, and the other one you said before. Envy. Whew, it's not that easy to remember them all. Why do you ask?'

'I think seeing that awful couple eating made me think of gluttony,' she says.

'Research, I assume.'

'Everyone and everything,' she says with a cheeky wink.

'Sounds ominous.'

'It is.'

Pictures in Vanessa's head of her characters, their voice, the softness of their skin, the sincerity with which they speak, honesty in their approach to life, give kudos to her vision in voice and require effort in the execution of perfection.

'I love this,' William says, touching the button on his steering wheel. *Unforgettable.* 'Is this the Natalie and Nat King Cole version?' she asks.

'Yes.' He looks at her with such passion, she feels she might melt.

Pulling up outside her apartment block, they're still laughing about the voracious couple back at the restaurant. William semi-parks and steps from the vehicle to see Richard already on standby. Nodding respectfully, he hands him his keys in case he needs to move it. Taking Vanessa by the hand, he turns to Richard and says, 'I shouldn't be too long.'

Judging from Richard's persona, Vanessa takes comfort in assuming Michael hasn't been lurking about and seriously doubts if she'll ever hear from him again. *He is not a man that likes to be caught out on anything. It should be smooth sailing from hereon in.*

Upstairs, Vanessa offers William a drink. 'Wait. Wait. Wait. Better still, do you trust me to surprise you?'

The first few chords of Sting's 'Shape of My Heart' fill the room.

'Go on then, surprise me. It's your night.'

'Good.' She's feeling chuffed she's on a roll. *This man makes me happy.*

'This is a bloody great song. The words are brilliant, "sacred geometry of chance". Sting is such a talented writer.' He looks across at her framed photographs, notices the picture of the man he'd seen the other night is gone, and inwardly grins. When Vanessa returns from the kitchen with two small glasses and a chilled bottle of French Sauterne, William seems suitably impressed and offers to open the bottle.

She gratefully hands it to him and watches as he eases the cork out, then pours.

'Good choice, Vanessa, I enjoy a bloody good Sauterne from time to time. It's a great end to a delicious meal.'

'I thought it would be a nice change.'

'Did you know Sauternes are the rarest of all dessert wines? The actual process is nothing short of marvellous.'

'How so? What's so unusual about it?'

Delighting in its rich golden yellow colour, he holds his glass to the light.

'You know what, I've figured it out,' she says, tapping her forehead like a research scientist who has discovered a cure for a deadly virus.

'What's that?'

'Whittaker, you're a bloody sybarite,' she proclaims.

'I can't be.'

'But you are.'

'I can't be,' he says.

'Why?'

'Because I don't even know what a bloody sybarite is.'

'A sybarite is one dedicated to a life of sensuous luxury.'

'Guilty as charged.'

'See.' She holds her glass up in acknowledgement.

'When one is referred to as a wine connoisseur, they're usually called an oenophile,' he says, confident he has resurrected himself of any ignorance.

'Okay then, you're an oenophilean sybarite,' she teases.

'Not sure, but in any case, they're both great words.'

'Indeed!'

'Honestly, Vanessa, I don't know much about wines at all. What I do know is simply learnt from restaurant ramblings.'

'Well, you'd never know it from that wine collection at your place.' *I love his passion for the finer things in life. Metrosexual, Elizabeth used to refer to them as. Men with large, disposable incomes, stylish, handsome, and heterosexual. If Elizabeth has such a predisposition for metro males, why on earth did she fall for Michael, a middle-aged, overweight barrister? He's just so far removed from being the stereotypical. Epiphany! It's no secret Elizabeth tries to emulate me and everything I do. Clothes, décor, any idea she can turn her hand to and, it would seem, Michael. Well, now she has him and bloody*

Constance to navigate around, and let's not forget his smelly feet. She can have the lot!

She focusses on William enjoying the wine. *Talk about timing. Here I am with quite possibly the most eligible man in Sydney, and virtually overnight, everything has changed, and it would seem for the better. It's too good to be true. Talk about out with the old and in with the new.* 'I'd like to make another toast. To new beginnings,' she says.

'New beginnings.'

In a secret part of her, she's thrilled with how things have worked out.

Without saying a word, he reaches for her glass and sets it down on the coffee table, next to his. Pulling her to him, he literally takes her breath away, whispering 'Vanessa,' and kisses her hungrily.

The chemistry between them is intensely felt and she'd never realised a kiss could be so consuming. Soft, luscious strokes with his tongue. The more his mouth moves hers, the more she wants.

He draws a long breath and picks up both glasses, handing hers back.

She meets his gaze.

'You know we need to start focussing on the book awards coming up,' he says, seductively keeping up his scrutiny.

How can a man be so sexy even when he talks about work? 'I do.'

'That's why I think you should seriously think about coming away with me. You deserve some down time before the hype begins.'

She gives him a sideways glance. 'I'm not so sure going to Bali with you would actually equate to down time.'

'I promise,' he says, a twinkle in his eye.

She grins at his sincerity but is equally doubtful of his intent.

'Well, thanks for the nightcap but I need to head off. I believe you'll be gracing us with your company again tomorrow. You'll actually be meeting my father for the first-time.'

'Oh good! It will be nice to finally put a face to the man.'

'Oh, and for the record, he surfs.'

'Oh?' She gives him a quizzical look.

'You asked me back at the restaurant if I surfed.'

'Oh.' She laughs, still uncertain as to why he's mentioned it.

'That's why Dad likes to come to Whale Beach on the weekends; so he can surf.'

Vanessa is not usually up on gossip, but like most Sydneysiders, she couldn't avoid hearing bits and pieces about Montgomery Ralph Whittaker's libertine ways.

'William, thank you for a wonderful evening and I will give some serious thought to going away. Let me sleep on it.'

'Of course.'

'I really like Bali. I've been there many times as far back as I can remember. My mother lived there once upon a time.' She thought it too silly to reveal she was conceived there.

'Oh, I look forward to hearing all about it.' He wipes the taste of Sauterne from his lips as they walk to the door, pecks her on the cheek, and says goodnight.

Closing it gently behind him, Vanessa leans up against the closed door and holds her hands to her chest in contemplation. *Wow!*

She wakes with a splitting headache and immediately spots the bag with Michael's law books sitting over by the bedroom door. Having decided to drop them off to Elizabeth on her way to her meeting, she'd put them in a bag before going to bed. *Oh, what a way to start the day. But it's got to be done.*

She glances at the bedside clock. 'Bugger! It's already eight.' She rubs her temple and remembers she has at least half an hour of work to do on her manuscript before heading out. 'Why have I got this bloody headache?' *Perhaps it's from the Sauterne.*

Before docking at the computer, she grabs a bottle of cold water from the fridge, takes a couple of pain killers, and waits for the pain to subside. As soon as her blurry vision eases, she begins tapping away:

Immersed in her work, it's easy to lose track of time, so when she glances at her watch, she realises it's already time to take a shower.

Feeling the need for something colourful, Vanessa throws on her new emerald green, cotton dress. It's simple, but classic, so she adds fuchsia pink court shoes to set a cheery tone, noticeably bright, and in some ways, symbolic of the way she is feeling about her future. Vanessa grabs her handbag and the law books, takes the keys from the door, and closes it gently.

Stepping out from the lift and into the unusually busy foyer, Richard gives her an acknowledging nod.

'Morning,' she says.

Vanessa passes another couple in the foyer who are waiting by the lift.

'Good morning,' she says happily.

'Morning,' the gentleman says in a deep, sophisticated voice accompanied by a stern smile.

Passing Richard, she holds up the plastic bag and whispers, 'Good riddance to bad rubbish.' The penny drops and he gives her a knowing look. Not that it's any of Richard's business, but Vanessa knows he never liked Michael.

'You have yourself a great day, Ms Albert,' he says.

'Thank you, Richard, I plan to.' She cruises out through the open doors believing Michael is not her equal.

Richard looks around the empty foyer, and with a closed fist, discreetly punches the air. 'Yes!'

Shocked by the shrill screaming emanating from Elizabeth's apartment, Vanessa nervously stops to catch her breath midway up the pathway. Her heart instantly starts pounding. *This is much more than a lover's quarrel.* She hesitates to venture any further. It's strange, the feeling that suddenly seizes her. *Here I am at Elizabeth's dropping off Michael's things.*

Taking a deep breath, she decides to get this over and done with, and ventures a few steps further, attempting to place the books on the doorstep as discreetly as she can.

Through the open window, Vanessa confirms Elizabeth and Michael are involved in a full-on screaming match. Michael has sweat streaming down his brow, resembling someone with dengue fever, and to Vanessa's amazement, Elizabeth is jabbing her fingers at his chest, giving him a bloody good dressing down.

Oh my God, this is so volatile. She attempts to make a swift get away. Vanessa lives on high alert since the attack, and any form of aggressive behaviour makes her extremely nervous.

Michael catches a flash of something bright moving across the verandah. 'Wait,' he says, pushing past Lizzie.

'What? Wait? No.' Elizabeth's head shifts in stages as Michael flies through the open the door. Angry, and in an almighty huff, she reluctantly takes refuge on her sofa.

Given her meeting is scheduled in twenty minutes, Vanessa is on a mission and isn't in the mood for confrontation. She tries to flee, but Michael's too fast and flies out the door, grabbing her firmly by the wrist with such a grip of desperation, it scares her. 'Michael, let go of my arm. You're hurting me,' Vanessa cries, her eyes widening as she looks past him directly into Elizabeth's red swollen eyes.

Elizabeth stares back, horrified, legs tucked beneath her as she clutches a cushion. They glare at one another for the longest moment. Vanessa instantly arcs up. 'Here's a tip. If you suffer from debilitatingly low self-esteem and crippling loneliness, get a dog next time,' she spits at a shocked Elizabeth, who turns her head away in shame.

Interjecting, Michael snorts, 'I can explain, Van. Please.'

Totally disgusted, Vanessa looks at him for the very first time. 'Michael, you are so grotesque. You're just like your mother, and at what cost? How much ugliness can you cram into one family?'

Appalled by her outburst, he falters in his step and let's go of her arm. 'What about my stuff?' he says, struggling to engage her.

'What stuff? It's all there!' She points at the books. Keen to terminate any angry diatribe, she attempts to make a final dash.

He surges forward again. 'She doesn't mean a thing to me,' he blurts out, much to Elizabeth's shock.

'Don't care,' Vanessa says, resolute in believing he doesn't deserve to be heard.

Elizabeth stands in the open doorway and calls out, 'Why don't you both piss off?'

'Put a leash on your cat,' Vanessa says, repulsed.

Michael stands stoic in his resolve, ignoring the women's outbursts, arms outstretched, pleading for Vanessa's forgiveness. 'I beg you, Van. It will never happen again, I promise. Please. you have to forgive me.'

No resurgence of love wells. Instead, she looks at Michael with contempt. 'Did the pair of you ever stop to think of the consequences, or did your sexual proclivities simply override your sense of morality?' Deep down she knows she is not in any position to take the moral high ground, but in truth, she is probably sadder about losing Elizabeth than him.

'I'm sorry, Vanessa,' Michael pleads.

She isn't about to bend on the matter, nor be cast aside, only to be taken up again as a narcissist's refuge.

'Give me another chance,' he says.

She views his every plea as deceit and desperation. *He may not have any pride or self-respect, but I do, and he's free to leech off Elizabeth now.* 'Maybe you should have thought about this before you started fawning around with her.' She looks down her nose at Elizabeth in the doorway.

'You're not so innocent, grovelling up to the Whittakers,' he says contemptuously.

'You can't possibly compare that to the stench of you screwing my best friend.' She can't believe she can spit out something so loathsome. *Oh, well, I've said it now, and if the shoe fits …* Though Vanessa is guilty of her own indiscretion, she still feels this is different in some ways, given Michael's disgusting behaviour towards her virtually pushed her into the arms of another.

'Michael, you are a lost soul.'

'Look, let's start again. Please, I'm asking you to give me another chance.'

'There's only one problem,' she says.

'What?' He quickly darts around in front of her in the hope of stopping her from leaving.

'It's all bunk.'

'Please, Vanessa, I'll change.'

You'll never change. With that overwhelming thought, she has a sudden twinge of concern for her friend and half-turns, looking back at Elizabeth. 'Get away from him while you still can because he'll do it to you too.'

The shocked look in Elizabeth's eyes says it all. She knows these are the last kind words she'll ever hear pass Vanessa's lips.

Vanessa looks back at Michael with pity. 'Once upon a time is over. I am sick and tired of your hollow promises and verbal drivel. You have no idea how beautifully you've re-aligned my life. In fact, I really must thank you, Michael. Now get out of my way. I have somewhere I need to be and it's where I'm wanted and appreciated.' She pushes past him.

Feeling exposed, his tone instantly changes. Waving a spiteful finger in the air, he yells, 'You're all high and mighty now. You think your imagination has brought you independence, don't you?'

Looking back over her shoulder, smiling sarcastically, she raises her eyebrows. 'It has.' Knowing she'll never have to deal with either of them again, Vanessa holds her head high and walks off. With a complete disconnect from the dysfunction that has shackled her for years, she is now full speed ahead into a new and exciting relationship. She is in no way surprised by Michael's behaviour, but she always believed Elizabeth to be her closest and most trustworthy ally. This act of deceit has put a nail in the coffin. *The seven deadly sins and associated pitfalls. Evidently Elizabeth's been consumed by envy and Michael by lust.*

'Good morning, gentlemen.' She feels like pinching herself, standing before these three remarkable men, looking at their dazzling brown eyes. Even with her best fashion armour on, it's still nerve-wracking knowing the dynamic trio are there for her.

Thornton inquires, 'So how is my favourite author this morning?'

She feels her face blush when William steps forward and greets her with a kiss. Visibly proud, he is quick to introduce her to his father.

'Hello,' she says, extending her hand.

Montgomery is a little different from the other two. *Mm, nice tan. Probably from all that surfing.*

'Ms Albert, it's a pleasure to meet you at last,' Montgomery says.

Gosh, he has such a beguiling, baritone voice. The sheer sound would make any woman fall in love. 'Yes indeed. Please call me Vanessa.' She's surprised at how visibly moved she feels by someone she's never met before.

Tall, muscular, but slim, the shadow around his scalp tells her he isn't bald, but it's the beginning of summer, so his head is shaved. Clad in a navy linen suit teamed with a stylish, open-neck white shirt, he looks sharp and smells of Oud oil.

He's not your stereotypical mature male, that's for sure, and certainly doesn't look anything like his mid-sixties. Mm, a sense of relaxed refinement and sophistication; he's a man who gets better with age. Vanessa senses a great sadness in him too, someone who has suffered the slings and arrows of scrutiny, both personally and professionally.

Like William, the media have had a field day with Montgomery, his affair sadly well documented. His wife, aged sixty-three, regrettably passed away recently from breast cancer. Her decline had been swift, but shocking, and within three months of being diagnosed, she was gone. Jacqueline's understated, tailored wardrobe had made her a style icon with Sydney's elite and had ensured her entry into exclusive circles. Her endearing appeal had been her down-to-earth manner and her kindness of heart. Most notably, she'd channelled her energies into philanthropy and away from the limelight. She had been known for her mischievous sense of humour.

It's evident Jacqueline Whittaker hadn't taken her husband's affair lightly, but she had been determined to hold her marriage together for the sake of their five-year-old son, William. When Montgomery's affair became public knowledge, everything broke loose. Everyone knew her to be a devoted, hands-on mother, giving love and attention to her only child. Undoubtedly the loss of his mother had a big impact on William.

The interlude had taken place overseas while he was on one of his worldwide surfing safaris. Being an offshore affair, times past had afforded Montgomery the ability to take off overseas surfing, leaving his wife and son alone.

It was believed his mistress was a beautiful woman who bore him a love child, a daughter. No secret Monty loved her deeply, notwithstanding pressure from family, but he returned home, leaving the other woman alone and pregnant.

This had not come without its challenges and Monty was left heartbroken, and apparently never got over it.

Jacqueline accepted his betrayal with outward equanimity, but things were never the same. Monty had indulged her willingly to try and win back her happiness – clothes, travel, jewellery, anything she wanted – but she'd still had to live with the shame that a child had been born from the affair.

It was a huge cross to bear, but Jacqueline knew she couldn't hate him forever for loving another and remained loyally by his side until she died. Still, scandal is never far from the door, and he remains forever the man that cheated on his wife. The press had rehashed the scandal recently, referring to Jacqueline's emotional circumstances causing her to become ill and eating away at her quite literally.

Vanessa remembers one of the headlines:

Sadly, Jacqueline Whittaker died knowing her husband, Montgomery Whittaker, still loved another.

For that very reason, William likes to keep details close to his chest and rarely likes to speak of his mother. For fear of sounding like she's prying, Vanessa feels it's far too early to discuss his Jacqueline with him. After all, when she has mentioned her, William appears noticeably heartbroken and deliberately changes the line of conversation.

There is a knock at the door and William steps across to open it.

'Here's Bryce now,' Vanessa says as her media lawyer steps inside.

'Gentlemen, Vanessa.' Bryce takes the liberty of sitting on the couch next to his client.

Vanessa spots a bottle of champagne on ice over by Thornton's desk and feels it's either awfully civilised or somewhat decadent to consider drinking before noon.

Thornton breaks her train of thought. 'Do you realise what day it is, Vanessa?'

'Why yes, I believe it's Thursday, but this all looks so interesting.' She glances across at two young women dressed in black who have just appeared.

One woman begins pouring the pink champagne into delicate crystal flutes, the other slides an enormous silver platter of delicious canapés from the sideboard and begins passing them around.

'Dom Ruinart,' Bryce says. 'Impressive.'

'Yes, 2004 Rose Millesime,' Thornton says proudly.

'Very nice.' Bryce raises an eyebrow.

Thornton nods, holding up the morning paper and begins reading aloud:

'"One of the nation's most thought-stirring writers. *A Woman of Courage* is written from the heart, like dipping your pen into an artery, and is a sure winner." Quote unquote.'

Vanessa reluctantly steals her eyes away from William and tries to focus on Thornton.

He picks up a broadsheet:

'"I am doubtful of their exactness, but some autobiographies fit too perfectly into the story of one's life. Vanessa T. Albert lays bare all that we tend to conceal in ourselves. Genius."'

Montgomery smiles. 'Yes, I saw that this morning. If I'm not mistaken, Robert Taylor wrote the review on the upcoming awards.'

William chimes in and says, 'I read in The Book Guru column "the plot is thicker than a hearty minestrone".'

They all laugh.

How did I get here? Right on the heels of that thought, *I'm here and I better act professionally and act like I belong here.* At times, Vanessa still couldn't shift the self-doubt. *I'm not entitled to it. What do I do with this?*

Being an artist brought with it a certain vulnerability, and if you're doing well, it's really scary, and in order to do well, you have to make a lot of mistakes, and when you make mistakes, you get scared.

'Well, Vanessa, we believe there's no ceiling on your talent. It's grown exponentially. At Whittakers, we are acknowledging and celebrating your phenomenal success to date and know this is just the beginning. So given the prompt success of your first book, and having read your latest manuscript, ahem, we'd like to sign you a second book deal.'

William interrupts. 'The Audacity of Men is a sure winner.'

'But it's not finished,' she says, abruptly interrupting.

'Yes, I know, but the story is most ambitious, and we want it,' Monty says firmly. 'Just not sure about the title.'

'Oh, that's only the working title. Keeps me fired up,' she jokes.

'It's a substantial deal too, if I may say so? We love the manuscript, Vanessa. It's written with a thousand miles of bad blood that has a real hook to it, something the reader will be able to sink their teeth into,' Thornton says.

'We realise it requires more work, but the body of it's there, so it's clear we need to sign a deal,' Monty says candidly.

Thornton looks at Bryce. 'Are you happy with our offer?'

'Yes, I just have one query.'

'What's that?' Monty is certain there isn't anything to query.

'Well, Vanessa says she's not finished this current manuscript, and yet there's another contract for a third book.' He holds up more paperwork.

Thornton interrupts. 'Yes, that's right. Is there a problem with that?'

'Not from my point of view, but it's up to Vanessa.' Bryce looks her way.

Knowing she has at least another two or three books in her, it isn't a problem, but given she hasn't been brought up to speed with some minor changes to the contract, she's a little hesitant.

Thornton takes the high ground. 'You, my dear, are quite a *tour de force* and about to become a very wealthy woman.'

'Oh, my goodness,' she says, flushed. She puts a hand to her chest.

A proud William nods her way.

'Well, hasn't this been a day of surprises.' She's aware they're not privy to this morning's event.

Montgomery hands over the contract papers with a pen and asks her to go over them.

Designer pen in hand, she turns her attention to the contract papers. Leafing through, she is delighted when she sees a substantial monetary figure, together with a print run of 400,000 copies. 'Oh my,' Vanessa says, feeling flattered.

'Vanessa, it's all in there, but take your time to go through it,' Bryce says reassuringly.

She takes comfort in knowing Bryce has gone over the contract thoroughly and given the go ahead to sign on the dotted line but heeds his advice to go through it. 'Thank you,' Vanessa says, blanking out the conversation now transpiring between the men. After a time, she looks up and asks, 'How long do I have to finish it?'

'That's up to you, but we, of course, would like it as soon as possible. Say inside three months. Then you can get started on the third, and you have twelve months to complete it,' Monty says.

'I see.' She returns to the contract as Bryce steps across the room to chat with Thornton. Having gone over the paperwork as thoroughly as time permits, and knowing Bryce is confident things are in order, Vanessa is assured it's on point. Bryce has been her entertainment solicitor since the beginning and she trusts him implicitly, happily signing the appropriate pages, then raising her champagne glass to share a toast. 'Gentlemen, I believe we have a deal,' she says, taking the men by surprise.

She's grateful for this life-changing opportunity, but it's always a tension and balancing act between levering your work and being fresh and new. *Thanks to Michael, I know exactly what my third book will be about and its title.* 'Gentlemen, if I may make another toast?' She's always afraid of the next thing, but for now the words and ideas keep rolling in. 'Here's to my next manuscript, Moving Beyond the Ultimate Betrayal.'

Caught off-guard, they all glance at one another.

'There's far too much going on behind those pretty lashes,' William says, pleased she already has ideas for the third. He responds to her toast. 'Cheers! You are amazing.' William quietly sits down beside her and squeezes her thigh.

Thornton smiles approvingly, secretly wondering if there might just be another type of celebration in the making, and no one could be more pleased than himself.

'You do know the market for romance novels is huge, hungry, and international. But I'm certain you know what you're doing,' Monty says.

'She sure does.' William is tingling with pride.

Vanessa doesn't want to let the cat out of the bag yet and tell them she's already working on a romance novel as well. *Better to keep that one under wraps for the time being.*

'Oh, and darling, do you mind putting your initials at the bottom right-hand corner of each page,' William says, looking down at the papers.

Vanessa finishes initialling the rest of the contract, and on the last one, she signs off with a great paraph. 'Nice pen,' she says, attempting to hand it over.

'Keep it. It's yours,' Monty says, passing her the gold-encrusted Cartier case.

'Oh, another one,' she says, surprised.

It's a thing with Whittakers to give their authors a pen on signing a contract, but unlike the first, this is a particular status symbol. With its signature sapphire cabochon at the top, it's not to be underestimated; an instrument that doubles as collectable art and continues to pen. A firm talking point.

'I'll treasure it,' she says, holding the pen to her chest with both hands.

Thornton suggests they all head out for lunch to celebrate.

'Sorry, gentlemen,' Bryce says, 'I have to get back to work.' Closing his leather briefcase, he bids farewell. 'Enjoy your lunch and I'll talk to you soon, Vanessa,' Bryce says, looking back over his shoulder.

I know Thornton likes to take his authors out for a meal after signing, but it's a treat to be going out with all three men.

Comfortably seated in one of Sydney's top restaurants overlooking the harbour, discussions continue over a sumptuous lunch of freshly shucked oysters and poached salmon.

Following several glasses of white wine, Thornton gives Vanessa his full encouragement to take a much-deserved break and go off to Bali with William the following week.

Vanessa can't seem to wipe the smile from her face, thrilled with the prospect, and after so much turmoil of late, she feels she's part of something bigger.

'Go away, celebrate your rest and each other,' Thornton says, smiling at the beauty who has evidently waltzed her way into his family's hearts.

Her eyes widen when Monty adds, 'You really should go; downtime is key when we all work so hard.'

William is quick to react. 'So does that mean you will come away with me?'

'You'll be surprised how quickly I can pack.'

'Great!' William clinks glasses with her.

Behind rimless specs, Monty's face grows reflective, more genial than expected, and he unexpectedly interrupts the celebratory atmosphere. 'Vanessa, you do know as soon as you two get back, with several award events coming up, you'll be on the go more than ever?'

'Yes,' Vanessa says excitedly.

'Good timing, huh,' Monty says.

'Which, need I remind you, are the National Book Awards,' William says proudly.

It's not about winning or being an acclaimed author, it's about getting the word out there, but then Vanessa had come to realise infamy brings with it the power of the word. *So bring it on!*

By the time dessert arrives, it's been decided the happy couple would leave for Bali in five days and be away for seven nights.

Vanessa stipulates she has one condition; she must be allowed to write for at least four hours a day, every day.

William frowns. 'I know. But I also know that when some writers are in the throes of creative fever, he or she scarcely notices the passage of time, so let's make a toast to four hours only.'

'Deal,' she says, looking him in the eye.

'As long as I'm allowed to set a task-driven stopwatch?' he says, hand outstretched in search of a handshake.

'My, this is a day of deals,' Thornton says, throwing back a heartfelt laugh.

Enjoying the passionfruit soufflé with Pina Colada ice cream, she feels completely transformed in the presence of these men.

Giving Vanessa a loving look, William mouths, 'You're incredible.'

Slightly embarrassed, her attention quickly returns to dessert. Salivating, she tells herself this will be the last sweet thing to pass her lips before setting off on holidays. When the handmade chocolate truffles arrive with coffee, she sighs in temptation.

'Vanessa, would you like one?' Monty asks, sliding the small silver dish towards her.

'Oh, I shouldn't but ...' She takes a milk chocolate ganache with fresh pistachio. 'Mm, delicious.' The smooth creamy texture teases at her tongue, followed by the distinctive earthiness of the nut.

Outside the restaurant, it's farewell air kisses all round. A chuffed Vanessa parts company, having decided to stay in town for a bit of retail therapy.

'Talk to you this evening,' William says, kissing her cheek.

After such a relaxed meal, Vanessa finds the city crowds almost overwhelming, but with a new contract in hand and love at the fore, she is resolute in taking herself off for a well-deserved shopping splurge. While wandering through the stores, she thinks about all the countless times she's been to Indonesia, assured this trip will be very different. With humidity high, a much-needed downpour is threatening, so Vanessa makes a beeline for the eye-wateringly exclusive Chanel store to try on bathing suits. Deep in thought, she pushes the heavy glass doors open as two young women in workout wear are exiting, their designer handbags swinging by their sides. *Gee whiz, Lycra has even made it to the city. What next?* She enjoys the relief of the busy store's air-conditioning.

No sooner inside than something catches her eye: a bikini, the most exquisite sky blue you could ever imagine. *Oh, I must try it on.*

She signals to a store attendant, who is more interested in following the well-heeled tourists around. The manager eagle-eyes the staff member, and in a huff, she reluctantly approaches Vanessa.

'Do you have this in a size 34?' Vanessa asks.

The woman checks the swing tags. 'Yes, madam, we do.'

The attentive store manager approaches holding a length of sheer fabric. 'I believe this will make a delightful ensemble, madam.'

'Oh yes!' Vanessa holds the end of the fabric up to the light and admires the silky texture. The selected pieces are immediately placed in a heavily draped cubicle.

'When you're ready, madam.'

Spinning around in the designated space, Vanessa, very pleased with the set, suddenly spots her scar in the mirror, causing her to catch her breath and stop for a moment of contemplation. *Heck! If those girls can get away with wearing midriff Lycra in a business district, I can wear a bikini on holidays.* She knows it's time to move away from her body panic. Since meeting William, Vanessa has felt a bit more sanguine about the scar and views it as a symbol of survival and inner strength. With genuine acceptance, she dresses and makes several other instore purchases, including the very skimpy bikini. *Perhaps it's a symbol of things to come.*

Vanessa decides to pop in to one of the major department stores. She wanders around looking at summer fashions, but sadly nothing really catches her eye. Out of disappointment, she heads downstairs to the lower ground floor, avoiding eye contact with the beautiful spritzer demonstrators offering sprays and small sample cards. Vanessa wants a particular body cream without arousing anyone's help. Unfortunately, by the time she ventures back up the escalator, she's been atomised with at least three different perfumes.

Passing through the accessory department, a delightful, floppy raffia hat with fringed edge takes her eye. *Very 50s. Will look good with my big, black, cat's eye sunglasses.* She tries it on, looking in the nearest mirror available.

A sales assistant appears behind her in the mirror. 'May I help you, madam?' the woman asks.

Different store, different service. Vanessa decides to make the purchase. 'Thank you, yes.'

Pleased with her new acquisitions, she orders an Uber. Thankfully the strong breeze brushes her clean by the time she hops in the car. To her disappointment, the stench of curry hits her nostrils. No thanks to a deodorant tag hanging from the rear-view mirror, she is so overwhelmed by the density of the pong she can scarcely breathe, feeling she might throw up from sensory overload.

Traffic is heavy this time of the day and vehicles are crawling across town to the sounds of horns blasting here and there in frustration, so by the time they finally pull up outside her apartment, she's relieved to get out of the car.

In the foyer, Richard greets her cordially. 'Let me help you with those bags.'

'Thank you.' She hands him the lot.

'Looks like you've had yourself a great day, Ms Albert.' With his free hand, he reaches behind the counter and holds up a bunch of pink peonies. 'These came for you this afternoon.'

'Oh, Richard, they're superb.'

'Yes, they are indeed, Ms Albert.' Richard holds the lift doors open and helps her to her apartment, setting the designer bags down inside the open doorway and handing her the flowers.

She hasn't closed the door yet when Richard pokes his head out from the lift. 'Looks like a big storm is brewing, so be sure to close your windows this evening, Ms Albert.'

'Thank you, Richard. I will.'

Her mobile rings from her bag. Setting the flowers down, Vanessa is conscious of not tripping over the carry bags as she answers the phone.

'Hello, Vanessa speaking.'

'Hello, Vanessa speaking,' her mother mimics.

'Mum, give me a minute could you, please?' She hurries to move everything away from the door and closes it. *All I want to do right now is run a hot bath, relax, and get into bed with my book.* She places the phone to her ear again. 'Sorry about that, Mum. What's up?'

'Darling, I got your text message. Sweetheart, I'm so proud of you and this new book deal, I told you Whittakers would love your stories.'

'Yes, you were right. Come to think of it, I never did ask why you were so insistent I go to Whittakers.'

Her mother is silent.

Vanessa kicks off her shoes. 'You never cease to amaze me, Mum. How do you know anything about publishing?'

Diana cuts her short by tossing a million-and-one questions her way. 'Mothers always know best. Who are you going away with and what will you say to that foolish man, Michael?'

'Mum, stop, will you. I've only just got in the door. Can I call you back tomorrow?' she pleads, knowing this is going to be a very long conversation.

Acutely aware she hasn't spent much time talking with her mother in recent weeks for no other reason than being busy with life in general, it's not foremost in her mind to tell her about the recent split. *I need to be in the right headspace if I'm going to share this business about Elizabeth and Michael. I'll deal with this later.*

Diana senses her daughter's reserve. 'Okay, darling, when you can. But make sure you call me before you leave for Bali. Remember I'm going away up to North Queensland to Aunt Sarah's next week and it's not the best reception up there, particularly where she lives.'

'I will, Mum. I promise.'

'And darling, if you can't sleep tonight, call me.'

Vanessa clicks off slightly annoyed. *Right now, I'm not in the right head space for Mother's ramblings.* Vanessa loves her mother dearly, but like a lot of mothers and daughters, their relationship can sometimes be combative. Living in the shadow of Monica's death, Vanessa understands her mother tends to cling, but the downside of that is she comes across as overbearing.

It's no secret Diana had both her daughters out of wedlock, and after

Monica's death, several failed relationships followed. This resulted in Vanessa being taken in yet another direction every time her mother met someone new.

But Vanessa's biggest peeve would have to be when her mother met and married James Goodall. Jim was your average-looking guy, but he had a huge inferiority complex and often went out of his way to put both her and her mother down to make himself feel good. Which was another reason why Vanessa would escape to her bedroom to write.

After spending years struggling to create a stable environment with the man, it finally fell apart and thankfully Diana left him.

CHAPTER FOURTEEN

Vanessa wakes from a peaceful dream. Happy, she decides to open the drapes, instantly drenching the bedroom in sunlight. The pink peonies catch her eye, causing her to smile.

She hears the birds in the trees outside her window banter back and forth. A particular breed seems to be saying 'give me a break'. Vanessa can't help herself, throws in a cheerful chorus, 'Give me a break,' and opts to make a cup of tea.

Going back to bed with her laptop and notebook, she inputs the details she'd penned the day before. Her head is full of ideas for this current manuscript, so she sets to work making the entries.

William is right, my character needs a more suitable Christian name, elaborate but nevertheless suitable. She goes through the alphabet systematically: *Alan, nah, Bobby, nah, Thomas, nah.* Coming up blank, she concentrates on the plot instead.

Her fingers race nimbly across the keyboard. After several edit ideas, she's on a roll and continues further into the story. At the smell of coffee wafting through the open window, she takes a break. Saving to file, she hovers over the cursor: Shut Down, click. Silence.

Vanessa tosses on her workout wear, ties her hair back in a ponytail, and heads off to Joe's café.

Writing really is the stuff of dreams, she muses, striding up the hill. Thinking back to the romance piece she's secretly been working on, she wonders if life is imitating art, or art is imitating life – questions she all too frequently asks herself, knowing her present circumstance is enabling her creativity.

Stepping through the shadows in the doorway of the bustling café, the loud tinkle of the bell never ceases to surprise. 'Hi, Joe. That bell gets me every time.'

'Ay, Vanessa. The usual?'

'Yes please, Joe.'

'To hava here or taka away?'

'Here.'

'You notta worka today?'

'Yes, Joe. I work from home, remember.'

'Ah, thatsa righta.' He looks bemused.

Being a hardworking Italian immigrant, she knows her work is not in his scope of thought. His forte is creating an effervescent atmosphere where people like to gather and linger over fabulous coffee.

She gazes at the stainless steel and glass cake display fridge. *Biscotti, almond ricotta cake, strawberry tarts, something lemony, all lined up for the kill. Bloody hell, and let's not forget the amazing cakes on offer.*

Looking around, they're mostly Italians. Aside from a few English-speaking patrons, at least one other language is in the mix – Greek. A cosmopolitan hub. *We really have become one world.*

Joe observes her over the top of his espresso machine as she removes a chair from a two-seater table, indicating alone time, and places it at the nearest vacant table. He remembers the time an elderly man asked if he could sit next to her. She kindly nodded, but the man was profoundly deaf and proceeded to open the newspaper and do the crossword puzzle, which he completed by asking Vanessa every single question in a tone that disturbed her morning hiatus. Joe looks over the burr of the machine and notices Vanessa close her eyes, smile glowing as a cool breeze blows across her face.

Unaware of his attention, she opens her eyes sharply to the outside sound of an angry Aussie woman haggling with a street vendor, a total contradiction to the Italian repartee inside. She's pleased to be sitting by the open window. 'It's so hot outside, Joe.'

'Summer is a-coming.'

A man's voice interrupts. *'L'estate e' arrivata.'* He looks at Vanessa across the café.

Oblivious to how much attention her appearance commands, Vanessa looks at Joe. 'What did he say?'

'Summer is here,' Joe says with a smile. He sets down her coffee plus a chocolate croissant. 'Thatsa on the house.'

'Oh no, Joe.'

'No. You eata. Youa too skinny.'

She laughs warmly.

'You wanna some water?'

'Yes please, Joe.' *This is such a welcome reprieve.* She takes a sip of coffee.

Vanessa looks outside again, paying close attention to a sedan moving slowly over a speed hump, music blaring from the open windows. The middle-aged woman driving is at odds with the loud, distorted noise booming from inside the vehicle. When Vanessa spots the badly damaged tailgate, rusty from long-term neglect, she questions whether some people assume responsibility for anything in life, or perhaps it just isn't a priority.

Joe returns with her water, then sets about his business in silence. The sudden ring of her mobile is an unwelcome distraction, but her annoyance quickly fades when she realises it's William.

'Hi. Vanessa, it's such a beautiful day. I'm wondering if I can steal you away for a picnic?'

Wow! That sounds great. The weather is perfect. 'Ooh! An adventure. I'd love to.'

'Good. I'll organise the food and wine; just bring your beautiful self.'

'Gosh! Sounds like fun.'

'I'll pick you up in one hour. Does that give you enough time?'

'Perfecto,' she says, starting to sound like Joe. Vanessa finishes her coffee and leaves the money on the table. 'See ya, Joe. Thanks for the croissant.' She holds it skyward in a paper napkin. 'If you don't mind, I'll have it a bit later.'

'Here, putta in this.' He hands her a white paper bag.

In seconds she's out the door and headed home. Glancing at her watch, she decides to cut through the local park to save time. Listening to the happy sounds of children playing, she strides past a medium-size dog that has a quirky face, like he's smiling, and he gets busy bothering her guarded paper bag.

A gust of wind whips through an over-hanging tree, spraying last night's raindrops across her sunglasses, causing the salivating pup to sneeze. Vanessa pulls her glasses from her face and wipes the lenses on her t-shirt. Placing them on her head in frustration, she continues to fast-track it home. Not wanting to waste a minute, she decides to bolt up the steep stairway inside her building, bounding two steps at a time. Inside, she strips off, leaving her damp sweat gear and runners on the laundry floor. *I'll deal with that later.*

A quick shower to freshen up. She dries off her hair and redoes her ponytail, then tosses on a simple turquoise sun frock and sandals, adding a pale pink lip gloss to her fresh look.

She takes two bottles of water from the fridge and stuffs them, and the croissant, in her tote bag. Grabbing the house keys as she goes, she jumps in the waiting elevator and presses the ground floor button as William pings to say he's downstairs.

Perfect timing.

She races through the foyer and spots him behind the wheel of his car, roof off, appearing to be organising music.

'Hi, beautiful.' He looks up from the screen momentarily. 'Music needs air, so I put the roof down.' Stylishly dressed, he is in a light grey t-shirt, crisp white cotton shorts, and orange suede loafers.

She laughs, grabbing her cap from her bag before tossing the tote on the back seat and climbing in. She's about to hand him a bottle of cold water when suddenly a shiver courses through her body, causing her to wiggle her shoulders. 'Oh, someone just walked over my grave.'

'Boy, that's an old expression. I've not heard that in a long while.' He eyes her flaunting the shapeliest legs as her dress rides up. 'You are so goddamn beautiful.'

She smiles, never tiring of his compliments.

'How was your morning?' he asks.

'Great. I did some work, then went for a walk, had a coffee, and now I'm here with you.' She touches his thigh as he places his hand over hers.

Headed south, across town, it takes them about an hour to clear the city traffic. Once they hit the freeway, William picks up speed, coursing down the fast lane.

'Where are we going?' She twists in her seat to face him.

'You'll see. Somewhere where there's no ice-cream or souvenir stands.'

She clasps her hands in prayer. 'Yes!'

The route is clearly familiar as he drives with only half his attention focused on the road, the other half on her.

'How lucky are we to have such a glorious day!' She takes in the surrounding scenery. *I love Sydney, but weather permitting, I really do enjoy getting out of it.*

'Fabulous!'

Vanessa isn't sure he's necessarily talking about the weather, but she loves his boundless energy and enthusiasm that seems to make fabulous things just happen, and all seemingly effortlessly.

They sit content in their silence, loving the bright sun and limitless blue sky as the softness of the music adds to the peace and serenity.

Suddenly a bunch of P-platers come from nowhere and drive past at high speed in a black convertible four-wheel drive. Muscle-bound guys in the front and two gorgeous young women in the back are all trying to talk over the music booming out from the car speakers.

'Well, they won't last long,' William says, referring to the speed at which they are travelling.

A large earth mover runs alongside their car and William realises the truckie is peering in. Judging from the look on his face, he is scoping Vanessa through his dark Ray-Bans.

William tries to speed away. The P-platers assume he's trying to race them. Eventually he decides to hit the gas and manages to get away from both vehicles. At a safe distance, he slows down and places a hand lovingly on Vanessa's thigh. Keeping the speedometer just above the legal limit, William replaces his hand on the wheel.

A few kilometres on, they veer off the freeway, the road stretching out across open country. The distant roar of cars dissipates, and they eventually turn off into a heavily wooded area.

'Hear that?' Vanessa sits content, admiring the cultivated, green pastures.

William slows at a cattle grid. 'Hear what?'

'It's like switching off the volume.'

A little further on, to her delight, black and white cows graze on the other side of a rocky stream. The couple cross the gurgling stream, a mind-blowing swimming hole to the right under a shady canopy of trees.

'I used to swim in there when I was kid,' he says happily.

'William, it's so pretty.'

Eventually they come to a quiet place that opens to verdant pasture. Vanessa shifts in her seat, taking in the beautiful scenery and the neatness of the grass where the flat-rock stream meanders on past several overhanging willows. 'Wow! From the main road, you'd never know this was here.'

He nods in agreement.

'You used to come here as a child?'

'It belongs to my family.'

'You are full of surprises.'

He angles the car under the overhang of a large, leafy tree. Unexpectedly, dozens of galahs fly out of the tree, startling Vanessa, who looks up at their beautiful pink feathers, a spectacular sight as they fly off.

'They flock together in the trees to escape the heat, and considering there's water nearby, it's a perfect haven for them.'

'They're beautiful.' She watches them over head.

William turns the music off and seems content just sitting in the car for a minute. 'I love it here. I love the quiet. It's a special place that's been in the family for decades. Gramps bought it a long, long time ago. Dad used to bring me here often; he thought it might be a nice, quiet getaway for us. I think he was worried that if we stayed in the big smoke all the time, I might become a wayward teenager, so weekends were spent here while I was growing up. Truth be known, I got up to more mischief here than anywhere else. I thought you'd enjoy having a secluded picnic here.'

'You're not kidding. It's spectacular.' Vanessa notices a sandstone homestead in the distance. 'Is that part of the property as well?"

'Yes, it's the caretaker's cottage, but he's not there at present.'

She loves the way the manicured garden stretches out in front of the house.

'He's gone into town for supplies, or some such, and won't be back until tomorrow. He usually has a few drinks in the local pub, crashes there for the night, then drives back in the morning. When we leave, I'll take you back the other way and show you the family home.'

'Hope he doesn't buy milk.'

He looks at her quizzically.

'It would spoil if he bought it today.'

William shakes his head with a laugh. A solo kookaburra suddenly joins in. Pointing to his feathered friend, William says, 'He's with me. That's what the cows are for, silly.'

'I knew that,' she says with a tilt of the head. Hopping out of the car, Vanessa notices the sweep of rugged hills way in the distance. She can see power lines looping from house to house, a series of telephone poles to the fore, all at odds with the surrounding vista.

As she helps William unload, she notices a pair of his runners in the boot and it triggers a thought. 'William, I saw something really sad today.'

'What was it?'

'A For Sale sign on the local notice board.' With a puppy-dog expression, Vanessa wiggles an index finger. 'Baby Shoes for Sale, Never Worn.'

'That is pretty sad.'

'I know. It brought a tear to my eye.'

'I bet.'

I have no idea why I shared that.

William takes the picnic hamper from the boot. He hands her a taupe rug, softer to the touch than expected.

'This is cashmere, designer no less.' She fingers the beautiful, cream, cable-edge stitch.

William suggests they sit down by the river under an old willow. 'This looks like our kind of spot: secluded, cool, and soft enough for us to spread out.'

She smiles, lifting the rug in the air and letting it fall to the ground, then kneels and lets out a contented sigh.

'That's a big sigh.'

'William, there's no doubt in my mind that being surrounded by nature gives a much-needed perspective on where we fit in the world.' Vanessa sits looking around at the sun, filtering down through the leaves of the trees, creating playful patterns of light and shade as William sets about laying out the picnic. 'It's so crisp and clean out here.'

'This is my earthy getaway.'

Looking into the distance, Vanessa remarks on an old stone ornamental building. 'What's that? It's beautiful.'

'A folly.'

'A what?'

'It's what is known as an architectural folly. It's quite old actually.'

'It's charming,' she says, looking at a curved branch of a gnarly old tree reaching out as if presenting the moss-encrusted stone form. She pulls her phone from her bag and takes a picture.

'Gramps had it shipped out from England, stone by stone, and had it rebuilt here as a gift to my grandmother.'

'Oh, that's so sweet.' She turns the phone on him and lines it up for a snapshot.

'He loved her so much …' His voice drifts off.

'You're a romantic lot, aren't you?'

'I guess we are. I used to enjoy hanging out there as a kid.'

'Is that where you got up to no good?'

He casts a telling smile. 'Mischievous teen.'

She fishes through her bag, pulling out her leather notebook, and scribbles away, happily taking notes of her surroundings, then pauses a moment, tapping the pen to her bottom lip in contemplation before crossing it all out. *I'll come up with something better later.*

William raises a bottle of wine. 'I have Sancerre, some grapes, cheese, an assortment of meats, and a French bread stick. Thought we'd go Parisian today.'

'Sounds great.' She looks across the river at the cows. 'Are they Parisian as well?'

'If you want them to be.'

She doesn't respond, looking at him quizzically.

'Dutch mostly; they're what you call Holstein Friesian.' He places the bottle down to rest against the corner of the basket.

This is like something out of a storybook. She reaches her hand out to gently brush the tips of the grass and jots down a couple more things, like the smell of the grass and the architectural design of the folly, before energetically jumping to her feet like a teenager.

William stands and places a warm hand in hers, spinning her around like a ballerina, then holding her to him.

A short distance away, the water bubbles and sings over smooth, earthy pebbles as the cows, with their distinctive piebald pattern, look on curiously. Tipping her head back towards the sun, Vanessa feels an unexpected trickle of perspiration slip between her breasts, almost exciting her. 'Can you hear that?'

'What?'

'The hush.'

A cow lifts its head and breaks the silence with a loud moo.

'She's saying hello to you.'

Vanessa grins and begins to hum a tune: *Hi ho, the derry oh, the farmer in the dell …*

William suddenly realises what it is. 'You are too cheeky for your own good, Albert,' he says, nudging her playfully.

She laughs and wanders down towards the water, urging him to take in the sweep of the valley. The vale is covered with trees, some reaching to amazing heights. There are large red and white gums, oak, fir, lemon, apple, and mulberry. The grass, perfectly manicured, is seemingly tamed by the cows grazing, huddled together like lovers in one spot.

'Why do cows do that?'

'Do what?'

'Huddle.'

'Lots of reasons: socialisation, protection against bugs and predators —

'You're starting to sound like a fact sheet.' She lets out a belly laugh and tries to sing. Farmer in the Dell. Hi —

'Albert, you set me up.'

'Well, all this greenery will do me. There's nothing like the Australian countryside.' She spots a magnificent line of fir trees ahead.

'You really like it here, don't you?'

'Yes,' she says, looking up.

He watches as the sun applauds her form through the sheerness of her dress. She turns back to him. 'Do you know what a fir tree symbolises?'

'I'm sure you're about to tell me.' He watches her walk to the water's edge.

'High esteem; it's a symbol of honesty, truth and forthrightness because of the way it grows on the straight and narrow.'

'Albert, you are a fount of information.'

'Oh, I don't know. You seem pretty up on cows.'

He wraps his arms around her waist from behind. Lifting her ponytail, he delights in gently kissing the back of her neck and whispers, 'I'm up on you.'

'Mm.' She feels the rush of goosebumps across her skin and turns, attempting to kiss him, but he surprises her by gripping her waist and lifting her onto the low rise of the slope.

They sit, side by side, letting their feet dangle in the coolness of the stream, watching the ripples of water run across their toes.

'I feel so free when I'm with you,' she says seriously.

William cups her cheek, and gazes into her eyes. 'This is how I always want you to feel.'

A cow peers across the creek and suddenly breaks the tranquillity by letting out a long, objecting bellow, triggering hysterics. 'Talk about stealing the moment,' she says, pulling back. 'I'm hungry.'

'Well, there's a start.' He helps her to her feet. They go back and plonk themselves down on the rug.

The sweet melodic sound of nature is almost as comforting as the warmth of the blanket. 'I'm so happy.' She closes her eyes, relaxing her head back towards the sun, and relishes the blaze that graces her cheeks.

'Such unbridled joy,' he says as Vanessa throw her arms back on the grassy verge.

She can't ever remember being this contented.

He notices her nipples harden against the softness of her dress. 'May I take the liberty of pouring you some wine?'

'I think that's an excellent idea.' She opens her eyes and looks at him.

William grabs the bottle and is about to pour when he notices an odd-looking bug having taken up residency. He shakes the glass gently, trying to coerce it out and onto the warm grass. 'Come on, you thlippery little thucker,' he says with a jovial lisp.

Vanessa laughs, impressed by the care he takes to remove the offending critter. He pours the wine and grows serious. 'To our glorious future. The best is yet to come.'

Vanessa is so moved by his words and the longing expressed in them. They clink glasses and she watches him carefully set about placing the food onto a large wooden platter.

Tugging at a bunch of rich green grapes, he leans across the board and pops one in her mouth.

Biting down, the taste is sharp on her tongue, filling her mouth with a bitter splash. She discreetly discards the offending fruit into a nearby bush.

While she watches him unwrap the cheese, she notices the sunlight, shimmering through the leaves of the trees onto William, and catching the side of his face.

He looks up, studies her for a moment, grins and goes back to setting out the gastronomic selection.

Vanessa gets to her feet and gives a twirl of happiness, allowing her dress to lift cheekily as she raises her glass to the afternoon sun. 'Here's to the best day ever.'

'Here's to the shapeliest legs I've ever had the good fortune to view,' he replies.

'And thank you,' she says, looking his way, as if it is something he is giving her.

'If I'd known you'd like this place so much, we should have packed a light bag and stayed the night.'

'But what would Farmer Brown say on his return in the morn, to find us knee deep in lust in his bed?' She gives a childish dip of her shoulder.

He laughs. 'Well, we wouldn't actually stay in his cottage when we have our own homestead over the horizon. I'll show you on our way home.'

She flops back down on her belly. 'Well, that's no fun.'

'You are a tease.' He seizes the opportunity for a quick kiss.

A nearby grasshopper leaps in fright, so William tosses a light cloth over the food, moves in behind Vanessa, and delights in rubbing the length of her legs, working his way up to the crease of her warm thighs, watching the softness of her skin goose up. 'Have I ever told you you've got the best butt I've ever seen?'

'No,' she says, cheekily looking over her shoulder as his warm hands move across her cheeks. 'Mm. That feels nice.' She feels him provoke in a teasing manner.

His silence excites her as he fondles, moving from her firm, round cheeks back down the crease of her inner thighs again. Feeling her heart pounding against the ground like it might explode, she doesn't dare move, anticipating his next as the sunlight intensifies, filling the space around them. She no longer feels self-conscious, only the need to share this time with him.

He shifts his hands to her inner thighs, moving slowly, and slides her panties to one side in a form of a reveal to gently caress the warmest of spots, listening to her sigh. 'A work of art,' he whispers.

Relaxing to his touch, the sensation is sublime. He gently caresses the silken folds, and her lips begin to swell. 'Mm,' she sighs. *The freedom of being exposed in nature in such a way is so exhilarating.* She is aware of the distant bird chatter as she parts her legs with a little movement.

Aroused, William shuffles out of his shorts and lets the length of his penis rest against her for a moment. He takes pleasure in gliding his hand over himself, then her moist lips, lingering, caressing for a moment, teasing slightly. She's so wet, he can't wait any longer. He strips off completely and lies back down, close enough for her to feel the warmth of his arousal.

'I want to do things with you I've never done before,' he whispers.

I do too. She's exhilarated by his offer.

With the delicious sounds of desire, the driving force of want so great, he suddenly rips at her panties, tearing them off with one swift movement, discarding them on the grass.

Caught up in the carnality, she sighs, seeing her tattered panties lying alongside. *What is this man doing to me?*

His silence provocative, he slides her dress up over her head and discards it.

A light breeze blows at their nakedness. William's hand, soft and warm, gently traces the outline of her back, then further afield, allowing his passion to unfold slowly. The sensual threat causes her to gasp in anticipation as he whispers, 'I want you.'

His voice dark and edgy, she surrenders under his force as he suddenly turns her around in one swift movement, feeling herself flush as he presses his hungry lips to hers.

William has the most sensual mouth she's ever felt, but it's the innate sensuality captured in his eyes, his every gesture, that thrills. Her mind is gone as they search each other's eyes. Feeling her moisture, he gently slides inside. The rhythm sets the tone as he suddenly grips a handful of her hair. His tongue in her mouth, swirling: wriggling against each other, teasing, tantalising.

He pulls back, eyes intense. 'I want all of you,' he whispers, driving deeper as his fingers tighten around her hair. 'Oh, Vanessa.' His scent, strong and masculine, sweat drips from his body as he gains momentum. His hips lift again and again, his muscular body trembling with need.

The chaos of his thrusts makes it impossible for them to kiss, but his warm breath against her neck drives her crazy with desire. She locks her ankles around his calves and tilts her pelvis forward, taking him deeper ...

Their bodies tense, then release, tense again, then the ultimate release, and they both cry out with desire.

'My God!' he calls in satisfaction. Still holding her, he catches his breath before falling back onto the rug, body quivering with satisfaction.

Quiet prevails for a moment as they lie there with their fingers intertwined, not wanting to let go.

'Are you okay?' he asks, curling himself around her body for a kiss.

She nods, her eyes telling; she couldn't be happier.

'I'm crazy about you.' He searches her eyes.

Vanessa is without words, resting her head on his chest, listening to the accentuation of his voice against her eardrum. Enjoying the sunshine and each other, they remain in the moment until Vanessa breaks the wonderment. 'My, it's so quiet here.'

'That's the beauty of this place.'

'My God, William, I've never made love outside before.' She looks at him contentedly.

He laughs when she cups her hand over her mouth like a naughty girl. 'Come on, let's eat.'

'Let's.'

'Would you like me to make you my French specialty?'

'Mm. Yes, please.'

William doesn't concern himself with dressing, nor does she bother to fetch her strewn panties: no point. She sits up, watching him walk to the stream and quickly plunge, before surfacing and brushing past her dripping wet. *He looks content.*

Vanessa steps down to bathe. She smiles as a farm vehicle breaks the quiet. It's too far away to worry, so she continues frolicking in the water, turning back to see William now tearing off a large chunk of a sizeable baguette.

Breaking it open, he lathers it with herbed butter and adds various other ingredients: prosciutto, brie, pepper arugula. He closes it and sets it to the side to prepare another. Cornichons, saucisson, and pate are also set out on the wooden board.

As she approaches, he looks up and throws her a towel.

'Thanks. I like your style.' She dries off, feeling her tummy rumble. 'Have you ever been to Paris?'

'Yes, many times.' He hands her the much-anticipated baguette and a grey linen napkin. 'Start, don't wait for me.'

'This is so naughty. I'm pretty sure the gods are against it,' she says, taking a bite.

'Vanessa, you would love France: the gastronomic food, café culture, the chic clothes, the incredible sights. It's the global centre for art. It's a place with hidden treasures that excite your every sense. It grips your heart romantically.'

'I need to write that down.' She fishes inside her handbag for her notepad. Instead, she pulls out a paper bag. 'I brought you something Parisian.'

He looks inside. *'Voila,* a croissant. *Je vous remercie.'*

'Au chocolat.'

'Oh, you speak French?' He laughs, setting the sweet treat to one side.

'No. But you clearly do.' Caught up in the moment, she forgets about making notes and takes another bite of her baguette.

'Enough to get me by when travelling.'

'Italian, French; what other surprises do you have up your sleeve?'

'You'll have to stick around to find out.'

'I might do that.' She looks like she's been swept away in a dream.

He grows serious. 'I'd very much like to show you my world.'

She feels a shift in her heart so intense it almost frightens her. He leans forward and gives her a kiss. They laugh and chat, enjoying the warmth of the sun on their naked bodies.

After lunch, Vanessa walks down by the edge of the river, standing naked like a Pre-Raphaelite painting. He watches as she skips a pebble in a lazy arc across the water, where it lands with a rich plonk.

'You've done that before,' he calls, impressed by her precision, just as a cool breeze suddenly lifts her hair, blowing it upward. 'Picture perfect.' He pretends to take a snapshot.

'I never want to leave.' She's aware the day is getting away from them. Balancing on two large, smooth river stones, bathed in the last of the sunlight, she waves her arms to steady her footing. *It's happy and dazzling here.* She climbs up the riverbank and spots her torn panties on the grass.

William suddenly picks them up and waves them in the air like a prize.

She laughs. 'You owe me.'

He likes her childlike sense of humour. 'Any excuse to take you shopping.'

Dressing, she slaps her thighs cheerfully. 'Oh well, I'll have to go home panty-less.'

He finds her cheekiness refreshing. 'Oh, and you'd hate that?'

'Yep, panty-less for the ride home.' Her eyes glitter with amusement and she allows her dress to drop over her head and down her body, slowly.

CHAPTER FIFTEEN

The last few days have simply flown by.

Before Vanessa left home, she did a swift repack to lighten the load of luggage, making space for a spot of shopping. She learnt, long ago, one of the biggest mistakes people make is thinking you'll be incredibly creative on holidays and wear that piece you've never worn at home.

Now lounging comfortably up in business class, she gives a sigh of contentment and happily snuggles up to William.

'That was a big sigh.' William smiles down at her cheek resting comfortably on his shoulder. 'More champagne, Ms. Albert?' asks the flight attendant.

'No, thank you.' Vanessa looks up at the pretty brunette.

The attendant looks at William in the aisle seat. 'Mr Whittaker?'

'Yes, thank you. Could we also have some water, please?'

'Certainly, sir.'

The attendant pours carefully, froth reaching the exact spot, then ducks away for the water.

'Don't you just love flying?' Vanessa asks.

'I do.'

'What's your favourite destination, other than Italy and France, of course?'

'Gee whiz! There are so many places I like: choosing a favourite is a difficult call.' He clears his throat. 'In saying that, I definitely love Bali for the relaxation, food, and the people. I think the convenience of getting there within a reasonable amount of time, not suffering jetlag, is a big plus. Having the luxury of regular staff, you know, means they're aware of your likes and dislikes, and that's always a comfort.'

'William, I have to admit I'm feeling very naughty for taking off like this.'

'I think I need to offer you plenty of opportunities to get in touch with your inner adventurer.'

'You think?'

The flight attendant returns with two glasses of water and places both on William's tray. Handing one to Vanessa, the overhead music clicks off and a very loud woman booms over the speaker:

'Ladies and gentlemen ... oh, pardon me.' She turns down the volume. 'My name is Vanessa and I'm your chief flight attendant. On behalf of Captain Richards and the entire crew, welcome aboard Garuda Indonesian airlines flight 3407, nonstop service from Sydney to Denpasar.'

'Hey, another Vanessa.'

'No, there's only one,' William says, laughing.

'What's so amusing?' Vanessa looks at William chuckling as her namesake continues with the announcement.

'This is going to sound absurd, but I once knew a guy in high school called Richards and his parents gave him the Christian name Richard.' He laughs again. 'Richard Richards.'

'Did he get Dick Richards?'

'No. The kids at school called him Double Dick.'

They burst out laughing, trying to muffle the sound as several serious-looking flight attendants, awaiting instruction, stand at attention down the aisle.

'Now we request your full attention as we demonstrate the safety features of this aircraft.' The flight attendants simultaneously hold up life jackets like synchronised swimmers and proceed with their Safety Demonstration.

Vanessa leans in and whispers, 'I can beat that.'

He listens, focusing on the movement of her sensuous lips.

'I once knew a Pam at Dicks Publishing House and she married a Mr Enis.'

'Right?'

'Her email address was p.enis@dicks.com.au.'

William and Vanessa try desperately to stifle their laughter but simply can't contain themselves.

'You're not serious?'

'Deadly.'

The nearest flight attendant, bearing the name tag Daisy, a tall giraffe of a woman, gives then a withering look. Knowing how absurdly they're behaving makes it even harder to control themselves.

'Flight attendants, please prepare for take-off,' the captain says.

The plane slowly taxies along the tarmac for a bit, then turns right, lines up and comes to a slow stop, ready for take-off. Vanessa covers her mouth like a petulant child and doesn't dare look at William. It's a welcome reprieve when the purr of the engine becomes an enormous roar, making it difficult to hear their laughter.

Vanessa rubs William's upper arms excitedly as the plane begins to move along the runway, then picks up speed and starts its ascent.

'Here we go,' William says, as the acceleration pushes them back in their seats and the plane goes into a straight climb.

A few minutes in, Vanessa looks out the window, thinking life in Sydney already seems so very far away. She relaxes, looks across at William and mouths, 'Thank you.'

'My pleasure.' He squeezes her knee.

Passing through clouds and finally levelling out, the captain turns off the Fasten Seat Belt sign and announces, 'You may now move around the cabin. However we recommend you keep your seat belts fastened while seated.' The attendants immediately set about preparing to serve lunch. Soon the combined aromas of savoury, sweet, and spice fill the cabin.

Vanessa considers the preceding days. 'Hey, I have a bone to pick with you,' she says.

'What's that?'

'You forgot to show me the homestead the other day.'

'Oh. Well, I felt it was better to get you home before you got cold.'

'Cold? The day couldn't have been warmer.'

'Yes, but need I remind you; you didn't have any panties on.'

'Oh.' She purses her lips. 'It was fun.'

'Mm. Tell me about it.'

'What are we planning to do while we are away?'

'Well, I hope you've packed plenty of panties.'

'Oh, William.' She nudges his arm.

Shifting in his seat, he grows serious. 'I plan on getting to know as much about you as I possibly can.'

She smiles at the thought. 'I love that this is all so impromptu.'

'But I thought you said you feel very naughty.'

'Always.'

'You know the problem is that most people try to clear the decks and get their lives sorted before they feel they can indulge in travel.'

'Guilty as charged,' Vanessa says.

'Has anyone ever told you you're crazy?'

'Never. They wouldn't dare.'

She is amazed at how truly connected she feels with him and her heart warms.

'I'm going to teach you how to live life like there's no tomorrow.'

'Deal!' She feels like he already has.

'Are you hungry, darling?'

'Smells good. Are you?'

'I could eat something. Yes.'

The flight attendant takes drink orders and offers a variety of nibbles to start.

'I've never asked, but you don't have any siblings?'

'No,' she says in a way that tells him don't go there. Vanessa can't bring herself to talk about Monica. It would mean she'd have to say her name and tell him all about her love and loss. It would be simply too much to bear.

A couple of wines in, having enjoyed a light meal of Sous Vide chicken breast and salad, they finally nestle back in their seats to relax. William decides to watch an action flick while Vanessa grabs the opportunity to get to work on her current manuscript.

When she opens her laptop to start, her creativity seems to be lacking at first. She keeps tapping away in the hope something will spring, and it usually does. Inspiration can come from anywhere, and in Vanessa's bizarre pinball-machine mind, words or simple sentences are triggers. It can be totally random or unrelated, but often works, and then she's off and running.

An email suddenly pops up on her computer about a cancelled doctor's appointment and she notices it signed off by the specialist's nurse. The word sparks an idea:

> Nursing a broken heart after discovering her ex, a German bodybuilder named Anton, is now dating her sister's best friend, Lindy. Heir to tens of millions, ironically, she's been disowned because of her love of Metaphysics and other mysterious life forces.

Yes, I like the name Anton for this character. She takes a moment to look out the window and observe the interesting cloud formations. She smiles at one which looks like the big, white writer's quill she keeps on her desk to remind her of Monica collecting bird feathers, as well as her vast collection of shells. She mumbles under her breath, 'Life can change in a moment, and you never know when it's coming.'

He shifts his gaze to her and nods. 'It certainly can.'

'Either you have supersonic hearing or razor-sharp intuition,' she says.

He leans across to steal a kiss, only to be halted by her question.

'Do you ever miss a trick?'

'Never!' He plants a big, smoochy kiss on her lips.

When the cabin lights dim, they recline their seats and try to get some shuteye.

I can't believe I began my journey with William only a matter of weeks ago when he quite literally bumped into me. It's incredible given how much has happened in and out of the relationship. Seems like a lifetime ago. Vanessa drifts off into a blissful sleep.

An hour or so later, she stirs when the passenger behind her, clearly intoxicated, stands and decides to discuss world peace with his co-traveller in a loud voice on his way to the bathroom. Annoyed, she opens her eyes and soon grasps she won't get back to sleep, so decides to use her frustration in a more positive way and write.

William is also awake and reading a glossy magazine.

'What are you reading?'

'The Robb Report.' He snaps it shut, giving her his full attention.

She stymies a yawn.

'Wow! You were really out to it.'

Instead, she stretches. 'I know. I was dreaming I was on an aeroplane with a very handsome man, and on my way to some exotic location, until this buffoon behind me spoilt it.'

'I'm surprised you got any sleep at all. He hasn't shut up the entire time.'

'You didn't sleep?'

Raising his eyebrows, he shakes his head. 'No, for the very same reason.'

'Some people are so self-unaware.'

'Ignoramuses, if you ask me.'

For the rest of the flight, William is content with reading while Vanessa thrashes out an angry fight scene.

When the overhead lights come on, the captain makes an announcement on local time and the temperature in Denpasar, the flight attendant approaches and interrupts with a tray of cold, white hand towels. William takes two, just as there is another announcement.

'Ladies and gentlemen, as we start our descent, please make sure your seat backs are upright, tray tables are stowed, your seat belt is securely ...'

Vanessa zones out, having heard it dozens of times before.

It's a smooth landing in Denpasar and as they taxi to their holding dock, William turns his cell phone on to check his voice messages. There are several business calls, but one is from his father, wishing them both happy holidays and reminding him to pick up some fresh coffee beans from the civet farm. William screws up his face.

'Is everything okay?'

'Nothing to worry about. I'll explain later. It's my father.' He grows somewhat serious. 'Now that's someone who is crazy.'

She takes him at his word and laughs.

It doesn't take long for Vanessa to feel the outside heat penetrating the aluminium walls of the aeroplane, a reminder she's now on holidays. Removing her blue cashmere wrap, she folds it neatly and places it in the front pocket of her travel bag.

'Ready?'

'Sure am.' *I feel so spoilt, having the benefits of sitting upfront and the flight attendants passing your bags to exit swiftly.*

The heat is evident as the handsome couple make their way down the stairs of the terminal. William holds their Australian passports as they line up amid a bustling crowd at the checkpoint. Once they are through, he notices an airport staff official, standing at the entrance, holding an A4 white board which reads: Mr William Whittaker and Miss Vanessa Talbert. He smiles across at Vanessa in acknowledgment of the typo and they proceed through the express customs area to collect their luggage.

Pointing out the relative pieces, the small Indonesian man dutifully takes the bags off the conveyer belt and waves them through customs. They're then led out to Ketut, their driver. Mid-afternoon and the air is a giddy mix of languages: Indonesian, Italian, English. People hurry to load their bags into queuing cars and taxis.

A group of young German backpackers block the pathway, determined to post their every move on social media. Ketut politely pushes past them with a half-smile, grabs William's and Vanessa's luggage and hauls it to the rear of his car, jamming in their duty-free bags. Doors closed, they are relieved to be away from the chaos outside and beginning the half-hour drive to their villa.

Initially Ketut is relatively quiet, focusing on navigating his way through the already bumper-to-bumper traffic of the enormous carpark, only stopping to pay the small fee at the toll booth. Ketut nods to the man and says, '*Terima kasih*,' then proceeds with caution. The calm that washes over his face is evident as he looks up and smiles in the rear-view mirror. 'Welcome back to Bali, Mr William.' He pops open the glove compartment and hands over two sealed hand wipes.

'Happy to be back, Ketut. Thanks.'

Ketut diverts his attention to the beautiful woman in his car.

'Have you been here before, Miss Talbert?'

'Please call me Vanessa.'

'Yes, Miss Vanessa.'

'Yes, many times, Ketut.'

'Oh, you must love Bali, Miss Vanessa?' His smiling eyes swing from the road to the rear-view mirror like the Feng Shui pendulum hanging from it.

'Yes, very much.' She smiles warmly.

Ketut puffs up his chest in proud proclamation. 'Good, good.'

I'm already starting to come alive. Vanessa turns her attention to the outside chaos of people struggling to get home. It's a familiar sight: locals with etched faces grateful for day's end; people being jostled along with the seething mass, holding their ground in the dusty streets. They move through scattered rubbish, mangy dogs, dilapidated shacks, and stores that some call home: some on foot, some on motor scooters or heavily loaded work trucks. Men and women piled high like the sandstone they've quarried throughout their long, drawn-out day. Even through closed windows, the toot of horns adds more din to the endless noise of the streets.

Life in Bali, in part, is often dirty, smelly, and laborious. Tourists are often unaware of the pain of the Balinese, but Vanessa knows the masses are not to be pitied. Most spend their waking hours toiling with scant opportunity for development of individual talents and interests, except for prayer, but overall, they appear content.

Vanessa notices a smooth-faced elder on her haunches, blinking compulsively, stirring a pot on a portable gas cooker. Nearby the ground is strewn with papers and empty bottles. She smiles at an incense stick burning in a tin can, filled with sand, on a blue plastic mat, a symbol of her dedication to Hinduism.

She couldn't help but feel humility for these hard working, kind, happy souls filled with pride even though their community is not wealthy, and the great majority live on the verge of poverty. Others, even some lawless spirits, perhaps holidaymakers, might seek adventure or set up transitory dominion, racing alongside, all in a human whirlpool. But there is an infinite beauty about the place, a magic that attracts tourists and locals alike. Of course, like all popular places, Bali suffers to a certain extent for being appreciated.

Vanessa opens the window just enough to allow the city smells in:

familiar, comforting, pleasing, and at times confronting. Having lost her sister in a tragic motorbike accident in Bali, it somehow brings her nearer to Monica. *Perhaps her glorious spirit somehow lingers in paradise.*

Vanessa allows the feeling to settle, pleased it's a very different time and the beginning of her holiday with William, and very much looking forward to seeing Bali, Whittaker style.

'I love the smell of these places,' William says, like he's always in tune with her thoughts. His hand rests comfortably on her thigh, gently stroking the crease of her beige linen trousers, 'and I love how the people embrace life.'

It's so special to be able to share thoughts and beliefs with a like-minded soul. One day I might tell him what Bali truly means to me and why it's always held a special piece of my heart.

'Here we are,' announces William as Ketut navigates down the busy, boutique-lined streets of Bali's hip Seminyak. He suddenly turns down an absurdly narrow laneway and around the bend, where he slowly approaches an automatic, swing-arm gate across the entrance to a small, private carpark.

Peering through the tinted glass, Vanessa can't contain her excitement as several smiling staff make haste towards the vehicle. Exiting the air-conditioned car is an instant assault to the senses as the heat hits Vanessa's face and the sound of distant surf washes ashore.

Vanessa is handed a chilled towel. She smiles at the calm with which the staff move, evidence life here generally beats to a serene rhythm.

The couple are led down a short pathway in the direction of the ocean. The smell of incense wafts through the air as they pass an exquisite Balinese floral offering lying at the foot of a stone Buddha statue.

'Canang Sari,' William says as they step through the ancient timber doors of the opulent villa.

Vanessa peruses the resplendent sanctuary with its sprawling lawn and tropical gardens. The heady scent of flowers throughout the grounds is intoxicating; frangipani, white jasmine, and champaca, which has an almost fruity scent often used as a base ingredient for making perfume. *Clearly no expense has been spared. Even the planning of the private estate surrounding the villa is elaborate.* Vanessa is struck by a magnificent queen palm soaring over this peaceful haven. On previous visits, Vanessa has seen many villas in Bali, but nothing quite like this. *This is where the traditional meshes with the modern: the luxury villa with its cutting-edge architecture and the lavish gardens has been built recently. It really is in keeping with the sumptuous style of everything the Whittakers do, but not in a pretentious sense. Everything here is calm and understated.*

Before them is an enormous, private infinity pool. At the end, the magic of falling water in such a mystical space is the garden's main feature. It's designed as a complete hideaway, but step outside the villa and it's a metropolitan hub with some of the best restaurants in the world right on their doorstep.

'This looks like the set of a Puff Daddy pool-side music clip,' Vanessa says jokingly.

No expense has been spared in this ideal sanctuary, which is serviced by no less than nine locals who will cater to Mr William's and Miss Vanessa's every whim: unpacking their clothes, drawing baths, making dinner reservations – you name it. The staff do it all to ensure the experience is one of unparalleled indulgence.

'It doesn't get any better than this.' William smiles at Vanessa, then in the direction of three female staff waiting to assist.

Vanessa gives a nod as one steps forward, places a pink and white frangipani behind her left ear, and says softly, 'This means you are unavailable.'

Vanessa feels herself blush as the women observe William lifting her hand and gently pressing it to his lips. She instantly remembers being young and her mother explaining that frangipanis are an icon to the Balinese and show the sanctity of the heart.

'This is where I come when I want a little fabulousness and a lot of beauty.'

'I get it,' she says, amazed.

'While we're away, all I'd like to do is relax, swim, drink cocktails by the pool, read a great book, and work our way through the fabulous restaurants.' William squeezes Vanessa's hand.

'Love it.' She follows him down the stone pathway.

'Good.'

'What book are you reading?'

'The Catcher in the Rye.'

'Salinger. An all-time classic.'

'I'm all-in for a good classic.' He pushes open the heavy glass doors of the bedroom.

Pausing inside the doorway, Vanessa's eyes dwell on the centrepiece of the thatched-roof bedroom, an intricately carved bed, and is thrilled. It reminds her of being mesmerised as a child, staying with Aunt Sarah in tropical Queensland, who has a four-poster almost identical, with a canopy of muslin to keep insects out.

It warms her heart, knowing that she'll be cocooned in William's arms, as she eyes the beautifully carved, stand-alone side tables. *Mm, no drawers. No Gideon Bibles in here.*

William startles her when he suddenly tosses his hand luggage on the perfectly made bed, oblivious to the heart-shaped arrangement of delicate pink flowers on the white cotton sheets. 'Why don't we take a swim?'

'Love to.' Vanessa feels the need to reboot before dinner.

They change and head back outside to find Yudi, their personal butler for the duration of their stay, pouring fresh guava juice.

William strolls into the kitchen, takes a bottle of vodka from the duty-free bag, adds a healthy splash to each glass, and takes them poolside.

In the shade of a palm by the edge of the pool, Vanessa notices a silver tray and a fresh banana leaf on ice laden with handmade chocolates, decorated with the most beautiful, candied flowers. The delicious treats make her smile. A glittering blue morpho butterfly flits slowly past, the whisper close enough to almost tickle her nose. *Perhaps it's a sign of good things to come, or perhaps its Monica's spirit acknowledging my presence: hopefully both.*

She couldn't resist taking one of the sweet delicacies and is delighted as the rich scent of chocolate assaults her senses and caramel oozes from its centre.

'Aren't they to die for?' William says.

'No. This is to live for.'

He laughs, feeling almost tempted to have one, but decides to wait for dinner.

'Miss Vanessa, Mr William, would you like me to arrange a massage for you before dinner this evening?'

He looks at Vanessa, who is embarrassed she's unable to speak as her mouth is full of delicious gooeyness. 'No, thank you, Yudi. We really don't have enough time. If possible, would you organise for us to have them every morning after breakfast.'

Knowing he likes his breakfast served promptly at nine, she confirms. 'Yes, of course, Mr William. Say half ten?' Yudi often endearingly refers to William as 'boss man'.

'Perfect.'

Vanessa swallows the delicious treat and smiles at Yudi, admiring her level of professionalism, then grabs her phone to take some pictures.

Places like Bali are such a reprieve from the daily grind of day-to-day living back home. Here is where hours are dictated by things infinitely simpler than the demands of the city. Here you can take time to leisurely doze in a hammock under the soothing tropical sun and aromatic scent of the surrounding gardens or stroll along the beach at sunset before an evening cocktail.

Both submerged in the pool, William takes Vanessa in his arms as the quiet washes calm over their bodies.

'Ah, this is the life.' She feels the tensions of everyday leave her body as she floats easily next to William.

'Happy?'

'Mm, very.'

'A beautiful woman like you should always feel happy.'

Vanessa can't get over his level of devotion. Emerging from the pool, she indulges in another chocolate.

'Good, huh?' He watches her recline on the sunbed with her drink.

'I'm so grateful to have eaten that,' she says, taking a sip.

'Trust me, it's written all over your face.' He steps out from the water and his gaze turns sultry. 'Grab your drink,' he says, taking her by the hand.

Feeling his need, she follows him through the heavy glass doors to the outdoor cabana-style bathroom. Seeing the dark stone bathtub filled with floating rose-petals appeals to her romantic notions, but William has other plans. Shaded by a huge, overhanging frangipani tree filled with tropical flowers of white and yellow, William turns the shower on to full capacity.

When the heat of the water hits the flowers, Vanessa delights in the rich, heady, floral fragrance it gives off.

Without words, William buries his face in her neck, then kisses her mouth, making deep plunges with his tongue, licking, and tasting her lips. The steam rises around them as they peel off their bathing suits and he kisses her lips once more, cupping her breasts, then bends to kiss them tenderly. Turning her to face the tree, the last of the days ray's glisten through the umbrella-shaped branches onto the curve of her body. Looking at her exquisite form excites him, feeding his passion, fuelling her desire.

'I love your body. So elegant, and sexy as hell!' He soaps her back with the flat of his hand, then moves seductively over her skin.

Feeling his erection throbbing hard against her cheeks, William grips her hips and begins circling, positioning himself, his need rising with every move, growing heavier, deeper, reverberating in the air as he teases at her.

Surrounded by a walled garden, protected from the wind, they're so caught up with one another that they're not concerned if they could be heard by the outside world. He lathers his cock, the sexual threat making her gasp in anticipation.

'I'll go slow,' he whispers.

Bent forward with need, her eyes settle on the dense curve of the tree. She positions herself and grips the narrow trunk, looking back at him fixedly. He eases inside in long movements, then more rhythmic, the branches of the tree shaking with the force of their bodies, and she pushes back, writhing beneath him with pleasure.

Her excitement creates the need to face him, but she dares not break the momentum, enjoying the passion of the moment. Their sighs grow louder with each thrust, escaping through the heated mist, transient with every laboured breath. Biting down on her lip, Vanessa closes her eyes, lost in ecstasy, and suppresses the loudest moan as all-consuming desire gathers.

His strength, his masculinity is utter pleasure, pulling her body to him, coaxing her closer and closer to orgasm with every thrust, then backing off slowly, teasing.

The excitement builds again with his every movement. His moans become more primal, stronger, sonorous with need, until she's about to come, edging nearer.

He picks his mark.

Breathing heavily and sensing his focus, she reaches round, grabbing his thigh and pulling him in deeper.

'You're mine, Vanessa. You're mine!'

With one long, deep, pleasurable sigh, she catches her breath and is elevated to her toes as they shudder to a slow, deep, grinding halt, anchored to him as one.

William doesn't move, enjoying the sensations coursing through his body as he grips her waist, enjoying the suppleness of her skin in his hands and appreciating the warmth and texture of their entwined thighs.

'Are you okay?' He turns her to face him. Gazing into her eyes, he rests his forehead to hers.

'Yes,' she murmurs as he kisses her voraciously with the hunger of a man lost in the passion, their silence screaming of love.

Vanessa gives a little moan.

Parting his lips from hers, he stays near. 'I keep thinking this is a dream.'

Her silence is met with the warmth of his love.

'Vanessa, you've released a fire in me I've never felt before.'

In loving gesture, she places her hand on her naked chest. No need for words, her eyes give off a soothing warmth.

The moment is broken as a scooter zooms past through the laneway on the other side of the high wall.

'Better get —' Williams attempt to speak falls flat as a barking dog suddenly breaks the intensity of the moment and tickles of laughter fill the space. 'I'll get Ketut to drop us up the road for quiet dinner at La Lucciola,' he says, drying off. 'It's a balmy night, so after dinner, I thought we could walk back along the beach.'

Take me anywhere. 'Great idea.' She watches him step inside and throw himself on the bed, naked.

Stretched out, his gaze follows her as she pulls on the skimpiest of thongs and steps into a blue, silky dress, pulling it up slowly in a teasing manner.

'My, my,' he says, engaged by her beauty.

I love the way he says that. She steps forward and sits on the edge of the bed, holding her hair off her neck.

He runs the zip up her back, kissing her nape.

'Come on, get dressed.' She shrugs her shoulders from side to side. 'Otherwise, we'll never make it out of here.'

'I can't help it. You drive me crazy.' He bounces off the bed.

'May I get you some drinks?' asks the slender Balinese woman.

'Yes, thank you.' William looks towards Vanessa. 'Darling, what would you like?'

'Long Island iced tea, please.'

'And I'd like a Mojito, lots of ice, lots of mint.'

'Ooh! We are on holidays.' The beach is lit beautifully by the lights of the restaurant, drawing Vanessa's eye upwards. 'The sky here is almost as beautiful as Whale Beach.'

'I think it's called vacation magic.' William notices her eyes sparkling in the light. 'Vanessa, in the short time I've known you, I don't think I've ever seen you look so happy.'

'I am.'

A young Asian couple in their twenties, hand in hand, are shown to the only empty table available, next to Vanessa and William.

'Ah, don't you love young love.' She watches the young man pull his girlfriend's chair out.

'There's a lot to be said for old love too, you know.'

'Hey, who are you calling old.'

'No, I didn't mean that. Remember the elderly couple at the restaurant on our first date.'

'Ah, yes, our business dinner,' she says cheekily.

'Got me.' He raises his eyebrows as the waiter returns with their drinks and the menus.

'You know my mother started coming to Bali over forty years ago?'

'Really?'

'Apparently this is where she met my father.'

'There you go, young love.'

'True. She looks across at the rolling waves on the shoreline. 'Can you imagine what it must have been like back then?'

'Different altogether, I'd imagine.'

'Yes. I was conceived here in Bali. Unfortunately, I have no idea who my father is or whether he's still alive,' Vanessa says sadly.

'What? Here in Bali?'

'Yes.'

'It's kind of sweet I've brought you back to where you were conceived, don't you think?'

'You are a terrible romantic, William Whittaker.'

'It's your fault. You bring it out in me.'

She gives him a pensive smile.

'It must have been awful growing up not knowing who your father is?'

'It's like ... something is always missing.'

'I bet. Couldn't your mother fill you in?'

'Oh please, I've tried.' She's quick to deflect. 'Now, William, you promised to let me have the time to write while we're here, so I'm thinking tomorrow ....'

He throws his hands up in the air in protest. 'Come on, we're on holidays. Let's take it one day at a time?'

She makes a face. 'A promise is a promise.' She shakes her index finger.

'I know but —'

'Okay. So, inspire me.'

'If you aren't feeling inspired by all this beauty, something's wrong.' He fans a hand at the magnificent vista before them.

She swings forward in her seat, placing a hand on the table. 'You're so deliciously cheeky. I love it!'

William places his hand protectively over hers and leans towards her.

'You're not exactly on a deadline, Vanessa. You only just signed the deal last week and already you want to get back to work.'

'You heard your father and grandfather. They'd like the manuscript as soon as possible so I can get started on the next.'

'That doesn't mean tomorrow.'

'You're incorrigible. Here's the thing, William. Inspiration is badly behaved. It strides boldly into our lives without knocking, and once it forces its way in, acts as if it owns the place. Then when it feels inclined, it simply vanishes.'

'It's not going to vanish, Vanessa.'

'Well, it doesn't always come when we call for it either.'

'Something tells me there will be no settling of notepads this week.'

'I hope not!'

'Are you prepared to venture further afield than the villa?'

'Yes, of course.'

'Good, because after our massages tomorrow, I'm taking you on a seawater sensation.'

'That sounds intriguing. A yacht? Cruiser?'

'So do you think you could hold off from writing for a bit?'

'Maybe.'

'It'll give you plenty to write about.'

'Maybe.'

'Come on!'

'Heck! I don't want to cheese my publisher off.' She winks.

'Never!'

'I like to think so. A seawater sensation, huh. Sounds interesting. You are full of surprises, William. Where is it? A beach somewhere?'

'Not exactly, but it is located overlooking the beach: Jimbaran Bay, in fact. Have you been there?'

'Yes, many times, but as far as a seawater sensation ... What is it?'

'Well, it's part of a resort situated on top of limestone cliffs. They have one of the world's largest aquatic seawater therapy pools. The water comes from the Indian Ocean and is warmed to optimum temperature to provide so-called curative properties. Is that research enough for you?'

'Mm. Sounds amazing. And sounds like something I should write about, so bring it on.'

'There's about a dozen massage stations that you move through and hydro-pressure jets bubble like geysers around your body. It is so relaxing, and what's more, you're meant to drop a couple of kilos through the experience. Not that you need to lose any weight.'

'You're a very persuasive man, William.'

'I know.'

'After all those chocolates this afternoon, I think I might take you up on the offer and opt for working off the kilojoules, rather than sitting at my computer.'

'Oh, believe me, we'll be working them off,' he says with a glint in his eye, reaching for a menu. 'Let's order.'

CHAPTER SIXTEEN

'Good morning, Miss Vanessa. Good morning, Mr William,' Yudi says in a soft voice that almost sings to you.

Watching the handsome couple cross the perfectly manicured lawn, Yudi dries her hands quickly and steps out from the kitchenette to greet them, giving a half-bow.

William pulls a wicker chair out from the table.

Vanessa admires the beautiful setting, delighting in the freshly prepared tropical fruit displayed on a large celadon platter. The smell of freshly roasted coffee hangs in the air, adding to the allure. *Why is it that everything is always better and brighter in Bali? Sunshine. Sunshine really does make things taste better.*

'May I pour you a coffee?' Yudi asks cheerfully.

'Yes, please, Yudi,' Vanessa says.

'Darling, I know you prefer tea,' William says. 'Yudi, do we have any English Breakfast here?

'Yes, of course, Mr William.'

'No, coffee's fine. I'd like to try it,' Vanessa says politely.

'Okay, good. This is what dad keeps messaging me about.' He watches Yudi pour steaming hot coffee into two celadon mugs.

Holding the handmade mug to her nose, Vanessa inhales. 'It smells amazing.'

'I thought the Italians had it all stitched up until I came to Indonesia,' William says.

'That's a big call.' She's conscious of him waiting for her to take a sip.

'The beans come from coffee berries which have been eaten by the Asian palm civet and pass through their stomach intact. The cat defecates it whole and —'

'I'm sorry?' Vanessa almost chokes at the thought.

'Don't worry, they're thoroughly washed. Farmers dry them in the sun then lightly roast them to produce this aromatic coffee. I like it because it's not bitter.'

Vanessa sets the mug down and says in astonishment, 'Let me get this straight. What are you telling me?'

Yudi covers her mouth with a tiny, weather-beaten hand, giggling at Vanessa's reaction.

'You've been to Bali before. I naturally assumed you'd know all about it.'

'No, because I'm not usually a fan of coffee.'

Suitably entertained by her guests, Yudi retreats to the kitchen.

Hearing the scurry of little feet, Vanessa looks up to see a gecko hanging his head over a wooden beam. 'A tokay!' she cries, pointing at the small reptile, his colourful skin a green and blue pattern with orange spots. 'Don't you love the unique sound they make at night?'

'What? That wah-wah noise.' William laughs.

'No, it's more like a to-kay, to-kay, sound, hence their name.'

Yudi giggles again from the kitchen.

'Evidently we are very amusing,' William says. 'Yudi, do we have any natural yogurt?'

Yudi reappears. 'I'll get some from the main kitchen, Mr William.'

'I don't want any, but by all means if you do?' Vanessa says, with a gentle hand gesture.

'No, we're fine for today, Yudi, but could you please make sure we have some tomorrow morning.'

'Yes, Mr William.'

Vanessa looks past the swimming pool to see two staff members entering the main bedroom with buckets, brooms, mops, and all manner of cleaning essentials. She marvels silently at their humble efficiency and wishes she'd thought to bring gifts for the staff from Australia.

'William, could you imagine every day leaving your world of poverty and spending it in this sort of luxury? It's unfathomable,' she says in a low whisper.

'There are a lot of people less fortunate than the team here.'

'Yes, of course, but they work so hard, I can't help but feel sorry for them.'

Yudi reappears and proceeds to serve an a la carte breakfast fit for the most discerning of tastes. For Vanessa, a strawberry-pecan pancake with crisp bacon, pure Vermont maple syrup and sweet butter. William, a three-egg omelette with fresh mozzarella, mushrooms, and thyme.

All this lovemaking has made me ravenous. She picks up her fork and takes her first mouthful. The sweetness of syrup, mixed with butter, ignites her tastebuds. She swallows. 'Yudi, this is breakfast bliss.'

Yudi giggles again at Vanessa's play on words. 'This pleases me, Miss Vanessa.'

'Oh, it's delicious.'

'Thank you, Miss Vanessa. Please enjoy.' Yudi humbly disappears into the kitchen again.

It's evident Yudi delights in the banter between the couple and simply can't wipe the smile from her face. She's never seen Mr William so happy.

The Balinese have such strong family values and the staff have often questioned why he isn't married, sometimes even worrying about him, so Vanessa's presence pleases everyone enormously. Yudi is very much looking forward to sharing the wonderful news with her colleagues during her lunch break.

Vanessa lifts her coffee cup to her nose, smelling the aroma again before taking an intrepid sip.

William gauges her reaction. 'Too strong, too hot, perhaps not your thing after all.'

'Mm. No, it's very good.' She nods her head, sensing William's relief.

The calm of breakfast is disrupted by a pleasant chime.

'Doorbell,' William assures her.

A short, stocky, competent-looking Indonesian man appears carrying a newspaper. 'Mr William, welcome back.' He places the paper on the table away from the food.

'Arif, my friend.' William stands to greet the man with an enthusiastic handshake, patting him on the back with his free hand. 'Vanessa, this is my dear friend and villa manager, Arif.'

'Pleased to meet you, Miss Vanessa, and welcome.'

'Thank you, Arif.'

Out of esteem for her boss, Yudi appears in the doorway. Arif nods with a warm smile, signalling she can return to her duties. It's evident the man is well respected.

'Arif, come sit with us. Would you like a coffee?'

'No, thank you, Mr William. I won't intrude. I just wanted to say hello before you get on with your day. Please, if there is anything you need, let me know.'

'Thank you, Arif. Oh, I got your email. I'll come and see you in the office in the next couple of days about those amendments.'

'No hurry, Mr William. When you are ready.'

'There is one other thing. I thought we might head out on a Hobie Cat one day while we're here.'

'Mr William, let me or one of the other staff members know when you would like to do that, and we will arrange it.'

Arif steps away politely. William thanks him profusely as he exits the villa.

'Nice man,' William says.

'Wise too,' Vanessa says.

'Oh, so you know what his name stands for, huh?'

'Yes. Fitting.'

'Vanessa, you never cease to amaze me.'

A warm fuzziness washes over her. There's no need to explain she has the fondest childhood memories of a driver, Arif, that her mother hired. He would often take she and her sister to a local store for ice cream and let them sneak a lolly or two without telling their mother. He was a kind man and she's never forgotten his pock-marked face filled with grief when he was told of Monica's death. 'What's with the Hobie Cat?' Vanessa queries.

'Guests have access to a whole bevy of amenities to suit their travel style. Tennis, paddleboards, kayaks, and I thought a small catamaran, with a mesh hull that guarantees you'll get splashed, might be fun.'

'Bring it on. Sounds like a welcome reprieve from this heat.' She fans her face with her hand.

'There's method in my madness because you won't be able to take your notepad with you.'

A tiny bird swoops in, landing on the opposite edge of the table near the newspaper. Vanessa laughs when Yudi rushes to shoo it away. The bird hesitates, assured it's not in any danger.

'I'm done.' Vanessa places her fork down on the almost empty plate.

'Yes, I'm with you. Yudi's cooking is too good.'

Yudi bows and begins clearing the plates.

William and Vanessa decide to sit out on the lawn to relax before having their massages. It's a glorious day and the sea breeze coming off the ocean gives them much relief from the Indonesian heat.

Vanessa gazes at William peeling off his t-shirt and reclining on a lounge, patting his washboard stomach. *I must be dreaming.* She tosses her sarong skyward, deciding to take a swim before the masseuses arrive. She plunges into the pool and kicks hard to swim to the surface. It takes her off guard to find him kneeling by the side of the pool, waiting to give her an unexpected kiss.

'You are adorable,' he says.

They're interrupted by the sound of the chime. Two Balinese women appear, all smiles. From a distance, they bow in the couple's direction, then proceed to set up their tables, slipping batik sarongs over them in preparation.

Slightly embarrassed, Vanessa breaks free and moves to sit on the pool steps, tying her hair up in a chignon, securing it with a band taken from around her wrist.

William looks on admiringly. 'I'm in heaven,' he mouths, approaching with a fluffy white towel. William wraps it around her body and gives a gentle squeeze before moving across to the tables.

Vanessa is a little apprehensive about having an open-air couples' massage. The silence, and the fact they are both face down with two strangers rubbing their almost naked bodies, makes her feel vulnerable.

The women begin simultaneously. Every long, fluid stroke of the masseuse's warm hands soon induces a sense of tranquillity. The delightful chirping of nearby birds gives a peacefulness to the surrounds and the couple are soon overcome with the headiness of the aromatic oil.

Vanessa soon relaxes, in harmony with her mind and body, knowing they're far from prying eyes and feeling secure with the man she trusts beside her.

When the treatment comes to an end, the masseuse lies a sarong over her and places a gentle hand on Vanessa's shoulder. 'Madam, please take your time and sit up when you are ready.'

'Thank you,' she whispers, allowing the feeling of serenity to continue for a moment longer.

William sighs and sits up, so she opens her eyes and decides to join him. Wrapped in the sarong, Vanessa has a gentle stretch before sitting next to William. 'Gosh! I fell asleep.'

'Mm.' A faraway look in his eyes, he watches the masseuse pour two cups of cool cranberry tea as he signs the notepad presented to him by the other woman.

'Same time tomorrow, sir?'

'Same time every morning.'

She smiles, taking notes with a small pencil and pink pad, rebooking them for the next five mornings.

Vanessa observes the woman dismantling the tables and neatly folding the sarongs.

'Are these handprinted?' Vanessa asks, reaching to touch the fabric, admiring the distinctive hues on the cotton.

'Yes, madam.' She nods shyly.

Vanessa thanks the women and retreats, with her tea, to the warmth of a sunbed. Her little bird reappears on the lawn. She grins, wondering if it's another sign from Monica.

When the Balinese women leave, William ensures the gate is locked before diving into the pool, startling Vanessa with a loud splash. She lifts her sunglasses and laughs.

'You coming in?'

'Not yet,' she teases, letting her hair down as she heads off into the bedroom. She reappears with her laptop and nestles back in under semi-shade. Turning her computer on, the sudden boom is an immediate assault on the senses. 'Sorry,' she mouths his way.

'It's okay.' He dives under the water as if to escape.

She quickly checks her emails, finds there's nothing too pressing, and makes a quick diary entry: *Where I am sitting now, I know no pleasanter place to dream away a sunny hour, couched in the garden of Eden with my love.*

'Honey, jump in. It's beautiful.'

It's an offer she can't refuse. 'Okay, here I come.' Stepping down into William's loving embrace, he pulls her close. The freshness of the water encircles them. The sun, in stark contrast, is warm on their shoulders.

'Feel relaxed?' William asks.

'Yes, that was wonderful. The woman I had was very good. What about yours?'

'Excellent!'

She brushes his wet hair back behind his ears, notices a birthmark, and on closer inspection is startled to see it's a small, dark map of Africa like Monica's. 'Oh, you have a birthmark.'

'Yes, just like my father's.' William grows serious and his voice softens, causing Vanessa's attention to be diverted. He whispers, 'Now that everyone has gone and the gates are locked, I have you all to myself.'

'That sounds ominous.' She gives him a peck on the cheek.

He lowers his head, and embracing his broad shoulders, her lip's part under his hungry kiss. His gentle, swirling tongue mixes with hers. Overflowing with sexual energy, she feels his arousal beneath the water and surrenders easily to his dreamy seduction. He pushes her bikini top to either side of her breasts, exposing her nipples taut with need. 'Damn, you have beautiful breasts.' They're not big, but round and firm.

She wraps her thighs around him in compliance.

Feeling her nipples hard against his chest, he wades through the water towards the steps and sets her down carefully. Slowly, one by one, he pulls the strings of her bikini bottom in an exaggerated manner and lets it float off. His gaze locked on hers, he steps out of his bathers, revealing his form, his erection flexing in reaction to the sight of her splendour.

Kneeling on the step, she wraps her hand around his penis, the oiliness of their skin so sensuous, she moves it over her pelvic bone to find her pleasure. Teasing gently, she delights in watching him ease inside. Burning with need, Vanessa tosses her head back. Allowing her hair to stream behind her in the water, she stares up in ecstasy at the clear blue sky, her long, silky neck calling him to run his tongue up the length to her open mouth. Arching her body into his, she looks back at him while they move their hands along one another's bodies.

The hunger in his eyes, his every gesture, turns her on more and more as the cool water laps rhythmically around them. The sun beating down on them, an overhanging palm sways with the wind in tempo with their bodies.

Teasing him with her body, she shifts her gaze downward, focusing on his movements, his form exciting her every desire.

'You need this as much as I do, don't you?' he says with a resounding moan, enjoying her boldness as she parts her legs a little further in acknowledgement. William grows more intense, pressing his forehead to hers, and slows his movements so she can see more of what she wants.

'Oh, William.' Her voice is a mere whimper as her legs begin to tremble. She lifts her hips to meet his movements, allowing him to move deeper.

'That's it, my darling.' Knowing she's near, he stops, but doesn't pull out, and Vanessa catches her breath. 'Relax, baby,' he says seductively.

She can't, too caught up in the lasciviousness of it all. He murmurs words of pleasure in her ear, sending her insane with need. 'William.'

The sound of his name spurs him on, and he picks up the pace again.

'My God!' she calls. The sudden rush of adrenaline surges, more intense this time. Gripping his body, intoxicated by lust, she throws her head back and calls out his name as a sudden warmth fills her body. *It's wonderful. It's amazing. It's William.*

Glowing with love, William holds her close for a moment before kissing her tenderly.

If I was a betting woman, I've just fallen pregnant. Knowing he felt it too, looking deep into his eyes, she waits for the words to fall from his lips.

'I love you, Vanessa.'

The tiny muscles at the corner of her mouth pucker up, ripples of joy spread across her face, and her heart warms, hoping this dreamlike romance will never end. He kisses her again for what seems an eternity.

'Are you okay?' he asks.

'Never happier.'

'I hope so, baby. I have big plans for us.' He breaks free.

'Darling, what time do you think it is?'

She looks up at the sun and squints. 'According to my calculations, it's just gone twelve.'

He laughs.

'Well, you did ask.'

'Come on. It must be time to get ready.'

'Let's go!' She gathers up her bikini pieces and steps out of the pool.

William suggests they take some extra clothes to change into at the resort. 'That way we can stay on for drinks and have an early dinner at one of the restaurants.'

'How do you do that, William?'

'Do what?'

'You really are the master of avoiding boredom. And you do it without even working at it.'

'Well, I can't resist an audience of one, and you happen to be the one.' He places a noisy pucker on her rosy cheek, then pulls back. 'You got some colour today.'

'Not too much, I hope.'

'Just right.' He kisses her shoulder.

Showered and dressed, Vanessa tosses a colourful kaftan, some stylish sandals, and a couple of necessary toiletries into a big straw tote. William opts for a black linen shirt and trousers, with black leather slides, and pops them into her bag as well. *Very trendy.* Vanessa applies a stick of lip balm in the mirror and throws on her large, floppy raffia hat and black cat-eye sunglasses.

Along the path, they pass several staff members who are in and out of the other villas, systematically going about their daily chores. Each takes the time to smile and bow to the happy couple.

Vanessa squeezes William's arm. 'Do you know the other villa owners?'

'I own all of them.'

'Oh, really.'

'Yes. We rent them out, but the one we're in is for our personal use only.'

'Nice.' *The expense guarantees exclusivity and the thrill of unexpected encounters.*

Waiting by his vehicle, Ketut opens their doors. Vanessa sighs as the air-conditioned car is a welcome relief.

'Buckle up,' William says, noticing Vanessa hasn't touched her seatbelt.

As they head off across the island, Ketut begins to chat.

'Did you enjoy breakfast, Miss Vanessa?'

'Yes, Ketut. Thank you.'

'My wife very good cook.' He looks pleased with himself, placing one hand on his small, bulging tummy and rubbing it.

'Yes, she is,' William says.

Vanessa looks at William, then back at Ketut. 'Oh, so Yudi is your wife?'

'Yes.' Ketut nods his head enthusiastically.

'Well, you're a very lucky man, Ketut.'

'I know,' he says proudly, and the car fills with laughter.

'Well, I, for one, won't need to eat again until this evening,' Vanessa says. It's lunchtime, so as they pass a series of small houses, she notices many people of all ages cooking over fires on the street.

'If you get puckish, the hotel can organise something for you,' Ketut says.

'Peckish. The word is peck-ish,' William says, politely correcting Ketut.

Ketut laughs, shaking his head and correcting himself. 'Peck-ish.' He looks in the rear-view mirror for William's approval. Ketut keeps one eye on the road, one looking back at William and Vanessa. 'My wife is right; you make perfect couple.'

'Thanks, Ketut. I think so.' William squeezes Vanessa's hand.

The winding turns force Vanessa to grip the handle over the door. Ketut hits the brakes suddenly when a small, half-naked child steps off the kerb like she is about to run across the road. Vanessa lurches forward, stifling a squeal as the little girl steps back, turns, and runs inside an open street stall. *Children and traffic always bring back bad memories.* She watches the mother wave her hands in the air, yelling in Indonesian and gently tapping the girl's bare bottom as she flies past.

William squeezes her hand again. 'It's okay, honey. She's okay.'

Ten minutes out, on the outskirts of the city, hordes of street kids appear at a set of traffic lights. Beggars, shaking their bracelet hands, start tapping on the window as the car eases to a stop. The poor souls, dressed in dirty, tattered rags, anxiously repeat, *'Tolong, tolong, tolong.'*

Vanessa focuses on a girl of around ten holding a completely naked, snotty-nosed baby on her hip. Their eyes lock.

'Don't put the window down,' Ketut urges.

'It breaks my heart to see them beg,' Vanessa says.

'I know. Their desperate faces can be quite overwhelming,' William says.

'They mostly come from the east,' Ketut says as the lights change.

The couple watch as the children dodge the traffic to join their mother waiting over on a grassy patch to the side of the road.

'See, there's the mother hiding under that tree.' Ketut points across the busy street. 'They're sent out to beg from the tourists so they can take money back to their village.'

'So sad.' Vanessa wipes a stray tear from her eye.

'But they don't get the money; somebody else does,' Ketut says, annoyed.

'The saddest part about it is they miss out on schooling and are often abused. If they don't make enough money, they're not allowed to go home, so they're in a very difficult situation,' William says.

A solemn Ketut nods his head in agreement.

By the time they reach the resort, Vanessa is relieved to get out of the confines of the vehicle. Ketut knows the drill. He'll wait outside the resort for them until they are ready to return to their villa later that evening. Most drivers do so, unless specified otherwise, as every resort has a specific carpark area for the drivers to hang out and chat while they wait for their guests to finish enjoying themselves. It's a pleasant way for them to kill time.

A staff member dressed in the hotel's signature uniform – short sleeve batik shirt and long grey shorts – approaches to transport William and Vanessa, in a golf buggy, directly to the aquatonic pool a mere two minutes away.

The couple hop in the open-air vehicle and Vanessa leans into William. 'It always amazes me how things happen seamlessly in Bali, without much fuss and what appears to be little communication. Somehow it works.'

'That's part of the beauty of Bali, right.'

As they exit the cart, another scoots past at high speed, almost running William over. Vanessa screams in fright and their driver yells in Indonesian. The other driver waves a dismissive apology.

'Are you okay, sir?'

'Yes, I'm fine.' William takes Vanessa's arm. 'Let's go.'

Inside, two staff are swift to appear, offering cold hand towels and cinnamon tea. It appears word has already got out about the incident outside.

'Is everything alright, Mr William?'

'Yes.'

'When you are ready, sir, would please you fill out these forms?'

'I'll do that.' Vanessa reaches for the pages, grabbing a nearby pen as the man bows and retreats to his outdoor desk.

William is grateful.

'See, he even knows.' Vanessa rubs William's upper arm as he struggles to smile.

William takes a moment to settle before they're shown to the change rooms.

'I'll meet you back here at the pool when you're ready, darling,' William says.

Vanessa steps out into the starting area in an aqua blue one-piece. She doesn't see William at first and is amazed by the enormity of the pool. Then she sees him entering the pool.

'Are you okay, honey?' She submerges herself in the water and is immediately struck by the heat and power of the whirlpool.

'Yes, I'm fine. Let's forget about it and enjoy ourselves.' Their hands float out to touch one another, fingertips to fingertips, before William grabs her hands and secures his grip.

A tall, uniformed pool attendant appears, as swift as he is dictatorial, ordering them to push through the rushing, oncoming current. 'Move, move, move!'

His voice is somewhat out of character. She looks at William for support. Feeling almost weak by comparison, Vanessa slips away from William's hold. Laughing at her own frailty, she struggles to move through the water, giving him no alternative but to follow.

William takes her hand again, helping her to the first hydromassage station where the bubbling jets pummel their bodies. She rests, as a means of gaining strength, before moving on through the labyrinth of seawater to the next station.

The pool attendant appears again, waving his enormous hand.

'Okay, okay, I'm going,' Vanessa says, feeling almost bullied. 'This is incredible, William. I've never seen anything quite like it before.' Barely audible over the noise of the jets, William has to lip read.

'It's different,' he yells.

They manage to make it to the next bay, and while the attendant focusses on unsuspecting newcomers, they take the opportunity to catch their breath.

Vanessa tilts her head playfully and asks in a seductive manner, 'So do you come here often, handsome?'

He frowns. 'I think the heat has sent you a bit gaga.'

She rolls her eyes. 'You're no fun.'

'Let's keep going, otherwise this will take forever.'

'Not if the Stasi has his way.'

He tosses his head back, laughing aloud. 'Come on. I'm hanging out for a champagne. It's a shame they don't serve drinks in here.'

'I'd love to see you carry them.' She screws her face up, then smiles at the absurdity of the idea until they reach an elevated relaxation station, where four white sun lounges are lined up facing the Indian Ocean. Basking in the sunlight, half-submerged in warm, shallow water, she entertains the idea of a cold drink.

With an open hand resting on her brow, shading her eyes from the intensity of the sun, she says, 'Now I could go a champagne.'

'I told you so.'

'I'm sure this is all very therapeutic, but it's like being in a hot bubble bath.' She finds the warmth almost seductive.

He smiles, brushing a hand through his wet hair.

'I feel so decadent lying here watching those poor souls out there on their little canoes. It's like we're sitting in a postcard.'

'Boats,' he corrects her.

'You know what I mean.'

'Those poor souls get to live here in paradise.'

'Not the same.'

'I don't know. From what I can see, they all seem happy.'

'Maybe?' She leans in and rubs his upper arm.

Looking at the flush of her cheeks, he says, 'You're such a softie, baby.'

'Am I?'

'You know you are.'

She thinks about what he's said and the sincerity with which he said it. Vanessa doesn't really want to move, but she's starting to feel a bit waterlogged, so suggests they move on.

'Yep. When we're done, we'll shower and jump into our zippy little golf cart and head on over to the bar on the other side of the resort.'

'Lovely. I'm ready now.'

'The Cliff Bar opens around five.'

'A civilized hour by any standard.'

'It's an amazing place perched on a rocky outcrop at the base of the bluff. An ideal spot to take in the ocean view. It looks straight across the peninsula towards Kuta. With a bit of luck, there will be a live DJ playing this evening.'

'It sounds amazing!'

William notices another couple approaching. 'Come on. Let's keep moving.'

'Okay.' She pulls her torpid body off the lounge. Pushing their bodies through the current, they work their way to the end and hop out to change.

Dressed, they take the trip across to the resort's boutique area for a spot of shopping.

'We've got an hour or so to kill before the bar opens.'

'If you don't mind, I'd like to see if they have any lightweight sundresses.'

'It's a great boutique, so I'm certain you'll find what you're looking for.'

Noticing his watch, she runs an intimate hand along his arm. 'I've not seen this before.'

'Royal Oak.'

'Royal what?'

'Audemars Piguet Royal Oak. Mother gave it to me.'

'Scarce wrist candy, no doubt?'

'You are far too switched on for your own good, Albert.'

It's been a long hot day, so by the time they leave the store with their shopping bags, the early evening sea breeze blowing towards the cliff face is welcome relief.

'Perfect weather for a summer drink.' He's pleased to be heading towards the bar.

At the cliff top, there is already a lengthy queue of tourists.

'Is it happy hour?' she asks.

'Baby, here it's only ever happy hours,' he says, glad he called ahead to his friend, the manager, to arrange V.I.P. service.

On announcing his name to the gate attendee, the couple are immediately ushered past the waiting crowd, on to an inclinator, and down the cliff face to the bar perched on a bold spur. They are guided through the excited patrons and shown directly to their reserved outdoor table.

'Compliments of Mr Lockhart,' the attendee says before returning to the inclinator.

Vanessa takes her lead from those luxuriating around her and removes her sandals, placing them on the soft white sand under the table and reclining on the cushioned cane lounge.

A striking young Asian woman approaches. 'Sir, my name is Wayan and I'll be your waitress for this evening. This is our cocktail list, sir,'

'Oh my.' Vanessa looks at the menu the length of her arm.

'What would you like, darling?'

'Oh, I'll have one of those.' She points across at the tall cocktail glass, more like a vase, on the next table.

'A Rocktonic,' Wayan explains.

'Make that two, and something to nibble on as well, please. We haven't had lunch today,' William says.

'Perhaps the homemade potato crisps or chicken popcorn or —'

'The crisps.'

'Yes, of course, sir.' The waitress retreats to the nearby bar to place their order.

'You look stunning, darling. I'm so happy I brought you here.'

'William, look around you. In this honey haze, everyone looks like a movie star.'

'Yes, well, you're my Oscar winner.'

Vanessa laughs at the way William never shies away from giving her a compliment, something she isn't used to.

The waiter returns with their drinks and steps to the side so as not to obstruct the view, waiting for William's credit card.

William tips his glass in Vanessa's direction and watches her take the first sip.

'Mm, fig and gin. This is delicious.'

William catches her staring across at an extremely stylish group of international travellers. 'You know it was Igor Cassini —'

'Oh, the society columnist for Cholly Knickerbocker?'

'Yes. Well, it was he who invented the term 'jet set' in the late 1950s for people who gave off a sense of luxury and power through speeding around the globe.'

She knows the story well but delights in listening to William tell it.

The light shimmers across the water and everything rapidly changes to a spectacular mix of burnt orange, pink and blue. As the sun announces its descent, the music noticeably changes, and the theatrics of the landscape feel like you're privy to an enormous Tim Storrier painting. An intense blaze of gold sweeps across the sky and the only give-away you are not part of a magnificent oil painting is the distant voices of the fishermen bobbing around on the water below.

Then all goes still. A disturbing hush rolls across the water, before an enormous wave crashes against the cliff face, causing the wave to rise in an explosion of sound as the sun slips down behind the horizon.

How magical. William witnesses her eyes widen and sparkle. It would be wrong to say they were falling in love; they were already in love from the very first day.

'This place is absolutely breathtaking,' She glances across at a young couple on the nearby table holding each other closely and looking longingly into one another's eyes. The woman mouths the words, 'I love you.'

I'm in goddamn heaven.

Immediately after the theatrics of the sunset, the mood becomes more upbeat, taking on a whole new vibe as the DJ spins various chill-out tunes.

Vanessa looks at her cocktail. 'Boy! This is a meal in itself.'

'Well, you better have an appetite because the best is yet to come.'

'William Whittaker, when have you seen me turn away food?'

'True.'

A beautiful Balinese woman, in a modern version of a traditional sarong, approaches their table. 'Mr Whittaker, Miss Albert, my name is Kirana and I'm here to take you across to dinner, if you're ready. Please sign here, sir.' She presents the black bill fold.

With a great flourish, William signs, takes back his card and hands the woman the folder.

She passes it to another staff member standing off to the side. 'Follow me please, sir.'

Holding hands, Vanessa wonders if William has noticed the way the two of them move together: along the beach, over drinks, at dinner. Unsure of where they are going, she happily follows the charismatic woman through the crowd and along an elevated, sandy pathway that leads to a wooden jetty cantilevered out over the water.

Glowing tiki torches and ceremonial umbrellas line up like soldiers standing to attention in black-and-white check uniforms along a breathtaking private pier. Vanessa realises this is where they'll be dining and tingles with excitement as soft music from bamboo xylophones, and the sound of the ocean, set the tone.

Halfway along, an eager Balinese waiter approaches with a broad, toothy grin and nods at his colleague, indicating he'll take over from here.

'Good evening, sir, madam. My name is Agung. Follow me please.'

'Oh, William, this is lovely. I noticed the pier in the distance as we were coming down the inclinator, but I had no idea what it was for. How fabulous.' Her excitement spills forth when they're taken to the candle-lit, stand-alone table for two.

'I've not eaten here before, so it's a first for both of us,' William says.

Over the next couple of hours, they are presented with a five-course dinner: freshly shucked oysters, deliciously seared scallops in coriander butter, spicy Indonesian crab, and finally, grilled red snapper with spices, followed by the most fabulous dessert imaginable, passionfruit cream cloud with a compote of Bedugal berries.

Several glasses of champagne later, and after toasting to their future happiness, William surprises Vanessa by pulling a small red box from his pocket and placing it on the table. He cups his palm around the case and gently slides it across.

'What's this?' She notices the gold Cartier insignia.

'Open it and see.'

She slowly tugs at the fine red and gold crested ribbon, her excitement evident as she opens the lid, and gasps. Inside, glistening back, are a pair of spectacular emerald, natural pearl, and diamond ear pendants.

'I hope you like them?'

She is spellbound! 'They're delicious,' she says, as if commenting on Yudi's breakfast.

'When you agreed to come away, I wanted to give you something special. When I saw them in the window of Cartier, quite by chance I must add, I knew they were perfect and you had to have them.'

'My God, William, they're beautiful,' she says under her breath, elbows on the table and hands folded to her mouth in disbelief.

He grows intense. 'The emeralds remind me of your magnificent eyes, the pearls, the lustre of your skin, and the diamonds, the sparkle within.'

As if not hearing him, Vanessa can't take her eyes off them.

'Since meeting you, Vanessa …'

She looks up at him, a tear in her eye, and listens.

'… you've given a rhythm to my existence. I love you so much.'

'Oh!' she says, visibly moved. 'William, I don't know what to say …'

'Darling, there's no need to say anything; it's written on your face.' He reaches for her hand and presses it to his lips.

In disbelief, she murmurs his name again.

'Let me help you.' He removes the simple gold hoops from each of her ears, placing them on the white linen tablecloth. She looks down at the jewellery, at the sparkling diamonds staring back. Placing one at a time on each of her earlobes, he says, 'My grandfather has a beautiful quote, Vanessa. Let's see, it goes something like this: "Love is the expression of one's values, the greatest reward you can earn for the moral qualities for which we have achieved."'

'Ayn Rand.'

'Yes. How funny you know it.'

Later that night, they made love like never before. His lips found every inch of her body in all the ways she wanted.

CHAPTER SEVENTEEN

Lying under the shelter of the soft, canopied bed, Vanessa squints her eyes for a moment, remembering the candlelit glamour of the night before; sharing an intimate dinner and William giving her those exquisite earrings before returning to the villa and making love all night. *No, it's not a dream. That was the most exotic night of my life.* Staring up at the ceiling, she notices the little gecko just like the one from the day before looking down at her with alert curiosity. *Are you the same one?* She chooses to ignore the little reptile's beady eyes.

William's unexpectedly anxious tone comes from the garden, alerting her that something's not quite right. As his footsteps fade, she struggles to hear his low, mumbled words, but she's certain he's dealing with a business dilemma back home. Without giving it much thought, she throws back the sheet and strides into the shower.

Tracing back over the events of last night, Vanessa remembers the bar was abuzz with tourists and ex-pats, and a large group from Italian Vogue completed the scene with their eponymous style. *Cocktails were delish. Mm, the sweetness of the fig. Dinner was superb; you can never go wrong with spicy Indonesian crab. Shouldn't have had the dessert though, but what the heck. I'm on holidays.*

She dries off, readies herself for breakfast, and checks the earrings are securely locked in the safe. Stopping momentarily at the glass doors, she pulls her hair from behind her ears, pushes the door open, and emerges into the sharp, bright light. She can't read anything in William's eyes as he continues to talk to Yudi. Instinct taps her on the shoulder. *Something is up!*

Yudi pours Vanessa a fresh cup of coffee, making idle chit-chat about the glorious weather they're having. Vanessa leans across to kiss the unusually quiet William, notices a bowl of yoghurt on the table, and thanks Yudi.

'Morning, darling,' she says.

He doesn't look at her, but rather through her.

She marshals a smile. 'Is something wrong?'

'Oh, a family thing back home regarding my father. I'll talk to you about it after breakfast.' He barely spares her a glance.

She can't pinpoint his mood. Under the casual manner, there is an edginess she doesn't like. 'I see you like the coffee.'

'Yes, it's very smooth.' She takes a sip.

He's scarcely touched his food, and given it's a somewhat moody and silent breakfast, she barely touches hers. They sit at the table a little longer in silence, before finally giving up on the pretence of eating.

William sets his cutlery down and says, cotton-mouthed, 'Vanessa, I need to tell you something.'

'Obviously it's serious. I know we haven't known each other very long, but I don't mind telling you you're frightening me a little. Okay, so let's chat.'

William politely thanks Yudi, then takes Vanessa by the hand, leading her across the lawn and back through the bedroom into their private courtyard. 'Sit down, Vanessa.'

She sits on an outdoor chair and leans forward, elbows on knees, her face in her hands, but she isn't prepared for the harried look on his face as he paces the outdoor space.

'Vanessa, why did you choose to come to Whittakers with your manuscript?'

'What?'

'How did you hear about us?'

'I pitched my story to you guys because I'd been told Whittaker's are the best publishing house in the country, if not one of the best in the world. Why?'

He says nothing, but she notices a change in him. 'What I'm about to tell you will be very unsettling.'

Icy fingers of dread close around her heart. *They're going to cancel my contract.*

Outside the high wall, a dog breaks the stillness with its sharp, carping bark. She remembers seeing the village dog yesterday as they drove out from the villa and had made a mental note to avoid it. Feeling his frustration, her thoughts are ricocheting all over the place. *He's found out about Michael.* 'Okay. What's up?' *Perhaps he's had a private investigator trace my background. After all, there is a lot at stake for families like this.* Nervously preparing for the worst, she suddenly sneezes. *Not now.*

'You need a tissue?'

'Yes, please.'

He grabs the box from the nearby bathroom.

They fall silent.

Oh well, I hadn't planned on telling him about Michael, believing it should be left alone, but life is full of messy bits, and hopefully William will understand why I've taken the path of secrecy.

Feeling somewhat manic, William takes a tissue, wipes his streaming forehead, and tries to recover his composure, focusing on how to calmly explain the situation. 'I'm sure you've heard about my father's very public affair over here in Bali some forty years ago?' He stops briefly, drawing a breath, then continues. 'It has been a shadow that has dogged my father throughout his adult life.'

'You know the old saying, scandal is nothing more than gossip masquerading as news,' she says, trying to ease the situation.

'Please listen.'

Vanessa looks at him, his resolve unnerving. His eyes challenging, his chin set firm, she feels confused, but somewhat relieved this isn't about Michael after all.

'Well, she was a young Sydney woman who lived here in Bali at the time and sadly fell pregnant to my father.'

Vanessa frowns.

'By all accounts, he adored her; in fact, they were mad for one another. However, it was complicated because he was still married to my mother.'

She pulls a quizzical look.

'I was small, not quite five-years old, and my grandfather had just had his accident, complicating the issue. Initially my parents were his primary caregivers. You see, my father was needed in Sydney until Gramps could regain his strength and independence.'

This is all rather vague.

'It was an extremely difficult time. My grandmother had recently died, and everyone was coming to terms with my grandfather living out his days in a wheelchair, and of course Dad had to take charge of the publishing house. Understandably my father was torn, especially when this woman, Diana ...'

She felt a shift in her stomach. There it is: the sound of dread.

William is conscious of the exact moment his unruly words hit home.

After that, his voice is a blur, and she hears him as if from a distance. With uninvited clarity, Vanessa feels an icy chill course through her heart as her mother's name passes his lips again, and she wonders if this is the first sign of reality encroaching into their idyllic relationship. Thoughts come at her at a dizzying pace, and she deliberately turns her head so he can't see her face. *Wit, or at least that's how I pictured it.* Benumbed, she looks back at William in horror as the facts pile up in her head like building blocks. It's all coming together so fast, too fast. William's lips are moving, but she can't quite comprehend the here and now. *Mother always called him Wit. It must be short for Whittaker.*

He watches as Vanessa tips her head slightly to one side, as if she is about to collapse. Her squinting eyes begging and threatening to water, she waits for the words that might signal some relief. Finally, in disbelief she utters, 'Are you serious?'

'No. I mean yes,' William says firmly. 'Deadly.'

Vanessa hears her heart pounding inside her head. It's like being shouted at through a loud hailer when the horn of the instrument is uncomfortably close to your ears. Even if she could make the noise stop, it would be a while before she'd recover from the residual deafness. Her face, suddenly alert, grows agitated as she tries to make sense of what he's saying. 'No ... no ... no.' She rolls an agitated fist to the middle of her forehead, then sighs and looks up. 'That means you ... me ... we ... are ... It's too grubby to think about!'

It's so hot, and with no breath of fresh air to break the stillness, she feels like she might throw up. Instead, she slumps in her chair. A distinct sound rushes from her lungs, a sound not heard since her tragic fall.

A deeply concerned William watches her drag a shaky hand through her hair. Saddened by what he sees, he sits on a nearby chair and helplessly stares as the tears roll down her cheeks. He's never seen her cry before and seeing her in such pain is killing him. He tries to scoop her up in his arms.

The immeasurable hurt in her eyes touches his heart, but instead of returning his embrace, she initially pulls away, not wanting to be touched.

'Vanessa, I genuinely love you, but there's a good chance we are quite possibly …' Horrified by the thought, he can't bring himself to say it.

With nowhere to turn, she unexpectedly gives in to his embrace.

'Diana …' His voice wavers, feeling her body tremble. He can't bear to see her like this, but it needs to be said. 'Diana was my father's lover. Your mother and my father had an affair which resulted in you, Vanessa …' His voice trails off.

For a moment, she squeezes her eyes shut. *Wait.* She tenses up. *He and Monica have similar birthmarks.* 'Mon …' She simply can't bring herself to say her sister's name and places it in the recess of her mind.

Feeling her relax, William releases his grip and waits to hear what she has to say. 'I wish that bloody dog would stop barking. I can't hear myself think.'

Is it even possible? She looks at him pleadingly. 'William, please say it isn't true, this isn't real. It can't be.'

Locking onto his hand, her voice grows more urgent. 'But we weren't to know. How could we?'

'Vanessa, it's unnatural.'

Her mouth drops, trying to define their forbidden love. 'William, if this is true, this …' She twirls her index finger. 'My God, this is unthinkable! Our love for one another is not 'that'. It can't be.' Filled with doubt, going over and over particulars in her head in the hope they've missed something and not wanting to see what it truly is, she grows silent. *How can this be?* She tries to compose herself, dabbing beneath her eyes with the wet tissue. *When William touches me, I feel he's touching my soul. This is not the love of siblings.*

A plane circles overhead and the roar of the jets mysteriously silences the dog.

'Thank Christ for that,' William looks up, then back at Vanessa to see her mouth quivering with emotion.

Scrunching her eyes closed, she begins to sob.

'Everything has been taken from us now forever,' he says, devastated as her anxious sobs grow with each painful breath in hyperventilating bursts.

Shocked, she catches her breath in her throat, trying to stifle the sound. Of all the comments he's made so far, this one stings the most. Detachment at the fore, she dries her tears.

'Nothing can be done from Bali. We need to get home as soon as possible, before the press find out. They're always snooping around, so we don't need the scandal. If they catch a glimpse of us here together, they may look deeper and find out more.'

'William, it doesn't get any worse than this.'

'No, it does not. I spoke to my father this morning and had Donna book our flight back this evening.' He notices a leftover tear trickle down her cheek.

'I hear you.' She hastily wipes her cheek.

'We're booked on the 11.00 p.m. flight. Let's get you home and sort this thing out.' His words ring with abandonment.

Vanessa changes tack. 'Don't you think the best and most secretive place to be is here?'

'My darling, if we don't leave here tonight, it may very well mean social suicide.'

She feels her chest tighten. 'But there's nothing concrete yet.' Vanessa wants to fling herself into his arms, bury her face in his shoulder, and let him protect her from the world.

'No, but we have to treat it as such until we know otherwise.'

Mother's nihilistic lifestyle choices have always screwed things up, but this will go down as her greatest achievement yet. She's really poisoned the well this time. She lets him pull her to him, his hand curved beneath her hair, along the back of her neck, holding her still while his lips cover hers. She can't fight it, melding her body to his, terrified she may never feel this intimacy again. She needs his kiss, his touch, his love.

'I love you,' he says.

Her eyes grow silent in acknowledgement as a surge of emotion, that feels as much like loss as love, comes over her. But knowing the secrecy of their love is paramount now.

Fearing someone might recognise them, the plan is to spend the rest of the day in the villa. All Vanessa wants to do is go back to bed and die. However, she decides to keep him company by the pool. What was once a place of tranquillity, suddenly feels hostile as they sit, side by side, in disconnected silence. Time seems to dwindle away at an agonising pace.

Vanessa decides to try and read her book while William buries his head in his magazine. 'Is that the magazine you were reading on the aeroplane?'

'Yes.' He closes it enough for her to see the cover.

'Robb Report; what's that about?'

'Modern luxury.'

'Of course it is,' she says, tongue in cheek. 'Told you when we first met you were a sybarite.'

He tries to smile.

Vanessa decides to go in for a swim. As she walks across the lawn, she feels his eyes upon her every move. She slips into the water at chest level, deeper, until it is around her chin, and closes her eyes. Feeling a single tear slide from the corner of her eye, she submerges. Returning to the surface, William suggests they go inside and pack soon. There's a moment of silence as she steps out of the water, and wrapped in a comforting towel, reclines on a lounge.

Sensing the awkwardness, after a time William looks across at her reading. 'Okay?'

There is a moment of silence. Holding a finger at the end of a sentence she's just read, so she doesn't lose her place, Vanessa looks up. 'Reading good books ruins you for enjoying bad books.'

Both are painfully aware of the disconnect.

'I wasn't talking about the book.'

'Oh ...' She stares at his magnificent face and studies his features for likenesses.

'Vanessa, I know you're not happy about going back, but we have to get home and tidy this thing up.'

In all the years of plotting stories, I could never have come up with something so absurdly ironic as this scenario.

It's hot and hazy, but dusk brings a hint of relief as they step inside the air-conditioned room to pack.

Vanessa watches William toss both their suitcases onto the bed simultaneously and open them one at a time. 'Is this a comfortable silence for you?' She throws her new frocks into her bag.

'I'm sorry.' Realising he's been a bit sharp, he looks up. 'I'm so confused.' He grows quiet again for what feels the longest time.

At the end of the day, the relationship I have with myself is the only permanent one. No separation. No breakups. No divorces. Only me! 'There's more in the bathroom that needs to be packed.'

'I know,' he snaps back and marches into the bathroom, where she hears him throwing things about.

When he emerges, she can't help herself and has to say something. 'My God, William, that means Monty is my father and Thornton my grandfather.'

He looks at her pensively. 'It kind of focuses the mind somewhat.'

She's not seen William like this before and decides to leave him well alone to resume packing while she takes a shower.

By seven, their luggage is already in the car. They walk in silence along the dimly lit pathway to where Ketut is waiting in the carpark.

As a precaution, William sits up front, staring blankly ahead, praying the press won't be at the airport, while Vanessa sits alone in the back seat feeling like her heart is about to break. *I feel like I'm on the verge of a heart attack.*

There is pin-drop silence in the car with a very confused Ketut behind the steering wheel, stark contrast to the hustle and bustle outside. It's dinner time and tourists in Seminyak are headed in all directions to the well-lit restaurants vying for their business.

Vanessa is thinking about the quixotic dreams she had of marrying

William one day, when suddenly she is startled by the bright lights of the airport.

'We're here,' William says, acutely aware of Vanessa's silence throughout the journey.

Ketut exits the vehicle as Vanessa looks out the window and swallows her tears, dabbing her ring finger to the outer corner of each eye.

William turns and looks over at Vanessa in the back seat. 'Ready?'

With a tentative smile, she nods, tucks her laptop under her arm, and they hop out into the evening humidity and rushing commuters. The surrounding chaos almost knocks her to the ground.

'Ketut, would you do me a favour and tell Arif I'm sorry I had to leave at such short notice, but I'll email him this week and make sure Yudi cancels our massages?'

'Certainly, Mr William. I will do that for you.'

Bidding goodbye, William presses a fold of money into Ketut's sweaty palm, thanking him with a strong handshake.

'Travel safely,' Ketut says sadly.

Vanessa is trying her hardest to stay strong, but with the constant noise of the airport traffic jam and sounding horns, she finds it an irritating distraction. She grabs the telescopic handle of her grey suitcase and waits for William to do the same. They approach the airport's automatic doors like they're approaching enemy lines and hurriedly walk through the busy international terminal.

Struggling to keep up, Vanessa finds William's stony face unnerving and doesn't dare speak. *Leaving the island of love and peace. Very different to the way we arrived.* Standing in line at the Business Class Check-in, Vanessa tries to break the ice. 'Why is luggage always heavier when you leave your destination than when you arrive?'

'Shopping.'

'What? Two lightweight summer frocks.'

He doesn't bother to respond.

After checking-in, everything moves quickly. Thankfully there are no paparazzi present, so things run smoothly through passport control. Breathing an exaggerated sigh of relief, William silently strides ahead through the duty-free area to the Premier Lounge.

Contrary to the busy terminal, to Vanessa's surprise, the lounge is empty. 'No one is here.'

'Better still, no one even noticed us.'

Scanning the service area, she eyes a four-pillared Balinese Temple which houses several bains-marie filled with Asian delicacies. The cold options are sandwiches, tropical fruit, rolls and fresh salad. *No bar!* 'I think this might be a dry bar, William.' They are both in need of a drink before boarding the aircraft.

'Heaven forbid! That's not to say we can't get a drink.' They settle for two armchairs in the remotest corner of the room and drop their carry-on bags. Waving a hand, William asks a waiter for two white wines, and he swiftly obliges, setting down two cardboard coasters in readiness.

In the quiet, Vanessa starts to over-think, feeling vulnerable and a hell of a long way from home.

The waiter quickly returns and sets down two small wines. 'It's better than nothing.' William leans forward and clinks Vanessa's glass, still on the table. 'Cheers.'

She nods, watching him drain his glass.

'I can't tell you how relieved I am that there weren't any photographers about. Let's hope we have the same good fortune when we land in Sydney.'

What good fortune? She feels like he's being unusually circumspect. She closes her eyes, pondering the paparazzi's fascination with the Whittakers, especially William, having to live his life under a microscope. She opens her eyes to a gulping sound.

A young Asian woman, settling at the next table with a porcelain bowl of greasy noodles, is slurping through her lips.

I guess good manners is not her thing. Vanessa seeks relief from the coolness of the overhead air conditioning. Looking around, she notes the lounge is starting to fill. A pair of very attractive, middle-aged women approach, smiling William's way, only to take up the seats parallel to theirs to sit and stare.

I want him like the rest of the world wants him. She looks for signs of life behind William's dark glasses, but he appears blank. *People notice him, but it's not as if he deliberately draws attention to himself. It just happens. Is there any escaping the absurdity of the situation?* She takes a much-needed sip of lukewarm wine.

Looking at Vanessa and then up at the air-conditioner, William asks, 'Aren't you cold.'

He's alive! 'No,' she says, watching him grab his lightweight sports jacket from his carry-on and shrug into it.

'That's feels better.' He zips up.

Nothing feels better.

CHAPTER EIGHTEEN

After poking at an inflight meal of some type of Indonesian rice dish, Vanessa tries to sleep. It's been an arduous day and she needs rest, so with a deep-seated feeling of melancholy, she puts her headset on and scrolls through the choices. *I will never understand music you have to struggle to listen to.* She flicks until finally settling on a soothing jazz station, figuring if ever she needed something to help her through the flight, this is it.

Vanessa sleeps fitfully, waking every half hour to the sounds of disconnected bits of music coming from her headset. Jumbled dreams, nonsense that patches together bits and pieces of her life, past and present, translated into strange sketches. The last image is one of touch, a soothing, pacifying caress of a firm hand stroking her arm. Struggling to surface, she's reluctant to open her eyes and keeps them closed. Sadness prevails.

'I love you Vanessa,' she hears him whisper.

Leaning up against William's arm, her fear subsides fractionally, knowing he's still here, and aware of his lovingness.

'Rough night, baby?' he asks solemnly.

Struggling to sound normal, she opens her eyes and looks up at him, but her voice is weak, and tears begin to pool in her eyes. 'Oh, it was awful.' She's mindful she must look ghastly. 'My mouth is dry,' she adds, thinking the rice she had must have been very salty.

'I'll get you some water.' He signals the nearest flight attendant.

Vanessa sits up slowly, but her body feels frail. When the water arrives, she holds the glass with a nervous hand and gulps it down in one go.

'Do you want another?'

'Yes please. I'll go and freshen up first.' She grabs her bag, steps past him and heads to the restroom. Behind the locked door, she gathers her composure, anticipating what lies ahead, considering the uncomfortable parallels. When she returns, she looks decidedly refreshed.

'Are you okay? Not long now, honey, and we'll be landing.' He sounds too pleased for her comfort.

Giving him a nod, she sits back down. 'We never made it out on the catamaran.' She tries to lift the tone.

'We never did a lot of things,' he says regretfully.

Staring bleakly out the cabin window, she notices the dense cloud cover. Shivers of uncertainty crawl up her back. Right now, her victories felt hollow. *What use are they when something as unforeseen as this is in play?* She can't bear the thought of losing William.

Unlike the flight across, the return has been sombre. Other than a tall, thin, middle-aged businessman with grey hair and the two young women from the lounge, business class is almost empty.

Vanessa looks past William and observes one of the women acting oddly, giggling loudly. Her sober companion appears embarrassed by her friend's behaviour. *That pair will never travel together again.*

Obviously on a turn-around flight, the very same flight crew are in service again, all rubbernecking it from the galley. The couple's sunny mood has changed dramatically, evident they're dealing with some sort of crisis. Graciously the crew dare not ask why the short stay in paradise, but it doesn't go unnoticed. The couple are still holding each other tightly, however this time there is a shift: no laughter.

'William, how did your father come to find out Diana is my mother?'

'I have no idea, but knowing Dad, he's been fishing.'

'Why?'

'This is what we need to find out.'

She understands it's imperative to sort this mess out, and hopefully without the media finding out, but with the weight of dread hanging heavily, she has a cocktail of feelings going through her head.

If William's not my brother, the Whittakers will still never welcome me into the fold, given Mother's affair with his father.

Noticing the light has gone from Vanessa's eyes, bearing witness to her fragility, William locks hands with hers like a starfish, leans in and shares his feelings in a low whisper. 'I do adore you. I want you to know that.'

She responds in a soft tone, 'I do. And you need to remember there's nothing to be ashamed of, William. How could we have known?'

He refrains from speaking.

'Sometimes life takes unexpected turns, and we have to soldier on,' she says sadly.

William kisses her troubled brow, then tilts her head upward so she's looking at him directly. 'When you're about to lose something precious, you protect it even more.'

Vanessa could cry, instead she chooses to stay stoic in the face of adversity. Feeling quite anxious, she hangs her head for a moment, looking at William restlessly patting her wrist. *How am I expected to simply dispose of my affections towards this man?*

A quiet but cheery-faced Daisy strolls past making last minute checks. Looking discreetly at the couple, she gives Vanessa a considered smile.

William turns to Vanessa and whispers, 'We started this journey to bring together what we love most: each other, and all that is meaningful in our lives. We wanted to see where this would take us. We tested the elements in ways that intuitively felt right. You need to know I am not going to give up on that. I, for one, know you are made of tougher stuff, kid. There's no questioning the depth of my love for you, but we both know this is the calm before the storm and we will need to draw on one another for strength.'

As the plane circles for landing, a baby deep in the back of the aircraft stridently wails, only adding to Vanessa's anxiety, so when the aircraft finally begins its descent, she's pleased for the mother and child.

William leans his chin on her shoulder and takes a deep breath, then kisses the crook of her arm before checking his watch; it's just gone seven.

When they land, Vanessa notices the tarmac is wet like it's been prepped for a movie shoot.

The loud ding of the seatbelt sign clicks off. Vanessa feels like a hibernating animal plucked too early from its den.

William jumps up to gather their overhead luggage.

As the door opens, Vanessa moves out from her seat, catching William's pleading eyes. and they reluctantly exit the plane. Vanessa's heart is pounding, but she tries to stay emotionally detached as they blend in and walk unnoticed with the mainstream.

Past the travelator, towards the passport check, it soon becomes apparent several flights have landed at the same time and they are relieved customs officers aren't about to dilly-dally, quick to process weary travellers carrying duty-free bags of cigarettes and vodka.

'Busy, huh?' William says, collecting their baggage from the carousel.

To their surprise, they are immediately waved through bag check, then straight through the automatic doors to where all eyes are upon them.

Vanessa goes into sensory overload as they're thrust into the unwanted paparazzi limelight and blinded by the lights of the cameras.

Click, click, click.

'I'm nervous.' Vanessa's breath catches in her throat, as one cameraman dashes up in front of them, inching back as they walk.

William's acutely aware she is shaking and unable to cope with being gawped at. 'Just look at me,' he tries to reassure her as they're shoved into the midst of the mob.

'Albert are you and Whittaker an item?' asks a young, bold photographer over his horned-rimmed spectacles.

'Over here, Vanessa. Is it love?' someone calls through the crowd.

The paparazzi are aflutter with details of the couple's recent movement and it's evident Vanessa doesn't like every aspect of her life being on display.

'You look good together,' says a gentler reporter closest to them. The woman catches Vanessa's eye and smiles as Vanessa recognises her sentiments.

At fever pitch, another goggle-eyed journalist asks, 'How long have you been seeing one another?'

Struggling to not be separated, her heart is pounding. To the previously obscure Vanessa, the sudden attention is all a bit much. William remains a picture of calm. but shows signs of relief when he finally spots his driver.

'Scott!'

'Sir,' he says, opening the back door for the couple.

The horde close in around the car. Click, click, click.

'Are you okay?' William pats her hand and gives it a squeeze.

'Yes, I'm fine.' *Why didn't he jump in the front seat this time?*

'Good.'

'I always get a fright when strangers call me by my name. I think, how do you know me.' *Protection; he's jumped in the back to protect me.*

Cameras are still pressed up against the windows either side of the car, clicking away as Scott carefully pulls away from the kerb.

'Undoubtedly these photographs will be in the Sunday tabloids,' William says, smoothing down his jeans.

'The trouble is, though, the newspapers think they're sacrosanct," Vanessa says.

'We'll see this time.'

Vanessa knows he's had a gutful of them, but this is a whole new ball game now.

William has never hidden anything from his grandfather, but he's already decided it's imperative to get some straight answers from his father first, and the fastest way to do that is to get to the office asap.

'Publishing house, please, Scott,' William says.

'Yes, sir.' He looks in the rear-view mirror, nodding.

Vanessa knows William detests the tangled, complex, and often destructive actions of their respective parents. *Wasn't it enough that his father ruined his mother's life, let alone Diana's, with his selfish actions? Nothing good has come of that affair, a poison that ruined two families and is now threatening to destroy a third. Though William's concerns are directed towards the family, this one may simply prove far too difficult to be resolved.*

The sun burns though the early morning cloud cover, but the city is already alive with people bustling everywhere. As soon as Scott pulls up, the couple are out of the car and fast lining it up to the office.

Pleasantries brushed aside, the couple sit, side by side, at the enormous walnut boardroom table. Monty remains standing, leaning up against the sideboard. He settles a look on her that is friendly enough but has a no-nonsense undertone. Donna takes coffee and tea orders and sets out a large tray with a mix of various breakfast pastries on the walnut table. The sugary scent is an incredible assault to Vanessa's rumbling stomach.

'Look, this won't take long,' Monty begins, like it's of no consequence.

A person is one thing in business, something quite different in private, and judging from the hesitant look on Monty's face as he forces a smile, it tells Vanessa it's just struck him how much she looks like her mother.

Not that it matters; Vanessa is too distracted by the assortment of cinnamon buns, donuts with grapefruit curd and citrus sugar and quinoa-banana muffins, the ultimate sticky buns causing her tummy to do crazy somersaults.

'You are bringing out the big guns today.' William grabs a napkin and picks up a crispy apple-oat fritter, one of Gramps' all-time favourites.

His father laughs. 'Just keeping in the good books.'

Vanessa has better things to think about. *I'm going to have one of those savoury fondue babkas with a cup of tea.*

William places his fritter back down and grabs a plate for Vanessa. 'What would you like, darling?'

'Babka,' she whispers and looks at him like she's seeking approval. Vanessa cringes at the thought she is quite possibly sitting in front of her father, which causes her to pause.

Anxious glances are exchanged as Monty smooths a nervous hand across the top of his bald head.

It isn't the joy she anticipated, and she takes little comfort in knowing she's perhaps finally found the family she's longed for her entire life.

They're about to discuss the latest revelations when Donna reappears with a tray and the aroma of coffee fills the room.

Monty pipes up. 'William, did you remember to get the coffee?'

He looks at his father incredulously. 'Dad, really? Are you fucking kidding me?'

'No need for the language, son.'

Vanessa appears to be on the cusp of speaking. Instead, she is taken aback, having more concern for William. Not much headway is made in the first half-hour. At nine sharp, the office doors swing open to Thornton in his motorised wheelchair. He grins but seems bewildered at the small gathering in the imposing room. Acutely aware of all the temperaments in the room, Vanessa forces a sorry smile.

'What's going on? I thought you two were in Bali having a romantic holiday,' Thornton says, surprised.

Vanessa doesn't respond. *Sometimes it's better to stay quiet.*

Thornton turns his attention to his son. 'Monty, aren't you supposed to be in the Stockdale meeting this morning?'

Monty clears his throat. 'Father, we have a small situation.'

William shakes his head at his father. 'We have a small situation. Now there's an understatement!'

Conscious of being examined by Monty, Vanessa sits motionless for much of the time, except periodically fiddling with a large, gold cocktail ring on her right hand. *Life has always been about extremes for me.*

Thornton picks up on Vanessa's discomfort, flashes her a warm smile, and asks that everyone else calm down. 'Now, now, there isn't anything that can't be sorted. What's going on? Did the damn paparazzi hound you two love birds out of Bali?'

Ignoring Thornton's question, a concerned Monty peers at his father and declares, 'Speaking of which, Father, you shouldn't be here.'

'Why?'

'That chest cold of yours? You should be home resting.'

'Oh, it's nothing.'

'Nothing until it becomes pneumonia again.' Monty sets his cup and saucer down, observing his father wiping his sweaty brow with his white handkerchief.

Vanessa knows only too well the body isn't designed to live with prolonged immobility, and given Thornton is unable to use his diaphragm fully, he's prone to regular bouts of infection.

Thornton ignores his son's concern and sets about having Donna cancel all his appointments for the morning, then insists on knowing why they're all there and the apparent urgency, but Monty and William are too busy bickering to respond.

In frustration Thornton hollers, 'What on earth are you all bellowing about? Will somebody please put me in the goddam picture.'

Everyone is feeling vulnerable, but for the very first time, Vanessa is aware of Thornton's hard edges and finds it unnerving. *And I thought meeting the Whittakers was going to be a giant gateway to maturity.*

A slew of responses and Thornton is finally brought up to speed.

Vanessa is deep in thought when suddenly she hears Thornton say, 'How did you come to that conclusion?' She looks up but has no idea what is happening, other than William pleading with his father.

'Dad, this has got to be sorted. Do you hear me?' His request hangs in the air.

'Indeed,' states Thornton sternly, looking his son's way.

'We've committed no crime. Besides how much of this really matters?' Vanessa cries.

Monty cocks his head as if she's just spoken Swahili. The others look on in disconnected quiet and she is made to feel very small amongst the tribe of men.

The sum of her mother's actions has clearly left the Whittakers reeling, and Vanessa now sits precariously on the edge, wondering how much ill will this family harbours towards Diana. Vanessa's eyes dart nervously towards Monty, as he reaches beneath his glasses to rub the ridge of his nose, and she wonders when he ceased contact with her mother. *From where I'm sitting, he doesn't seem to have any sentimental attachment, and certainly no indication of anything other than detached curiosity. Is it possible that Monty has expunged all memory of Mother?*

'Have you lost all common sense? Seriously, are you all insane?' Monty goes on the attack. Monty's tone is insensitive, but no one dares dignify his outcry with further comment.

Vanessa certainly doesn't need to fill the air with words.

William takes her hand. 'Darling, if we've broken the law —'

'Impossible!' she cries, looking up. 'I've never broken the law in my life.'

They catch one another's eyes, aware of the gravity of the situation.

Having looked up to these men, it's a very weird feeling to think they may well have the very same blood running through their veins as me.

'Well, that may or may not be true, but it's sure as hell going to be the media's narrative,' William says.

'Christ almighty!' Thornton says. 'Let me think for a minute.'

'It's a bloody business, but I can't see any way around the problem. We need to speak to Diana immediately to clarify things.' Monty lights a cigar.

'Put that bloody thing out. Do you want to kill me?' Thornton says in disgust.

Monty clears his throat and stubs out the offending cigar.

'But what about us?' William asks, looking to Vanessa.

With a lame attempt at wisdom, Monty takes to the floor. Pacing, he looks at the couple and says, 'People are always really romantic about new beginnings or fresh starts. Look, I know this has only just come to light and something like this can certainly level you, but you will get past it, I promise.'

Vanessa could think of any number of reasons not to look at Monty right now. Instead, she focuses on William, who looks like he's going to string his father up by his words.

In an attempt at defusing the situation, Thornton ignores Monty's unsuccessful shot at romantic wisdom. 'Without stating the obvious, you need to keep this thing quiet, because if the press gets hold of it, the outcome could be catastrophic.'

'They're already onto us, Gramps,' William says. 'The press was at the airport this morning asking questions.'

'Asking what?'

'Oh, whether or not we are an item.'

'Christ! What could be more paparazzi perfect than the spiciest author and the hottest publisher seen returning together from overseas?' Monty says, tossing his hands in the air like a petulant child.

'Well, at least they didn't ask us if we were brother and sister,' William says sarcastically.

Vanessa could feel anxiety roiling in her gut.

'That's enough,' Thornton says. 'Certain words lead to a slippery slope, and I don't like to go down that road. I do know all the paranoid ramblings going on in this office won't help solve this today. Just let the dust settle for a day or so. I need time to fathom this thing out.'

Here is this self-made man, whose colossal literary enterprise has made him not only famous, but one of the wealthiest men in his era, and he has no answers?

With the low hum of the motor, Thornton turns his chair in Vanessa's direction. 'For the time being, Vanessa, I'd like you to go about your business like it was before you met William. Hell, you could have both been returning from a promotional tour, for all they know.'

'From bloody boiling Bali,' Monty volleys sharply.

It shocks Vanessa to see the look of concern on their faces, but Thornton chooses to ignore another outburst. 'For now, you and William need to keep a safe distance from one another and don't talk to any media.'

The gravity of the situation is not lost on the couple, but Vanessa is now made to feel like an imposter, a nobody.

'The problem will be if they dig deeper, Gramps,' William says.

'I know. Bear with me here.' He turns to Vanessa. 'Where is that boyfriend of yours?'

Hurt wells in Vanessa's eyes and a bitter taste fills her mouth. There is a short pause, knowing Thornton has a way of finding people's weak spots, but she never believed she'd have to come face to face with it.

'Michael something or other?'

Ouch! There's that stern English exterior William was talking about. Feeling the whole weight of the Whittakers is like an interrogation. With much throat clearing and nervousness, she utters, 'Sorry,' looking across at William and feeling his trusting eyes on her.

He stands and places his hand on her shoulder as a means of protection and she tilts her head so her face rests on it as a thank you.

'Michael Keats-Dickens, I think his name is?' Thornton says in a formidable tone.

This is landmine hopscotch. Thornton's forthright declaration floors her. Looking up at William for a sign that this is news to him, he seems unmoved. Feeling like she's been thrown under a bus, Vanessa thinks she should say something redeeming, but instead, tears form a bright line of silver along her lower lids. William squeezes her shoulder reassuringly and she says in a low whisper, 'He's out of the picture.'

'Pity,' Monty says.

William looks at his father indignantly. 'You really are something else. Come to think of it, Dad, how did you find out Diana was Vanessa's mother?'

Monty suddenly looks guilty. He clears his throat. 'I had someone look into it for me.'

'But why?'

Monty squints. 'Because I've never seen you look so goddamn happy before.'

'So?'

'Well, I decided if Vanessa is going to be a part of this family, then I needed to know more about her.'

'You decided. Christ!'

'Well, it's a bloody good thing I did.'

'If you ever bothered to read a book in your life, you'd know all about her – and how remarkable she is.'

'Paparazzi,' Vanessa says under her breath.

'What?' William says, reacting.

'That's how the paparazzi's found out about us.' Vanessa registers a mild protest at Monty's stupidity.

William looks at his father again in frustration.

'Okay, okay, okay. That can't be helped now,' Thornton says. 'You need to stay low, concentrate on writing, and let me focus on the rest.'

It's going to be hard not seeing William. She knows this is the time to bring out the smaller version of herself.

Thornton organises the company's driver to take her home and asks Donna to accompany her downstairs. 'The rest of you are to stay here for further discussion.'

As much as Vanessa is loath to leave William, she's just as loath to hang around.

Stepping forward, he pulls her to him. His eyes big and sad, William hugs her hard and she has the overwhelming need to say don't forget me. Instead, she kisses his cheek and walks out.

'Stay strong, baby. I'll be in touch,' he says, watching her leave.

Feeling dismissed, Vanessa sits dazed in the back seat of the car, hesitant about what to do next. *What a mess. But he'll find a way. He isn't the type of man to sit and lament things.*

Looking through the window, the streetscape appears as a moving picture. A toddler yanks at her mother's arm as she steadies an empty pram. A small, fluffy brown dog, anchored to a street sign, strains at its leash, barking at the child in distress. The toddler weakens her grip.

Vanessa manages a smile, then looks straight ahead, acutely aware Scott sits in polite professionalism and isn't about to make unnecessary conversation. Arriving back at her apartment, Richard isn't anywhere to be seen. She is relieved as she knows when she is sad, not wanting to make anyone else sad, she typically closes herself off. She makes a quick dash to the waiting lift, luggage in tow, keys at the ready, and opens the door into a world of silence so thick, it falls upon her like a woollen blanket. As soon as Vanessa closes the door, a dark pungent smell catches in the back of her throat and she realises she hasn't thrown out William's flowers. *Lucky I've come home early.* She races to open the balcony door to let in the fresh air. *There is nothing lucky about any of this.*

As she disposes of the flowers, a knot of pain starts in her forehead and spreads behind her eyes, the weight of the morning coming down hard. She tries to ignore it, but gradually and relentlessly, it pulses and pounds inside her skull, and a sense of nausea takes debilitating hold. Fearing she might be sick, she lies down, only to wake an hour or so later in a cold sweat.

Grateful the headache has passed; she strides back through the living room and slams the balcony door on the sunshine. The weather has cleared, it's beautiful outside, but the serenity of the day, the birds, and warm sun seem to be mocking her, so she prefers to stay in the comfort of the air-conditioner.

I think I'll take Thornton's advice and lie low for the time being. He clearly has his reasons, so I'm not about to tell Mother I'm home yet. Privacy is a deep thing for Vanessa, and fortunately for her, she hadn't told her mother who she was going away with in any real detail. Being so busy of late, circumstances have inadvertently prevented her from discussing anything at great length.

She looks out the kitchen window in a semi-daze. *In a short space of time, my whole life has changed. Discovering Michael's been having an affair with Elizabeth, I've met the love of my life, who just might be my brother, and to top it off, I've found the one man I've longed to find – my father.*

'Christ!' She throws her hands in the air.

Vanessa stirs, and suddenly feels anxious, realising she'd had an extremely vivid dream about Monica for the first time in years.

Aware of beads of sweat trickling down between her cleavage, she turns to look at her bedside clock and is stunned to see it's 11.54 a.m. *The day's half gone.* It's enough to launch her out of bed and relocate to the office armchair, logging on to her computer as a means of distraction. Instantly a barrel of disturbing lyrics come rushing forward:

> Words can surprise, delight, or be a rallying cry, but nepotism favours family: *en famille*.

Feeling momentarily emotional, she stops and curls up in a ball on the chair, staring ahead at the screen, hoping she won't be accused of such a thing if she's to become part of the Whittaker clan. Aware of the tight knot in the pit of her stomach, she picks up a cushion and hugs it close, hoping for the feeling to disappear. Having been shut up at home for two days, she's never felt more alone and desperately needing to know what William's thinking. *This is bordering on cruelty. Surely he'll call soon.*

Having absolutely no contact from any of the Whittakers, she's starting to feel a terrible torment and yearns to be put out of her misery, no matter how bleak the outcome. *One minute I'm among them, the next I'm cast aside.* Vanessa reluctantly prepares for the worst: to lose William's affections completely. *All this romantic idealisation. Perhaps it is time to rip the band-aid off. He might have simply walked away. Besides, he's way out of my league!* 'I'd have to be crazy to think I could aspire to be a part of the Whittaker family.'

Vanessa moves around the house like a zombie, indifferent to everything: making her bed, having a shower, everything. She heads into the kitchen to make some fresh juice. Looking down at the orange goop and seeds in the press, she suddenly feels sick again. She glances at the overhead clock; it's now gone half twelve. She reaches for a bottle of wine.

Placing the glass to her quivering lips, she sculls, then heads for the couch with her laptop. She learnt long ago, when something slips under your skin, the best remedy for getting over it is to write. She realises she hasn't opened her online diary since the Garden of Eden in Bali, but all she manages to muster is:

Nothing noteworthy today.

She bursts into tears.

Right now, she needs a place for this to land and she snaps the computer shut, sitting in contemplation.

Strange, no other calls either, other than the odd text message from the girls, thinking I'm still away.

She tries to imagine what William is doing and has half a mind to call him. Instead, she walks into her bedroom, looks at the clothes strewn all over the floor, and comes to terms she's still only half-unpacked. *So unlike me, but it's not necessarily a bad thing.* She picks up a t-shirt and dries her eyes with it.

The landline suddenly rings, startling her. Trying to calm her nerves, she doesn't answer immediately and stares at the phone, fearing it might be her mother. In anguish, Vanessa picks up on the last ring. 'Vanessa speaking.'

'Hello darling,' William says with an intense sigh.

Her heart sinks to her feet. 'Hi,' she mumbles sadly.

There's a long silent pause as they listen to one another breathing.

William clears his throat. 'Vanessa, I need to see you as soon as possible. Are you busy?'

'William, we can't.'

'Why?'

'Because the idea is absurd.'

'I feel you need me, and I know I sure as hell need you.'

Even though the thought of seeing him feels like going down a rabbit-hole, she weakens and says, 'Yes. I'm beside myself, William. I'm going out of my mind here alone, trying to bring some sort of semblance to this madness.'

'Okay, I'm on my way. Do you need anything?'

'Yes, you.'

'See you soon.'

Vanessa feels his smile down the other end of the line.

A short time later there's a gentle tap on the door. When she opens it, Richard is standing alongside William.

'Oh!' she says, surprised.

Richard is taken aback and has a particular kind of stare, a look he often gives strange visitors to the building. 'Oh, Ms Albert, I told Mr Whittaker I was under the impression you were still away. My mistake.' He turns to William, 'My apologies, sir,' and retreats to the lift looking a little confused.

William crosses the room and sets down a bottle of wine.

The emotions of the last couple of days wash over her like a tidal wave and she bursts into tears.

'Oh, darling, come here.' He takes her in his arms and kisses her tears. 'I've missed looking at you, He wraps his arms around her like he'll never let go and tilts her head up to kiss her, staring for the longest time, as tears stream down her cheeks. He wipes them away with his fingers, like he's trying to make it all better, and she stops crying.

His face seems changed: worn and tired. Holding her gaze, she's forgotten what his eyes could do, what they make her do as the heat radiating from his body engulfs her. She tastes his desire, but pulls back slightly, and shocks him when she says, 'We shouldn't.'

He steps away and they grow awkward in their silence. He reaches for her again, but she doesn't move a muscle.

'You've spoken to your mother, haven't you?'.

'No, what would make you say that? My mother doesn't need to hear about any of this until we're absolutely certain we share the same father. Christ! Saying it out loud makes me feel sick.'

'To be frank, I have no idea why you haven't contacted her.'

'I can't. She's away.'

'Where? In the Bermuda Triangle.'

She may as well be. She knows she's probably off grid. The truth is Vanessa hasn't even attempted to call her mother, concerned that if she is able to pick up, Diana would want to discuss Monica, and it's too much to bear thinking about.

'Why would you even question the possibility? Think about it: the dates, Bali.'

'M ...' *Monica. Every time I try to say her name, it catches in my throat.*

'Not to mention the money my family paid in alimony.'

'What money?'

'Darling, I shouldn't have mentioned it. Forget it, it's nothing.'

'No, you've said it now. What money?'

'Well, it's a fact, Vanessa.'

She stares at him blankly.

'Anyway, let's not go over this now. Forget the money. I've missed you terribly and I need a drink. Boy, do I need a drink,' he repeats under his breath.

'I'll get the glasses,' she mumbles, crossing to the bar.

William pulls the chilled wine from the brown paper bag and before pouring, pops the bag in frustration. 'For the first time, it doesn't seem right to toast.'

They sit close and William declares, 'Darling, I need to feel close to you.'

She knows what that means.

'No one will know.' He's surprised to feel her flinch.

Their needs are the same, but she doesn't answer.

'Maybe I should leave.' He stands unexpectedly. When she pleads for him to stay, he stops short of opening the door.

This is wrong on so many levels. In truth, she's terrified of breaking their bonds of affection.

'We need each other more than ever now,' he says.

As much as she wants him, she can't bring herself to tell him.

'Vanessa, darling, I'm here for you if you still want me.' Ignoring her silence, he places his hands around her waist, pulling her gently in, kissing her tenderly. Tasting her salty tears, the moisture only hastens their desire. 'I will not live without you, Vanessa. One way or another, we will be together.'

Her eyes beam a love for him that seeps into his pores. William's words are like everything else she loves about him, steeped in sincerity, and no matter how anyone scorns their circumstances, she wants nothing more than to feel his naked body against hers.

Taking her by the hand, he leads her into the bedroom, the door returning to a soft close.

CHAPTER NINETEEN

Having snatched at threads of sleep, Vanessa wakes befuddled, and nervous about-facing life in general.

The scent of him lingers. She looks out the window from her bed and realises it's pitch-black. The sound of rain is deafening. Beside her, the bed is empty, and she stares at the place where he has been.

He's gone! Squinting and cursing, she rolls to the other side and searches the bedside table for the free airplane mask she usually wears in the early hours, puts it on hastily in the hope of nodding off again, then slumps back down onto the pillow.

Too late. Her brain kicks into gear and she ushers a smile at the thought of William's initial suggestion: 'we could curl up and watch a movie, eat burgers and fries'.

Instead, they had made love all afternoon.

Vanessa presses her face into his pillow and keeps it there for the longest time, wanting to be weighed down by his body again. All she can think of is William. Moving in a dream, she reflects:

His body, long and strong, his chest broad, his erection enormous, William slowly kisses away her tears as their naked bodies touch in sensuous connection. Her mouth opens slightly, begging to be kissed. He presses his lips to hers; her mouth opens to his tongue; he licks in, fuelling her desire as a trailing hand slowly outlines her delicate hip, across her silky-smooth skin to her thigh. William gazes down at her smouldering eyes, her lips ripe and wet from his kiss. He feels the heat radiating from her body as she gives off a mute sound of pleasure. Hard at her side, she sighs with need as he runs his hand across her pelvis, then down her body to gently part her legs. Wanting to enjoy her, he moans with desire and tastes her. The muscles in his arms bulge as his fingers gently circle the fragile folds: touching, exploring, arousing, teasing. Every touch expands her consciousness. Everything's heightened. His perfection is her reality. The self is gone. Time stops. There is only now, moving in a dream.

Lying on her rumpled bed, Vanessa lifts her eye shade and realises the quilt cover is a sea of scrunched-up tissues.

She notices a novel left face down on the bedside table and remembers burying herself in the pages after he left. Not able to see the words through her tears, she eventually gave up and dog-eared the page. *Gosh, this is not like me.* She remembers the analogy: closing a book with a bookmark is like pressing the stop button, whereas leaving the book facedown means you've only pressed pause. *Is that what this is, a pause in our love?* She lets out a long sigh. She hadn't wanted him to leave, and he hadn't wanted to go.

Until recently, Vanessa had moved to a kind of aloneness, but since meeting William, an emotional transformation has changed her life. The chemistry between them is so exclusive, she wants only him. With an un-beaconed future, she'd rather die than be without him.

Sure, it's easy to get caught up thinking your world is the only thing that matters, but how many people wake up one day and are faced with the possibility that the person they're romantically linked to is their sibling.

She cringes at the thought and pulls the sheet over her head, instantly transporting herself back to when she was little, playing hide-and-seek in her mother's wardrobe amongst her long, beautiful kaftans, silk scarves, and hippy beads. Silent as her mother called her name, she took delight in being very still, the soft, silky textures calming her skin as she breathed in her mother's scented clothes, a heady mix of ylang-ylang and patchouli.

Ironically, she wishes she could crawl inside again, take refuge, and wait for this horrible mess to go away. But there is no mother's cupboard for shelter and no magic wand to make things right. Laid bare, Vanessa realises she must stay on track, silence her fears, the one's that constantly come to the fore telling her life is pretty messed up. Sure, she's crawled her way out of many a crisis before. Even when Bruno's anger surged to a frightening pitch, threatening to kill her, she managed to hide her fear. Now it's a different kind of fear, one she's not felt before, a fear of losing the one person she believes to be her soul mate.

Peeking out from behind the sheet, Vanessa switches on the bedside lamp and the light floods her bleary senses. Staring at the small bookshelf in her room, she loves the way the books are all colour-coded and set in some sort of chaotic order.

The gilt edge of her orange diary catches her eye, poking out from the bookcase like a reminder to revisit. Originally penned with romantic tales of honeymooning in Italy with Bruno, she realises she hasn't opened it since they were married. *I believed I was happy then.*

With every female instinct rioting inside her, she pushes back the covers and places both feet flat on the carpet. Reaching across, she grabs the memoir in the hope it might hold answers to why she seems to have a knack for messing things up, then slides between the sheets again. *Perhaps by revisiting the past, I might gain some sort of insight from its scribbled contents.* She props herself up amid the pillows.

She's taken by surprise when a small, pressed rose falls from the deckle-edged pages, reminding her of her wedding in Sicily. Refusing to accept its painful representation, she places it to the back of the book and settles in to read.

At the beginning, a little of what she's written is indecipherable, like perhaps she'd had too much wine that evening. After a time, the words seem to leap into form as if they've come alive, like a drop of water to a neglected plant, dragging her thoughts away from the withered rose.

Rome

Sunday 4th May

Our 1st day in ancient Rome, arriving early we shower after check-in & head up the Via Del Corso to begin the day shopping.

She remembers visiting the Pantheon and Trevi Fountain, then taking in evening Mass at Basilica St Marcello.

Gazing up at the decorative ceiling and along the ornate walls, it's like walking through the pages of a bible.

A flood of memories triggers all manner of thoughts, and how she made little notes and sketches of things that caught her fancy, like mosaic flooring – carpet for eternity – Roman frescoes, and religious paintings.

Gelato, gelato, gelato … yummy!! I plan to have some every day!
Ever since Audrey Hepburn and Gregory Peck enjoyed gelato together in the 1953 romantic comedy, *Roman Holiday*, the Italian ice cream has been permanently linked with romance.

I can see why Fellini said, 'Rome is the most wonderful movie set in the world …' He's right! I have no idea how reading this will help in any way, but it's worth a try.

Monday 5th May

Our body clocks are out so we naturally wake early … just gone five in fact and we decide to go for a walk …

Yes, sharing those empty, stone-paved streets with only a few street-sweepers and smiling as we ran past a young, romantic couple sitting on the Spanish steps, clearly on their way home from the evening before.
I remember the view changing with every step as we headed towards Villa Borghese, that beautiful park north-east of Piazza Del Popolo. Once the estate of Cardinal Scipione Borghese, and where Bruno carved a love heart with our initials into the trunk of an elm tree. If only I'd known what was to come.

Sicily

Wednesday 7th May

Pick up hire car, a brand-new Peugeot Bruno aptly names Penelope …

We make the 40-minute drive to the extraordinary hillside town of Taormina, where we will soon wed.

Check into The Grand Timeo, an extravagance dating back to 1873. This was the first hotel ever built in Taormina situated on a spur of the hill which overlooks the sea. It is immersed in parkland, which backs onto the rosy ruin of the Greco, Roman Amphitheatre.

Our deluxe double room is magnificent and overlooks the bay of Naxos, so we decide to sit on the terrace and enjoy a drink. Sipping away on Dom Perignon looking out across to snow-capped Mount Etna, it is picturesque but a grim reminder this is earthquake region.

I call mother as it's her birthday. Like everyone else, she too had refused to travel to Sicily for our wedding, the conversation is short and guarded.

Ah, there it is! No one came to our wedding because no one trusted Bruno. Why didn't I realise that? Perhaps I chose not to. Instead justifying everyone's absence due to long-distance travel.

Taormina

Friday 9th May

We drive to Messina, the city of the straits and have breakfast at the Port of Sicily. It's close connection to the continent has always given it an independence from the other cities of the island. Yet, throughout history its position made it not only a power to be reckoned with, but also vulnerable to invasion dating back as early at 281 B.C.

When Mamertines, lawless mercenaries of Agathocles, seized it by a subterfuge, held it against Pyrrhus which brought about the first Punic war. Then, again in 1061 it was captured by Robert Guiscard a resourceful Norman adventurer.

His bravery, villainous mind, and fierce fighting, lead to the successful capturing of Messina giving him control over the strait.

On to Milazzo on the northwest corner of Sicily. At the end of town is a 13th century Spanish Castle, once ruled by Frederick II in 1239. It was originally a castle until the first Parliament of Sicily was housed here, then a hospital and finally a prison from the late 1800s–1963.

Taormina

Saturday10th May

In the afternoon our hotel manager organizes for us to go down to the sister hotel Villa Sant' Andrea, an old Villa dating back to 1830, built by an aristocratic family from Britain.

The hotel still holds precious paintings and valuable antiques from its early days and is situated in a park of subtropical vegetation with its own private beach below on the Bay of Mazzaro. After sunning ourselves on the pebble beach sipping on Mai Tais, we then take a boat cruise to Grotto Azzuro. We enter through a small stone portal into another world lit by azure lights, simply breathtaking! The skipper singing, Ciuri Ciuri a popular Sicilian folksong, meaning flowers, flowers, cannot drown out the echoes of history in these remarkable stone walls.

Returning to our hotel I soak in an oil bath, sipping a Vino Bianco, while Bruno plates up a delicious spread of antipasto for dinner, prosciutto, olives, artichokes, and pecorino cheese with a loaf warm ciabatta.

This wonderful man will soon be my husband.

My God! I'm about to marry this monster and I'm calling him wonderful. Love can be so blind. All this talk about food is making me hungry. Soup season is supposed to be over, but with this out-of-season chill in the air, I might order a chicken ramen from Suki's. Wait. No, I won't; there's some chicken in the fridge.

Tossing a bathrobe on, tying the cord as she goes, she heads into the kitchen. The light of the fridge illuminates the kitchen as she tears at a piece of chicken schnitzel, the garlic-ness rich on her tongue. *Mm, not as good as Suki's ramens, but nevertheless tasty.* She feels almost undignified, standing at the sink eating with the fridge door still open. She reaches in for a chilled glass and pours a chardonnay. The chill of the wine washes the saltiness down. She rinses her oily fingers with liquid soap and returns, with her wine, to her dimly lit room, painfully aware she reeks of garlic. *Lucky William's not here.*

Vanessa decides to light a candle, then stands by the window like a lost soul watching the twitching flame and its reflection. Pressing her head against the cold pane, there's little relief from the coolness as she looks down on the wet footpath below, lit by the streetlamp. There's not a soul in sight and everything looks moody. She watches a small wattle tree moving about in the wind like a thick woollen hat. Negative thoughts worm their way through her head, causing her to tear up again, so she opens the window in the hope it will dry them up, then takes another sip of wine.

Weighed down by an invisible load, a man's loud sobs can be heard through the rainy gloom, echoing off the glass and concrete surface outside the building, bringing with it deeper dread. *I hear you, buddy, but not my monkey, not my circus.*

A heavy splat of rain hits her cheek just as a red convertible sports car zooms past in the rain, the decibel levels off the scale, Elton John's words never more apt: "I guess that's why they call it the blues." She closes the window in haste.

The wine is quick to go to her head. She's liking the sensation and decides to pour another before running a bath. Still intent on finding answers, she grabs the diary. *Answers to what?* She looks down at the book in her hand.

Her concentrated effort is to heap precious insight as to why she continually chooses unavailable men. *Perhaps it's a lack of a father figure? This level of insight could be the subject of a whole new book.* She knows she'll never write it. She perches her glass and the journal on the edge of the bath, then leans over the tub, swishing a hand in the water before dropping her robe. It lands heavily at her feet and she steps into the tub. Reclining back, she drops beneath the water, slipping into a sad case of isolation by trying to wash away the crying feeling. Resurfacing, she continues reading:

Taormina

Sunday 11th May

We start the day with a brisk walk throughout the town along quaint streets interwoven with little alleyways. As fresh white linen blows about in the breeze on balustrades overhead an old woman peers out watching the children playing below and sympathetically looks across at us, the travellers, to which we look back with such regard.

I read Italian cafés are the soul of the nation, where arguments are won and lost, the day's news is debated, and gossip comes alive. So, why not today, the day is bright and beautiful, and we find the idyllic spot to sit outside alongside the now bustling locals.

Bruno holds my hand tightly and says, 'You will be Mrs Vanessa Salvi tomorrow.'

Midmorning we head out to the fabulous seaside village of Cefalu' for lunch. Leaving Taormina I see a sign on the opposite side of the road, Syracuse 104 km. Considering Bruno's parents are from there and his extended family is virtually next door, I wonder why we don't go visit. However, having been told his mother is the direct line to the Mafia, I don't dare ask.

Cefalu has retained its medieval appearance with very narrow but ever so charming streets. The buildings are of elaborate architectural decoration with numerous churches throughout the town, and with the charm of its old houses clustered along the white sandy beach is what makes it so scenic.

On our way back to Taormina we stop off in Enna, which has exceptional views over the mountains and valleys of Sicily. This beautiful town is the highest provincial capital in Italy and well worth the visit. It dates to 859 A.D. and is the home of Castello di Lombardia, an ancient fortress.

Stopping off at a corner deli we purchase salami, prosciutto, olives, and cheeses to have with the fresh bread we bought at the roadside stall earlier … this will be dinner tonight.

Big day tomorrow … fingers crossed we get some sleep!

Big disastrous day is more like it! When I consider his mixed ancestry and given Sicily's illustrious history, there must be a whole collection of individuals in embryo in Bruno. It's difficult to believe I once trusted this man who was loving, humorous, self-respecting, but that same greedy, shameless lowlife went on to cause me so much misery!

THE WEDDING

— A New Chapter in our Lives —

I'm not going there. The fear of facing this chapter is too great. Deep in thought, she climbs out of the bath, pats herself dry with a towel, and decides to put her favourite silk pyjamas on.

This imposed silence from Thornton is bordering on the ridiculous. I should call him tomorrow as I really need to get back into work.

Ambling into her office, she hesitates at the doorway. Even her desk looks depressed, papers strewn all over the place. Unlike the rest of her apartment, this is a cluttered space, but she likes it that way. Right now, it gives her a sense of acknowledgment of her existence, an extension of herself.

Considering what we writers do with our time, sitting all day at our desks, we're the most unadventurous souls on earth. She looks at a dead red rose hanging limply over the lip of a small, willow pattern jug, which brings her back to William and how he holds her heart. *I miss his scent, his touch, the sound of his voice: even his only imperfection, the turn of his skinny ankles.*

In despair, she shrinks down the wall and sits in the corner by the desk. Staring out at the sky into the darkness of night, she's mildly displeased to see the rain has stopped. It had suited her melancholy.

In the past I've always created a protective pseudo-self, choosing men who have a superficial capacity for intimacy. You could say I have a certain type. It's always been easier that way, rather than give of myself entirely. But with William, it's different. I've allowed myself to open my heart and love him unconditionally, becoming a part of him literally.

She elects to return to the inner sanctum of her cocoon-like bed. Whenever life's trials and tribulations threaten to overwhelm her, she clambers into the safety of her beautiful, king-size bed, her go-to, a safe place away from life's demons. She remembers her aunt saying, "It's a Celtic tradition of taking to bed. For small dramas, a day in bed will do it." *At this rate I'll need a decade!*

Pre-dawn light, a red-eyed Vanessa wakes with a dim memory of thunderstorms rolling through the night. She's unexpectedly startled, unable to ignore the shrill ring of the telephone in line with her ear.

Very few people ever call me at home. 'Hello, Vanessa speaking.'

'Vanessa, it's Thornton Whittaker, dear. Is it a good time to talk?'

'Why yes.' She glances at the clock boldly displaying 6.35 a.m. and is swift to prop herself up against her pillows, hoping to sound alert.

'Sorry to call you so early, but I need to see you in my office as soon as possible, say around 3.30?'

'Today?'

'Yes.'

'Of course.'

'Good, see you then.' He promptly hangs up.

Vanessa knows it isn't a question, but rather a polite order. *Thornton obviously has his own theories about this complicated situation and wants to air them, or perhaps it's business as usual? I'll soon know.* She lies there listening to the sound of the engaged tone.

Vanessa brushes a small piece of lint from her navy, pinstriped suit and glances at her reflection as she passes the dazzling glass and marble office block bearing the name Whittakers. Entering the building, she's surprised by the number of people waiting by the lift and her anxiety is elevated. She's grateful it is quick to arrive and steps in, only to notice every button has been pushed. *It's going to be a long ride to the top …*

Walking down the imposing corridor, she spots Thornton's secretary coming out of his office, who stops to hold the door open for her. 'He's waiting,' she says with a kind-hearted smile.

The warmth in Thornton's eyes meets her gaze, his composed face an expression of power, and somewhat eases the tension. 'Vanessa, please sit. Are you okay?' His eyes are full of reassurance.

'I've had better days. I'll help myself to some water if I may? Would you like one?' She glances back at Thornton.

'No, thank you, dear. I'm fine.'

Seated, she takes a sip and pretends to be interested in a particular book jutting out from the shelf.

'Is everything alright?'

She is quick to reveal. 'I won't lie; I need some good news today.'

'I know that, dear. That is precisely why I've called you in.'

'I'm glad you did; in fact, you beat me to it.'

He nods.

'I'm still madly trying to get the complexity of my main character right in this draft.'

He looks almost surprised. 'Vanessa, we can discuss that another time.

I think you know this is not about business. For the moment, my priority is you and William. My dear, what I have to say must stay between these walls until we can be absolutely certain I am on the right track.'

'Yes of course.'

'Look, I'm going to come right out and say it. I don't believe for one minute you and William are related. In fact, I'm so certain, I'm willing to stake my reputation on it.'

She's taken aback.

'I know you mean a great deal to one another.'

Despite the many pinch-me moments I've had during the course of my burgeoning career, this one would have to take the cake, sitting here in Thornton's office having a deep and meaningful about my love for his grandson. Focus, Vanessa, focus.

'Look, I'll start at the very beginning. When you first came to us with your manuscript, I had no idea you were Goodall's daughter. Why, there was no way I would even think of putting the two of you together. Yes, I knew your mother as Diana Albert once upon a time, but she's had the surname Goodall for what? Well over twenty-five plus years?'

'Yes, that's right.'

'In fact, no disrespect to your mother, but when she married that fellow – what was his name?'

Vanessa doesn't get a chance to respond. Instead, she reflects on her stepfather, remembering how they loved to jump into the river together off the pier of his holiday house. She could only breaststroke, but she did it extremely well and he encouraged her every time to swim out past the markers.

Later, when he got busy with her mother, she'd sit on the riverbank and make necklaces with seedpods and gumnuts, anything she could find to free herself from the sound of their tumultuous lovemaking.

'James. Yes, that's right. James Goodall. The twitter-pated senator, we called him. Anyway, that's neither here nor there, but at the time, we all felt there was nothing good-all about it. In fact, it was all bad. By that I mean Diana hasn't exactly been thought of in glowing terms around here.'

'With all due respect, this is my mother you're talking about.' She feels a slight contradiction inside.

He raises an unsteady hand in the air. 'I know, I know, but needless-to-say, it did set the cat among the Town Hall pigeons.'

'Sir, can you appreciate this is all very awkward for me?'

'I realise that, but she also received quite a bit of alimony from us over the years. However, at the time it was thought easier to pay the enemy than keep the gossip nourished.'

'Mother led me to believe my father never knew of me and certainly never paid a cent towards my upbringing.' She observes his disgruntled cough, holding his hand to his chest. 'Mr Whittaker, you have to understand, from my perspective, this is all such a shock.'

Thornton arches his brows. 'Vanessa, please call me Thornton. I know what you're saying you believe to be true, and this is precisely why I asked you here today. I don't believe for one minute you are Monty's daughter. Yes, yes, I know all about the affair in Bali forty odd years ago, and a child was born from that affair, but I don't believe for one minute that you, my dear, are that child.'

Vanessa dares to try to utter her sister's name, but it's stuck, and she simply can't.

'I believe, Vanessa, your father is someone else, someone none of us know of. And I would go so far as to say, Diana may not even know herself.'

She's incensed by his comments, but her instinct for self-preservation is too strong, so the thought of mentioning Monica is far too painful at this point. She knows Thornton to be a good man and clearly invested, but he hasn't exactly provided her a soft place to land. *Avoidance is key.* 'The only way to sort this whole thing out is for me to do a DNA test or talk to Mother.'

'Well, my dear, I've tried calling your mother, but her phone just keeps going through to message bank. Perhaps you could make headway.'

Vanessa isn't the least bit surprised. 'She's away, up at my aunt's place just outside of Cairns, and it's pretty poor reception where she is.'

'Right. Look, it's a long bow, but I'm prepared to draw it, which means if I'm right, you and William are free to do whatever it is you choose.

Vanessa, given your mother's word is not pure of thought around here, at the end of the day only a DNA test will reveal the absolute truth.'

'Have you told any of this to William or Monty yet?'

'No, and I won't. I feel confident there will be less to puzzle over once you have the test and try to discuss this with your mother, and you need to do all the above sooner rather than later. There's a lot at stake here and if you don't speak to her, I will find a way.'

Vanessa grows nervous.

'Believe me, dear, I'm not about ruining families, but rather finding solutions. When I see the way my grandson looks at you, I know how much he is hurting. It's time your mother did the right thing by you, and this family, and fesses up, even if it is to her own detriment.'

At this point, Vanessa's head is swimming.

'What's most important is that you and William stay out of the public eye until this is all sorted. But rest assured, if your mother doesn't come clean, I will get to the bottom of this one way or another myself.'

She inwardly cringes.

'And please, please, speak to your mother in person. Do not, and I repeat, do not discuss any of this on the telephone!'

Got it!

Thornton's parting words are thought provoking. 'Vanessa, remember this. All parts come together for a reason and what drives us away can sometimes be the very thing that can bring us back.'

CHAPTER TWENTY

By the time Vanessa steps out of the publishing house, a damp wind is blowing down the street and fast-moving grey clouds travel past a barely visible sun. She's been with Thornton for over an hour and the conversation has been so intense, she hadn't noticed the cloud cover forming. She dodges a woman attempting to put her umbrella up as she scurries past. Heavy drops hit her face and the distance blurs as she rushes to the safety of her car.

Everything has happened so quickly that Vanessa is feeling physically and mentally exposed. *Is it worth it? Of course, it is.* She looks at herself in the rear-view mirror. *No amount of sleep seems to be helping lately.*

Vanessa attempts to buckle up, struggling with the latch repeatedly. 'Jesus, I must get this seat belt fixed.' She catches her breath and sits in the car in contemplation for a moment. *With so many conflicting voices in my head, I need to clear my mind, but at least I know Thornton is supportive of my relationship with William. He's like a comforting mantle on a stormy day and his support of mother in the past is nothing short of remarkable. Is he that forgiving?*

While she appreciates her mother's bohemian lifestyle, it isn't her take on life. She often questions her mother's snafu decisions. *If all this is true, and I have no reason to doubt it, it means mother extorted money. How could she have done such a thing to this family, but more importantly, why?* She knows these are questions that ultimately need answers. *I need to figure out how to approach her and not run off on a tangent. I've never been able to discuss my sister with her, so I think a DNA test is the best way to go.*

Unfortunately, Vanessa couldn't get in to see her trusted doctor until the end of the week. In the meantime, Thornton said he'll investigate, but suggested Vanessa get online to the Registry of Births, Deaths & Marriages and have a good look for any listings of babies having died either the year before or that same year. *Whilst not telling mother feels somewhat underhanded, it's nothing compared to what she's done.*

Vanessa starts the car. *I don't like the thought of being alone tonight, plus there's absolutely nothing at home to eat. Maybe Francesca and Georgia are free? The camaraderie of close girlfriends really would be nice, and given Elizabeth's no longer on the list, dinner for three is in order. I know they have busy lives, and I don't want to burden them with this whole sordid mess, but I really need them around me right now. Heck! That's what friends are for. Besides Georgia is wickedly funny, and always up for a drink at short notice, and Francesca is probably still in the city working anyway.*

When she calls the women, proposing they go to the Mosaic Bar, the meet is sealed for 6.30 p.m. under the guise of celebrating Vanessa's second book deal.

Vanessa is first to arrive at the bar. Knowing the others aren't far away, she orders a pitcher of vodka martinis. Waiting she can't help overhearing the conversation, next to her, from one woman to another, about men in general.

'We're no picnic ourselves, you know,' the older woman replies.

Vanessa smiles across at the woman, thinking of several she could name off the bat, Elizabeth at the top of the list.

The sight of her friends' gorgeous faces instantly lifts her spirits and it's hugs and kisses all round.

'Gosh! It's so good to see you guys,' Vanessa says warm-heartedly.

'How was Bali?' Francesca asks.

'Interesting.'

'Oh, do tell?' Georgia asks.

'Let's have a drink first.' Vanessa says, needing to deflect.

By the time the jug is almost empty, the sonic levels in the bar have soared, so it's unanimous they take their drinks and move through to the dimly lit restaurant, rather than brave the elements by going further afield.

Georgia asks, 'So who is this fellow you went away with?'

'Who said anything about going away with a fellow?'

'Well, if you were to go away with anyone else, it would have been us, or Lizzie.'

'Yes, do tell,' Francesca says.

Vanessa observes Francesca's remarkable brown eyes. The girls are armed with a quiver of questions, but considering what's happened, Vanessa has no intention of going into any detail. She strategically changes tack by blurting out about Michael and Elizabeth's affair.

'What?' Georgia says.

Vanessa painstakingly goes over all the sordid details. The girls are shocked into silence.

'At first it was difficult for me to negotiate the tangled crosscurrents of pride and hurt. You know, the usual things, but it has given me plenty to think about.'

'Whoa! Hold up there, girlfriend. There ain't nothin' usual about a girlfriend stealin' your man,' Georgia says in her strongest southern drawl.

'I know.'

Georgia goes in again. 'Are you sayin' Elizabeth, our Lizzie, has been screwin' your Michael?'

'Yes, that's precisely what I'm saying.'

'Connivin'.' Georgia narrows her eyes at the thought.

'Excuse me while I drop my martini in slow motion.' Francesca waves to the waiter for another pitcher.

Hearing Vanessa has fallen prey to the vitriol of yet another insensitive man, and with one of their very own, the girls are livid.

Vanessa places a hand on both friends.' It's okay. I'm okay, truly I am.'

'Will she stop at nothing?' Francesca shakes her head.

'So, what will you do?' Georgia asks, genuinely troubled.

'Well, they can have one another, as far as I'm concerned. Better I find out now, than walk down the aisle with another buffoon.'

'Honey, you were never going to marry that man. But lordy, lordy, wonders never cease,' Georgia proclaims.

'True,' Vanessa agrees, 'but I haven't exactly been an angel either.'

'Honey, I don't need to know what it is you've done, but it sure as hell couldn't be anywhere near as bad arse as what they've been doin',' Georgia says candidly.

Though stunned by Elizabeth's betrayal of their dear friend, Georgia and Francesca look at one another and can't quite grasp Vanessa's obvious level of indifference. Other than looking tired, she seems almost unperturbed by the whole grubby situation.

Michael had hit on both women, at one time and another, so it isn't surprising to them. Nevertheless, it's a hard pill to swallow.

Vanessa's friends have discussed many times their wish the success of Vanessa's first book would make her wise up to the less scrupulous among the opposite sex. They had hoped it would be a way of venting through the pages and growing stronger during the process.

'Anyway, enough about them, its onwards and upwards,' Vanessa says.

'So long as you're okay, honey.' Francesca offers a sympathetic hand.

'Yes, truly I am.'

They look at each other, holding their glasses mid-air. 'Cheers!' They take a sip simultaneously and then slam the glasses down on the table, laughing. It's a thing the girls delight in doing as a means of cheering one another up whenever there's an issue in the group: good, bad, or indifferent.

'So what's been happening while I've been away?'

'Well ...' Francesca stalls. Her mind is clearly working overtime in search of worthy conversation.

'Guess what?' Georgia pipes up.

'What?' Francesca's relieved.

'I've decided to have my breast implants removed.'

'What?' Both shriek at once.

'Well, isn't this a night of news? We need to get together more often. My life is so boring compared to you two,' Francesca replies.

'Stop. Your life isn't boring,' Vanessa says.

'Yep, going, going, gone in a few days' time! I've already booked in for surgery. That's it, I'm over them.' Georgia squeals with delight, looking down at the offending appendages.

'But why? I think they're fabulous, I've always envied your breasts.' Francesca gazes at her Georgia's chest.

Georgia cups her DDs. 'Here, have them.'

'Seriously, why?'

'Because I don't want to be looking down the barrel of fifty with a matronly chest and too scared to go under the knife, that's why.'

'Fair enough.'

'Look, Paul made me get them years ago and I've never been comfortable, so I figured it's time to close that chapter and start anew. Besides I think large breasts are out and I want to be built for speed, not comfort,' she says light-heartedly.

'Seduction,' Francesca says.

'What?'

'More like built for seduction.'

Laughing and talking over one another, Vanessa sits bathed in the familiarity and concentrated dose of oestrogen her friends bring with them. The waiter returns with a fresh pitcher.

'Right, I'm calling it. Charge your glasses, girls. It's official. Big breasts are out, and little ones are in,' Vanessa says.

'I'll toast to that.' Francesca excitedly holds up her glass and cups a tiny breast with the other hand as another waiter sets down a platter of antipasto.

He notices and cheekily grins at Francesca.

'Oh! Did you see that? He's cute,' Francesca checks out the waiter's butt as he walks away.

The girls have never understood why Francesca doesn't have a man. Vanessa puts it down to too goddamn gorgeous and remarkably clever. The laughter is so loud, three businessmen at a nearby table look across flirtatiously.

Georgia looks at Francesca. 'Interested?'

The girls do a reassessment.

'Nope.' Francesca bursts into laughter again.

'Wait, wait, wait. Do you remember that time we were out on Robbie's boat, and you fell into Sydney Harbour with all our handbags?' Vanessa asks Georgia.

'Need I remind you, you never let me forget it.'

'Tell me,' Francesca says. 'I haven't heard this one.' 'Why are you bringing this up again?' Georgia asks.

'Oh, that vulgar woman on the boat that day who kept flashing her very large breasts at Robbie,' Vanessa says.

'Please, I'm not that well-endowed, am I?'

'Tell me about the handbags,' Francesca urges.

'Oh, this was before we met you, I think?' Georgia looks at Vanessa for confirmation.

'Why do I always seem to miss out on all the fun?'

'Because we're meant to be more mature now, I guess.' Georgia puts a finger to her cheek with a smile like a southern belle.

'Seriously, that so doesn't make any sense,' Francesca says.

'I'm being sarcastic.'

Vanessa couldn't wait to tell her story for the umpteenth time. Leaning into the table, she spreads her fingers, palms facing downward, her hands hovering just above the table, pleased to have a captive audience. 'Well, we were all out on Robbie's big cruiser and it had been a huge day on the harbour. I think there were probably about twenty-five people on the boat. It was late at night, and most had been dropped off out the front of his place, me included, with the plan to continue partying.

'Meanwhile, the captain, another friend of Robbie's – Ian, I think his name is – and Georgia here,' she says, nudging the American's arm, 'head back out to anchor the boat offshore and clean up. Well, everyone was so pissed, a lot of us had left our handbags downstairs in the galley. Georgia thoughtfully decides to gather up the bags, then steps off the boat into the dinghy. Unfortunately, she misses and ends up in the drink. The bags quickly fill with water and our good-hearted friend here,' another nudge, 'refuses to let go of them and starts to sink into the abyss. Ian instantly reaches down, pulling her up by the scruff of the neck, and drags her, wringing wet, into the dinghy. Luckily, he saved her tiny little arse and our precious bags.'

'I wish I had a tiny little arse,' Georgia jokes.

'Oh, shoosh. You do,' Vanessa says.

A very serious Francesca looks across at Georgia. 'Jesus, you could have drowned.'

'Yes, trust me, we know,' Vanessa says with a measure of concern.

'Bloody hell, we can all laugh about it now, but it wasn't funny at the time. You're right, I could have, because there was no way I was going to let go of those bags, and I'm not exactly a good swimmer.'

'Especially when you're drunk,' Vanessa says seriously. 'When they arrived back at Robbie's, I saw Georgia walking across the lawn barefooted, looking like a drowned rat, water still pouring from a dozen bags. I zeroed in on my brand-new Gucci tote and absolutely freaked out!'

'What?' Francesca exclaims.

'Never mind, Georgia, all I could think of was that our mobiles and makeup were all ruined, and my bag would never be the same again.'

Georgia adds, 'I was barefoot because when Ian fished me out of the water, I lost a shoe, so he took off the other one and tossed it into the water. When I asked why, he said, "Well, one's no bloody good to you."'

'That's hysterical,' Francesca chuckles as she falls back in her seat, clasping her hands.

With her heart warmed, Vanessa beams across at Georgia.

Back at home, Vanessa thought about the evening and how catching up with the girls had certainly helped lift her spirits, and she's grateful they had the good grace not to revisit the question about Bali.

Readying herself for bed, Vanessa catches her naked reflection in the bedroom mirror and notices how much weight she's lost. What's more concerning are the puffy eyes staring back at her. *The girls are right. I do look tired. Maybe I should get my breasts reduced too? Nah!* She crawls into bed, exhausted.

The next morning there's a knock at her front door, so she tosses on a robe and races to open it. She's surprised to see Richard standing there with a gift box.

'Just arrived,' he says, handing her the medium-sized box. There's a card attached and she opens it to find a beautiful, handwritten poem inside by e. e. cummings:

> I carry your heart with me
> I carry it in my heart
> I am never without it,
> Anywhere I go you go, my dear.

How special to hold a handwritten note. She places it to her heart for a moment before setting it down on the coffee table and opening the box. She's enchanted to find a sacred white lotus flower with another small card that reads: A symbol of purity and beauty, I Will always love you.

This is undoubtedly a bright moment in an otherwise difficult week.

A wall of thoughts hits her, of love and life, and being down at Whale Beach on the private terrace of William's bedroom. Off to the side was a beautiful pond filled with superb lotus flowers.

She replays the conversation about the charming plant and how, whenever his mother felt despair, she delighted in watching the lotus emerge from the water to reveal its exquisiteness. Such a pure flower held special meaning for his beloved. His mother had told him, 'The flower slowly and magnificently emerges over a three-day period and majestically blooms in the morning until mid-afternoon.'

Feeling a lone tear stream down her cheek, Vanessa watches it fall ponderously onto the flower. She decides to take it outside and put it in a large stone cistern.

She'd set the water feature up some years earlier for her three goldfish and instinctively, these same fish race to the surface and gather around, expecting to be fed.

Wiping away her tears, she looks down at Mack with his celestial eyes, her favourite black goldfish, knowing how intelligent he is. 'I give you credit, Mack. You're a bold boy and you never fail to make me smile.' She shakes her head in affection, setting down the water lily. 'Yes, Mack I'm happy to see you too.' She watches him investigate, and wonders if the love she shares with William will have a rebirthing. Heavy-hearted, she lets out a sigh.

Suddenly she hears a mosquito, like an overhead drone, and stares as it lands on the lip of the pond. 'Hey, buddy, if I were you, I'd get out of there quick smart before Mack has you for breakfast.' Vanessa has no sooner finished her sentence when Mack gobbles up the parasite in one swift movement.

'Well done, Mack.' She chuckles and reluctantly heads back inside to log on to her computer.

Bringing up Registry of Births and Deaths, she types in key words to see if there is an application form and notices a section on stillbirths. Vanessa punches in the relevant information, her mother's name, the year of the baby's birth etc. Sadness overwhelms her when required to enter the father's details. She leaves it blank, and hits enter. Nothing, except to say there is no record.

The second attempt, she adds Montgomery Whittaker's name and hits send. Still nothing. Vanessa tries every possibility but continues to come up blank.

Out of sheer frustration, she decides to wait to see the doctor. She attempts to work, but after a few short bursts, she opts for a more low-key piece of work as a diversion.

The Man Who Saved my Life
Compassion seems an emotion seldom shown to one another. The sheer magic of Alexander's work could not be attributed to a formula. All he knew is …

Stuck a moment, Vanessa sits tapping her designer pen on the laptop before adding:
… such a decision could destroy your soul.

CHAPTER TWENTY-ONE

The unrelenting rain throughout the night had caused Vanessa to sleep fitfully, but when she wakes, it's cleared up somewhat, so she decides to get moving early. By the time she's back home from her coastal power walk, the clouds have lifted and it's a bright gem of a day.

She stops at the mailboxes. Buried amid the flyers and catalogues, she finds a handwritten letter addressed to her in the most beautiful copperplate. On the back, she's delighted to see a smiley face alerting her to the sender.

In a flash, she's inside her apartment, tearing at the envelope and reading the first line. She can't help spontaneously waving it about with excitement, letting out a huge sigh. Reading further, it's so heartfelt, tears spring to her eyes. William is openly sharing his feelings about his plans for their future and declaration of everlasting love. Her heart skips a beat. *I love this man so much.*

Her first impulse is to call, but instead she decides to text a simple message thanking him for the touching letter.

As she's texting, he calls. 'You got the letter!'

'Yes, I was just texting you.' The love she feels wells inside beyond anything she's ever known.

'Please try to stay calm,' he says.

'William, I can't see why your father isn't fast-tracking this. He has his people.'

'Trust me, he's on it, but we have to be careful it doesn't leak to the press.'

'William, remember we shouldn't even be talking on the phone.'

'Yes, I know – but I have to see you.'

Telling her he's at a loss without her, William suggests she heads up to Whale Beach so they can discuss things face to face.

His irresistible offer releases the tension in her body and she agrees to drive up a bit later.

'If you leave by four, you'll miss the school zones and the peak hour rush.' He also stresses to be vigilant she's not followed.

'Will do. See you soon.'

'Looking forward to it. Oh, and when you get to the house, be careful of the next-door neighbours. God forbid, don't engage in conversation with them.'

Hugging the coastline, Barrenjoey Road draws Vanessa on. Her blood shot eyes dart back and forth from the rear-view mirror to the side mirrors, considering what will happen when she gets there. *Is it possible to love someone so completely, you're prepared to take on the world? When it comes to loving William, I would seriously reconsider my fundamental beliefs.*

Her heart begins to race as she navigates along the final stretch into Whale Beach. At the top of the cliff, she takes the hairpin turn to the left and catches a glimpse of the house.

Don't engage with the neighbours. Mm, I'm keen to hear the full story about that pair. She pulls up the distinctive driveway, pleased the gates are already open. *William's world is so seductive; this whole situation seems surreal: this magnificent home, this incredible view, this wonderful man. Dreamlike.*

After checking her lip gloss, she turns off her car, then looks to see if anyone is about. Grabbing her overnight bag from the back seat, she slides out and locks the door. With insomnia her new best friend, she stumbles on the entrance stairs. Gripping the handrail, she realises the door is slightly ajar. Stepping inside, she lets the door shift back softly on its return as William comes rushing into view from the terrace, fussing nervously with the buckle of his belt. *He looks like he's just stepped out of a Ralph Lauren photo shoot.*

Vanessa knows the pressure is showing on her face, but at this moment she is succumbing to euphoria, giving him a grin as she approaches.

Holding her overnight bag in front of her with both hands, she stops for a second, catching her breath. Her much-vaunted shyness evaporates completely. 'Nice.' She looks down at his feet, admiring his brown croc-skin boots as a means of easing the tension.

'Nice dress,' he says, yearning to embrace her.

The dress fits snugly, and with no bra on, she's acutely aware her nipples are showing through the fabric. 'Yes. My boyfriend bought it for me in Bali.' She drops the bag at her feet.

He immediately closes the scant space between them, pressing to her and hugging so tightly she thinks she might stop breathing. 'How are you, sweetheart?'

'I'm okay. You?'

'Missed you,' he says, not wanting to let go.

'Missed you too, baby.'

'I love you so much, Vanessa.'

Knowing he still cares gives her an enormous sense of relief. 'I love you too, William. But I have to say it feels weird being here, considering what we've been through.'

His smile is filled with sadness. 'I get that.' He tilts her head with a gentle finger and kisses her long and hard with such desire, she feels her knees give way. William reluctantly releases his grip and hands her a glass of wine. 'Here; I thought you'd be needing this.'

'Do I ever.'

'No hiccups on the way down?'

'None. Oh, William I need to feel you.'

'Mm. I'm hearing you.'

Knowing she's a sensual woman and deserves to have all her needs met, he picks up her bag and leads the way.

'Shall I bring the wine?'.

'Yes.'

Upstairs, William pushes the bedroom door open with his boot and drops her bag just inside. She sets the wine down on the bedside table. Standing close at the end of the bed, she smells the delicate aroma of his fever.

He leans in, burying his face into her neck and whispers, 'I am going to make love to you all afternoon.' He brushes his mouth gently to hers, causing her skin to goose up. 'Kiss me, darling, kiss me.' He presses his mouth to hers, exploring tenderly as if searching for the first time.

She's aware of his body, long and hard against her, and imagines his hips moving with hers rhythmically.

Almost swaying, he slowly peels off her dress to reveal her ivory panties. 'Beautiful.' Guiding her down onto the bed, he kneels next to her. Her feverish breath quickens, giving off a weak moan as he runs a nurturing hand across her décolletage, never shifting his gaze. Her nipples tighten as he takes his time to tenderly explore the curves of her body. 'I need you.'

'Do you?' She looks at him longingly.

He knows her play and hastens to stand, kicking off his boots, pulling his shirt over his head in haste, then ripping off his jeans. Naked, he stands at the end of the bed. 'My life centres around you for the rest of my life.'

He's gorgeous!

Lying down, he whispers in her ear, 'But first I need to pleasure you.' Leaning into her body, he buries his nose in the soft, fragrant silk of her hair, stroking it gently. 'You're mine. Do you hear me? Mine.'

The command in his voice sends shivers throughout her body and she waits in anticipation for him to kiss her again.

Their mouths mesh, not in slow seduction, but desperate hunger, before he kisses a path along her jawline to her neck and sweeps a gentle hand across her pelvis, feeling her warmth through the softness of the silk. Knowing exactly what she wants, he moves down her body, admiring her form. Reaching her slender thighs, he stops.

'Oh, William,' she groans.

'Shh! Let me love you, my darling.' He slowly peels off her panties and gently parts her legs. In the intimacy of her body, he delicately tastes at her desire.

She closes her eyes, lost in the sensation. Catching her breath, her body arches into him and gently rocks. Hearing him moan, she reaches down, the tip of her nails on his back as sounds of muted pleasure hang in the air. She whimpers, 'Oh, God!' Gazing up at her face, she's a vision of ecstasy as her moisture pools.

Tasting her deeply, his mouth fills.

'I need to feel you, William,' she says, looking down at him. Her eyes are lit with fire as longing fills her heart. *I've waited a lifetime for this man.* Her urgent hands pull him towards her, feeling him travel patiently up the line of her body.

Feeling the softness of her skin, he's hard and wanting, but he tempers his lust, fixing his gaze on her eyes and satiating himself with her scent.

Perplexed by the urgency in her eyes, he plans to treat her tenderly and go slow. Holding his gaze, he gradually runs his index finger down the bridge of her nose to the tip, before kissing it. Then he reaches down between their bodies, positions himself and presses into her slowly.

When William starts to move, she holds him tight and whispers, 'Don't be gentle.'

In a tone vibrating with emotion, he tells her, 'You're mine, every bit of you. You're mine.' His promise resonates with love.

Her inner thighs squeeze him tightly and their rhythm meshes: her breath laboured, his deep and slow.

Arms wrapped around him, her sex clenched firmly around his erection, she presses a kiss to his shoulder and hugs him to herself.

Feeling her fervour, his lovemaking becomes more urgent.

She lets out a long, desperate cry of passion. 'Show me I matter.'

He muffles her cries with a gentle hand as his eyes rake her form, lusting after her love.

She pushes up into him. 'Oh, God!' she gasps.

Driven by their need, he starts to ride her harder, faster, deeper. Her heart is throbbing. His breath heavy. Their love endless. She stiffens beneath him and his legs lock, tipping his head back for a moment, allowing the climax to roll through their bodies, every moan echoing desire, sending him crazy.

He catches his breath, and she feels every inch of him vibrate and shudder to almost a stop, her limbs slipping away from his body. Hushed, he places his head on her heart for the longest moment, relishing her comforting breasts and listening to her breathe.

Audibly breathing in rhythm with her, he shifts his body, a tender smile already in place. He lies alongside her and scoops her up into the warmth of his arms. 'I love you, Vanessa, with every fibre of my being.'

Locked in his embrace, loving his masculine scent, she's never known a man to hold her the way he does. *Never!* She feels a tear on her face as he clings to her. She lies there, awake while he sleeps, thinking about how much she loves him and how unfair life can be at times. They could have such a wonderful life together, but right now they are being tested.

Catching his breath, he rolls onto his back and turns toward her. Reaching across, he gently strokes her hair, then kisses her shoulder.

'You were really out to it.' She's watched him sleep for 20 minutes.

He yawns and grows serious. 'It's important that you know we will sort this out, one way or another.'

One way or another. She feels abandoned by his words. 'Yes, it has to be sorted.'

'Baby, don't look so miserable.'

'I can't help feel sad for us,' she murmurs. Her eyes begin to water with emotion.

William leans across and gently kisses away the tears. Tilting her chin, he says, 'Don't cry, baby. All you have to do is keep your chin up.'

In a way, she is glad she's able to cry because she hasn't for the longest time, until William made her feel safe enough to do so. He has gifted her that much.

'It will all work out, I promise.' He looks longingly into her eyes, searching.

Vanessa gently strokes his jaw line, concerned by the dark circles under his eyes. 'Darling, you look exhausted.'

'I know. This is unknown territory for me, Vanessa. I've never been faced with anything quite like this before.'

'None of us have. And me being here isn't good either. Your grandfather would have a fit if he were to find out.'

'He knows.'

'He does?' She frowns, her heart racing.

'Yes, he knows, but he's the only one who does. Look, he's not stupid, Vanessa. He understands fully. I'm certain he knows more than he's letting on. He even gave me his blessing. Besides I needed to see you myself to make sure you were okay. I can't risk losing you. I've only just found you.'

'You won't lose me, William.'

'Good.'

'What do you mean, he knows more than he's letting on? What else did he say?'

'Can't quite put my finger on it. But he did say as long as we were discreet, and until we have proof to the contrary, he totally understands my need to see you.'

'He is such a remarkable man.'

'Look, he is such a by-the-book-type of guy, there's no way he'd be okay with us seeing one another if he thought otherwise.'

Noticing Vanessa's hair has dried in a snarl beneath, William attempts to shift it from the nape of her neck.

As he leans across, she spots his birthmark again. *I need to tell him. Say it, goddamn it!* But she simply can't bring herself to speak of Monica. Instead, she shifts her focus to the birthmark itself, as a means of deflective safety.

Other than knowing her sister hated hers, the significance of birthmarks never really concerned Vanessa until recently, when she decided to investigate, only to discover they're simply blemishes on the skin. There are two types; vascular, which are red, pink, or purple, and not hereditary, or pigmented, which are usually brown like William's.

She was also surprised to find a spin of folklore:

According to legend in Spain, Italy, and some Arabic countries, birthmarks are caused by the unsatisfied wishes of the mother during pregnancy and mean wishes or whims. *I wouldn't dare tell William, given his fragility about his mother.*

'Vanessa, I promise to never do anything to hurt or imperil your relationship with your mother, but I simply cannot understand why you are delaying in talking to her.'

'I know, I know, but you don't know my mother, and trust me, it's just easier to get a DNA test.'

'Okay. Well, I'm sure you have your reasons,' he says, bewildered.

'We need to get this thing resolved sooner, rather than later, so we can get on with our lives,' he says.

Speak up and tell him about the birthmarks. Instead, she changes tack. 'Years ago, I saw a documentary on how it goes against human nature to be attracted to a close relative, like a sibling or a child. Apparently, we're genetically coded not be sexually attracted to one another because our scent is nature's deterrent.'

'Fascinating, considering that was the first thing that drew us to one another – and your extraordinary beauty, of course.'

'I'm serious, William. We need to look into this further.' She's, a tad perplexed by his flippancy.

As the day draws to a close, they're not in any great hurry to move, and are still relaxing on the bed, looking out at the endless sky as it fades into a beautiful, soft pastel sunset.

'Isn't that stunning,' he says.

'Incredible!'

'Come on, let's get something to eat. I'm starving.' He jumps up and grabs a couple of bathrobes.

'I'm loving the 'W' on these robes, by the way.' Vanessa looks down at the pocket, then clasps his hand as they head down the stairs.

'It's not what you think.' He's slightly embarrassed.

'What?' she teases.

'My father bought them when he was staying at the W hotel.'

'Yeah, yeah. Blame Daddy.'

He laughs at her sarcasm and switches on the kitchen lights.

William happily sets about prepping dinner while she races back upstairs to grab her laptop from her overnight bag.

When she returns, William gives her a questioning look.

'What?'

'Nothing.' He shakes his head as she sits on a stool at the bench and connects to the internet.

'Darling, I forgot to ask. Did you see the neighbours on the way in?'

'No, darling, I didn't. What is it with those people? You've got me so curious. Do tell.'

'They're pains in the butt.'

'But why?'

'It's a little questionable when every time me or my father end up in a tabloid, that ugly lump of a man isn't far away.'

She cringes.

'Which is on a regular basis.'

Palms open, she says, 'Precisely. Will, he's your neighbour.'

William ignores her sense of logic. 'Dad has this theory.'

'Oh?'

'Yes, Mauri used to work at Consolidated Press as a journalist and we're sure he still has contacts there, so for a kickback, he fills them in on our movements.'

'That's being paranoid.'

'Maybe?' He shrugs, observing her looking down at the computer screen.

Vanessa suddenly looks up. 'William, I've found it. According to New Scientist magazine: "disliking the smell of close family might be part of the mechanism that helps prevent incest." I knew it. This proves it, William. We couldn't possibly be related. Nature simply wouldn't let it happen.'

The look on his face makes her feel she's starting to sound somewhat bonkers, but she can't help looking back down at the screen:

'"Particularly notable is the fact that opposite-sex siblings dislike each other's smell, while same sex siblings do not."'

'Really!' he says, now seemingly interested. William places the paring knife down on the cooktop and walks around the bench with a glass of wine, placing it in front of her. He kisses the top of her head as a measure of calming her.

'Come on, William, I need you to be serious.'

'I'm going to make fish and chips. Are you okay with that?'

'Yes.'

She feels his weight as he leans over her shoulder, focusing on the details on the screen. He's so near, she feels the tickle of his skin and hears him sigh before spinning her around on the stool and making direct eye-contact.

'Look, Vanessa, while this is all very interesting, I'm afraid it doesn't prove a thing. We still need solid DNA proof, like bloody blood samples and blooming hair samples. We need to be tested.'

'William, I'm booked in to see the doctor the day after tomorrow.'

'Good. If it turns out we aren't siblings, and Gramps certainly doesn't think we are, then we'll be able to spend the rest of our lives together.'

His words resonate.

'Vanessa, this is the first time I've ever felt true love and I will not lose you.'

Unexpectedly, there's an almighty crash outside. William looks around, puzzled, and heads out to see what's happened. There's nothing on the terrace. On a hunch, William walks across to the dividing wall and peers over to see Mauri on the ground, with his slumpy wife alongside him, and the ladder strewn across the lawn.

'You right there, Mauri?' William calls, trying to disguise his hilarity.

Arms and fat flaying everywhere. 'Yes, yes, sorry to disturb you, Will. Just trying to fix something here,' Mauri snorts.

'As long as you guys are okay.' William waves a nonchalant hand in the air, heads back inside and pushes a switch, turning on all the surrounding mood lights.

'What happened?' Vanessa asks.

'Those bloody idiots next door obviously trying to peep over the fence and Mauri fell off his perch.'

'Are they alright?'

'Yes. Just a couple of bruised egos.' He tends to dinner again.

She laughs and decides to shut the computer off.

'Hey, you were going to enlighten me about my painting,' he says, genuinely interested.

'Well,' she takes a sip of wine, 'Lempicka was a Polish painter who lived most of her adult life working between France and the U.S.'

'When I bought her, I was provided a detailed account of the work, but seeing you're so interested, tell me something I might not know.'

'Did you know she was married in St Petersburg?'

'No.' He looks up from the potato he's peeling.

'I would have to say her most famous painting is another self-portrait, "Tamara in a Green Bugatti", circa 1929.'

'You really are into this artist.' He dips the fish in the batter, with a knowing grin.

'My all-time favourite.'

'This is "Portrait de Marjorie Ferry". 1930, I think.'

'1932, to be exact.'

'And not to be mistaken with dear old Marj next door,' he says, looking out to the fence line.

'Trust me, she's no "dear".' Vanessa knew he must have paid millions for the painting but wouldn't dare ask such a question. *Sydney gallery owner Tim Olsen said, 'Being wealthy is not always a passport to buying whatever you like when it comes to high-end art, unless you are prepared to pay well above the market price.'*

'So, who did Marjorie marry?' He looks up from the pan.

The sizzle of the oil requires Vanessa to elevate her voice. 'William, you need to know these things.'

'Why, when I have you?'

'Boy! That looks good, but fattening.' She eyes the contents of the pans.

'This is precisely why you need to stick around.' He takes the pan off the heat.

'So I can get fat?'

'No, so you can share your infinite knowledge.'

She laughs.

'Go on,' he says, genuinely interested.

'Marjorie Ferry was, in fact, an artist herself who married a wealthy financier, and he commissioned this painting to show off her large cabochon ring.'

'The one in the painting?'

'Yes.'

He plates up, then sprinkles sea salt over the food. 'Come on, let's eat.'

He carries the plates towards the deck. 'We can continue this outside.'

Having discussed the artist's many works over the finest bottle of Pouilly Fume, the rest of the conversation is light and laidback.

'Dinner was fabulous, William.'

'It's the first time I've ever cooked battered fish.'

'You could have fooled me; it was delicious.'

'Idea. Do you feel like having a spa?'

'Good idea. I'm really beat.'

'Well, I'm up for an early night, if you are?'

She grins. 'I've never known you to have an early night in the entire time I've known you.'

He winks.

For the rest of the evening, their time is spent laughing and sharing moments of great passion and eroticism, the distant roar of the surf finally serenading them off to an exhaustive sleep.

The next morning, William stirs, feeling the overwhelming need to make love to Vanessa before she leaves. Spooning her body, he presses himself close, his hand exploring her warm, silky skin, gently coaxing her from a deep sleep.

Feeling him near, ignites her with desirable pleasure.

'Vanessa, I need to love you, my darling.'

'Mm,' she murmurs, tilting slightly as a flutter of excitement and expectation races across her body. She reaches around and grips his muscular thigh, pulling him in closer. It's an unspoken desire they have, knowing when and how to touch one another. Loving the warmth of his body's closeness, she adores the way it curves with hers and feels him bury his face into the ridge of her shoulder, kissing the outline as he spoons her in the most intimate way.

With his breath warm on the nape of her neck, her breathing slowly meets his. 'Oh, William.'

'Yes, baby.' He turns her to face him.

When a slice of morning light filters through the edge of the drapes and she sees the want in his eyes, she gently kisses the outline of his lips. Her breasts beneath, cushioning him, she waits as he positions himself.

'I love your body. Sexy as hell,' he says, feeling between her legs, her moisture calling him in. His voice is raspy from sleep.

'Not yet.' She licks her lips and kisses until moisture pools on his tongue, driving him crazy. 'I love you, William Whittaker.'

In that moment, nothing was of any consequence. Vanessa knew where she belonged. Right here.

Cradled in his arms, he feels her reluctance to move and sensitively asks, 'Are you okay?'

'Yes, baby.'

'I know I will never love anyone else but you.' He smooths a strand of hair away from her face, saying it with such certainty, it makes her heart skip, and she knows then, nothing can ever tear them apart, not now, not ever.

After showering, the couple delight in cooking breakfast together. Vanessa makes coffee and tea, then preps the chives. Slicing the loaf of fresh, wholewheat bread, she pops it in the toaster before heating the stove.

A knob of butter in the pan melts slowly until it's frothy, while William, in direct contrast, frantically whisks the eggs.

'Hey, I'm glad you're not that brutal with me.' She touches his wrist to steady on.

With a saddened grin, he heeds her warning, then adds the diced herbs before pouring the beaten eggs into the pan.

'I'm really good at making scrambled eggs. Can I take over?' She eases the wooden spatula gently out of his hand.

'Sure.'

She loves cooking with him in the kitchen, but she is acutely aware he's feeling anxious today. Stirring slowly, circulating the eggs, she brings the mixture from the edges of the pan, while glancing at William hastily buttering the toast and placing a slice on each of the plates in readiness. *He's already showing signs of stress at the thought of us being separated.* 'Almost ready.' She tries to sound upbeat.

He doesn't answer.

'Silky and slightly runny.' She turns off the heat and spoons the eggs onto the toast.

They decide to keep it simple, staying inside and eating at the countertop. In a trance-like state, William puts the finishing touch with a sprinkling of black pepper.

'I'm going to head off soon if you don't mind?' She's aware of the uncomfortable silence that has descended upon them.

'Sure, honey. I need to get some work done as well.'

Vanessa starts to load the dishwasher, but William's quick to reach across. 'Leave it.'

'You sure?'

'Yes, absolutely. The cleaners are coming this morning. They'll be here in 20 minutes.'

'All the more reason I'm out of here.' Vanessa races upstairs, quickly gathers up her things and finishes dressing. She meets him downstairs.

William reluctantly takes her bag and walks her to the car. 'Drive carefully, baby. I'll call you later today. Are you right to get the car out?'

She feels his concern.

'Darling, I'm a big girl. I drove the car in, so I can certainly back it out.' She kisses his hand through the open window.

'Hey, buckle up.'

'I can't; it's broken.'

'Are you kidding me? You drove all the way here without a seatbelt?'

'Look, sometimes it works and sometimes it doesn't, but lately it's the latter,' she says sheepishly.

'Well, we need to get that fixed asap.'

She likes that he refers to them as "we" and touches his hand in acknowledgement. 'We will.'

'I'll get Phillip to book it in with Mercedes and he'll call you to arrange another car.'

'Okay, darling. Thank you.'

'You're a naughty girl.'

She winks. 'I know.'

He watches as she starts the car and manoeuvres down the steep drive. He's worried her face is a little bit lonely, a little bit lost. Waving her off, he knows he needs to fix a lot of things.

Heading down the stretch of road, Vanessa looks at the enormous homes on either side and can't help thinking some seem to be jutting out from the cliff face like human stickybeaks. Amid these spectacular homes is the odd beach bungalow from days of old, original residents who sought their patch of beachside bohemian heaven before the big money came flooding in.

She passes a small group of joyous teenagers waxing their surfboards on a vast stretch of perfectly manicured lawn, and warmly smiles. It reminds her of her uncle and his friends when she was a young teen.

A few metres down the road, she notices a young boy, then a woman and a man, walking at a distance from one another. The boy, about twelve, is carrying a surfboard under his arm and stops suddenly to look out at the wave sets. The woman continues walking about a dozen paces behind the man. Like the boy, she's wet and just come from the beach and her appearance, while stylish, is relaxed. The man, to the contrary, is dressed in clothes from the night before, his sandy feet bare and he's carrying his dress shoes. He stops and turns, alerted by the crunching sounds of gravel underfoot. He notices the woman, in a sheer, lemon sundress barely covering her damp, green bikini, and pauses to wait. They know one another.

You never know what goes on in other people's lives. Vanessa watches, curious as she drives past filled with all sorts of mixed thoughts, and wishes she could stay longer, causing her to feel especially lonely.

Out of nowhere, a shabby vehicle screams past and overtakes, tooting at the pedestrians and causing Vanessa to jump in her seat. It's loaded with surfboards and passengers, alerting her that she needs to concentrate on the journey ahead.

CHAPTER TWENTY-TWO

The second Vanessa closes the front door to her apartment, it feels like a warm blanket has been wrapped around her. She sets the car keys down and is surprised by a thick layer of dust that has settled on the surface of the console. *Time to clean house.*

Instead, she dumps her overnight bag in her room and decides to spend the day being kind to herself and doing what she loves best: write. *William calls it an obsession. I figure one person's obsession is another's devotion and given the last few days have been so tumultuous, it's important I knuckle down and regain my momentum.*

While waiting for the computer to reboot, she plugs her phone in and sits arched over her desk, drumming her fingers on the mouse pad in contemplation. Fingers poised at the keyboard, the screen lights up, but she just stares in disconnect before deciding to set down all the stuff she swore she'd never tell. A moment of dialogue and she's off and running:

> The self-loathing and insecurity I felt while waiting for
> test results …

Tapping away at her secrets, her words quickly string together: sounds, colours, smells, voices even. Biting down on her bottom lip, she rereads what she's written. *On second thoughts, too sad and way too messy.* She highlights a flurry of words, then deletes. She decides to attempt something of greater relevance, but after an hour or so, throws the towel in, admitting defeat. *Blocked! This is getting to be a habit. I'm just way too restless to concentrate, so this, my friend, is a complete waste of time.*

Being a voracious reader, she scans the bookcase in a desperate bid for something to facilitate her creativity. It's only mid-afternoon, but she climbs into bed anyway and revisits *Letters of Note*, never tiring of the fascinating stories contained within the Shaun Usher series, a thoughtful collection of letters written by some of the most influential, inspiring people of our time. Like Virginia Woolf's heartfelt suicide letter to her devoted husband, which sadly turned out to be her final piece of writing, expressing her love and gratitude for his patience towards her.

With a tear in her eye, she sets the heavy book down and tries to nap. *That bloody dog!*

'Nietzsche,' she hears the owner softly say, more like a token warning than a reprimand.

Who calls their schnoodle Nietzsche anyway? Must write a formal complaint to strata. That poor thing needs training.

Feeling edgy, she peels herself from the tangled sheets and grabs her travel diary. Sitting cross-legged on the floor, her back pressed firmly against the bedroom wall, she opens the book to face that audacious day.

— New Chapter in our Lives —
THE WEDDING

New chapter in our lives: more like the beginning of the end. At the time I had no idea how foolish I was to marry such a wickedly disturbed man.

Taormina

Monday 12th May

Following a delicious breakfast of eggs Benedict, we prepare for the ceremony. It is a stunning day and Mt Etna is so impressive, watching over us on our day of days.

Huh! Like the man I married: volatile!

Bruno goes on ahead to the town hall, and a few minutes out, I'm driven slowly through the streets of Taormina in a silver Mercedes decorated with a large silver bow on the bonnet. As tourists cheer and blow kisses of good will through the car windows, I feel like Lady Diana seated comfortably in the back, dressed in a slim-line cream Galliano gown with a few simple flowers in my hair.

Following the intimate ceremony, photographs are taken in and around the town square, and following much fanfare from onlookers, we return to the hotel for a wonderful lunch out on the terrace. We sip Veuve Clicquot in celebration whilst dining on lobster, prawns, and sea bass under the shade of an enormous cream-coloured umbrella, and make a toast to Mt. Etna, our only guest.

What was I thinking? I married into a family known for its secrecy: an organised crime syndicate, the Mafia.

Rubbing her tired eyes, she reflects on what she'd written, all those years ago, when her heart was full of love, dreams, and aspirations. Page after page of pseudo-happiness, as if looking for a hidden sign that may have prevented the tragedy that later befell her. Re-reading reminds her of the heavy heart that once penned these shallow words, keeping her company throughout a very lonely honeymoon. It had been her comfort then, and in some twisted sense of logic, she tries to seek its comfort now.

She decides to make a cup of tea and move back into her office. She sits at her desk and opts to fly through the pages of Sicily, stopping when she reaches London. As she skims the part where they hire another car, Robyn the Range Rover, she is reminded of Bruno's only redeeming feature, his sense of humour.

His mood could turn on a dime, and she remembers one evening, where they were clowning around discussing the way their dog, Bonnie, liked to slurp his water, then rest his snout on the edge of the bowl. In the background, the American sitcom *Sex and the City*, a program he believed undermined men, had come on the screen.

Wham! With the click of a finger, Bruno had snapped and threw her up against the wall to prove his point. A terrified Bonnie lifted his head from the bowl, visibly shaken.

'Boy, I'm so grateful that hellish existence is behind me,' she says aloud.

On the following page, she's reminded of happier times in the English countryside. First destination, the Queen's weekender, Windsor Castle, built by William the Conqueror in 1070.

We stop and have pies and peas in the local café, opposite Windsor Castle. I wonder if Queen Elizabeth ever walked the streets of her local village, so I ask the Cockney storekeeper, pouring gravy over my kidney pie.

I still remember that quirky little Pommy with his distinctive East Ender accent.

'Ur, luv, course. Use to see Mum aroun' 'ere a lot,' he says, sounding like Michael Caine, the Cockney who conquered the silver screen.

However, I have a sneaking suspicion he's been asked the same ridiculous question thousands of times and decided to tell 'the geezers' what they wanted to hear.

Good on him. What's life without a bloody good fairy tale.

On to Stonehenge, built 3000 B.C. The surrounding area is where Thomas Hardy wrote his masterpiece, *Tess of the D'Urbervilles*.

We arrive in Bath, having travelled across the Salisbury Plains and the beautiful Wiltshire countryside, and check into The Royal Crescent, hailed as the most majestic street in all of Britain. This graceful arc of 30 Georgian terraces was built in 1767, and one fine building is a hotel and our home for the next couple of days.

Our next leg of the journey is Cheddar Gorge to taste, you guessed it, CHEESE! Sadly, it's not to be. Bruno's mood changes again, and for no apparent reason other than he doesn't want to stop the car.

Following an hour of awkward silence, we arrive at Longleat House, circa 1568, where 900 acres of the 9,800-acre estate opened as a safari park in 1966. The clouds suddenly open and it's teeming as we enter the animal enclosure, but that doesn't stop a lion and lioness mating. 'Bravo!' Bruno says suddenly. and "out came the sunshine and dried up all the rain …" And just-like-that, Bruno's mood lifts and he starts communicating again. Go figure.

Then off to the Cotswolds, where we stay at the remarkable Buckland Manor, dated 600 A.D. The most amazing hotel experience of our trip. Following a hearty breakfast of Scottish porridge with The Famous Grouse Whisky, we set off on a cold countryside walk to the local village about an hour away. As a reward, we indulge in homemade apple pie and hot English tea.

Vanessa bounces the heels of her palms gently on her desk. 'Enough! This is a goddamn waste of time.' She throws her hands in the air in a gesture of surrender. 'That's it. I'm hungry.'

She decides to go out and get something sensational to eat. Dressed in a pair of faded jeans, fitted white t-shirt, and navy Vans, she ties her hair up in a simple ponytail. You'd be forgiven for mistaking her for being much younger than her years. She tucks some cash and her credit card into her back pocket and grabs her door keys. *Check phone, check sunnies.*

Outside, all is lively on the suburban, treelined street, the late afternoon sun greeting her as she makes her way to the nearby shops. Down one small laneway and out onto the main drag, she passes the local wooden flower barrow, its fanciful folk-art designs on the sides, and is reminded of how much she likes living in the area. Being able to get ice cream late at night and cinnamon buns early in the morning appeals to her whimsical side.

On an impulse, she checks her phone. *Nothing.*

Rounding the next corner, she hears 'Raaaaahhhhhh!' A cacophony of noise coming from the local day-care centre. A couple of smart-looking young mums emerge, chatting to one another, pushing prams with newborns, holding their boisterous kindy-age children's sandy hands.

Smiling, she escapes the noise by pushing open the door of La Bastide, her local French delicatessen. The bell over the entrance alerts the owner and she's immediately greeted by the irresistible smell of excess: mouldy cheeses, olives, salamis, and much, much more.

'*Bonjour,*' sings a fat, cheerful French woman dressed in a clean, white dust coat. The colourful poke of a rich, silky collar from beneath and the jangle of a Cartier Trinity bracelet, with matching ring on her fat pinky, reveal so much more about the woman.

'Bonjour,' Vanessa replies in her best attempt at French.

'Can I help you?' asks the woman huffily.

She hates not being able to speak French or Italian. *Right now, I wish I was fluent in French.* Vanessa gazes through the glass display. *Oh dear! Everything seems so essential, so delicious, so necessary.* Vanessa has no idea where to start, but doesn't dare move awkwardly, like the timid outsider alongside her.

Given it's for one, and evident the French woman has seen this expression of confusion before, the storekeeper decides to help. Fresh *foie gras*, a wheel of brie, cheddar cheese for sharpness, and at the woman's suggestion, one of France's oldest cheeses, *Fourme D'Ambert*, made from cows' milk. Without asking, the woman grabs a freshly baked breadstick from the back wall and places it on the countertop.

Vanessa looks at the refrigerator and taps her lips thoughtfully. *Ah, why not?* She reaches for a bottle of Sancerre, pays the woman, and with a smile, waits patiently for her change.

'Au revoir,' Vanessa says, thinking it's all a matter of attitude.

'Goodbye,' says the dour woman, turning to serve another.

Out on the street, Vanessa passes a teenager looking indistinguishable by gender, reminding her of the latest *Vogue* edition showcasing a transgender fashion spread. *A refreshing break from convention.*

Another pit-stop; she pops into her favourite florist, Mon Cherie's, where they have the most phenomenal heirloom roses. *Nature's little works of art.* She plucks a bunch from the bucket of water, and holding them to her nose, inhales their delicious scent.

A young, slender woman in a floral apron appears and takes the flowers, shaking free the water. 'Beautiful choice.' She flashes a sunny smile, grateful Vanessa recognises quality, rather than buying from her opposition. Vanessa likes that the florist wraps the roses in matching sangria tissue paper. She hands the woman a fifty dollar note and is surprised when she's handed back thirty.

'On special,' the woman says with a flirty grin.

'Thank you.' Vanessa feels herself blush.

Flattered, she turns to leave, stepping over a group of local kids playing hopscotch on the footpath. Their banter is in overdrive as they suck on enormous, sugary snakes dangling from their mouths, allowing their chalky hands to remain free. Vanessa smiles at their little mate, sitting kerbside in the gutter, desperately trying to finish his rainbow-coloured ice cream before the afternoon sun destroys what's left.

Last stop, she grabs the daily newspapers at the corner news stand. *My God! These stands are almost a thing of the past.*

Headed home, she peruses the hive of activity on the streets, basking in its public form of theatre, starting to feel a bit like her old self.

In stark contrast, on the street corner is a scruffy old man sitting on the pavement with his head tilted forward and a tattered hat at his feet, begging for donations. Vanessa places the thirty dollars she has in the hat and the man looks up unexpectedly, with pleading eyes, and thanks her. She can't help feeling the depth of his sadness and gives him a knowing smile of kindness. He ushers a forgotten grin, and she goes on her way.

When she gets back to her block, her rumbling belly sends her hastily up the stairs. *If I can't spend the afternoon with William, I'll do the next best thing and eat darn good food.*

Having poured a glass of wine, she sets out small portions of the delicious goodies onto a heavy stone platter, a treasured gift from her beloved grandmother. Quite by chance, she grabs a white linen napkin that reads: To Brie or Not to Brie, that is Not a Question.

Tucking a piece of the French stick under her arm, she chuckles at the irony and heads out to the terrace to sit in the late afternoon sun. Draping the napkin on her lap, she takes a sip of wine and studies the platter's spread. With her growling tummy telling her to hurry up, she delights in scooping up a runny lump of ripe, oozy brie and savours not only the flavour, but it's delicious texture on her tongue. 'Oh my God! This feels like a very grand thing to do indeed.' The blade cuts through a sliver of the *Fourme D'Ambert*, revealing the cream-coloured interior marked with plentiful blue veining. The texture is creamy and yielding on the tongue, and distinct notes of butter and cream complement the spicy mould. 'Mm! Delicious! Great suggestion.' She holds her glass up to the gods, tears at the bread, lathers a bite-size with a healthy serve of *foie gras* and takes another sip. *Ah! That's good.*

Vanessa sets her glass down and begins flicking through the newspaper, randomly turning the pages. Aware this is a momentary reprieve from her concerns, she's not surprised to find a photograph, William and her at the airport, in the social pages. *The tabloids are well and truly onto us now.* The caption reads: Author, Publisher cosy return.

And if that isn't enough, she reads the piece in the Guess Who Section: What famous female author has recently been spotted out and about, dining across broader Sydney *and* abroad, with her high-profile publisher?

People seem so preoccupied by us, but why? Whichever way you look at it, I guess I'm the author and he's the publisher. Her mobile suddenly jolts her out of the pages. 'Hello.'

'Vanessa, sorry to bother you, but it's Montgomery Whittaker, Will's father. Have you seen today's paper?'

I know who you are. She eyes the ring of the wine glass on the newspaper. 'Yes, I'm looking at them right now.'

'I don't want to alarm you, but the last thing we need is to be accused of nepotism.'

'I understand.'

'Good. Are we still on for our meeting tomorrow afternoon here at the office?'

'Yes, definitely.'

'I don't want to concern my son or my father any more than they already are, but would you mind coming in, say, half an hour earlier, so we can have a quiet chat beforehand? I have something I'd like to say to you in private.'

'Yes, of course.'

'Good.' He lingers. 'Look, I don't want to say too much on the telephone, but as time marches on, there are obvious questions surrounding your future with my son, and a lot needs to be discussed as to where you and he go from here.'

'Yes, of course.' She's annoyed by his patronising tone.

'I'm not certain you understand the seismic scale of this situation?'

There he goes again. She clears her throat.

'Are you okay?'

'I'm trying my best,' she says, exasperated. Monica's name still doesn't make it from her lips.

'Good girl. See you in my office tomorrow then – at two.' He hangs up.

Good girl! There's nothing I hate more. Frustrated, she leaps to her feet, tosses the newspapers into the outside bin, and glances at her watch. *So much for relaxing. Less than twenty-four hours before I've got to face him.*

With one foot at the heel of the other, she kicks off her Vans, walks barefoot into the kitchen, and places the wine in the fridge. *Right now, feeling intoxicated is the last thing I need.*

She sets about putting the flowers in a vase alongside Monica's photograph. With a rush of melancholy, she tears up. *It's time to face this thing head on and get to a therapist. Darling heart, I've finally found the man of my dreams, but it is the most dreadful mess.* Staring at Monica's picture, she's truly concerned about her being the missing link. 'Please help me!'

Monica's innocent young face, aged ten, stares back. Vanessa has the queerest feeling in the pit of her stomach that her sister has deliberately drawn her to the photograph. 'But why?' The landline's strident ring. She's in no mood to chat and lets it go through to message.

'Monica, I mean Vanessa, Mum here. Can you call me back asap. I have barely any ...' Her voice trails off with concern, followed by a loud click. Gone.

It's time to get back to work. She ignores the call. Opening a file on her computer, a brainstorming session ensues. Vanessa taps away at the manuscript, making relevant changes enthusiastically.

CHAPTER TWENTY-THREE

Stepping onto the busy street, Vanessa's unexpectedly distracted by the splat of plump raindrops on her silk blouse, signalling a late summer storm is barrelling through. *The humidity is unbearable.* She reacts swiftly to a middle-aged man thoughtlessly shaking his umbrella beside her, as he steps inside the building. *Some people are so totally unaware.*

Hurrying back to her car, she braces into the wind, manically juggling her leather tote, struggling to control her own umbrella. Vanessa flinches as footsteps pound behind her, relieved to see two young, carefree lovers, swinging their hands and giggling, as they run through the rain. Another pedestrian thuds past and steps off into the gutter, splashing her trousers, leaving a Jackson Pollock-like splatter on her cream pants. *Boy, it's not my day.*

Having spent an emotional hour alone with Montgomery, Vanessa couldn't help feeling worked over as he managed to control the entire meeting by homing in on the crucial problem at hand. At times he even sounded cold, almost hostile, but she recognised his fear.

William had rung to say he and his grandfather were detained across town at a business meeting but promised to call the moment they were done. They never showed.

As if her own uneasiness in the presence of Montgomery wasn't enough to deal with, she was subjected to matters relating to his affair with her mother. Without William's support, going over minute details had been quite difficult while still hoping Monty might shine some light on the situation. Instead, she's come away feeling exhausted. *Whilst Monty has many redeeming features, tact is not one of them. However, I can see why Mother was attracted to him.* Though awkward, he had pushed the point Vanessa speak to her mother and organise to meet with him asap. *I'll call her as soon as I get home.*

Out of the rain and in the safety of her car, Vanessa breathes a sigh of relief. She decides to call Francesca and confirm she's on track to pick her up around half-six, the plan being they go to the hospital to visit Georgia, who's just had surgery that morning.

The rain begins noisily pelting down on the roof of the car with a steady and consistent beat, making it hard to be heard. *I hope it doesn't hail; I need to get this baby home.*

Vanessa fires up the engine and tries buckling up, but again the locking clip won't engage. Frustrated, she makes two more attempts, before giving up, putting the car into gear, and pulling away from the kerb. Looking down at the dash, she has no idea how she's managed to put over 3000 km on the odometer since she bought it. *This baby rarely leaves the garage.*

Turning left onto the main drag, Vanessa sees the traffic lights turning amber, but certain she'll make it before they change to red, she speeds up.

Suddenly she hears the horrifying screech of brakes and the crude blast of an air horn. She looks to her right to see a B-Double truck, an enormous black beast, hurtling towards her. Her eyes lock with the truckie's. Her heart rate soars and defensive hormones surge into her bloodstream as the driver tries desperately to bring his rig to a halt. Under the weight of his load, the brakes lock, causing the truck to skid. To a chorus of angry horns, Vanessa screws her eyes shut, expecting the worst. Time is suspended as she waits for the impact of pain and oblivion.

Boom!

On the street, all eyes look up at the truck as it clips the rear end of the driver's side of the Mercedes, watching it spin precariously out of control on the slippery road and head rapidly towards a telegraph pole on the adjacent footpath. People are screaming and running in all directions.

Bang!

In a millisecond, it's over. To the passers-by scurrying for shelter, the scene is spectacular. It's like a bomb exploding. Startled by what they see, a loaded truck colliding with a vintage sports car, people look about frantically, checking for carnage.

Miraculously, no pedestrians are hurt. Shocked, they look to the wreckage. Dropping their umbrellas, individuals scramble to help. Others gather, transfixed, in the blinding rain.

Vanessa watches in horror as a man tries to yank open the door of her twisted wreck. *I know this feeling.* The life force begins to drain from her body.

Having come to an abrupt halt, the truck driver instinctively dials 000, simultaneously trying to release his seatbelt. It's locked. He's trapped, but his gaze never leaves Vanessa, watching as she loses consciousness and slumps in her seat. Her body goes limp. 'Help! Please help her,' he shouts desperately.

Vanessa is trapped. She's unconscious and the only thing the drenched onlookers can do is wait for emergency services.

One uniformed woman, a nurse just off shift, steps from behind the crowd, races to the car, and through the shattered window, feels for a wrist pulse but is unable to find one. Focused, the woman then places her index and middle fingers on Vanessa's carotid pulse, just below the angle of her jaw. She presses firmly. The clock is ticking. She feels a pulse and screams, 'She's alive!'

Suddenly they hear the sirens in the distance; emergency services are close. 'They're coming!' shouts a concerned man.

Vehicles arrive at the scene and sirens are switched off as emergency workers alight and jump into action. Onlookers move back slowly as police cordon off the area and fire fighters check for any vehicle fires, gas leaks or hazardous materials, exposed electricals or arcing of wires.

While a paramedic secures Vanessa's neck with a rigid cervical collar, another puts an IV cannula into the vein of her arm. Once she's stable, firefighters use the Jaws of Life to remove the door of the car. It takes only two minutes. Unaware of a pre-existing spinal fracture, paramedics know to assume the worst, the possibility of spinal injury from the impact. Taking extreme care to maintain alignment of her head, neck and spine, paramedics finally slide her out of the motor vehicle using a long spine board. They then secure her on a spinal fracture board and firmly strap her in for transit. A paramedic jumps in the back before closing the doors. He'll monitor her vitals while in transit.

By this time, the truck driver is freed from the wreckage and seems fine, but two paramedics place him in another ambulance and take him to the hospital for routine checks. There is much chat among the crowd as they begin to slowly disperse while firefighters and tow truck drivers go about sorting the wreckages.

En route, an officer calls the hospital's Emergency Department on the designated phone number. Staff are told the patient is a thirty to thirty-five-year-old female with superficial lacerations to her face and body, unconscious, with possible spinal injuries. Medics are given an ETA. A hospital team of on-call surgeons, anaesthetists, and radiologists immediately kick into gear.

On arrival, Vanessa is conscious. Cradled in agony, she fights back emotion and tries to dumb it down as best she can, only complaining of numbness in her legs. The paramedics give the handover to doctors in charge and a lumbar MRI scan is ordered.

'No, no, no,' Vanessa struggles to tell them through a haze of pain. 'I have metal rods and screws in my back, L1.'

Staff look at one another and a CT scan of her back is ordered immediately. The scan reveals not only the existing metal rods and screws, but significant swelling around the spinal cord. Thankfully no damage. Vanessa also has whiplash.

Vanessa opens her eyes to the sound of heavy rain. Her head is restricted by the neck brace, so she moves her eyes to her right, discovering her mother is standing at her bedside.

'Where ... am ... I?' Vanessa asks, terrified.

'You're in the hospital. You've been in an accident, sweetheart, a car accident.' Diana tries to hold back her welling tears, stroking her daughter's head gently.

Vanessa's face hurts and her body feels like it's been thrown against a wall, but she's alive. Suddenly she remembers her car being catapulted like a torpedo through the air, only stopping when it met with a telegraph pole. The car almost snapped in two and the detachable roof popped off on impact. Being an old car, it didn't have airbags, and with a dodgy seat belt, Vanessa took the brunt of the collision when she met the pole on impact.

'Where's …?' Vanessa struggles to say William's name, not realising he's sound asleep on a chair off to the side in a darkened corner of the room.

Diana strokes Vanessa's head. 'Please, honey, you need your rest.'

Heavily sedated, she drifts off to sleep again.

William stirs and strives to get his bearings but doesn't get to his feet in time.

Having barely left her side, he looks exhausted. On the day of the accident, William and his grandfather had left their meeting later than expected, William making numerous attempts to get hold of Vanessa to no avail.

When he got back to the office, he saw a report on the early evening news of a horrendous car crash not far from the publishing house. Recognising Vanessa's car, he immediately raced to the emergency room and was taken up to the ward.

Staff asked if he was a relative, but he chose to keep facts to a minimum, saying they were close friends.

The following day Diana landed back in Sydney, oblivious to what had transpired. She waited at the carousel for her luggage and switched on her mobile while simultaneously looking up at the airport news monitor. Straightaway she recognised Vanessa's car on the screen to the sound effect of her phone repeatedly pinging in her hand. The bottom of the monitor read: Famous author in hospital fighting for her life after horrendous car accident.

Shocked, she looked down at her lone bag on the carousel, immediately grabbed it, and rushed out to a waiting taxi. At the hospital, she was greeted by William. At first, she had no idea who he was. However, nothing could have prepared her for seeing Whit shortly afterwards, walking through the doors of the hospital pushing old man Thornton.

In the past, she and Thornton had come to blows on more than one occasion and Diana was acutely aware she wasn't thought of in glowing terms. None of this mattered though; her daughter's wellbeing was paramount.

They were interrupted by Vanessa's long-time surgeon, Dr John Stokes. 'She's very lucky, Diana.' He explained the CT scan of her back revealed the numbness in the legs was due to swelling around the spinal cord, but miraculously there was no permanent damage. 'There's nerve pressure, so she's going to need plenty of bed rest and cold compresses to reduce swelling. We may also use heat to help loosen the stiffness and sore muscles. We must avoid overheating numb legs and feet, as too much can exacerbate the inflammation.'

'Oh dear.' Diana held her hand to her chest.

'Look, don't worry, her stats are good, and in time, things will settle, and she'll be back to normal. But we'll need to keep her in hospital for observation.'

'When can she go home, Doctor?'

'One day at a time, Diana. For now, she still needs daily neurological checks and physio.'

'What about the whiplash?'

'She'll have to wear the neck brace for a few weeks.'

The following day, Diana and the Whittaker men are at the hospital in a nearby waiting room, seated together in a semi-circle, when Thornton decides to address the elephant in the room.

'Vanessa's not Monty's daughter, is she?'

There is a pause and Diana hangs her head. The stillness in the room is felt by everyone. 'No, she's not,' Diana says, looking up, forced to admit her failings.

William lets out an exhaustive sigh, relieved by the knowledge that Vanessa can't possibly be his sister, rather than concern at her mother's deceit.

Thornton listens as Diana turns to Whit and explains through her tears. Her voice starts at the back of her knees and reaches above her head. 'Our daughter is dead.'

Shocked, he sits silent, grappling with what she is saying.

'She died tragically in Bali, thirty years ago. We were headed to the beach, our scooter was sideswiped by an oncoming car, and she was killed instantly.'

'What?' Monty screws his face up, barely able to believe his ears.

She watches his eyes widen.

'How old was she?'

'10.'

Thornton says nothing, instead choosing to watch the conversation unfold.

'Diana, there are some serious questions about timelines here,' Monty says.

'No, there's not. The girls were born ten months apart.'

'Christ!' Diana's years of deceit are finally revealed. 'Diana, why would you live with such a dreadful secret – and for so long?'

She shakes her head sadly.

William is up and pacing the floor with a gamut of emotions: relief, anger, happiness.

'Please help me understand,' Monty says, staring at her in shock as she begins to cry.

'Because I love you so much, I couldn't let go,' she says, starting to sob.

He waves an impatient hand in the air, wanting this to all go away. 'That doesn't make sense. None of this makes sense. Why?'

'Truly I didn't,' she whispers.

'Truly you didn't what?' Monty asks, frustrated.

'Want to hurt you.' She looks pleadingly into his eyes.

Decades had passed since Monty left Diana and returned to his wife Jacqueline. Tragically, Diana was left to rein in her passion. Over the years, only small parts of her true self were revealed to the outside world. It had been a matter of survival, not selfishness.

'Why, Diana? Why didn't you tell me she died?'

'I Know. I know. I know. There's a lot of things I should have done.' She is up and pacing around in circles as William sits back down.

With scrambled thoughts, Monty steps across to the window and looks out.

'What sort of mother does that?' he says, turning back and rubbing his brow.

Diana tries to approach, but he steps back.

In disbelief, William watches the woman who had been his father's mistress, the woman he'd heard snippets of throughout his entire life. The woman who'd crushed his mother's spirit and caused so much misery. He is also acutely aware his father has never stopped loving her. 'What a mess!'. With an overwhelming need to get some fresh air, William walks out of the room to gather his thoughts.

Thornton chooses to stay.

'Losing you left such a void in my life,' Diana says, pleading with Monty. 'Whit, I still break down often and cry for the loss of our daughter. That always brings me full circle, back to the love we shared, and the reason Monica came into this world.'

'Christ!' He places both hands over his eyes.

Diana remembers Whit freaking out when she told him she was pregnant, and he still returned to Sydney, leaving her to go it alone, stricken with grief.

'I had a one-night stand not long after Monica was born and found myself pregnant again. Suddenly I had become responsible for two tiny humans, so I had to use the child support you sent each month for both my babies.'

Listening to how hard it must have been, Monty chokes back tears.

'By the time Monica died, well, I hadn't spoken to you for years, and aside from needing the money, in some twisted, fucked-up way, it kept me connected to you. As crazy as it sounds, I always hoped you would come back to me.'

'That's insane, Diana. You could argue, rightly, that ...' Monty is suddenly lost for words, shaking his head, clearing his throat.

'Please don't take Vanessa's trust away from me, Whit. You must make her understand, I'm begging you. I have nothing left.'

Silenced by her plea, there is no doubting the love he still feels for this woman, but to have kept his own daughter's death from him is inexplicable.

Seeing the pain cross his face, Diana's reaches for Monty, but he refuses and heads out through the open door.

Thornton sits in disbelief at the lengths this woman has gone to. 'My dear, secrets are like callouses on your heart. Lies are hard. You tell enough of them, soon your heart is numbed.' He watches her shrink into a chair. Still, Thornton's misjudged metaphor gives her the inner strength to gain moral high ground, and with clarifying certainty, Diana realises she doesn't owe this man anything.

Monty and William return twenty minutes later to see Diana and Thornton engaged in conversation with two of Vanessa's specialists.

When the doctors leave, William asks if there are any updates.

'No, not really. She's doing really well,' Diana says.

'Well, that's good news.'

'Yes, it is.'

Monty asks Diana to step out of the room for a minute.

'Dad, can I have a word first?'

'Sure, son.' Monty looks to Diana. 'Give me a minute. I'll meet you outside.'

When she leaves, Monty asks, 'What's up?'

'Dad, this woman clearly loves you. You have to realise she's not a person that's been shielded from life's hardships. She's had to face them head on, in all manner of ways. Don't go it alone because of some misguided perception of the woman you love.'

'In other words, don't screw this up.'

'Precisely. I've grown up watching your eyes searching for her everywhere. You must sort this thing out, once and for all. Only then will you recognise you have more in common than what divides you. She's here now, so don't blow it.'

'I hear you, son, I hear you.'

Monty pats his son on the back and heads outside to join Diana. Walking through the automatic glass doors, he spots her straight away. 'Let's sit over here.' He points in the direction of a lone bench.

Diana senses his mood has changed, a calm almost, and she is somewhat relieved.

They sit close.

'Jesus, Diana, what a mess we've made of this,' he says ruefully.

Too nervous to speak, she keeps her gaze downward.

'We're the only two people out here on this bench and you can't meet my eyes?' Monty says in frustration.

'I can't.'

'You have to. Do you know what my son just said to me?'

Diana shakes her head.

'He said, "Dad, you've never stopped loving this woman."'

She looks up. Diana places a gentle hand in his, grateful when he squeezes back. 'He's a smart boy, that William.'

'Yes, he is.'

She holds his gaze in thoughtful silence.

Monty looks at the woman he's loved for as long as he can remember. Even under the fine beauty lines, she is the same woman he met on that Balinese beach forty years ago.

'Whit, you must remember the love we shared?'

'Of course, I do,' he says, clearing the lump in his throat, 'but at the time, I simply wanted to immerse myself in the love affair and didn't really consider the repercussions.'

'Neither of us did. It was like an unstoppable wave.'

He squeezes her hand. 'Please believe you have never been far from my thoughts.'

Diana is certain he is speaking the truth, but she is also aware nothing will make up for the lost time and distance that has separated them.

Monty remembers how he felt when he first laid eyes on Diana. He watched as she stepped out of the surf, squinting her eyes and shaking water from her long, dark tresses. Realising she hadn't noticed him; he decided to stand next to her by the water's edge and chat.

'Do you remember what I said to you the first day we met?' he asks in a much softer tone. 'You were so reserved, to the point of shyness. I told you what a beautiful woman you were. I knew you hadn't grasped what I said, but I was so keen to take you out. I summoned the courage to ask you to dinner and everything after that was in fast forward. Our first date, I was feeling things I'd never felt before, and it was reinforced by the love you showed me over the ensuing weeks and months.'

After a few dates, Diana considered them a couple and soon fell pregnant. A terrified Monty returned to his wife and young son waiting for him back in Sydney.

She nods, pondering the gravity of the situation.

Monty remembers returning to Australia where certain details about the affair had already come to light. By then, Sydney's society A-Listers knew of the pregnancy.

William opens the glass door and peers out to see Diana and Monty deep in conversation. Clearing his throat, he interrupts, suggesting they come back inside so he can take his grandfather for coffee.

'Okay, won't be a minute, son.'

'I don't want to leave Vanessa alone in case she wakes up,' William says.

'Yes, I think we can all agree we could do with some coffee,' Monty says.

Looking back at Diana, a wall of forty years suddenly comes tumbling down and Monty realises how cruel it would be to put Diana through any more pain. 'I still love you, Diana. I've never stopped loving you. Please forgive me for what I'm about to say but staying away was the only way I could move forward with my life, for my father and for William. It wasn't so much for Jacqueline, but for them.'

'So you sacrificed us instead,' she says sadly.

'I didn't see it that way, Diana.'

'I thought we had more time. We were supposed to have more time, but then you were gone.'

'I would have been no good to anyone if I'd stayed. I had to leave. I couldn't stay in Bali and pretend I had no responsibilities back home. My father would have cut me off for good and we would have had nothing. I was a torn man and my only means of survival was to shut you out and bury myself in the business. I admit I went into denial, but there hasn't been a single day I haven't thought of you and Monica, and I certainly had no idea you had another daughter.'

'But you never looked back. Why?' she says, searching his eyes.

'I know this is no excuse, but I think I acted out of fear and broke things off. I'm sorry Monica died, baby,' he says, slipping a hand in hers.

'Whit, it was horrible. I've never gotten over it.' She begins to cry into his arms.

He squeezes her tightly for the longest moment, not wanting to let go. 'Let's not get into this now; there's plenty of time. Right now, we need to focus on Vanessa. Let's go back inside.'

He thinks about his feelings for Diana and the public outcry if they were to get back together again. If the press was to get hold of their relationship, it would mean professional suicide, but knowing he still loves her, it is his cross to bear and he is willing to shoulder whatever is to come next.

William soon returns to the waiting room, with Thornton holding a cardboard tray of coffees. 'All good?' William asks.

'All good, son. Go and be with your woman,' Monty says.

Vanessa's room is dim and silent. William comes in with coffee and tries to creep around the bed without making a sound, but stumbles on the tray table, causing her to open her eyes for a moment, then close them again.

She smells the coffee and gives him a vague smile.

Noticing how pale she is, William leans over the bed rails, kisses her forehead, and whispers, 'Darling, I love you.'

Tears weep from her closed eyes, but she's unspeakably happy to have him by her side.

'Darling, you're safe now,' he says, squeezing her hand gently. He kisses her bare shoulder and says, 'Doctors have said you will make a full recovery.'

The warmth of his breath on her skin is comforting but being heavily medicated, she drifts back into a deep, contented sleep.

An hour or so later, she wakes and appears to be more alert. William is not prepared to let her drift off again until he can share the wonderful news. 'I need to tell you something. Darling, we're not related.'

'Why? What do you ...?' She struggles to ask, her mouth dry from her meds.

'What it means is – my father is Monica's father.'

'What?'

'Don't you worry. I'll explain it all later.' He strokes her hair gently. 'Rest, my sweet.'

She manages a contented smile and closes her eyes. William takes a seat and leans back, exhausted. He tips his head up against the wall in thought.

Diana had explained that because of the associated trauma of losing her sister, Vanessa couldn't bear to talk about her, let alone discuss intimate details like the hereditary birthmark Monica and William share with their father.

A deeper understanding of her reluctance to talk about Monica was met with both relief and sadness by William, who promised to support her in any way he could to help her move through her grief.

Euphoric, the couple are now free to spend the rest of their lives together. William is determined to do whatever it takes to see her happy and content.

Vanessa wakes shortly afterwards, but this time she's terrified. Staring out from behind the rigid neck brace, she looks up at the bright lights on the ceiling. Confused and disorientated, and fearing she's alone, she feels the hot stabs of panic and heavy dread of Bruno making his way down the hospital corridor. She cries out in horror. 'Help! Help! He's going to kill me.'

William opens his eyes and leaps to his feet. 'It's okay, it's okay,' he says, acutely aware she's having a nightmare.

Her body is so tense, he gently strokes her matted hair and says, 'You're safe, baby. I'm not going anywhere.'

CHAPTER TWENTY-FOUR

The day is hot and steamy and the air conditioning in William's car brings welcome relief as Sydney's grey, sullen sky threatens to rain again. It has been an intense time, but William and Diana have managed to take turns watching over Vanessa. William decides to duck away and not to bother going into the office, preferring to use the time to race home to Vanessa's apartment to freshen-up.

During her time in rehab, things have often been laborious, and she's shown a whole new level of hard work. Slow steps, gripped handrails where her knuckles turned white, were regularly on the menu. William was always there by her side, reassuring her the intensity of the throbbing pain wouldn't last forever.

Bearing witness to her struggle, William tormented himself with useless speculation akin to if he'd called off his meeting that day and been at the office with her, she wouldn't have been in the accident.

He reverse parks, brushing ridiculous thoughts aside, breathing a sigh of relief knowing she'll be back to her old self in no time. As he races through the foyer, he tosses Richard his keys. 'Richard, I won't be long.'

'Sure thing, William. How is she?'

'She looks good. Stronger by the minute.'

Inside her apartment, he notices Phillip's been there working his magic and already cleaned up the mess on the terrace. He drops his clothes in the laundry and naked strides through the apartment towards the ensuite. For a moment, he stops and looks outside at all Phillip's handiwork. Knowing exactly how he wanted it to look, he'd had Phillip purchase the plants. The results are nothing short of spectacular. Richard, of course, had never been far away as the men set about landscaping the terrace and creating a whole new feel to the place.

Under the shower, William attempts to still his mind. The water cascades over his body. Closing his eyes, he decides to white light himself, a technique Phillip shared with him after his remedial massage course. Today's gratitude thought is he and Vanessa are now free to move forward with their lives at last.

Feeling somewhat revived, with whippet speed, William throws on some fresh clothes, grabs a small box from the bedside drawer and races out the door again.

Standing kerbside is Richard. 'Pass on my regards, William.'

'Always.' William waves appreciatively. Chewing thoughtfully on a peppermint, he looks at his watch before pulling out, anxious for Vanessa to be awake by the time he gets back. Hoping Diana doesn't leave before he gets there, he has just enough time to pick up the roses he's ordered. Initially he had been angry at Diana for passing Vanessa off as his father's daughter for all those years, thinking it was for mere financial gain. The more he'd thought about it, the more he'd realised they were both to blame, and William now has a much better understanding as to why Diana did what she did.

William calls the florist from the car and tells them he's two minutes out and could they run the flowers out to the car.

'Sure thing, William. I'm sending Jill out now,' the florist says, eager to please one of their biggest customers.

As William pulls up, the young trainee rushes out of the store, red-faced. and places the flowers carefully on the front seat.

'Thanks, Jill.'

'No problem, William,' she says coyly.

He's acutely aware she has a crush on him. The run is smooth from there and so far, he's managed to get green lights all the way. 'Thank God!' The thought is no sooner out of his head and the lights change. Waiting impatiently, William notices a young, attractive woman in a wheelchair being pushed across the road by her mother. The resemblance is uncanny. When the light turns green, he moves off, shaking his head. 'Bloody hell, that could have been Vanessa.' He cranks up the stereo as if to drown out the disturbing thought. 'Christ, I love that woman.'

William slowly merges into the parking station, angling his car around a line of waiting vehicles. The queue is long, but the attendant recognises him and places both index and middle fingers in his mouth, generating a high-pitched whistle, waving William around the cars.

'Mate, leave it over there. I'll look after it for you'

William nods and smiles as the attendant approaches.

'Thanks, bud, you've been a great help.' William says, pulls over, discreetly slips him a hundred bucks, grabs his things, and leaps from the vehicle, giving the attendant an air wave as he strides towards the hospital entrance.

In the throes of a heated discussion, Vanessa looks at her mother with disdain. She steadies herself with the forearm mobility frame, unable to contain her disappointment or her tongue any longer.

In contrast, Diana sits in silence for a time, staring down at the reflection of an overhead light on the surface of her black coffee. The epitome of hippy chic, she is dressed in flared jeans and a loose floral blouse, the beads on her wrist jangling as she puts the cup to her lips, taking a sip.

They're discussing the deep-seated issues and emotions that have been repressed for so long.

Looking up at her daughter with softened eyes, Diana says, 'Honey, please stay calm. Don't get worked up.'

'No, I will not stay calm at all.' *From a tender age, you taught me betrayal is the most heinous breach imaginable and look at what you've done.*

'What can I do?'

The usual gamut of emotions has no hold over Vanessa now. 'You can start by growing up.'

'Darling, drop it. I'm tired of going over this time and time again.' Diana sets her cup down on the table with a sigh.

The conversation begins to escalate.

'Well, Mother, this is a collision of your own making. It's where old meets new. Your impulsive past has come back to bite you. Secrets certainly have a way of rising to the surface. Until now, you have been unaccountably negligent. Things are going to change and whatever unfolds will be your responsibility.'

'Vanessa, stop this instant. You aren't strong enough. Please, darling.'

She fixes a deadly stare on her mother. 'I had no idea how unscrupulous you could be. Clearly, you're capable of anything. How you could have done this, Mother, is *way* beyond me.'

While Vanessa was growing up, her mother had a string of boyfriends until James came along, but she was still miserable and just assumed her daughter hadn't noticed. Vanessa has always carried the burden of her mother's actions to this day. 'Why did you betray so many people, including me? Do you really understand the gravity of your actions?'

Her mother watches Vanessa's knuckles turn white as she grips the handles of the frame.

'What? No shame or understanding of the fall-out effect of your actions? Believe me, Mother, the emotional impact will be ongoing.'

'You're being very harsh, Vanessa.'

Vanessa pulls a judgy face. 'Do you understand what you've done?'

'You've already asked me that.'

'Well?'

'Sometimes people do the wrong thing for the right reason.'

'That's insane!'

'Darling, what kind of an argument are you looking for? Me? Them? Who?'

Vanessa doesn't respond.

'Don't talk to me about emotional impact. At the time, I had two small babies, an enormous amount of stress, and no ability to filter any of it.'

Vanessa is under no illusion Monica has always been very much her mother's daughter, even in death. She doesn't even attempt to couch her words. 'Oh, so I was a substitute for my sister?'

'Don't be so cruel, treating me like an adversary. That's not fair. You know I have always loved you, Vanessa.'

Vanessa mutters under her breath.

'But you must understand I love Monica's father: always have and always will. I only wanted to keep Monty in my life. Separation is not dissolution, you know.'

'And did you love my father?' Vanessa says.

Diana doesn't have an answer.

Now privy to the fact Monica was her half-sister and she had a different father doesn't matter, as far as Vanessa is concerned Monica is her sister, and the best ever. Nothing is ever going to change that.

Extremely troubled by the turmoil, Diana softens her tone. Tears streaming down her cheeks, she pleads, 'I don't expect you to understand this now, but in time I hope you will forgive me and are better able to see why I did what I did. It was never meant to bring shame upon you, Vanessa.'

'I will never understand it. And stop with the vintage tears. Please leave. William will be here any minute and I need time to think.'

Diana struggles to wipe away her tears.

'How he or this family will ever forgive you, and accept me, is beyond me.'

'Darling, you needn't feel frightened or ashamed.'

'I am ashamed. I'm ashamed of you. Go!' She shoots her mother an angry glance. Vanessa is unaware her mother and Monty are on talking terms and very much in the process of forgiving one another.

As tense as it is, before leaving, Diana makes a last-ditch effort to make headway with her daughter. 'Vanessa, don't you think my mind replays the scene, frame by frame? The things I've witnessed, and what happened to Monica that day, are unimaginable for any mother. The image will never, ever leave me. Woman to woman, do you have any idea what that feels like to watch your own daughter suffer like that, knowing it was all my own doing.'

'Oh, I remember, Mother. I remember trying to sit very, very still so you wouldn't feel any pain. I was left to feel that if I didn't talk, didn't say her name, didn't make a sound, move, or even cry, then maybe you wouldn't realise she was gone, and I could spare you the intense pain I was shouldering.'

Diana knows her daughter is, by nature, a caring soul, but with such harsh words being spoken, a heavy silence descends on the room.

The sudden gaps in conversation reinforce Diana's sense of loss, and the pain she's caused, but she is pleased Vanessa is finally talking about it, knowing her daughter has never been able to discuss Monica, not even in therapy.

'Vanessa, I'm sorry for your pain, truly I am, but please, if you could try and understand why I hung on to whatever thread I had. Whether it was right or wrong, the only way I knew how, was through Whit.'

Vanessa calms herself, looking her mother's way. 'I simply don't understand you.'

'Vanessa, you're being very one-sided now. I thought you had a bit more heart. I tried to contact Whit years ago and talk to him, but every call, he shut me out and wouldn't let me explain. Maybe he didn't want to know. Maybe, maybe, maybe; so many maybes, but we're all here now. It's what we do from here on in that matters and it's time for me to get some goddamn emotional support.'

'Support! You've had more support than the Leaning Tower of Pisa.'

'Sure, the financial support was there, but a dollar doesn't weigh as much as the heart, Vanessa. You should know that. Darling, I may have to live with what I did to his family, but they have a different type of shame on their hands. Don't forget it was Whit who walked away from me. Monica never even had the chance to know her father.'

'Oh, please,' Vanessa says sarcastically.

Fed up with shouldering the blame, Diana blurts out, 'Do you know what Whit's parting words were when he went back to his wife, leaving me alone and pregnant in Bali?' She has her daughter's attention now. '"I will support this child, but you have to understand I never want to lay eyes on it."'

Vanessa feels saddened by Monty's choice of words towards her sister.

'Oh, and this one's a doozy: "I'm sure, in time, your life will go back to the way it was." So I continued to accept his financial support after Monica passed away because he never even asked to see her when she was alive. So don't wax lyrical to me about how wonderful they all are. If continuing to accept money meant you were taken care of, forgive me; a mother does what a mother has to do – for all her children.'

They are like strangers, standing there in the room alone with one another.

Vanessa grips her walker, observing Diana looking down at the floor. For the first time ever, she feels pity for her mother, but refuses to discuss it any further.

Diana looks up and says calmly, 'Vanessa, please put old ghosts to rest and try to accept who I am.'

Vanessa doesn't utter a word.

'Try and ramp up the better you and downgrade the negatives, if not for me, then do it for yourself. Judging me won't help either of us. What is done is done, and the only way now is to move on with our lives.' Diana takes one last look at her daughter and reluctantly leaves the room, making her way down the corridor towards the elevators. Eyes downturned, she doesn't notice William in the corridor, behind an enormous bunch of long-stemmed red roses, as he races past.

William notes Diana's look of defeat as she walks hunched over, face pinched, clearly upset, but chooses to leave her in peace.

At ground level, Diana makes her way outside, stops and looks up at the sun, fearing she may have lost her only daughter. She decides to leave the hospital for the day, knowing she may have to come to terms with facing more grief and pain. The truth is Diana is fiercely loyal to Vanessa and would die if she couldn't have her daughter's love and acceptance. Having lived with so much loss, her lies have been a heavy load to bear for far too long. Now that everything is out in the open, in some strange way there is a sense of relief.

William is pleased to see Vanessa up and about, confidently moving around the room with her frame. 'Hey, beautiful.' He places the flowers on the bed. 'How is my gorgeous girl?'

Vanessa tries to look happy, but instead she manages a pout.

'I saw your mother in the corridor. She walked straight past me in a kind of daze. I didn't know whether to say something or leave her be. Is she alright?'

'She'll be fine. Right now, William, I have nothing, other than contempt for her.'

'I see,' he says, saddened.

'Do you?'

'Vanessa, I know you've had some robust conversations with your mum of late, but there's no point in hating someone you love, really love. She clearly has her own reasons, darling. I think it's important you get to the bottom of why she chose to do what she did before you erase her from your life.'

'I know, but I'm so angry with her.'

He lowers his voice. 'According to Gramps, she and my father have been spending a lot of time together.'

'Really?'

'Honey, if they can bury the hatchet, maybe you should too. Yes, so let's take the emotions off the boil for a minute, shall we? They're old enough to sort it out for themselves.'

You're always so sensible. 'Oh, I've missed you, William.'

'What are you talking about? I've only been gone long enough to freshen up and come straight back.'

'I mean I miss you. I miss not being as close. I want *us* back.'

'It's only a matter of weeks, darling, and we'll be together again.'

'I'm so lucky to have you, William. Truly I am. I have no idea why you've stuck by me.'

'Because I love you. Vanessa, when you love someone as much as I do, you hold on to every wonderful moment. We have our whole lives in front of us now and I know we will grow old together.'

She feels his presence as rooted as a tree. Her eyes soften.

'Sit here beside me on the bed. Or better still, over there on the chair under the window.'

She does as he asks.

'Yes, that's good.'

'Ok, but you're acting a little curiously, William.'

He clears his throat, takes a deep breath, and bends down on one knee, an expression of intense concentration on his face.

Her heart skips a beat. *He's not about to do what I think he is?* She watches as he produces a little blue box from his trouser pocket. Vanessa cups her mouth with one hand and feels a well of emotion as her cheeks blush with excitement.

He pulls at the white ribbon and opens the box. 'Vanessa, will you do me the honour of marrying me?'

'What?' she asks, as if she hadn't heard him.

'I said will you marry me.'

No words.

He waits.

She offers a tear-choked yes. 'Yes. Yes, William, I would love to be your wife.'

He slides the ring on her finger. They seal their love with a tender, lingering kiss.

William reluctantly stops. 'Vanessa, this is an heirloom. It was my mother's.'

'Oh, William, it's divine.' She catches her breath at the enormous, emerald-cut diamond.

'I had the good artisans at Tiffany work their magic. I hope you like it?'

Vanessa knows marriage to be a never-ending journey, but one she will happily undertake with William.

Over a period of many weeks, Vanessa's been made to rest a lot as a means of reducing swelling and getting full sensation back to her legs and feet. Daily cold compresses and physio were part of the everyday plan.

William has been resolute in his commitment, and by her side every day to give her the love and support she's needed along the way.

'Sometimes this whole thing feels like it runs at the speed of molasses.' She grips the frame and flexes her foot.

'You have the strength and determination, Vanessa. I know you do. You'll see this through.'

'Yes, I will, knowing you are by my side, darling.'

The next day, William returns bright and early, surprised to see Vanessa already up and about. She is glowing. 'Wow! You're looking pretty perky today, darling.'

'I am. With that awful brace off, I finally managed to have my first good night's sleep in a long time. '

'I bet you did.'

'I feel I may have turned a corner at last. Isn't that strange?'

'That's what happens when you're truly loved.'

CHAPTER TWENTY-FIVE

The tabloid-reading public are abuzz about the couple's pending nuptials.

'How you are feeling, Vanessa?' calls one of the paparazzi.

The click of cameras is blinding as William wheels his wife-to-be away from the confines of the hospital.

'Over here,' calls another.

Probably someone at the hospital has clued them in. Vanessa gives a friendly wave. *My God! You can feel the hype in the air. I can almost touch it.* She savours the fresh breeze like a silky wrap, as the coolness strikes her face. 'What a glorious day.' She looks up from the wheelchair and clutches William's hand resting reassuringly on her shoulder. Vanessa is grateful to be moving on, but a little annoyed she's made to leave in a wheelchair. *Bloody rules. None of that matters now. I am going home. William and I are free to live our lives as we choose.* She smiles at the press.

Amid the crowd are other curious onlookers and several off-duty nurses, physiotherapists, Dr Stokes, and an elderly orderly, all there to say their goodbyes.

Vanessa waves and thinks about the bonds that have been established with these incredible people during her time in hospital, having a great regard for those who have diligently worked to restore her to optimum health.

'Who will walk you down the aisle, Vanessa?' asks a press agent.

Seeing there's no sure answer, Vanessa chooses to ignore the question. *The matter remains; who is my biological father? I may never know. It is a bloody good plot.*

During her time in hospital, she's decided to write a much kinder novel about the male gender. In the past, her words were weapons, but meeting and falling in love with William has softened her fundamental beliefs. *No more venting through the pages. Perhaps I'll even call it Finding True Love.*

Being unable to personally promote her first book thankfully hasn't changed a thing and miraculously, the paperback is still flying off the shelves, due in part to the press coverage about her accident:

Author, Albert, again critically injured.

With such gripping headlines, and given the past, the public naturally assumed Vanessa had been physically attacked. That much publicity sparked such enormous interest, the book has been rolling off the press, day in and day out, to meet demands.

As the orderly wheels away the chair, Vanessa breathes in the familiar leather smell of William's car, and when the seat belt automatically locks and pins her to the car seat, it feels strangely like freedom.

Vanessa gives a gentle wave of gratitude through the window as William pulls out from the parking spot. A whole range of possibilities fits comfortably into the couples lives now. The choices are endless, from residing in Whale Beach to living in her pad, or both. Even buying something completely different, nearer to the city perhaps. It doesn't matter; she has her knight in shining armour and nothing else is of any consequence.

'We need to start thinking about getting you a new car,' William says.

'Oh, William, there's plenty of time.'

'I know, but I'd like you to give it some thought.'

'I'm so sad the Pagoda was written off. I loved that car.'

'Darling, it's only a car. We'll get you another one.'

'I know,' she says, pouting.

William hears the familiar burble of a Harley-Davidson and looks to his right to see a guy dressed in black leathers on a very impressive, charcoal bike. 'Nice bike.'

'Fabulous!'

'My father has a Harley.'

'No way!'

'Seriously. Says he loves to head out into the countryside on it; it frees his taxing mind.'

Mm, interesting. Mother had always loved motor bikes up until Monica's accident and has never sat on one since.

'Mid-life crisis.'

'Couldn't he have bought a sports car instead,' she says.

'Trust me, there's no shortage of those.'

'Really?'

'I shouldn't have a dig about the bike because he's always liked them. As far back as I can remember. My mother used to freak out whenever he tried to take me for a ride on that thing, but I loved it.'

The drive home to her leafy suburb is such a pleasant one, Vanessa had almost insisted on walking. When they arrive, Richard is there to greet them both, lending Vanessa a helping hand from the car. Like a lot of people, Richard has been enormously concerned about Vanessa's wellbeing, but pleased William has kept him in the loop daily.

Over the scent of her flower-filled pad, Vanessa breathes in the aromas of home-cooked baking. 'What's that?'

'I'll tell you in in a minute but come over here first.' William quickly shows her a couple of things before guiding her across to sit on the sofa, where he places a beautiful, navy-blue cross-stitch rug over her legs.

'Oh, William, it's beautiful! I've always wanted one.' Not that she has a fetish for designer gifts, but more the thoughtfulness. 'It's divine.'

'I remembered you commenting one night down at Whale Beach.' He waves a hand. "No, no, it was at the picnic, wasn't it?'

'How could you ever forget?' she says, a twinkle in her eye.

William has planned her home-coming right down to the smallest of details, even filling her apartment with her favourite roses. He opens the terrace doors to reveal several dracaenas in the narrow garden bed. Vanessa showed him an article in a home decorating magazine recently, and he thought they'd work perfectly on her terrace.

'How did you get them in here?'

'Richard helped me, and Phillip.'

'Oh, that was good of him.'. 'So, you did all this with Phillip?'

'Vanessa, I know you feel at odds with him, but please don't. He's a really good guy.'

'I'm not, truly I'm not. It just felt strange seeing a man massaging you.'

'To be fair, darling, I gave him and his fiancée both remedial massage therapy courses as an engagement present. I told him the least he could do was give me one after he completed the course. But I can see how you thought it odd. Trust me, when you get to know our relationship a little better, you will be more at ease around him.'

'I'm at ease. There's no more bad juju here.'

He laughs. 'I'll give you juju.'

She spots something else over William's shoulder. 'Ah, herb garden.'

'Yes, the remnants of the latter hopefully taught you well.'

'You saw that?' She feels ashamed.

'Yes indeed.' He raises an eyebrow. 'These are sown in dehydrated, untilled soil.'

'A wall garden; how lovely.'

'Yes. Phillip set it up for you.'

No need to push the Phillip card. 'My goodness: dill, thyme, even oregano. Flowers?'

'Yes, edible flowers: violas. Just add water.'

'Got it. But I can't promise anything.'

William picks a purple flower, wraps his arm around her waist, and places it to her lips.

It's bitter. 'Yuk! They aren't very tasty on their own.' She laughs and decides to head back inside.

'That's home baking you smell. It's fresh this morning. I had Jo and Tess – you remember down at Whale Beach – prepare some delicious meals for us.'

'Oh, that's lovely.' She grateful to be finally sitting back on the couch. 'After that bloody awful hospital food,' she adds.

'Vanessa! I don't think you had a single hospital meal in the entire time you were there.'

'True,' she says sheepishly. Having been spoilt by her mother's remarkable home cooking, and incredible take-away William systematically organised from exclusive restaurants around town, Vanessa was never without choice. She notices there's a red vintage jewellery box, with a small deckle-edged card attached to it, sitting on the coffee table. 'What's this?' She peels off the antique note.

He smiles.

She reads aloud:

My darling Vanessa,
Life has never felt more complete since meeting you.
When I first held you, a blissful wave overcame me
I knew, then I was falling in love. Now, I know I have.

When he hands her the box, she realises it has serious weight and opens it carefully in anticipation. Staring back at her is the most remarkable emerald and diamond bracelet. 'Cartier!'

'1920s Art Deco. My grandfather thought it only fitting that you should have something special from our family.'

'But I have your mother's gorgeous ring?'

'I know, but Gramps wanted you to have this. *Vous êtes une famille maintenant.*'

She gives him a quizzical look.

'You're family now.'

'Not quite,' she sings, waving a cheeky finger.

'Gramps said now that we're engaged, it's only fitting you should have this. Ava would have wanted you to have it.'

'Your grandmother?'

'Yes.'

'It's beautiful!'

'He loved her so.' William places it around her wrist. Closing the clasp, the sound of the locking mechanism is quite impressive as it clicks shut securely. 'It looks beautiful on you.'

'I must call Thornton.'

'Plenty of time to do that, darling.' He gazes at her lovingly. 'Oh, and your mother wanted you to have this.'

Diana's left a box of a different kind, a much larger one, asking William to give it to her at his discretion. 'Hungry?' he asks, handing her the duck-egg blue velvet box.

'Famished.'

He retreats to the kitchen, respectfully giving her some time alone.

Vanessa looks down at the box for a moment, then slowly peels off the ornately hand-lettered card taped to the outside and holds it to her nose. It's been sprayed with her mother's familiar patchouli scent. *It's comforting.* She tentatively unfurls the letter and reads:

> *Vanessa darling, this is my gift to the love we share. You should go through this box when you're ready to not only forgive me but open your heart to our differences. This is a peace offering. I love you from the depth of mine, your loving mother, Diana x*

Vanessa lifts the lid and is astonished to find it's a celebration of her childhood. It's not like her mother to be sentimental.

Diana has thoughtfully collected an array of things throughout her daughter's lifetime, creating a kind of life map. Things ranging from photographs to costume jewellery, and even an old, navy velvet scrunchie. A light blue envelope with a water stain on the front holds a love letter from her first serious boyfriend, written when he was out of town visiting his aunt in Adelaide during school holidays. Another from that interlude in her life is a colourful postcard bearing cheeky, suntanned bikini-clad bottoms with scribbled script professing his undying commitment on the flipside, signed Love Jack. That time he was away on the Gold Coast with his parents.

Memories of greater and greater importance reveal themselves one by one. She's taken aback to see her sister's locked diary, in bold pink, Monica's favourite colour. The key is loose at the bottom of the box, but Vanessa has no wish to open the diary today. Closing her eyes, she can still see her sister doodling away in her bedroom. Finding it incredibly hard to hold back tears, she continues rummaging through the treasured possessions. *My God! A documented collage of my existence: things that matter.* She soon forgets to be annoyed.

Vanessa touches each item, one by one, of the various phases in her life. Too scared to use the velvet scrunchie, as it might destroy its integrity, killing off what little memories she has of being thirteen, she sets it to the side gently.

Flicking through the photographs, some of which have become crisp with age, she comes across a dog-eared snapshot of herself and Monica asleep on the beach in Bali. Tears cloud her vision again. Wiping them away frantically, she sniffles and looks up in thought, as if trying to catch a glimpse of her sister in fear of losing her again. Looking back at the snapshot of the two of them in happier, carefree times, she still remembers what her mother was wearing that day when she took the picture, a bright orange bikini.

Nothing is more surprising than a small, spiral seashell that her sister had presented to her the day before she died. Turning the shell between her thumb and index finger, she can still hear her sister teasing her to dive to the bottom of the pool for it:

'Go! Go, Vanessa. You can do it: swim to the bottom. You'll come back!'

When Vanessa finally found the courage, she took a deep breath, swam to the bottom, scooped up the shell, turned, then kicked with all her might and made for the surface. With one last kick, she broke through the surface of the water, arm reaching skyward, holding up the shell victoriously. From the edge of the pool, Monica beaming with pride, applauded her little sister's determination.

Vanessa remembers the next day, racing back to the hotel after Monica's passing, when to the staff's amazement, she jumped in the pool. It must have seemed strange, given her sister had just died. They watched as she anxiously swam to the bottom to recover the shell the girls had played with; in the hope it might bring something of Monica back.

Touching her cheeks, Vanessa realises they're saturated with tears. She kisses the shell before putting it back in the box for safekeeping.

She spots an old, faded Polaroid of herself. In the snapshot, she's tanned, dressed in a white singlet top and wearing a black felt, hippie-style hat. A bright green frog nestles between her developing breasts. Vanessa is thirteen and on a road trip with her mother to north Queensland. Her expression of disdain is noted. She remembers her mother's rhetoric: 'Don't sulk, Vanessa; it absolutely spoils your face.' The truth is, after losing Monica, she was never the same again.

She comes across a colour snapshot of her uncle, Harry, down at Bilgola beach, hanging out in the carpark with his mates, their girlfriends watching in the background. It warms her heart. She asked Harry, that day, if she could drive his car, an old, white GT Ford, his pride and joy, and remembers him sitting nervously beside her, having agreed to take it for a spin around the carpark. He observed as she gripped the wheel, revving the motor. Grinning across at him as she selected first gear, her body tensed as she pressed the accelerator and the car lurched forward, rocking back and forth to the cheers of their audience. She was sixteen. *I miss him so, especially the sense of knowledge he brought to my life.*

William clears his throat as he reappears carrying a tray. 'Here we go; a cool drink and some delicious sandwiches the girls prepared earlier.' He sets down the tray, looks up, and realises she's crying. 'Right. Enough tears. From today, it's onwards and upwards. Okay?' William sits alongside and gives her hug. 'Right, now tuck into one of these. Oh, and guess what? Later you have a choice of either Jo's lemon drizzle cake or her Banoffee pie. Believe me, the choice is a difficult one as they're both delicious.' He squeezes her hand. 'Come on, cheer up.'

He's right, it's time to get back into the current narrative of my life.

He reaches for a sandwich. 'I need to fatten you up.'

If I put on any more weight, I won't fit into any of my clothes. Could be the meds. Doctors did say everything would return to normal when things settle. She grows serious. 'What is Banoffee pie?'

He laughs. 'It's an English dessert pie made from bananas and caramel. Hence the name is a portmanteau combining the words banana and toffee.'

'A what?'

'Come on, you know what a portmanteau is.'

'No, I do not.'

'It's a blend or morph of words. Like brunch: breakfast and lunch. Or Brexit: Britain and exit.'

'Or, I know, anklet: ankle and bracelet.'

'That's it. Come on, Einstein. Eat up.'

'William Whittaker, you are full of surprises.'

'Oh, believe me, I haven't even started yet.'

It's such a relief to finally to be back home in my own apartment, and to think, William is staying here. Vanessa snuggles in on the couch and looks around the room.

Shortly after her accident, it had been agreed it made far more sense for William to bunk down at her place and be closer to the hospital, than endure long hauls back and forth to Whale Beach.

William steps out from the bedroom, breaking her chain of thought. 'Right, I'm off to the office. Is there anything you need while I'm out, baby?'

'No. Only you.

William leans down and plants a tender kiss on her lips.

'Mm,' she sighs, missing him already.

He stares longingly into her eyes. 'Have I told you that I love you today?'

'Only about half a dozen times, and it's only 9 a.m. But I'd like to hear it again.'

'*You'd* only *like* to hear it again?'

'No, no, no. I'd love to hear it again.'

'That's more like it. I love you, Vanessa T. Whittaker.'

'Well, who says I'm going to be Mrs Whittaker anyway?'

He pulls back. 'Christ! There's only ever been two Mrs Whittakers, my mother and my grandmother.'

She smiles at the thought.

'Of course, I'm biased and think Whittaker is a great surname, but it's up to you if you want to keep Albert. I'm happy with that.'

'I haven't really thought about it until now.' She looks down at her ring.

'Speaking of which, we need to go back and see Joe the jeweller to get your ring resized. I have no idea why it's so tight. I was sure I got it right the first time,' he says.

'I don't either. This weight gain thing is starting to bug me and the medications I'm on are causing me to have waves of nausea all the time. I'll ask the doctor when I see her again next week. She might be able to tweak my meds.'

'Better still, why don't you call your doctor today?'

'Good idea.'

'Oh, and if you get a chance, why don't you give Joe a call while you're at it and tee up a time for later in the week. If you make it late morning, we can go have lunch somewhere afterwards.'

'Great idea. His number is in my phone, so I'll call him a bit later.'

'Well, I'm off. See you late this afternoon and don't forget, if you need anything, call Phillip. He's in and around the city running errands for Gramps today and knows he's on call because I'm pretty much locked into meetings for most of it. I've put his number in your phone.'

'I'll be fine. Don't worry. Now go.' After waving him off, she rests on the couch before going out to the terrace with a cup of peppermint tea and sitting in a spot by the newly planted garden. *William has created such a tranquil spot for me and thank goodness that dog has stopped yapping. Nietzsche is either gone or had training.* She sets her tea down and listens to the familiar tinkle of the neighbour's wind chime. She closes her eyes for a moment. A slight chill ripples through her, so she heads inside to grab a sweater.

Feeling slightly nauseated, Vanessa decides to make some brunch. *Maybe it's the meds on an empty tummy.* She decides on something plain and pops a slice of bread in the toaster, grabbing the butter and Vegemite from the fridge, but covers her mouth with a trembling hand and tracks to the bathroom, fearing she's going to throw up. *It's unbearably stuffy in here.* She opens the window, taking a few deep breaths. It doesn't help. *This is weird.* she retreats to the lounge to call her G.P.

'You're not pregnant, are you?' Dr Wendy asks.

'Oh, I don't … Well, gee, I could be, I suppose.'

'Get that gorgeous man of yours to duck out to the chemist for one of those over-the-counter pregnancy tests.'

'Are they reliable? I mean shouldn't I come and see you first?'

'No, do this first, today preferably, and call me as soon as you have the results.'

'Okay, Wendy. Thank you.'

This is the sort of thing I would call Elizabeth for, not a man I barely know. I guess I have no choice but to call Phillip. She tries not to over-think it and dials Phillip's number. The number rings out, but she no sooner hangs up when he calls back.

'Oh, hi, Phillip. Sorry to bother you. Are you busy?'

'No. I wasn't quick enough to pick up, that's all. Are you okay?'

'Well, yes and no. This will seem strange, but are you able to go to a chemist for me?'

'Of course. What do you need?'

Silence.

'Vanessa, you still there?'

'Yes, I'm still here. Just a little embarrassed, that's all.'

'Don't be. What is it: tampons, condoms, anything? I'm a big boy. What do you need?'

'Well, I wish it was one of those. Oh, well I ...'

'Yes.'

'Um ...'

'Jeepers! You haven't got bloody head lice from that hospital, have you?'

She laughs. 'No, I don't have bloody head lice.'

'Well, at least I made you laugh.'

'Phillip, I need you to get me a pregnancy test, if you don't mind?'

'It would be my pleasure. See you soon. Any particular brand?'

'I don't think so. Just get whatever the pharmacist suggests, thank you. See you soon.' Her face is burning. A whole range of things flood her thoughts, and she can't help wondering what sort of mother she'll make. *What if it's twins? What a bonus! One like William, one like me. Better still, one like Monica. How wonderful.* she thought, given she was robbed of her sister.

While she waits, Vanessa puts the kettle on and makes a fresh peppermint tea for herself. A short time later, Phillip arrives with a brown paper bag. Vanessa offers him a cup of tea.

'No, I'm fine, I imagine you're in a hurry to check out what's going on.' He nods towards the package.

'Yes, yes, I am. Do you mind?'

'No. I'll be off then. See you later.'

'I'm sorry, Phillip, I don't mean to be rude.'

'Of course not.'

Knowing Phillip is William's rock, Vanessa has a much more positive take on him now. *As William says, he's like a brother to him, and evidently the feeling is mutual.*

Unable to summon the nerve to go to the bathroom, Vanessa sits on the couch, staring at the test kit on the coffee table. So far, she's only managed to pull the box from the bag bearing the name First Response. *I wonder what William's first response will be. I have no idea what his take is on children, but this little box could be a deal breaker. Given our lives are something like out of the bloody "Bold and the Beautiful", we've been too busy dealing with everything else to discuss children. Now pregnancy!*

William's reaction should be the least of Vanessa's worries, but still, it's troubling. *Maybe I should wait until he gets home, and we do the test together? No, the doctor is waiting for me to call back. This is unnecessary pressure. Perhaps I should have told her I'll call back tomorrow. That's what I'll do. I'll call her back and explain I need to do this with William.*

'Hi, Wendy. I have the test here, but I think I should wait for William to get home.'

'No, Vanessa. It's only you that needs to take the test.'

'I know that.'

'Vanessa, that's fine. Talk tomorrow, dear. All the best. Oh, and Vanessa, if it is positive, you are both very fortunate, so please don't take this blessing for granted, will you?'

'Yes, I know that. Call you tomorrow. Thank you.' She knows what Wendy is thinking; *People my age shouldn't take the gift of life for granted.*

Suddenly she rushes to the bathroom, kneels over the white porcelain throne, and throws up.

It's after five when the front door finally swings open.

'Hi, honey, I'm home,' William calls, shutting the door.

Home? Even though he hasn't officially moved in, she likes that he calls her place home.

Once they're married, they plan to reside at Whale Beach and keep her apartment as an inner-city base.

'Just practicing,' he says happily. He looks across the room and sees her semi-reclined on the couch. 'You look terrible, honey. Are you alright?' He spots the pregnancy kit on the table. 'Oh ...'

'William, I've been unwell all day, so I called Phillip. No, I called the doctor first and she suggested I might be pregnant, so best to get a test kit. I had no choice but to call Phillip.'

'Well, what are we waiting for?'

'I thought we should discuss things first. I realised, after speaking to the doctor, I really don't know your take on being a parent.'

'I think I'd make a terrific father and absolutely open my heart to a child. This is fan-bloody-tastic,' he declares. 'Come on, let's do this.'

She leverages herself off the couch, walks towards him and gives him a peck on the cheek.

'You know if it's negative, that's fine too.' She places a gentle hand to his cheek.

'Honey, as long as I'm with you, children or no children, I'm happy.'

She smiles up at him.

'But ...' his face lights up, 'but if you are, I think it's wonderful. So come on, get that little butt of yours in the bathroom and do the test.'

'Okay, well, give me a minute.'

'You do that, and I'll get the champagne.'

'Not for me, darling.' She stops in the doorway and looks back at William.

'Why not?'

'I won't be able to have a drink if I am pregnant, and I'm far too nauseated to drink, even if I'm not. Go ahead, you have one. You might need to have one for both of us.'

'Okay, honey, I'll wait a minute.'

Vanessa closes the door and sits for a moment on the vanity stool, staring at herself in the mirror, then takes a deep breath. *What do I really want?* Feeling personally overwhelmed, she is pleased William does want children. A few minutes later, she exits the bathroom with the test results in her hand.

William leaps from the couch. 'Well, what is it? Are we pregnant or not?'

She'd always thought it peculiar when couples said *we* are pregnant. She looks at him intently, holds the test up to show him. 'Yes, we are, darling.'

William's smile bursts into joyful tears. She has never seen such joy in his eyes. He hugs her tightly before circling the room like a caged lion, fantasising how great a dad he is going to be.

'I always thought this would be impossible,' she says, trying to calm the beast before her.

He says nothing.

'Darling, it's okay we'll be fine,' she says.

He rushes towards her. 'We are going to be better than fine; we're going to be the best parents ever. Think about it: amusement parks, camping, fishing, playing games, hide 'n' seek —'

'I'll get a World's Best Dad mug for you tomorrow.' She's a little shocked by his enthusiasm. 'And as for the camping, you can leave me out.'

'Come on!' he says, feeling his heart expand a hundredfold.

Throughout the rest of the evening, the phone never stops. Initially, William calls his grandfather, who is thrilled to bits, then calls his father. Vanessa decides to call her mother, but Diana has already been told the good news by Whit, who is sitting alongside her in bed. Diana is overjoyed she and Whit are going to be grandparents.

Vanessa's voice softens. 'Mum, are you okay?'

Diana knows it's her daughter's way of asking forgiveness.

'Of course, why wouldn't I be? I'm going to be a grandmother.'

'You know what I mean.'

'I'm fine. You'll soon realise, Vanessa, mothers are very forgiving souls.'

'I know. I love you, Mum.'

'Love you too, darling. Which reminds me, I must call Aunt Sarah now and tell her the good news. She'll be thrilled she's going to be a great aunty. Now, on a different note, are we still on for tomorrow?'

'You mean the wedding planner? Hang on a minute, Mum.' She holds the phone away from her ear. 'William?' she calls. 'Darling, are you still okay to meet Mum at the wedding planner's tomorrow at eleven?'

'Abso-bloody-lutely!'

Vanessa puts the phone to her ear again. 'Mum, did you hear that? I guess it's yes all around.'

'Sure did. Now I've already started writing out a checklist —'

'Mum! That's what the wedding planner's for.'

'I know, but it doesn't hurt to have your own list.'

'Mother, please —'

'Okay, darling, see you there. Bye for now.'

Vanessa decides to ring the girls. 'Hi, Georgia, I have something to tell you.' There's a lilt in her voice.

'Tell me you did not go off and get married?'

'No —'

'If you eloped, I will bloody well throttle you. I've already bought a brand-new dress for the wedding, and I'd recognise that tone of yours anywhere.'

'No! No! No! However, it is special news.'

'What? Come on, spit it out.'

'We're pregnant!'

'You're what? Oh my God! Oh my God! That's fantastic. Oh, I love babies. I wonder what it is. Have you called Francesca yet?'

'Not yet. I'm about to as soon as I hang up from you.'

'Quick, hang up, call her and call me back. Oh my God! I'm going to be an aunt.'

Her friend's words take Vanessa by surprise. *They aren't even related, and Georgia is already calling herself the baby's aunt. Love it.* 'Okay, bye.'

Vanessa looks at William smiling across the room. 'Come here,' he says, arms outstretched. 'Have I told you I love you today?'

'No, not since this morning, and I'd *love* to hear it again.'

William scoops her up in his arms. 'I love you. You, my dear, are the most amazing, irresistible, delicious, clever woman I have ever known.'

'Is that all?'

'No.'

'Seriously, William, life of late has been such a roller coaster ride, but this new level is wonderful.'

'Darling, I told you, it's the beginning of so many beginnings. Hurry up. Call Francesca. This calls for a celebration and I need to have you all to myself.' He hugs her as Phillip's name comes up on the screen of his mobile.

'Gidday, mate. I was about to call you.'

'Is it a good time?' Phillip asks.

'It's a bloody great time. In fact, it's a bloody wonderful time. I'm here with Vanessa. I'll put you on speaker.' William looks at Vanessa and signals to her, 1,2,3.

'We're pregnant!'

'Mate, Vanessa, that's the best news I've heard in a long time. Well done, guys.'

Vanessa cuts in. 'Thanks, Phillip, so much. Look, I've got another call to make, so if you will excuse me, I'll leave you boys to chat.'

'No problem, and again, congrats.'

Vanessa heads into her office to call Francesca. It begins with a shriek of sheer delight. Francesca, like everyone else, is so pleased for the happy couple and insists that she and Georgia call over tomorrow evening, after work, for a quick hi and celebratory drink.

'Remember though, I won't be drinking.'

'But we will be,' Francesca says cheekily.

Vanessa laughs. 'Okay, great. See you tomorrow at half-six. Would you mind calling Georgia back? I'm so tired and need to rest. It's all been a bit much for me really.'

'Of course. Will do. You go and share some quiet time with that hunk of a man of yours.'

'Oh, tell Georgia I'm sorry I didn't call her back, but I'm looking forward to seeing you both tomorrow evening. Thanks.'

Vanessa hears William's rowdy excitement from the other room.

My apartment has never felt more like home. She rubs her tummy and feels the bud of new life inside her.

CHAPTER TWENTY-SEVEN

Vanessa steps from the car. Her look is timeless, chic and classic, wearing a stunning cream Valentino gown. Her skin is porcelain, and her auburn hair is tied back in a classic Audrey Hepburn chignon.

Following a whirlwind romance, the bride-to-be is about to tie the knot with the man of her dreams in a beautiful outdoor ceremony on a sprawling, private clifftop estate by the sea. Of course, the paparazzi are there to make sure they capture every moment.

Her mother's eyes well. It's one of Diana's celebrated moments, seeing Monty entrusted to walk her beloved daughter down the aisle. Vanessa radiates as he steps forward, takes her by the arm, and says, 'Vanessa, you look stunning, my dear. My son's a lucky man.'

Diana smiles. Vanessa was always a happy little girl, happy about school, happy about sport, everything she ever did until she lost Monica, but a proud Diana has never seen her as happy as she is today.

It's a fancy affair, and the weather is exceptional, showcasing the panoramic views. A choir of six singers, performing Rachmaninoff's 'Vespers' in harmony, fills the space hauntingly as Montgomery guides Vanessa down the red carpet, surrounded by perfectly manicured, brilliant emerald, green lawn, towards the man of her dreams.

No, Monty isn't Vanessa's biological father, but Diana is swept away by the vision of seeing them walk together towards an arch of fresh flowers in hues of white and cream, the groom standing beneath beaming with pride.

In recent weeks, Monty and Diana have had many discussions, not only about decades lost, but of moving forward in life together.

'You know not so long ago; I was an impatient perfectionist. I wanted to go faster and do more and fix everything at once. And when you play a leading role in a large publishing house, you must be crystal clear on what's going to move the dial, what's a priority, and in what order we need to do things. But then I saw you again and realised – at what cost?'

Clearing his throat, he says, 'There have been times, Diana, when I thought you were just a dream. I was certain that was the only way I knew how to deal with things. But now I've come to appreciate I don't want to waste whatever precious time we have left. I know I'm not blameless. My mistakes have plagued me for decades and I've been unequivocally arrogant and selfish.'

Listening to him pouring his heart out, his words meant the world to her for so many reasons – love mostly.

'Sadly, my marriage to Jacqueline was complicated. We loved one another, but more like a brother loves a sister, so at times it was strained. When she died, I'll admit I felt numb. I thought about finding you but recognised it would be selfish of me after all these years. Then suddenly you were there. I'm done grieving and know it's time to move on.'

'I've never stopped loving you, Diana, and if you can find it in your heart, please give me another chance. I promise I'll never walk away again. I want to share the rest of my life with you.'

She catches an unforgotten breath and is about to say something when Monty suddenly holds his index finger up to her lips as a means of silencing her.

'Diana, before you say anything, let's get married.'

Feeling the pieces of her soul trickling back, she takes another deep breath.

'I swear I'll spend a lifetime making you happy.'

She grins. 'You know that means we have to try and repair a gap that spans over forty years.'

'That's a lot of making up to do, but I'm prepared to start again.'

'I don't mind being at the beginning of something special,' she says, causing him to smile.

'Late is a million times better than never.'

'I have time..'

'I promise, with all my heart, I will make it up to you in more ways than you could ever imagine possible.'

'It's not all your fault. I'm in search of forgiveness too. I should have —'

'Shh,' He touches her lips gently. 'Diana, what's the point of dwelling on the past. We must look forward; we're certainly not getting any younger. I've had a lot of time to think about this and I know I've chosen to be with you for all the right reasons.'

She was without words for the longest moment.

'I'll ask the question again. Diana, will you marry me?'

Realising her dreams will finally become a reality, her heart skips a beat, but this time she's quick to agree.

Diana has never stopped loving Whit and with new-found hope, they agree to work at rebuilding their relationship and aim to happily grow old together.

Plans are immediately put in place to wed in the coming weeks, the details under wraps until after their children's wedding.

In the presence of all their loved ones, Monty turns to his daughter-in-law-to-be and says, 'Vanessa, I am filled with pride and joy.' The celebrant asks, 'Who gives this woman to this man?'

'I do,' Monty says, proudly placing her hand in his son's as she looks adoringly into the eyes of her husband to be.

Monty steps back to join Diana, who gives him a kiss on the cheek.

With held back tears, Vanessa smiles at her mother in acknowledgement of their happiness, before turning her gaze to William.

'Let us begin,' the celebrant says, then looks out at the handsome crowd. 'You may be seated.'

The ceremony is heartfelt, and when it comes time for the couple to say their vows, Vanessa is first. 'William, you are my lover and my best friend.'

Then William. 'Vanessa, my commitment to you is complete. I will always hold our life together as my most valuable possession.'

You could hear a pin drop as the couple exchange their vows, declaring love and dedication before some of the city's most well-heeled people, a dazzling blend of their closest friends and family. The guests are enthralled when William presents a glistening band of diamonds to match her diamond engagement ring and it slips on perfectly.

In the late afternoon light, teary onlookers throw confetti over the couple as Lauren Woods' 'Fallen' croons out from the surrounding speakers and a dozen doves are released.

The scene is simply spectacular.

To the sounds of clicking cameras, the crowd begin mingling. Waiters in starched white jackets begin circling with trays of hors d'oeuvres: scallops wrapped in bacon, crab tarts, prawns, sturgeon caviar. Accompanying these delicious bites is an elaborate selection of wines, boutique beers, and champagne.

A sophisticated ice sculpture sits centre stage, vodka flowing down into frosted shot glasses to companion the freshly shucked oysters.

At Sydney's most cinematic moment, a golden pink sunset lights up the sky, then slowly slips below the horizon as everyone raises their glass in celebration.

Following this extravaganza, guests share lively discussions and are then requested to sit down for a stylish feast overlooking the ocean. The grounds are festooned with fairy lights and bowers of ivory roses hang like garlands. The tables gleam with silverware and crystal set out on white linen. Handwritten place cards mark every setting in signature black ink. As the guests are seated, they admire the scented, soft pink roses in small vases lining the centre of the table.

By candlelight, a sumptuous meal is served, prepared by one of Sydney's most acclaimed chefs, Wolfgang Thomas, as a string quartet plays specially selected music throughout dinner. The choice of entrées is roasted duck salad or small blue cheese ravioli, followed by filet mignon or lobster tail.

Over the tinkle of silverware, William stands, his breathtaking bride sitting silently, beaming up at her new husband with consummate pride. Before a captive audience, he makes a passionate speech recalling the first moment he saw his bride, and the space is filled with smiles of joy, none greater than Vanessa's.

William then introduces his best man, Phillip, who stands and begins by reading a poem by Sir Robert Sidney:

My true love hath my heart and I have his,
By just exchange one for another given:
I hold his dear, and mine he cannot miss,
There was never a better bargain driven:
My true love hath my heart, and I have his.

His heart in me keeps him and me in one,
My heart in him his thoughts and senses guides:
He loves my heart for once it was his own,
I cherish his because in me it bides:
My true love hath my heart and I have his.

As the band begins to play the couple's favourite song, "Begin the Beguine", the newlyweds take to the dance floor and the whir and ka-chick of cameras can be heard over the music.

Vanessa's spectacular *haute couture* gown is made of six metres of cream silk organza and William looks the epitome of style wearing an Italian light wool suit with a white gardenia in the buttonhole.

'I love you, darling,' he says, as he spins his princess gracefully around on the dance floor.

'William, I've never been happier,' she says.

Stylish women and formally attired men join them on the dance floor and there's much merriment amid the joyful laughter as the celebrations pick up the pace.

There is oohing and aahing when the first dessert course arrives, a chocolate sculpture served with fresh cream. The selection of fromage is a stunning showstopper including gruyere, gouda, fresh goat's cheese, and brie, as well as the sharper cheeses, cheddar, and pecorino. The sweetness of fresh berries, apple, pear, fig, and nuts naturally complement the cheeses.

Later, the guests are treated to a spectacular firework display and as the whole sky lights up, the couple cut the wedding cake under its spectacular glare. This architecturally inspired masterpiece consists of four tiers of fruitcake covered in white and cream icing. A variety of eight different types of flowers, each with its own symbolic meaning, are elegantly replicated by fondant flowers that adorn the cake.

The number eight also represents infinity and everything in the universe; on a personal basis, infinite love, energy, time, an endless abundance of all that is good, without disadvantage.

After dinner, the guests are served French liqueurs and velvety cognacs from the north of Bordeaux, Courvoisier XO and Martell Cordon Bleu.

To the delighted couple, their dreams have finally come true. Everyone wishes them the greatest of happiness and none more so than Thornton Whittaker. Thornton looks out across the water, holding back tears, the wedding reminding him of how he and Ava, in happier times, used to love going up to Whale Beach. He isn't, in any way, a recluse, but he has avoided going there for such a long time. He realises there comes a time in a man's life where it hurts to do the math and he decides to make a concerted effort to do so again, now that his two favourite people are together. Thornton has always been the focal point of the family, but at eighty-eight, it's time to open a pathway for a new generation and spend more time celebrating his family. Nothing really beats uniting people. With greater insight into Monty and Diana's relationship, unbeknown to anyone else, Thornton had recently called Diana into his office.

He'd always considered himself to be a good judge of character but acknowledged he may have missed the mark this time. Diana hadn't expected what passed from the old man's lips.

'Who am I to carry a grudge that spans some forty years. It's time to move forward and clear a path for future generations of Whittakers. As William's grandfather, this won't be possible if I continue to carry any ill will towards you, Diana. From here on in, I would like us to all work towards family unity.'

That was good enough for Diana, who took comfort knowing she'd finally found her voice and Thornton accepted why she did what she did as a young mother.

Thornton beams across at Vanessa, who is standing ready to throw the bouquet. He notices there is a special look in her eye. It's not just the adoring, awestruck gaze a bride has for her new husband, but one that tells you she has fought hard and triumphed over adversity.

'Ready, girls?' she says.

All the single ladies huddle together for pole position in anticipation. Even her Aunt Sarah, who had never married, and had flown down to Sydney for the wedding, joined in.

Vanessa turns and tosses the bouquet over her shoulder. As it hurtles through the air, she looks back to see Francesca leap to catch it mid-flight. Vanessa's face breaks into a broad smile and she throws her a kiss. Georgia squeals with delight while the other guests cheer in response.

Suddenly a tall, dark, handsome guy grabs Francesca by the wrist and drags her away from the excited crowd to the dance floor. Knowing she's in good company, Francesca's smile widens, and with a great sense of amazement, she willingly allows herself to be led, shooting Vanessa a knowing wink.

Vanessa has a flash of insight. *When you see yourself as a choice-maker, you take on the role of protagonist in your own life story. Its time Francesca met someone special.*

Vanessa moves through the evening feeling almost surreal, so when it comes time to leave, she and William circulate one last time, saying their goodbyes while holding each other close.

William nears his father and notices Monty's hand locked with Diana's.

In recent weeks, he's observed his father's out-pouring of love for this woman, exposing him to another side, a side of great depth and open heartedness. Sure, William misses his mother deeply, but having watched his father run two versions of his life, he takes comfort in knowing he is finally happy with this woman. To the outside world, his father has it all and wants for nothing, but to his inner sanctum, it's been one of confusion, especially by not being with the woman he truly loves.

All is ancient history now. Leaning in, he gives his dad a big hug, beams affectionately over his shoulder at Diana and mouths thank you.

She beams back.

It's midnight by the time the couple are ready to leave. Suddenly the guests and bridal party grow quiet and look to see Phillip pulling into the driveway in a brand-new Mercedes SL in the deepest navy with a big velvet bow in contrasting red on the bonnet, Just Married scribbled on the back window.

Phillip steps from the car and hands William the keys. Vanessa is taken aback when William hands on the keys to her. 'My wedding present to you, my darling,' he says.

She catches her breath, and he leans in and whispers, 'The seatbelts work in this one.'

She laughs and delights the onlookers by kissing him passionately, clapping going on around them.

He pulls back. 'Go on. What are you waiting for? Get in.'

Francesca is nowhere to be seen, but Georgia helps Vanessa with her gown, and she slides in behind the wheel of the car,

William taking the passenger seat. His grandfather's favourite Ayn Rand quote comes to mind again:

> Love is the expression of one's values, the greatest reward
> you can earn, for the moral qualities you have achieved …

CHAPTER TWENTY-EIGHT

It's early, and with morning sickness thankfully abating, Vanessa is snuggled up in bed alongside her new husband, who is enjoying a lazy morning lie-in reading the daily newspapers. Cradling a mug of peppermint tea, Vanessa takes pleasure in listening to the sublime sound of the waves below, feeling like the ocean exists only for them.

It's been over a week since the wedding, but because of William's work commitments, unfortunately they couldn't take off on their honeymoon right away.

Visions of white sand stretch for miles and miles and aqua clear water swirls vicariously around in Vanessa's head. *Shame we couldn't fly out sooner.* Bathed in morning light, she feels a flutter deep in her belly, presses her face against the warmth of her favourite porcelain mug, and scans the wedding cards disrupting the territorial lines of their bedroom.

She squeezes her eyes shut for a second then opens them again. *Yep, we're really married.* The cards in the room confirm she's not dreaming. *I should probably pack them away before we go.*

Grinning at her own silliness, Vanessa is suddenly winded by the baby's kick, causing her to splutter her tea back into the mug. 'She kicked!' With both hands lovingly clasped around her baby bump, she whispers, 'I'm here little one, I'm here.'

Looking at his wife adoringly, William says, 'It's too early, isn't it?'

'Yes, very.'

He reaches across, touching her tummy. 'Good morning, little princess,' he says, proudly.

'Well, we can't be 100% certain.' Having only had an ultrasound at ten weeks, the gender hadn't become visible yet, so it was still guesswork.

'I'm sure of it,' he says, hell bent on having a girl.

'Oh!' she squeals, with a tiny jolt as the baby kicks again, only harder this time.

'See, she's telling you so.'

Vanessa laughs. 'What? That she's a footballer.'

'This is the first time, isn't it?'

'Yes, but I'm only thirteen weeks.'

'I'm sure it's fine.'

'I know, but it's usually not until around the eighteen-week mark.'

'Then I guess we have another Vanessa on our hands, keen to make her mark.'

'I guess so.' She lets him have this one. *Whatever the sex, this is a meant-to-be child.*

The couple know it's a miracle she didn't miscarry because of the car accident, and were shocked the foetus wasn't picked up on the CT scan. As it turns out, she must have conceived while they were away in Bali. Vanessa would like to think it was the very first time he told her he loved her.

'You know, William, every agonising moment has been worth it to bring me here with you. With our own little blessing on the way, I now know being a mum was meant to be.'

He smiles.

'In some strange way, I feel I may have willed you to me.'

'Oh darling,' he leans in and kisses her cheek, 'I'm one lucky guy.'

'We're both lucky.'

The baby settles and William returns to his newspaper, leaving Vanessa deep in thought. *With a bubby on the way, I really wish Mother could remember more about my biological father.* Now everything is out in the open, she knows Diana would never intentionally withhold his identity, but she doesn't have very much to go on, other than spending a one-night stand with a tall, handsome man named David holidaying in Seminyak. His surname started with B, either Bay or Burns, but Diana simply couldn't remember anymore. He was a script writer or some such on leave from the United States, having just finished work on a popular television crime series, but she couldn't recollect the name of the program either. *Without a surname or a photograph, anything at all to go on, I'll never know.* Diana said he undoubtedly passed on strong genes, giving Vanessa her height, the green eyes, and a talent for writing.

William turns the page, and the headlines leap off the broadsheet.

Feeling him flinch, Vanessa asks, 'What is it, William?'

Silence.

Vanessa scans the page:

MURDERER'S POSSIBLE RELEASE AFTER SERVING ONLY SIX YEARS OF A TWELVE-YEAR SENTENCE FOR ATTEMPTED MURDER.

Supreme Court Judge Roy Ormond may give leniency to attempted murderer, Bruno Salvi. Mr Salvi may be released in time for Christmas.

She is paralysed.

In a split second, horror grips her by the throat and she's unable to speak, instead managing a gasp. Everything grows distant.

'Noooo!' she howls like a wounded animal rendered inert with fear, as if being sucked into a vortex. In a desperate need to breathe, Vanessa throws back the covers and flies to her feet. The energy surging throughout her body is frightening. Her fear filled eyes begin to water.

William tosses the sheet off and waits, worried that if he rushes to her suddenly, he'll send her into a tailspin.

Her lips quiver. A hoarse moan rumbles in her throat. The stark white of the vast bedroom feels cold and empty.

'Darling, please don't upset yourself. I'll make some calls and find out what's going on. Come, sit here on the bed. You must try and stay calm; it's not good for the baby, sweetheart,' he pleads, terrified by what he is seeing.

Ignoring his remark, she grips her tummy and seems to focus. 'No matter which way I look at this, I'm tethered to the past.'

'No, you are not.'

'No one's even bothered to contact me.' She looks at him in shock.

'I'm sure it's just a big mistake,' William says, now visibly concerned. He touches her quivering hand, acknowledging her pain.

'Mistake!' She cries and begins to ramble, her words barely audible, then looks past him and stares blankly at her mobile on the bedside table. Feeling a terrible sense of hopelessness, she looks his way again and says, 'I know you're not going to like this, William, but I need to call Michael.'

'Okay?'

'After all, he's had a longstanding career in criminal law and may be able to put me in the picture as to what I could or should do to prevent this from happening.'

Giving her his full support William doesn't hesitate. 'By all means.'

Over the years, Vanessa has often had torrid ideas of prosecuting Bruno for injury compensation, but as quickly as the torturous notions enter her head, she shuts them down. She grabs her phone, makes the call to Michael's mobile, and to her surprise, he picks up quickly.

'Hi, long time,' he says apprehensively.

'Hello, Michael, this isn't a social call. I need your professional advice.' She waits to hear his response.

'Go on. I'm all ears.'

'Bruno is about to be released from prison.'

'What? How do you know?'

'It's headline news.'

Vanessa hears the rustle of the newspaper as Michael scans the headlines. 'Oh dear.'

'For Christ's sake, Michael, we all know he's a dangerous man,' she says, infuriated.

'I know, I know, Vanessa. You won't get any argument out of me, but you're going to have to wait until I make some calls and get to the bottom of what's really going on here. I can't give you any answers until I have all the facts in front of me.'

Their conversation shifts back and forth for some time until Vanessa cuts it short.

'Okay. Call me back on this number as soon as you know anything at all.'

'Shouldn't take too long. Talk soon.'

She agrees, needing to know if she has grounds to fight this. Thoughts of wanting to exterminate her ex-husband swirl viciously around in her head. Having gone over the details with Michael as to whether it's even possible to delay, or better still, stop Bruno's upcoming release, causes her tummy to do somersaults. Vanessa turns to William who is standing patiently nearby. 'Michael has agreed to look into the matter. He says there's a slight possibility of preventing Bruno's release on the grounds he is capable of revenge, or worse still, murder.'

'Christ!' William looks troubled but remarkably calm.

'After sentencing, Bruno publicly swore he'd come for me one day.'

'Yes, I remember you telling me. Come sit down, let's talk this through.' William gently takes her by the arm and ushers her to the bed.

She sits close, feeling the heat radiating from his arm, and lets out a frustrated sigh, then looks at him pleadingly. 'This is all so wrong.'

'I know, darling, but you're stronger than your circumstances,'

She ignores his attempt at psychological insight.

'Michael said not to get my hopes up. It's highly unlikely, but we can only try.' Tears stream down her cheeks.

'What else did he say?'

'Oh, it's all gobbledygook to me, William. I don't quite understand it all. Perhaps you should chat to him when he calls back.'

'What's highly unlikely? Bruno seeking revenge? Or highly unlikely he'll be refused release?'

'Oh, he'll seek revenge alright. Michael seems to think he may have been given leniency because, well, he's rich, lawyered up, and obviously able to beat the system.'

'Mm, not good.' He stares down at the floor.

She feels his brain ticking over, knowing he's a deep thinker and isn't taking this lightly. 'They say lightning doesn't strike twice, but I feel like I'm reliving this nightmare all over again.'

'Darling, it will be sorted one way or another.'

'I'm not so sure, William. I've lived under a dark shadow for the last six years. Whilst this might sound very strange, I would have preferred not to have known of his impending release.'

'No, darling, we needed to know. It's important.'

'Ignorance can be a form of strength, or perhaps that just sounds naïve.

Sometimes you can be brave because you have no idea of the consequences. Now, unless Bruno is prepared to make some sort of murderer's confession, he'll be out and seeking reprisal. By all accounts, it appears my past is not keen to leave me.'

'You can't think like that, darling.'

'I'm going to take a shower,' she says abruptly, walking into the ensuite. Vanessa waits for the water to heat up, drops her negligée, and steps in as William walks through the open door, continuing their conversation.

'Sweetheart, I can't imagine what this feels like for you, but I do know he will never hurt you again as long as I'm alive. I promise you that much.'

His words do little to console her. *William is a darling, but coming from a life of privilege, he has no idea. He's underestimating Bruno and his ability to make life hell. I know, better than anyone, Bruno is very much a man who will seek retribution at any cost.*

'Look, it's an anxious time, but I know it's imperative we remain calm and stay focused. You're not alone anymore, Vanessa, so let me do all the worrying. I will make some calls first thing tomorrow morning when I'm back in the office, but for now let's try to enjoy our Sunday.'

Stepping from the shower, she struggles a smile, feeling their Sunday has been blown to pieces. 'William, we can't fly out next week. Not now.'

'Let's wait and see what Michael comes back with first, shall we?'

Throughout the next day, Vanessa gets several calls from reporters and a few tidbits which end up making the newspapers the following day. However, 24 hours later, the papers read:

> The latest chapter in this case has been reopened after six years. While the trial will open old wounds for Ms Whittaker nee Albert, the victim is insistent she will be present in court. Ms Whittaker states she fears her ex-husband's reprisal but feels it imperative she face him.
>
> Bruno Salvi received the maximum penalty for his crime and was convicted of causing grievous bodily harm with intent to kill the now famous author, Ms Vanessa

T. Albert. He left the scene of the crime in fear of being arrested by police. He was given a long prison sentence, but an appeals court in Sydney recently released a 100-page report that may free Salvi. It cast doubt that prosecutors had identified the motive or come up with any convincing evidence as to why he should serve out his full sentence. Prison authorities reported Salvi had been a perfect prisoner, and at this stage, there was no reason not to release him after only six years of a twelve-year sentence.

Michael calls and tells Vanessa not to do any more interviews. 'Vanessa, I have matters under control, but you need to keep a cool head and be patient until we meet in Chambers tomorrow.'

Since first seeing the headlines, the last couple of days have been an emotional quagmire, so when Thursday finally rolls around, it's with a touch of relief. Arriving promptly at ten, the couple make their way into Michael's Chambers. Unlike Thornton Whittaker's name, Michael Keats-Dickens is emblazoned across his door in distinctive, big brass letters. Tensions ease a little when Michael appears in reception and extends his hand to shake William's.

'It's a pleasure to meet you,' Michael says.

The feeling isn't mutual, but William would never be so rude, and gives an acknowledging nod.

Michael rests his hand on Vanessa's upper arm and leans in, gently kissing her cheek.

She feels like he's undressing her. Vanessa would love to ask if it had done him any good, playing up with her best friend, but pushes the absurdity aside. *What a lazy choice you were.*

'Come this way.' Michael guides them into his ostentatious chambers. 'Can I get you guys some coffee?' Michael asks, closing the door.

'No, thank you,' they respond in unison.

'So, Michael, what can you tell us?' Vanessa asks anxiously.

'Well, you're not going to like this one bit, Van.'

There it is.

'Vanessa, William, it appears Bruno has been a model prisoner and the justice system believes he's successfully rehabilitated and no longer a threat to society.'

'Society! What about being a threat to me?'

'I know,' Michael says sympathetically.

'Why can't we take this thing back to the courts?' she asks.

'Vanessa, a court battle may prove nothing.'

'Why?'

'Look, unless you are prepared to move mountains, and I mean literally move mountains, we haven't got a leg to stand on.'

'But it's okay I was left with a broken back,' Vanessa says flatly.

'Well, I can see the news certainly hasn't taken away your spirit, Van.'

There he goes again. She couldn't bring herself to look at him this time, instead she stares at her hands in her lap. *He might be a good criminal lawyer, but the man's an emotional idiot. How I was ever with him is beyond me.*

'May I interrupt here, Michael?' William says. 'This really isn't even an option for us, and I think I can safely speak for Vanessa when I say we would like you to move those mountains.'

'Right. Okay,' Michael says, 'if those are my instructions —'

'Look, money isn't an issue here, so if you can build a strong enough case as quickly as possible, I'd like you to represent Vanessa and engage a suitable senior counsel.'

'Yes, of course. I have just the man for the job.'

'And who is that?' William asks, very much in control.

'The audacious Anthony Terracini,' Michael says proudly.

'The best.' William turns to Vanessa. He knows he can't spare her from the pain, but he can afford to have the best legal minds in the country put together a stellar case.

Vanessa's stricken chest releases and the grace returns to her face. In the past, she'd heard Michael speak of Terracini in glowing terms and feels he's finally on the right track.

'Good. Do you think you'll be able to get him?' William asks.

'I know I can. This is right up his alley.' The meeting ends abruptly. Michael needs to act immediately and make some more calls. Once that's done, they must go to the parole board and put Vanessa's case that she is in fear of her life.

Out in the fresh air, Vanessa flinches when footsteps pound behind her. It's only two men, one in a dull grey suit, the other in a barrister's wig and robe. Deep in conversation, both men are carrying folders, and without breaking stride, they head in the direction of the nearby courtrooms.

'Gosh! I needed to get out of there and get some fresh air.'

'No kidding, Sherlock.'

'What?'

'Vanessa, it was written all over your face.'

'He makes my skin crawl.'

'Yes, I know, but he's bloody good at what he does.'

'I know,' She takes a deep breath.

They both catch the smell of tobacco and look around to see a man with a cigarette in the corner of his mouth, winking one eye to avoid the smoke while texting on his mobile. They move further away without saying a word.

Vanessa looks up and gazes at a few wind-smitten clouds making pale streaks across the blue sky. The breeze picks up, gathers the hem of her silk skirt, and whips it up, showing the length of her legs.

'Oh!' She grabs at her skirt.

A passer-by notices and eyeballs her intensely, smiling in admiration.

'Still got it, honey,' William whispers in her ear. It makes her laugh just when she needs it. 'Now that we're in the city, how about we have lunch?' William suggests.

'Yes, I think that's a great idea.'

'Okay, good, on one proviso.'

'And what's that?'

'That my beautiful wife doesn't spend the next couple of hours talking about Bruno.'

She pouts.

'Two hours, that's all.'

'Deal.' She kisses her knight in shining armour on the cheek. 'Where will we go?'

'Anywhere you like.'

Had Bruno Salvi known he was showering for the very last time, he'd have stayed in his cell and refused to enter the prison washroom at all. But the narcissistic Sicilian wasn't to know this was the last time for anything.

As his attacker neared his target in the steamy shower rooms, his height overshadowing his prey, he was swift, cutting and gutting the man that had planned a revenge attack on his ex-wife.

It all happened so quickly; his target knew nothing of the blade. The homemade shiv shot like an ice pick through the right side of his back, moving slowly up and under his rib cage, releasing the air from his lung. He was like a lamb to the slaughter.

A shocked Salvi slumped forward, gripping the brass faucet. Gasping for air, he hung on, paralysed, helplessly watching the opulent red water wash over his veiny, pallid feet and pool across the grey concrete floor.

The walls of the empty shower block echoed the silence with the captured sounds of the inmates, like the distant roar of an enormous waterfall from the prison yard. Mesmerised by a large crack in the floor, he was powerless as he looked at his life blood trickle into the stratum. Salvi was bleeding out.

This was not the freedom he'd expected. There would be no life outside the grey, faded walls of the hellhole he'd called home for the last six years. Instead, through the steam in this cold, stark washroom, without the strength to turn around, Salvi suddenly recognised the familiar smell of his aggressor.

'You Yank ...' Too weak to speak, his only thought was *you Yankee cunt*.

All he could see was the watery blood quickly reaching his attacker's white canvas shoes. Defenceless, he felt his cellmate, Brays, step back swiftly, careful to avoid the stream of scarlet.

The only freedom this 42-year-old would have today is when he was carried out in a body bag to the sounds of stomping inmates as they cheered, 'Man's dead! Man's dead! Man's dead!'

Identified to some as The Man, short for The Manipulator, he may have been a model prisoner on paper, but to those who knew him well, he was the stuff of Satan, getting his kicks from intimidating his fellow inmates and making their lives a living hell, filling his time with cruel amusement. Fuck 'em was his catch cry. With veiled threats, he lorded over any man who stood in his way – but not today.

Fellow inmates were happy he was leaving and to see the back of him, but his attacker wasn't about to let him go free. Salvi's murder had been planned with absolute precision by his cellmate, David Brays, who had suffered at the hands of this monster. Revenge had been planned right down to Salvi's final hours on the morning of his release.

For the last stint of his incarceration, David had been made to share a cell with Salvi since the brute was transferred to Sydney's Silverwater Prison two years ago.

Though Salvi was suspected of many murders, ludicrously he'd only ever been convicted of attempted murder and causing grievous bodily harm to his wife, Vanessa.

Sharing a cell with Salvi in the low security Dawn de Loas section, the situation had been untenable for David. He was made to endure months of Salvi's psychobabble about his carefully planned revenge attack. David, a good man at heart, was serving time for a white-collar crime and had never had blood on his hands before. As a reporter his crime was defamation against one of the criminals, he'd brought public light upon, not murder – until today.

Privy to Salvi's intentions, David hatched his own plan. Listening to Salvi constantly brag his plans to murder his already brutally injured ex-wife was all too much for David to bear. He improvised by fashioning a piece of Perspex into the shape of a blade and hid it in the prison yard until he could strike.

Call it what you like, stupidity perhaps, but knowing he was the man with the best opportunity to get the job done, David believed it was up to him to finish Salvi off. Like many, he'd heard Vanessa T. Albert's story, so by killing Salvi, he was able to prevent the senseless death of an innocent woman. With Salvi dead, David was severely aware, if caught, he'd be faced with the reality he'd be forever known in the prison system as a shiverer.

Certain no one had seen him, not even his victim, David let out a heavy sigh, calmly retreating from the shower block. Nervous as each door closed with a loud clang behind him, his heart pounding deep inside his chest, he moved slowly through the prison, not wanting to arouse suspicion, and headed towards the yard to join the other inmates. Relieved to be outside in the fresh air, he took a deep breath again, grateful to be in the overcrowded yard at last where, unaware, inmates were going about their daily routine.

The air was heavy with the scent of angry men, and this was strictly the social part of the day.

It was going to be a beautiful day, David felt, pacing steadily past an army of prison greens faded to various shades according to their terms served, as uniformed guards, dressed in blue, stood around dispirited, keeping watch.

Only just gone eight and it was already hot. Having come from the steamy shower block, David wiped his brow to see if he was sweating. Not a drop. He smiled across at Tommo, an inmate he respected, seated solo over in the shade, writing another love letter to his wife of twenty years. Having never married, David could only imagine what it must feel like when a loved one served a long-term prison sentence, especially for a white-collar crime. The commitment required by the spouse to stay in the relationship: immeasurable. Especially when the law doesn't allow conjugal visits. Suffering the indignity of this hellhole and watching your kids, often in their formative years, visit each month, that's gotta be tough.

He spotted two tall dudes shooting hoops at the old basketball ring. As they jumped about, dodging one another on the chalky outline that marks the baseline on the small court, the ball hit the edge of the ring, causing it to bounce off. One guy caught the ball and motioned backwards, lining the ball up at eye level and throwing it again. David wondered how they could stand the heat as perspiration dripped from their armpits. On the opposite side, David noticed the infamous four playing poker in the corner of the yard. He chuckled to himself at old man Carlo, an Italian immigrant who never lost. David sniggered, watching the other three listening to Carlo's pointy insults.

'You idiot, motherfucker!' Carlo was saying, raising a closed fist in the air.

David gave Freshy, the new kid on the block, a nod. He was pleased young Kurt, a blue-eyed blonde, had taken his advice and was sitting quietly off to the side with a book, trying to be inconspicuous until he got the true lie of the land. David worried for the small-framed twenty-year-old. Sentenced to six months in prison for repeated driving offences while disqualified, he had to co-exist amid some of the most hardened criminals imaginable.

'Keep your head down, kid, until I come out and say hi to you,' David had told him when he first arrived. 'That way the others will know you're okay and shouldn't bother you.'

Kurt discreetly glanced over at David, giving him a grateful grin.

David nodded back but was distracted by the sound of heavy barbells being dropped, followed by loud, grunting noises coming from the gym over by the toilet block. He peered at the men in white singlets showing off their muscles, taking testosterone to another level as they competed in weights, pull-ups, and push-ups.

David passed three shifty characters covered in jail pen-mark tattoos, often referred to as boob tats, an old Aussie colloquialism. The stooges were leisurely walking up and down, deep in conversation, ignoring David, who noticed one was sporting a recent, deep laceration to his temple, which had required several stitches. David made his way over to a pair of familiar faces playing racquet ball up against the yard wall.

'Hello, boys, how you going? Who's playing the winner?' he asked coolly.

'No one, Davo. You're next,' Peanuts, a short, thick-set fellow with a heavily scarred cheek said.

Suddenly the horn sounded, and an authoritative voice boomed from an overhead speaker. 'All inmates return to your cells immediately. I repeat, all inmates return to your cells immediately.' The shrill wail of a deafening siren was heard.

'Sorry, Davo, I guess it's not your lucky day,' Peanuts said.

David shrugged. 'That's the way it goes, mate. There's always tomorrow.'

David headed for his cell, just as Big Kev exited the gym in a pool of sweat, yelling out, 'Hey, Davo, wait up. Take a look at these babies; the guns are getting bigger, mate.'

Ignoring the sounding siren, Big Kev proudly exhibited the flexed bicep of his right arm as perspiration poured from his hairy armpit. David nodded approvingly, giving him the thumbs up, smiled, then shifted his view, purposely eyeing Baggy, a new prison guard seated up ahead, behind thick, heavy glass, watching the surveillance monitors of the yard. David fell into line, joining the motley queue to gain entry back to the main block.

Approaching the window, David tentatively asked the screw at the door, 'What's going on?'

The guard didn't make eye contact, 'Get to your bloody cell. Someone's been hurt in the shower block and we're going into lockdown.' The guard's behaviour was a stark reminder of the anachronism of the system.

David followed the other prisoners as they walked back to their cells. The cacophony of thunderous, clunking doors, commanding voices of guards, and unruly prisoners strident with anger, was an assault to the senses. As David passed several stony-faced guards, each salutation exchanged chilled him to the bone.

Alone with his thoughts and safely locked inside his cell, David began shaking uncontrollably. Sweat poured from his brow and he paced back and forth, the stark reality of murder setting in. As a meagre distraction, he anxiously switched on the television. Attempting to drown out his thoughts, he covered his head with a pillow, but his thumping heart kept his shame to the fore. An hour later, and still resting uneasily on his bunk, he heard the clatter of a tin mug against the cell bars.

An inmate yelled, 'Man's dead!'

Numerous tin mugs chimed in, building momentum.

A heavy voice called out, 'What the fuck happened?'

David remained silent as rock music blared from his television screen.

A distant voice replied, 'I don't fuckin' know. Last time I saw the cunt, he was in the shower block, happy he was goin' home for Christmas.'

The uproar built thunderously, hitting fever pitch, making it difficult for David to hear himself think. Incongruously, he felt somewhat protected by the level of noise.

Suddenly the steel doors to his cell swung open. Three prison guards, brazen-faced, standing strong, were staring him down. A startled David tried to leap to his feet but was pounced upon by one guard and forced up against the opposing wall. 'What the f—'

'Never mind what's going on out there. You're coming with us.' He was flung from his comfort zone and hurled along the cold corridor with brute force.

The sound of tin escalated.

The ringtone of the mobile startles an already anxious Vanessa.

'Hi, Michael.'

'Vanessa. Bruno has been murdered.'

She is astounded.

'Vanessa, are you still there?'

'Yes, I'm here. I'm sorry. Can you say that again?'

'What it means is he will not be released from prison today, at least not in the way we feared.' Michael hears her exhale. 'Bruno will never be a problem to you again, Vanessa.'

'I can't believe it.'

'Well, you better believe it.'

'How was he murdered?'

'Apparently a fellow inmate who had a grudge did it.'

'My God!' she says, hardly believing her ears.

She is too grateful to ask how or why and thanks him profusely for being supportive.

'Would you like me to speak to William?'

'No. That's fine.'

'You take care now, Vanessa, and don't be a stranger.'

'Thank you. You, too.' She's still holding the phone when she hears a click. An astonished Vanessa hangs up slowly and shocked, walks across the living room to William.

He is still madly in play, both the mobile and landline ringing off the hook with every legal mind he can muster, when he notices her dazed look.

Vanessa doesn't interrupt.

'Can you hold one minute, please,' William says down the line.

Her eyes are glazed over and Vanessa mumbles indecipherably.

'Sorry, darling, I can't understand you.' William holds the phone away from his ear, covering the microphone.

'Bruno is dead!' She could almost hear the cogs in William's brain ticking over. 'Somebody killed the savage beast.'

Still holding the mobile away from his ear, he asks, 'How do you know that?'

'I just got off the phone from Michael. Apparently, he was to be released today, but was killed this morning.'

Without acknowledging the person on the phone, William hits end call and places his mobile down on the table. Vanessa draws breath and begins sobbing with relief. He takes her in his arms, holding her close.

'Are you certain?'

'Yes.' She shakes her head in disbelief. 'Someone must be watching over me.' There is no furrow in her brow anymore, only serenity.

'My God!' William says. 'Incredible!' The rise of her tummy tells them the baby is kicking. Vanessa pulls back from William slightly, holding her bump protectively. 'Yes, little one, everything is going to be okay.'

'Told you we'd still make our honeymoon.'

She looks up at him, wipes away her tears and ushers a smile. 'Why are you always right, William Whittaker?'

'It's a gift.'

CHAPTER THIRTY

On the morning of their departure, Vanessa has to shake herself to remember this isn't a fantasy. *It's really happening; we're off to Tahiti for our babymoon, to a private island, no less …*

The lavish, long-range jet is waiting for them at a private airstrip and by the time the couple are strolling up the stairs, Vanessa is feeling like a superstar and taking in every goddamn Hollywood-style moment. *Impressive; I've never seen an aircraft like this. It's like a beautiful piece of sculpture.* In the doorway, they are greeted by a tall, leggy, blond supermodel with a striking smile.

'Hello, Mr & Mrs Whittaker. Welcome on board. My name is Charlie, and I will be taking care of you throughout your flight.' Her soft, dignified voice and piercing green eyes whisper not only seduction, but a wealth of confidence and knowledge.

Charlie. I love that name for a woman. Vanessa is too bedazzled to say anything other than hello.

Charlie shuts the door behind them and goes to work. Inside the sprawling aircraft, Vanessa sits on the edge of her soft, white leather seat, her eyes taking in every inch of this extravagant, high design interior, noting the layout has three functional zones cleverly divided by Art Deco-inspired contemporary furniture.

The galley, guest bathroom, and crew facilities are all forward in the first zone, while the dining and entertaining areas are situated in the second zone, or main salon. The third zone houses the guests' suite, which is complete with a full-beam main cabin, a full-beam bathroom, walk-in wardrobe, and office area all outfitted with a mix of Hermes signature leather and rich mahogany wood.

'This is a mile high lounge,' Vanessa whispers to William.

In the front cabin, through the open door, Vanessa sees two pilots preparing for take-off. Flight attendant Charlie presents a drinks list.

'Not for me, thank you,' Vanessa says. 'Just water.'

'What champagne do you have?' William asks.

'Krug, sir, or we have —'

'Krug, please.'

When it's time to take-off, Vanessa nestles in her seat against the softest of designer cushions and stretches her legs. Running a seductive hand along the plush white leather, she looks across at William, batting her eyelashes, and says, 'I'm in love.'

He can't help laughing. 'Buckle up, baby. You're in for the ride of your life.'

Once in the air, and having reached a safe cruising altitude, Charlie reappears and presents the menu detailing a slew of choices: fresh figs, Parma prosciutto, gorgonzola, vincotto, beef carpaccio, *Testun al Barolo* cheese, walnut pesto, celery heart, quail eggs, caviar and crème fraiche, and a selection of garnishes served with a shot *or* two of Beluga Vodka.

And these are just the entrées? The entire experience is tailored to us. Vanessa turns the page: duck, red grape, thyme and honey, lobster tail with garlic parsley butter, eye fillet, potato puree, wilted spinach, king brown mushrooms, Roquefort and chive butter.

My goodness, all this butter! I'm going to give the bubby a bloody coronary. Vanessa whispers across to William, 'Considering our destination, I'm surprised the menu isn't more fitting. You know, hearts of palm ...'

'It will be on the turnaround leg, I'm sure. Given we'll be having so much seafood over the next week, I assumed an eclectic choice would be welcomed.'

She smiles. 'And you assumed vodka shots only fitting for the father-to-be.'

'Of course. You're not allowed, remember.'

'So much for "we are pregnant",' she says, air quoting.

During the seven-hour flight, Vanessa gets quite a bit of work done while William manages to read a recent manuscript.

He lines the pages up, straightens the foldback clip, and releases a sigh.

Vanessa lifts her eyes from her laptop, giving him an inquiring look.

'No good?'

'On the contrary, it's a fascinating read. It's a true story about a boy, Baldwin Brown, who grew up in the late 1800s and wanted a dog, so he built one.'

'Not the art historian?'

'No.' He turns a frown into a grin. 'You do have a breathtaking range of interests, Albert.'

She laughs. 'So why couldn't he get one.'

'What?'

'A dog. Why couldn't he get a dog?'

'His mother claimed they couldn't afford to feed it because they were poor.'

'What? She didn't like dogs?'

'Apparently not. Anyway, this is written by the great grandson, Jack Brown, and tells of how Baldwin ended up working for the military.'

She bursts out laughing.

'What's so funny?'

She tries to gather her composure.

'What?'

'You're telling me Jackson Brown, the singer, is the great grandson of Baldwin Brown, the art historian.'

'You've lost the plot,' he says, trying to contain his laughter.

She shrugs her shoulders in a teasing manner before returning to her laptop. *I love stirring him.*

Following an indulgent lunch, they decide to retire to the sleeping area. William quickly falls into a deep sleep and Vanessa watches him. *I am the luckiest woman in the world.*

Vanessa wakes an hour later and sits up to find William is back in his seat, reading. She's feeling refreshed and keen to get back to work but is convinced she's been talking in her sleep. *Something about prams.*

After washing, she sits and turns on her computer, the loud, whirring sound from not turning the volume down when she keyed off last time, in stark contrast to the inner sanctum. *I always do that.* 'Sorry,' she says to William.

Charlie peeks her head out from the food prep area, waves an acknowledging hand, then steps out with a tray of fresh towels and two glasses of ice-cold water. 'Can I get you another champagne, Mr Whittaker?'

'No, thank you. Water's fine.' He takes a hand towel.

'Mrs Whittaker.' Charlie offers the towels and retreats to the front of the aircraft.

Vanessa looks across at William. 'Boy! Does it ever strike you how far we've come considering the hurdles we've faced.'

'Often.'

'Me too. My injuries, our parents, publishing my book – and how we met.'

'Books, plural.'

She looks reflective.

'My love, it's onwards and upwards from here.'

'I hope so.'

'I know so.'

In super-fast time, they are already preparing to land. Coming in on the tiny airstrip of the Polynesian island, the plane skims the tops of dense trees like a pebble skimming the surface of the water. The pilot executes the gentlest of touchdowns.

'I noticed you looking at that luxury yacht out there in the water.'

She nods.

'We can charter it if you like. They do these adventure treasure hunts.'

'Treasure hunts?'

'Yes. They're based on the routes of historical seafarers.'

'What? Like swashbuckling pirates of the Caribbean?'

'Precisely, except we're not in the Caribbean.' He chuckles.

'Perhaps we could find Marlon Brando's lost treasure.'

'More like Brando's lost wives.'

'How many wives did he have?'

'Three.'

'Well, you better stay on dry land with this one.' She holds her index finger up before gathering their things and heading to the open door.

Looking out from the top of the stairs, aside from basic terminal facilities, there's barely any sign of life other than the wave of the red-and-white national flag. Two vehicles appear from out of nowhere to escort them and their luggage across the island to where they'll be spending the next eight days.

When they arrive at the luxury resort, an official welcomes them to the island, and the couple are gifted frangipani leis via harmonic voices of a ten-strong choir greeting their arrival. Vanessa is brimming with excitement as she looks across the breathtaking, pristine beach stretching before them, framed by the skyscraper palms of this idyllic South Pacific Island.

'This song portrays our traditional Tahitian life and dialect,' says an attractive staff member bearing the name tag Poehei.

Vanessa tries to pronounce the woman's name.

'Please call me Poe.'

It's a short distance to their three-bedroom, Polynesian-style residence on the beachfront.

At the front of the villa, they are formally greeted by the tallest Tahitian man. 'My name is Metua and I will be your butler throughout your stay. Please don't hesitate to ask if there is anything you need.'

Inside, the open-sided living space has multiple dining and entertainment areas with doors that open onto a private outdoor patio and pool overlooking the ocean.

As staff set about unpacking their things, they decide to change into their bathers and take a leisurely dip in the serene lagoon.

Vanessa is finding it hard to wrap her head around this sort of luxury.

'So, my darling wife, there are two main restaurants here at our disposal: French, of course, or Japanese.'

'French, of course.'

'Good. Then I made the right choice.'

'You are too clever, my darling.' She runs a soothing hand across his cheek.

As the sun begins to fade and the sky slowly reveals the apricot tone of sunset, the casually dressed couple head to the open-air, lagoon-view bar for pre-dinner drinks.

'Bonsoir,' says the very tall, tanned bartender.

'Salut.' William pulls a chair out for his wife at the bar.

The bartender slides the drinks list across in front of them. 'My name is Pierre.'

Of course it is. Vanessa opens the folder in amusement and immediately spots what she wants. 'I'll have a flower sour mocktail.'

William looks at the colourful list. 'Is that because of the pretty picture?'

'Maybe.' She pulls a cheeky grin.

William snaps the drinks list shut. 'I'll have a Chivas neat, no ice.'

Pierre prepares her drink, adding a sprig of lavender.

'This is so beautiful.' She touches the lavender to release its scent and looks up at the bartender.

'So are you,' he says suggestively.

She catches her breath, in shock at his candour.

After drinks, they stroll to the restaurant. William, not usually a jealous man, says under his breath, 'So are you.'

She laughs. 'You should be flattered.'

He winks. 'I am.'

'He makes a good mocktail though.'

'Then he better behave so he can keep making them.' She hears music, soft and pure, hanging in the air, drifting across the water to the intimate setting with its beautiful tones of tropical light and sand.

An elegant gentleman seats them by the window. Vanessa rubs her hands together, interlocking her fingers. 'The surrounding moat gives the sensation we're floating on a lagoon.'

'I think that's the idea, darling.' He lowers a gentle hand to hers.

They stay motionless for a moment. 'Do you know how much I love you?'

She sits silent, studying the tears in his eyes, and can't believe how truly blessed she is. For several years, she has gained pleasure from being in control of her life, of where she went and what she did – going to bed late and getting up when it suited her, eating meals that suited her when it suited her – but now decisions needed to be made for three.

After dinner of cognac shrimp with *beurre blanc* and classic French Chateaubriand, they ask that the lemon citron dessert be brought to their villa and cosy up for the rest of the evening.

The following day, sipping on a fruit juice, Vanessa luxuriating in an enormous hammock under the shade of a coconut tree, she gazes at William strolling towards the water's edge. *My Adonis.* The sun is high, the beach is warm, the sand white and the weather is balmy. *What's not to love?*

William turns, catching her staring, breaks the quiet. 'Come on!'

It's an offer she can't refuse. She climbs from the hammock and tosses her sarong skyward, letting it land softly on the white carpet of sand.

He can't help feeling amused as she walks towards him. Embracing, they linger, her tiny bump holding centre court between them.

'She's been very quiet lately.' Vanessa rubs her tummy.

'Guess she knows we're on holidays.'

Vanessa breaks free, takes his hand, and they plunge into the coolness of the water. Underwater visions amid muffled echo sounds, they kiss before meeting the surface together.

'Nice?'

'Fabulous!' Her eyes shine.

In a warm, tropical kaleidoscope of colour, they float in contented silence.

Vanessa glances across. 'Why did you decide to come here, to this particular island?'

'Well, a few reasons. Aside from being transformative, I didn't want to risk being too far from home, considering our priority at large.' He glances at her baby bump just above the surface of the water.

'Whittaker, are you calling me large?'

'Never!'

'And ...'

'Well, I thought Italy might be a bit much at this stage. Better still, there's no reporters lurking about. What better way than to honeymoon, on a secluded island knowing there's a jet on standby 24/7. Oh, and by the way, Charlie's a nurse.'

'A nurse?' Vanessa's taken aback by his flawless instincts.

'Is there nothing you don't think of William?' She splashes him playfully.

'When it comes to you, nothing.' He shakes the water from his hair.

'Why didn't you tell me?'

'To be honest, I didn't over-think it.'

'Listen to you.' She knows he always overthinks things when it comes to her best interest.

They swim ashore to be met by staff bearing fluffy white towels at a secluded seating area for lunch on the beach. Tahitian crab, low in mercury and high in omega-fatty acids, is the order of the day.

They may be far from others, but Vanessa feels totally pampered and truly connected, looking out over the turquoise water.

'You love your seafood, don't you? I thought you were supposed to avoid seafood?'

'Not all seafood, only the ones high in mercury. Personally, I think it's a lot of baloney.'

'You're not concerned you might be taking a risk?'

'On this? Not in the least. I am worried if I have any more of those *Firi Firi* coconut things, I won't just have a baby bump.'

'What? The Tahitian donuts?'

'Yes.'

'You worry too much.'

William's no pressure approach is so refreshing, given Bruno and Michael were constantly telling me to lose weight. Vanessa has learnt women cannot cancel out part of themselves and play a man's ideal. William leans in with a glint in his eye. 'Hey, let's go check out the island after lunch and see what we can find.'

'Let's.'

Through the palm canopy, a few minutes out, they hear the distant roar of water like a gigantic beast. They eventually come to a glade, dazzling to the eye, and a lofty peak hosting an enormous, cascading waterfall in a sheltered bay.

'It's breathtaking.' Vanessa's face glistens in the rays of the sun, distant calls of exotic birds singing to one another. 'You'd be hard pushed finding a more beautiful and tranquil setting. I have no words.'

He wraps his arms around her, enjoying standing in the moisture-filled air. 'It brings home just how truly small we are compared to the rest of the world.'

'Let's go under,' she urges, feeling her skin goose up.

'Okay. But be careful. Here. Take my hand.'

William's hand feels warm and strong as they step cautiously around the rocky outcrop. Vanessa is initially hesitant, watching as William offers up his other hand, testing its force before ducking in under the shelf of water and leading her to safety.

Looking at his wife holding centre stage in a white bikini, he is overcome with happiness, a picture of health standing beneath the water with a nurturing hand to her tummy.

Without words, they strip naked together.

'I love you.' His words are barely audible beneath the roar of the water. He pulls her near, tasting the perfect fullness of her lips with such passion, she believes she'll never breathe again.

Gently pushing her back against the rock, his hands move around her breasts, gliding down to her belly, caressing for a moment, then down between her thighs, making her skin tingle. He tastes at her groin, kissing gently the slick folds of her skin, feeling her desire as anxious heat begins to build inside her.

When she opens her eyes, he's gazing up at her, kissing tenderly before moving up her body and taking her mouth in his. She turns to face the wall, his hands on her hips as she grips the rock, and they make love under the arch of the waterfall. Nothing could feel more magical.

He catches his breath and turns her to face him, holding her close.

'You are incredible.'

She gasps a little and hopes his passion towards her will never change.

They bathe under the waterfall until William gathers their bathers and helps Vanessa through the water's arc and down the rocky wall.

Looking at her naked body, speckled with droplets of water, primal pleasure suffusing his body, he has the sudden urge to take her again in the surrounding wilderness, and tries in vain to curb his desire. Watching her walk on, he has no restraint. 'Vanessa, stop!'

For a second, she felt something shift, then recognising his forthright tone, she turns and seductively leans up against the trunk of the nearest palm. He can never imagine not wanting her for the rest of his life.

Drowned in sexual and emotional pleasure, Vanessa and William barely leave their villa, other than back to their private, mist-filled patch of paradise after lunch each day.

One evening, the couple are treated to the beauty and drama of barefooted Tahitian hula dancers in traditional costumes, accompanied by three gentlemen on ukuleles, harmonising South Pacific songs closely related to the dances. Dramatic effects are added by thunderous drums, conch shells and harmonic nasal flutes to create a surreal experience.

Towards the end of the week, William asks the butler to have the kitchen organise a surprise picnic filled with delicious goodies, and a half bottle of Pouilly Fume for him, at their treasured spot. Unbeknownst to Vanessa, staff make their way, ahead of time, to a dry spot in full view of the waterfall and set up a romantic lunch for two.

While taking their usual mid-morning swim, William suggests they go for a walk before lunch.

'Sure,' she says, splashing him with water in a teasing manner. 'Why don't we go another way today instead.'

Quick-thinking William says, 'I definitely want to see other parts of the island before we leave, but I saw something unusual yesterday and would like to take another look.'

'Unusual?'

'Yes, a palm that I thought would work at home.'

Vanessa is always happy to go wherever he wants, as long as they're together. 'Sure.'

When they arrive, the scene is set, complete with table luxe and platters of food fit for the most discerning appetite. A staff member is vigilant to ensure none of the exotic locals swoop down from the trees and take part.

'My goodness, William, did you organise this?'

He smiles and pulls out her chair.

'If that is all, sir, if you don't mind, when you are done eating, could you place everything back in the sealed basket as island policy is not to feed the birds and animals.'

'Of course.'

Vanessa's attention is drawn to the branch of a nearby tree. 'Oh look, he's so sweet.' She's looking up at a white fluffy bird with a curious look in its eyes. 'He's one of the locals our friend was talking about.'

'You mean a permanent resident.'

He laughs.

'My, we've seen some incredible tropical birds and wildlife while we've been here.'

'Any wonder Marlon Brando never wanted to leave. Did you see that book on him in our room?'

'Yes, I was reading it the other day while you were napping.'

'Now there's a dude that knew a good thing when he saw it.'

'Are you referring to the island, the wildlife, or the women?'

'All of the above.'

'You're incorrigible, William Whittaker.'

'I try.'

The evening before they leave, the couple decide to have dinner tucked away in their villa, soaking up what little time they have left in paradise. Staff have lit candles throughout the pool area. The bed has been prepared, its crisp white sheets neatly turned down ahead of time, so as not to interrupt the mood.

'William, it's been a sultry and indulgent week,' Vanessa says, floating naked in the pool.

'Darling, just being here with you is a dream.'

After a time, he grabs her by the hand, carries her out of the water, and into the bedroom. Lying on the bed in a sweet cocoon of intimacy, barely touching, he gazes at her with hunger. She feels the warmth of his hand as he strokes the outline of her hip reflected by the candlelight.

'You are more beautiful by the minute,' he whispers.

She is quiet, enjoying his touch.

William closes his eyes and concentrates on the smoothness of her skin. Her breasts swell and her nipples feel incredibly sensitive, but his touch is sublime as he lulls her into a peaceful sleep.

The following morning, when it's almost time to leave, Vanessa can't help feeling a foreboding, staring out from the doorway at William lounging in the sun after having just made love to her in the pool after breakfast. *Our lives seem so perfect right now.* Tears blur her vision, and she has the tiniest notion things will never be the same again.

Eyes shut, William is still naked, a towel across his waist, looking as handsome as ever basking in the sunlight, so she decides to join him.

Hearing her approach, he asks, 'Are we all packed?'

'They're in there now.'

Her teary words cause him to open his eyes sharply. 'Oh, come here, baby.' He sits upright and reaches for her. 'Honey, we'll come back. I promise.'

'It's not that. It's just I love you so much.'

'Oh, darling.'

'Being here with you has been the most wonderful experience of my life.'

'Vanessa, I've said this to you before. We have our whole lives in front of us, and better still, there'll be three of us soon.'

'That's the thing, William. This will be the last time we'll ever be alone together,' she says, squinting against the holiday sun.

'Oh, sweetheart.' He hugs her close.

At one of Sydney's leading eastern suburbs bookstores, Vanessa is standing off to the side of the lectern that bears the bold black-and-white poster of her latest book as the store manager makes her introduction.

'Welcome, ladies and gentlemen.' The woman waits for quiet.

'Our remarkable author this evening needs no introduction as she is a powerhouse in her own right. Her incredible body of work, her creative life at large, and now her most recent work …'

Vanessa zones out while scanning the busy room filled with anxious people all present to hear her speak. It's a mixed crowd, just as Vanessa would have it. *I've come a long way since snagging my first book deal.* She twists her diamond wedding band around on her finger. *Two turns to the right, one to the left, for luck.*

Under the sound of applause, Vanessa thanks the woman, then steps up to the lectern and centres herself, waiting for her audience to settle.

Tucking a strand of hair behind one ear, she steadies herself, taking in a deep, calming breath as the crowd finally grows quiet, the majority seated on fold-out, wooden chairs while others stand at the back of the store.

Facing her audience, she feels proud to be standing there. Not that she's one for speeches, but she's proud to have come so far. She looks across at her healthy, newborn daughter in Diana's arms. The little girl had auburn hair like her mother and her father's olive skin and brown eyes from the moment she was born. Vanessa never imagined her heart could expand so much until she held her child in her arms for the very first time.

Watching her mother, who is radiantly happy looking down adoringly at her granddaughter, Scarlett Monica Whittaker, Vanessa realises just how strong a mother's love truly is. Diana appears calm, considering the heated discussion she'd had earlier with Vanessa and William about Scarlett not being baptised yet. *Christ! She didn't bother baptising me until after Monica died, so what's the urgency?* Vanessa looks to her husband, standing beside Diana and tickling his daughter's chubby little foot.

The sudden well of applause startles Scarlett and Vanessa watches as Diana is quick to calm her little one, methodically bouncing her, cradled in her arms.

Vanessa gives a reassuring smile, then turns her attention to the audience. 'Hello everybody, thank you for coming.' Pause. 'My name is Vanessa T. Albert-Whittaker.' More applause. 'I'm here to discuss my latest novel.'

The audience rise from their seats, turning back and forth, applauding in recognition.

Deep breath ...

THE END

ABOUT THE AUTHOR

Tracey Roberts is a Sydney-based retired art dealer, writer and author of *The Will to Live, the Courage to Die*, a non-fiction inspirational biography about her uncle who lived as a ventilated quadriplegic.

Following her books release in 2012, Tracey went on to conduct a major fundraiser titled the 'Blue Diamond Ball' in 2013 and successfully raised over A$128,000 for high-tech wheelchairs for Sydney's North Shore Hospital.

Tracey was awarded Drummoyne Woman of the Year as part of the 2014 NSW Women of the Year Awards for her book's legacy and fundraising.

That same year Tracey was invited to become a member of the Perry Cross Spinal Research Foundation and happily accepted. Like many, her dream is to one day find a much-needed cure for paralysis and as part of her work she is dedicated to seeing that dream become a reality in her lifetime and ultimately fulfill her promise to her uncle.

Her new book *Paralysed* is a romance novel which touches on various forms of paralysis, both physical and emotional, showing that it was possible for her lead character Vanessa to overcome both.